WEB OF
ANGELS

WEB OF ANGELS

JOHN M. FORD

TOR

TOR PUBLISHING GROUP
NEW YORK

WEB OF ANGELS

Copyright © 1980 by John M. Ford
Introduction copyright © 2024 by Cory Doctorow

A Tor Book
Published by Tom Doherty Associates / Tor Publishing Group
120 Broadway
New York, NY 10271

www.tor-forge.com

Tor® is a registered trademark of Macmillan Publishing Group, LLC.

Library of Congress Cataloging-in-Publication Data

Names: Ford, John M., author.
Title: Web of angels / John M. Ford.
Description: First Tor edition. | New York : Tor, 2024.
Identifiers: LCCN 2023051899 | ISBN 9781250269140 (trade paperback) |
ISBN 9781250269157 (ebook)
Subjects: LCGFT: Cyberpunk fiction. | Science fiction. | Novels.
Classification: LCC PS3556.O712 W43 2024 |
DDC 813/.54—dc23/eng/20231106
LC record available at https://lccn.loc.gov/2023051899

Our books may be purchased in bulk for promotional,
educational, or business use. Please contact your local bookseller
or the Macmillan Corporate and Premium Sales Department
at 1-800-221-7945, extension 5442, or by email at
MacmillanSpecialMarkets@macmillan.com.

First Tor Edition: 2024

Printed in the United States of America

0 9 8 7 6 5 4 3 2 1

"I HAVE A HORROR OF BEING OBVIOUS":
INTRODUCTION TO *WEB OF ANGELS*
BY CORY DOCTOROW

There's nothing like a first novel. The first novel is a vessel for every notion, eyeball kick, world-building conceit, character tic, and linguistic flourish a writer has ever conceived of. First novels are *thick* in a way that no subsequent novel will be. It's true that "every novel teaches you how to write the novel you just wrote," but your first novel also teaches you to write *novels*.

You're holding Mike Ford's first novel. It is a remarkable, innovative, strange, and dense book. It's not easy to read, but it is a stupendous book.

If you've heard anything about this book, it's probably something like, "John M. Ford wrote a novel that presaged all of the major themes and conventions of cyberpunk in 1980, four years before William Gibson published *Neuromancer.*"

That's not a bad hook, but there's a lot more going to the story.

Cyberpunk was already brewing when this novel came out. Gibson's debut short story, "Fragments of a Hologram Rose," came out in 1977, in a small-press 'zine, and it was part of a long-running foment in the field that sought to fuse technological speculation with avant-garde literary experimentation, a kind of successor to the New Wave movement, whose tide was on its way out.

Gibson was hardly alone in staking out this new territory. Brunner's *Shockwave Rider* came out in 1975, while William S. Burroughs's *Blade Runner* (which supplied the title, but not the plot, for Ridley Scott's 1982 film) came out in '79. John Shirley's proto-cyberpunk novel *City Come A-Walkin'* came out the same year as Mike's *Web of Angels*.

So cyberpunk's early stirrings were well underway when this book came out, and this book is part of the genre's pioneering early history. It is prescient—and not merely because Mike got lucky and called the network at the center of the book's action "the Web"—and it presages many of the real and fictional struggles of hacker heroes and antiheroes in the years to come.

However, the fact that this book was so prescient does not mean that it should be thought of as a shared ancestor of the cyberpunk we know today. Rather, *Web of Angels* represents a kind of sister species to the main line of cyberpunk—like *H. floresiensis* or *H. neanderthalensis*, a kindred species that coexisted with us *H. saps*, interbred with us, but vanished long ago. The themes in *Web of Angels* were largely forgotten and independently re-created by subsequent cyberpunks down the line.

There's a good reason that *Web of Angels* did not spawn generations of books that refined its themes: timing. You see, *Web of Angels* was published in 1980, and because it was published in 1980, it is mostly a book about *phone phreaks* rather than a book about *hackers.*

Long before we connected our homes and our pockets to the internet, long before dial-up online services and BBSes popped up like mushrooms around the country, long before the standalone PC arrived in our living rooms, the Bell System—the phone network—was the only way that everyday people could interact with a computer.

Every time you picked up your indestructible Western Digital phone—leased from AT&T at an exorbitant monthly fee, which the company was able to charge thanks to a law that made it illegal to use any other kind of phone—and dialed a number, you caused a network of lumbering electromechanical and fully digital computers at the phone company's "central offices" to perform computational work, connecting your phone to some distant handset.

For a certain kind of transgressive, curious, anti-authoritarian, and technically minded person, the phone network was an irresistible lure. Self-taught phone hobbyists figured out how to perform surreal and delightful stunts, like making a call between two adjacent payphones that transited through exchanges that stretched around the country—or the planet. They took over the primitive phone message systems appearing in large businesses and transformed them into party lines or communal voice mailboxes where like-minded souls could leave messages for one another.

They called themselves "phone phreaks," and their culture was the forerunner of hacker culture. Not every phreak became a hacker, and not every hacker trope, practice, and ethos owes its existence to phreaks, but the hacker of today would be a very different person if not for the phreaks that came before.

Phreaks differed from hackers in one very important respect: their relationship to the system they were exploring. Today's hackers investigate (or invade, or sabotage) any of the billions of computers that we have connected to the internet, and even early hackers had dozens or hundreds of systems to explore—computer systems used by the military, by insurance giants, by government agencies, by private labs. But for American phreaks, there was really only one adversary: the Bell System, AT&T, the Death Star.

AT&T was a cruel and remorseless monopolist. At the time that *Web of Angels* was published, the company had been fighting regulators over its monopoly practices for *sixty-seven years*, and two years later, the DOJ would finally prevail, shattering Ma Bell into several "Baby Bells"—the RBOCs ("are-bocks" or "Regional Bell Operating Companies").

The Bell System was twined around the state. As it predated upon and extinguished smaller phone operators across the country (especially the rural phone co-ops that were the successors to the New Deal's electrification co-ops), it cannily accepted "punishments" that required it to provide universal service across the country, and to ally itself with emergency services and the public safety apparatus, working with local and federal police agencies to develop protocols for criminal surveillance. (Years later, the Snowden revelations would make it clear that AT&T never halted this practice, and that it was far and away the most complicit and active commercial partner in the NSA's illegal mass-surveillance campaign.)

Anti-monopoly enforcers seek to guard the state from corporate power growing so strong that it usurps the power of the state. AT&T's shrewd strategy was to accept "punishments" that caused it to become a deputized arm of the state, the original too-big-to-fail American company. The DOJ *almost* broke up AT&T in the early 1950s, but then the Pentagon stepped in to rescue it, arguing that the US military could not effectively prosecute the war in Korea if AT&T was not left intact to serve as toolsmith to the US invasion force.

AT&T was thus rehabilitated from a predatory monopolist to a national champion, a guardian of safety and security. This, in turn, transformed the parasites, explorers, wreckers, and builders who trespassed upon its authorities into threats to public safety, to the national interest itself. AT&T's enforcers found enthusiastic allies in the American criminal justice system, who aggressively policed AT&T's network policies on their behalf. A 1981 episode of *WKRP in Cincinnati* features a comedic meltdown by Dr. Johnny Fever, who breaks a Western Digital phone and flies into a panic at the thought that "the phone cops" are coming to drag him away. The joke was not really a joke: phone cops and real cops worked together to break down doors and drag away "toll thieves" who figured out how to beat the company's high-margin long-distance rates.

The crime of "toll fraud" really amounted to "felony contempt of monopoly," but AT&T had a winning strategy for disguising its parochial interest in maintaining its monopoly pricing and control over telephone handsets, by conflating the organized crime syndicates that systematized toll fraud with the kids and weirdos who set up free conference calls and the basement inventors who created tone-generating boxes that let them defeat long-distance tolls.

It was a profitable sleight of hand for AT&T, one that provided cover and government support to harass, demonize, and even imprison the early phreaks.

Indeed, the first salvo in the hacker wars that were to come was fired by AT&T, when it sicced the FBI on some phreaker-cum-hackers who had posted a bureaucratic document describing the management of a local 911 system and sparked a nationwide wave of arrests, as documented in Bruce Sterling's *The Hacker Crackdown*.

The FBI's Hacker Crackdown marked a turning point, and not just in law enforcement's relationship to the anti-authoritarian, high-tech underground, but in that underground itself. Phone phreaks operated an oral culture—inevitably, since the fundamental unit of phreak social interaction was the phone call. Phreaks learned to be phreaks from other phreaks, and mentor-protégé relationships were common.

The Hacker Crackdown concerned an article published in *Phrack*, the seminal hacker e-zine that was founded in 1985—five years after *Web of Angels* (2600: *The Hacker Quarterly* commenced publication in 1984). The rise of BBSes and their archives of "tfiles" (text files filled with bragadocious accounts of daring hacker exploits, as well as manifestos and lies) and e-zines represented a profound shift in the hacker's journey.

With these files to hand, a hacker wasn't nearly so reliant on mentors: these documents (along with the painstakingly retyped internal documentation harvested from the dumpsters of Ma Bell, IBM, and other tech giants) were the raw materials of a self-directed study program, albeit one supplemented by online forums and chats, and the odd hacker get-together. (Phreaks *did* have some written culture, notably the *Youth International Party Line*—later changed to *TAP*—published by Abbie Hoffman and Al Bell in the early 1970s.)

The thing that makes *Web of Angels* such a book of its time—and so definitively a cousin to cyberpunk, rather than an ancestor—is how much of a phreak book it is.

Its protagonist, Grailer Diomede, learns to be a "Webspinner" after he is taken under the arm of a much more accomplished spinner. Their mutual adversary is Bell Stellar, a galactically metastatic version of Ma Bell, one that has actually devoured the state that once protected it, winning for itself the right to deal out lethal retaliation to anyone who threatens the integrity of the network that binds the distant worlds together.

Ford's hackers—the Webspinners—play Websets, strange computer terminals that interact with Bell Stellar's computers on their behalf. These are played like thumb pianos, by means of up to 256 sliding levers that have to be finessed with the skill of a pianist. These bear a striking resemblance to the Altair 8080, the first successful personal computer, released in 1975 as a kit that you assembled and programmed by means of switches on its faceplate. At the time that *Web of Angels* saw print, the Altair was in decline, being supplanted by the Apple II Plus, which was much closer in form to the PCs that we use today, with an alphabetical keyboard and a screen, rather than blinking lights.

In 1982, two years after the publication of *Web of Angels*, the US Department of Justice broke up AT&T, sixty-nine years after its first action to crack down on the company to end its strong-arm tactics. At the time, AT&T's apologists reacted with horror, claiming AT&T as America's national champion, its bulwark against the ex-fascist copycats of Japan, who would surely destroy America's tech sector if not held in check by Ma Bell (the Yellow Peril scare talk of the day is eerily familiar to anyone who's listened to Cold War 2.0 hawks rant about China).

In reality, AT&T was a boot on the neck of the American high-tech sector, and its breakup—along with IBM's twelve-year-long turn in antitrust hell, which tamed the company's predatory instincts—led to the creation of the PC industry and the network era. The cyberpunk era, in other words. An era where you could have your choice of computers at home, and not just interact with the central office's switching system by means of a standardized Western Digital phone that was the only device you were legally permitted to connect to the network.

We can think of *Web of Angels* as a contrafactual, a cyberpunk novel for a future that never arrived, one where AT&T once again rebuffed America's antitrust enforcers, where IBM slipped out of their grasp with its killer instincts intact. It's a cyberpunk novel for a world where we never got the forty-year interregnum between the breakup of AT&T and the rise of Big Tech, in which starved and demoralized antitrust enforcers allowed the internet to be converted to "five websites, each consisting of screenshots of text from the other four" (to quote Tom Eastman).

Ford's later work makes it clear that he quickly caught the zeitgeist of the cyberpunk we know today, and *ran* with it. His tabletop RPG work—notably *Paranoia*—was far more influential on cyberpunk aesthetics and tropes than this odd, out-of-place 1980 novel.

But that just makes this novel all the more interesting. It's a parable about a dystopia we thought we'd averted, but that we now seem to be living amidst. It is exuberant in the way of first novels, and messy in the way of first novels. It's a book that gives us a glimpse of Mike Ford before the varnish had dried, when you could still see the rough edges.

Ford hated laying things out plainly—he famously told editors who asked him to be plainer, "I have a horror of being obvious." In *Web of Angels,* we get a glimpse of Ford's theory of mind, the extent to which he assumed that everyone had his ability to spot and assemble subtle literary puzzle pieces. His later novels are far more accessible. This one can be tough sledding.

But it's worth the work. It is bursting with tropes for a genre that never emerged, a notional "phreakpunk," in which technological ronin are pursued by a single, remorseless tech giant that has fused with and supplanted the state. It's not a precursor to *Neuromancer,* but rather, the sole example of an extinct parallel branch to it.

Which is to say, it's a very Mike Ford kind of book. The guy was *extraordinary.*

Still to be haunted, still to be pursued,
Still to be frighted with false apparitions
Of pageant majesty and new-coined greatness. . . .

from Perkin Warbeck

FIRST MEASURE:

THE WEB

CHAPTER 1

THE DARK LADY

The boy ran for his life, across the City Juvenal on the planet called Brass. Past lights and mirrors he ran, through blocks of shadow and dark glass, short legs running, small heart pounding, seeking a street to hide him from those that came after; for if the City would not have him he would surely die.

(*Oh*, said the serpent, *thou shalt not surely die.*)

He was blond, dark-eyed, dressed in soft parti-colored felts and high glossy boots turned down at the tops. To his chest he clutched a box covered in gray leather, resembling a large book; held it with both arms, looking more often at it than at the streets ahead, fingers spread wide to grip as much of its surface as he could.

The City Juvenal sat on the shore of the great golden sea that gave Brass its name. It was a city of colors not too bright, of sins not too black, of comfortable means and reputation. Its people took Lifespan to stretch their years into centuries, and took other things to fill up those centuries, and sometimes quietly did certain acts that ended their Lifespanned lives all at once; but this was the City Juvenal, not New Port Royal or Granmarque or Wicked Alexandria.

So the black floaters over the city were a strange sight, like dark clouds the size of a man's hand, small shadows on the land. The Combined Intersystem Regulation and Control Executive was like a shadow. You could look away from it, or put it behind you, but there it always was; and the brighter the light shone upon it the starker and blacker it stood. The only way to be free from the shadow was to enter a darkness so deep that it was lost in the shadow of the whole universe.

The CIRCE floaters seined the city, all in pursuit of one small running boy, running before the edge of a net that tightened toward the sea.

When he entered Swann's Way, the old ones stopped chewing their cream pastries to look at him. Lips moved, hands went to brows.

"He's young."

"Not real, not real. Too many éclairs."

They floated around him on their singing Hellmann chairs, looking down on him.

"Are you a boy, or a Prousty surfeit?"

"He's an angel. He's a hologram."

"He's real enough; angels cast no shadows."

Cakes fell to the pavement. The boy looked at one, stepped toward it; but he would not take a hand from his box to reach out for it.

"He's hungry! He's not a dream. My memories aren't ever hungry."

"Mine are mostly of food. Are you edible, boy?"

"Tell him not to touch the pastry. I don't want to see the womb again."

The chairs, humming off the ground, closed in. The boy stepped back.

"His eyes! Look at his eyes!"

The Hellmann hum changed pitch. Fingers, heavy with gems and age, pointed.

"Oh, me. Running, he is."

"Running. My memories don't ever run."

"Who cares for real youth? Waiter! Champagne and éclairs—a hundred trays of them!"

A young man came out with a silver salver of memory-cakes and a silver-handled broom. He shook the broom at the shivering boy.

"Go on, please," he said, not harshly. "You couldn't outlast them anyway." The man set the fresh éclairs down and began sweeping up the scattered crumbs.

The boy ran on, watching his shadow shorten. The big red sun of Brass was soon before him, so he stared at the box instead. He was better than halfway across the city, and the city ended at the yellow sea.

He ran into Peridot Street, where the Goliards were dancing a late-afternoon step. They chittered and giggled, praising the right people, scandalizing the right names, drinking the right drinks with the right pills following after.

The boy stood no chance in the Dance of the Goliards, though he did not know it; he was not schooled in the steps.

He stopped, boots swishing and clunking. The noise caught the Goliardic ears, always alert for such a disturbance and thoroughly numbed to each others' voices anyway.

The Dance stopped in midturn.

Eyes roved over the boy, measuring his smallness. Daggers came out to pin him down, cut him up.

"He does not *Dance*."

"One, two, doesn't Dance, doesn't Dance."

A Goliard in a red-and-white uniform and boots like the boy's came forward, stepped round him. "If he's not one of us, he can't Dance and can't pay forfeit." The soldier dropped to his knees with a clank of deadly metal. He spoke very softly: "You can run, I can see. Can you shoot? Can you stab? If not, you must keep running." The soldier's eyes held the boy's, then moved low. His voice fell to a whisper. "Run, child, when I say. Live and Dance when you know how."

The man stood, smacked the dust from his knees. "I don't think he's what he appears at all," he said loudly. "Some sick joke, some juvenile whim—look! Does he bear himself like a youth?"

The crowd revolved to look, and murmured that he did not, that his carriage was wrong somehow.

"Of course. Joke or whim, but not youth! When was your Life-span given, sir? How many years have you been that age? *I* would not have stretched the time to my maturity." The soldier stepped aside, breaking the cordon of people; gave the boy an urgent nod.

Without nodding back, he dashed through the gap and departed Peridot Street.

He came to the Quarter, which could hide anyone and hid nearly everything. A gleam peddler scouting for a fad to start spotted the box in the desperate clutch and blocked the clutcher's path. The boy dodged, but gleam peddlers are of slicker stuff; a slippered foot went into his path.

He stumbled, boot tops flopping, then lost balance and fell, felt shirt gliding on the smooth stone veneer of the Quarter's streets.

Heads came out of dark Quarter corners, not wanting to miss a killing or be left out of a brawl.

"It's one of Ildrahim's dwarf pickers," someone said in the mutter that Quarterfolk favor.

"Na-na, 'tis that new cannon larkey, the devil's own child." Mutter again; a whisper is too sibilant, carries too far. The Quarterfolk have a saying that all ears are wrong save the one you're nibbling.

"Ah, your noses are full o' dream. It's none of our Quarterfolk. I want to know what's the commotion? Where's the jolly ruckus?"

The boy had come to a stop, had lost his tight hold on the case but not quite his grip. The gleam peddler was near, though, straddling him and reaching, hating to hurt a soul without profiting some thereby. Down came her arms, twinkling with plexy jewelry.

The boy's breath whistled, and he rolled, but his elbows slid on the pavement and he could not pull the case in.

Then the peddler's eager eyes opened in great surprise, and she lay down quietly next to the boy and did not move. Did not breathe. Only bled a last trickle from a star-shaped wound in her back.

The boy rolled away, scraping the gray package. At the end of the street, looming awful from so low a view in the setting sunlight, were two figures in black, almost human in shape. One had a hand outstretched, and something in that hand. The something moved down.

The boy struggled with his frictionless clothes, squirming on the ground. Keeping one hand locked on his case, he grabbed the peddler's clothing with the other, used her body to lever himself up. He hesitated, looked at the CIRCE pair, saw them walking toward him. The one with the quiet gun holstered it.

The boy stopped hesitating. He jumped up from the body in the street and in a few clip-clopping steps was at one of the thousand locked doors of the Quarter. He knocked, double-knocked, triple-knocked. There was a scuffling behind the door, but no other answer.

Another door: *rap, rap-rap, rap-rap-rap.* A bolt slammed hollowly home.

Another door, and this time the knock was punctuated by the double click of boots coming closer.

"Find another door," said the door. "Find another street, another city. Leap into the sea and swim to another world. That's CIRCE chasing you, lad."

The boy hung back an instant, then repeated the knock.

"Go away, boy, if that's what you are. We'll fight any man living, but CIRCE isn't man or living. We're scared, if you're not. Go away."

Black-gloved hands swung into view, impact gloves that stiffened a slap to break bones. Black boots shod with steel, black jackets and trousers of bulletweave. Black helmets with black shiny shields instead of faces.

There were human bodies beneath all the black—at least, bodies born of man/woman/creche unit. But on the march, with the wands in their belts black for kill instead of brown for stun or red for pain, with a quiet gun issued them, they were CIRCE with its boar tusks bared. Real pure nova death on the march.

And they were not so very far to the rear of a gasping boy with light hair askew and face gray-pale as the box he still pressed to himself, feeling his colored clothes burning his skin, the leather case heavy as a shoplifted sweetchip.

Behind him, CIRCE; ahead, the butter-colored sea and the sun now drowning in it; between, only one more place: Romany Court.

And Romany Court was still asleep.

The sour dust of the day was still settling on the pavilions and doorsills when the boy came there. The clean air of night would soon blow in from the sea, waking the inhabitants from their beds with the home soil spread beneath them. Then the streets would ignite, and those who dared would revel under the colored flames for as long as they could stand it, or until dawn.

But now there was only dust, and dark lanterns, and the boy with the black knights following behind.

He played dodge-me with them for five minutes, ten, trying to outlast the light. But however he turned in the high narrow streets, the click of their boots soon came after. Clever the black knights might not be, but determined they always were. And the doors were locked, the windows shuttered; not a whisper stirred.

It was twilight. Almost night. Down an alley the boy ran, case in both hands, head bent down, CIRCE behind him.

And suddenly ahead of him as well. No more fox and hounds, now. Piston and cylinder. Hammer and anvil.

He looked at the case, held it before him. Chest rising and falling, hair in his eyes, he put his thumbs reverently on the latches.

In the middle of the crooked street with death at both ends, an open door caught his eye: the slit in the cylindrical shell of a public Web terminal. And though it was no exit, he ran for it, as cornered people will. He reached the opening, shoved it wide.

Inside, filling the booth, was a man in coarse green cloth, a hood over his face. He held something golden in one hand. He looked taller than the sky.

With his empty hand the man slammed the door.

The boy landed on his backside, bringing his knees up and his arms in close. He looked right, left—

The black knights were gone.

"And what are you, there, on your back like a beetle? Get up, little tumblebug."

He got up, looked all round once more. The CIRCE killers had vanished entirely.

Before the boy stood a very black woman in a very white dress that reached to the ground. A blue shawl was over her shoulders, and her hair was gray.

She smiled whitely, spat on one thumb and rubbed it against her

forefinger. Her skin was lined and dry, like rubbed mahogany. The
stuff of her dress was rough, burlap or sacking; the shawl was glossy
metal-silk.

"They've not gone forever, little bug, but they won't be back for
a while. Come with me, now." She stretched out a knuckly hand.

The boy stepped back, turned to face the Web terminal, which
still stood closed and impenetrable.

"Come with me," the woman said. "There's not a thing for you
in there now."

He took another step, pushed the door open. The booth was
empty save for seat and keyboard and mirrorlike Web-screen.

The woman clucked her tongue. "Not any thing, do you see. I
would God to see how he does it, but he does. Now come with me,
little bug. You should rest. You want a rest, no?"

He held his gray case so that his knuckles swelled white.

She laughed. "And you may sleep upon that if it pleases."

He nodded, and followed her, but did not take her hand.

"I am Celene Tourdemance," she said.

No reply.

"I am not so of the night as the others here. Good for you, I
think; the black *samedis* might yet have found you, but they would
not have taken you home with them."

They walked from one end of Romany Court to the other. Shut-
ters opened as they passed, and steps were heard in the street as
night stole in. Romany eyes followed them. The boy looked once at
those dark eyes and did not again; few people did.

"How much farther?" he said finally, annoyance in his voice
painting over the fear in it.

"Right here." They were at a low wooden door in a white wall.
The door-panel was deeply carved, the wood strongly figured, and
when the woman put her hand on the old brass knob the boy
thought how similar in texture she and the door were.

It was dark inside, close but not oppressive, smelling of ancient
furniture and being long closed up. Thick cloth hangings covered
the walls, and small two-dimensional pictures with glass over them,

and strange things like cane-stalks and snakeskins. A furry rug had claws and a head with teeth and eyes. What light there was came from colored glass globes at an adult's eye level; he thought at first that they were Hellmann hoverlamps, but as his sight got better saw the chains that hung down from the beamed ceiling. One globe only was white and bright. It hung above a round table with two chairs covered in deep blue fibersilk.

Behind one of the chairs was a painted picture of a young woman, black-skinned, holding a ball in one hand and something rectangular in the other. He could see in a moment that the picture was of Celene Tourdemance, maybe a thousand Lifespanned years ago; and she was wearing a silver crown. He moved closer, to see the thing she was holding in her left hand.

"Come, come," the old lady said. "There is all the time for that later. We will ask later."

Between the cool and the darkness and the curious music of her voice, he was suddenly very tired. He took off his boots, which felt wonderful once done, and lay down on a couch with feathers puffing out at its corners, which felt better still. She tried to cover him with a brocade shawl, but he turned it back to his waist.

He had seen the painting close, just for an instant. The white thing was a card, with a colored picture of a man; and for that moment it had seemed that the man was dressed like him.

He fell asleep with the gray case under his head, still in one hand's grip.

> > >

When he awoke, she had nutmeat pie and hot strong coffee waiting for him. He ate quickly but carefully, watching crumbs and drips, conscious that Celene Tourdemance observed him. When he was finished, he pulled on his boots, put the case under his arm, and sought the door.

"Not now," she said. "We are not done together, yet; and besides, it is day again. The *samedis* will find you in the day, tumblebug on a white stone. Come here. Sit down at the table."

He looked at her, his dark eyes wet and full of the frustrated loathing of the child betrayed by adults.

"Ah, no, why look so hard at me? I do not keep you for myself. I keep you for the future, and if the cards fall right, for yourself too. I am Celene Tourdemance, or does that not mean anything? Did your mother never read the cards?"

The boy blinked several times. Nothing leaked from his eyes. He looked from the woman to the old painting, looked back and forth. In a moment he saw that both held the card with his picture.

He went to the table and sat down, keeping the case in his lap and his hands on it.

"No, no, put your hands on the table. Bring the Web device up, if you must watch it so closely."

He did so. Then, suddenly, he popped the latches and opened it. It was a new set, and elaborate; a portable programming set with sixty-four keys, a detachable Ariel, and many other controls. Public sets and pocket Ariels had only sixteen keys—and that was enough to reach across the whole of the Ercon. The screen, plain silver while the set was off, was curved for depth. The maker's plate, gold, read SPECIALLY BUILT BY BELL STELLAR COMMUNICATIONS CORPORATION FOR—the rest of the plate was blank.

"You need not fear I will steal it. I do not trust the instantaneous-thing. My messages come through the cards . . . the synchronous device. Here, this is your card. Hold it a moment. Go ahead, take it; see if you like it."

He took the card in one hand, ran his eyes over it. It showed a man dressed in colorful, floppy clothes and boots turned over. He gazed intently up at the holder. He held a goblet that was like two pyramids joined at the points, with jewels at the weld.

The boy turned the Webset to see himself in the screen. His look went from card to mirror, picture to reflection, to the painting on the wall, to Celene Tourdemance.

"Does he look like you?" she said.

"He's dressed like me."

"Ah, you have the Sight; I should have guessed." She laughed, a sound like deep-throated wind chimes. "Don't you look at the clothes. They are just what we wear. We can dress like many things, if not like ourselves. I could dress like you, and I did, long years ago. And all of the young men followed me *all* a-round. But that is not my card, and never was. Now you tell me: Does he look like you?"

It took him a moment more, a long stare at card and mirror images. "Not like the mirror," he said finally. "But yeah—yes, he does."

"Why not like the mirror?" He had not before noticed her eyes, but he did now; they were bright witchy eyes, not like the Romany eyes but scaring him much the same way.

"Be-because when you look in the mirror, you see you, and you know it's you because it's a mirror, and it's your re-flec-tion . . . but it's not how you think you look. It's not how you look when you think of yourself." He held out the card to her. "This is how I look with my eyes closed, you know?"

"I know."

"When I have dreams."

She nodded.

"My Lady Tourdemance, is that how you found me, in the street?"

"Not 'Lady,' for I am not. You must call me 'Celene,' or 'Mistress Celene' if you must. And I will call you 'Page of Cups,' for that is your card.

"And no, Page, I did not go looking for you; but yes, in a way. Do you remember the green man, yesterday, who would not let you in?"

"Yes."

"It was him the cards sent me to—I thought. This was his card once, oh, long ago. I thought it was him I would find. But it was you."

"Couldn't it have been both of us?" The boy's eyes went to the picture of paints, and the card in the young woman's hand.

"It could have, but it was not. This is no more his card, as silly Mistress Celene again forgot. Mistress Celene, forgetting the cards could change; *ah*, ha."

The picture held the boy; there was something about the face of the young woman there that was missing from the Mistress' hard grained one.

"Was he your lover?" he said suddenly, and stopped his tongue.

She nodded slowly. "All my sadness, all my joy," she said, "came from loving a thieving boy.

"But you are the Page of Cups now. Put the card down, Page. Cut the deck with your left hand—no, left—and put your hands on the table. Very good."

She put out a finger to the card, gave it a quick tap. The figure of the Page began to move. He raised the cup to his lips, drank it down; held it forth again, and the liquid rose. A fish's head peeped out. He drank, was replenished.

"Page of Cups—if you will. Or Jack of Hearts, Daughter of Waters, Deeping Son, Blood's Eleven, Knave of Wounds.

"Now, Mistress Celene," she said (he knew not to him), "we will see if your silliness has departed." She tapped the card again, a movement almost too quick to see. The Page stopped still in mid-swallow.

"Page of Cups drinking," she said, again to the air. "Neither filled nor emptied."

She drew another card, turned it, tapped it. It showed a man in armor on a white horse, cutting the air with a sword. At her tap the horse had stopped with all four feet off the ground.

"This covers you," she said. "Knight of Swords, unsupported. You ride quickly, and for vengeance; but you may fall."

Another card: a blindfolded woman holding crossed swords. "This crosses you. Two Blades reversed. Beware judgment. Beware the law."

He fidgeted. He knew what he had seen yesterday, and what she had seen.

Another card: a boat, bearing a man and a woman and six huge swords plunged into the deck. The man poled the boat across a roiling sea. Waves broke left, right.

The card held its motion with a breaker poised above the boat and its passengers, ready to swamp all.

"This is beneath you. A terrible voyage."

Another card: a great heart pulsing from black to red, dripping blood where three swords transfixed it. When the card held steady the heart was shrunken and black.

"Behind you, death. Death by water, death by air or space. Not your death, but that of someone you traveled long with."

The boy was not moving now. His hands held the table as if shackled there. His eyes were on the glistening inks of the colored cards.

"So many Swords," she said, her voice under strict control.

"This crowns you." A man in a red and white gown, waving a white wand. "The Juggler. Or the Magician.

"This is before you." A man working at a golden disk, in a room lined with seven more disks. "Apprenticed to the Juggler. Perhaps less danger then. . . ."

Another card: a golden wheel spun, letters and symbols around its rim. Winged creatures watched from the corners; they were up-side down. Riding on the wheel were a lion with a human head and a man with a head like a wolf's. When the card stopped, the wolfman was uppermost, the lion beneath.

"The Wheel reversed, the Jackal-God high," she said with a hiss of breath. Then, more softly, "All my sadness . . . all my joy . . . this is what you fear."

Turn and tap: a man on a riverbank, picking up and planting three staffs. He stopped with a wand in each hand and one in the ground.

"This is outside you. A merchant or master with more than he can handle. Do you see that third wand?"

He abruptly realized she had spoken directly to him. "The third wand?"

"He would keep all the wands, but he has only two hands, do you see? And his eyes are on the river, for his ships are passing."

"Is the wand for me?"

"It is planted in the earth. You will be able to take it, when you meet him. But remember, it will fill one of your hands as well.

"Your hope." A cathedral, and a pleased workman with metal coins in his hands. "You want to be a craftsman. That is why you must take care to keep your hands unencumbered."

"The next card is the future, isn't it?"

She nodded. "And you would turn it, would you not?" She pushed the deck toward him, tapped it. "Now turn. I have put in my skill."

He turned the card with two fingers. Woman and boy were silent.

A robed figure lay prone on a beach. Ten swords pinned it to the sand. A small wave rolled in, washed around the body.

"Not a card of violence. I am Celene Tourdemance, and I say so. It is the old spirit slain, but look; here comes the tide, and it brings the new soul in from the sea."

The boy sat back, well back. Whatever spells had bound him were broken. "I really have to leave," he said. "Do I owe you any magic? I have some."

The woman's look had changed as well. "I do not read for money. I read because I am a reader.

"You say you have to go, because of the Ten of Swords. You will not go for an hour yet, that is what I say. In an hour it will be dark, and then you will go. And then, will you see the Ten? No, you will not, for it is your final future. To reach the Ten you must pass the Juggler, and the Eight Coins, and the man with Wands. You must run beneath the Wheel, and draw the three swords from your heart.

"You are not even a knight, yet; just a page, still drinking from the cup. And you think the cup is the Grail of blood, but it is just a glass of sorry wine."

And, once again caught between the cluttered walls and the sound of her voice, he said something he had not said often, even for a small boy: "Yes, Mistress Celene." He sat down and latched his Webset. She gathered up the cards and set them each another cup of bitter coffee.

He opened the set again, enabled it. The screen shimmered with multicolored static.

"Can you use that?"

He nodded.

"Without the black knights, the *samedis*, finding you?"

He paused.

"You see? The swords, they have not fallen yet. Do this. When you leave, go to the skyport by the sea. No other. Find a ship of the line Rina Rosenfeld owns—that would be Starwinds. Take the first Starwinds ship. No other."

"Where will it go?"

"I would God I knew. But if I do not know, will the *samedis*? Do not ask me any more, now. Drink your coffee, and leave when the streets are full."

She stood up, pulled her shawl over her head, and tucked the deck of cards into her sleeve. "Good-bye, now. When next you have a reading, remember you are the Page of Cups, and tell them who told you so."

She paused at the door, said, "Not until the Romany come out," and left.

He waited a few minutes, until he was certain she was not coming immediately back, then opened the Webset and enabled it.

BELL STELLAR COMMUNICATIONS CORPORATION
WEB LOGON 40/12/00 16.22.18
GNOSIS COARCA CODE
??

And he stopped. He had a Gnosis number he could use, enter safely because it was not his own.

But what good would it do him? He knew one trick and one only, and for it they were chasing him.

But he wanted to use the set. He rested his fingers on the keys he knew, touched some of the controls that he didn't understand. Just one brief prayer to BellStel. But whom did he know to make the call to?

Only a page, still drinking.

He banged a fist on the keypanel.

SLW34P appeared on the screen and
IMPROPER ENTRY
:REPRISE
GNOSIS COELCE CODE
??

disable, he typed, and the screen went silver again.

Not yet, he thought, *not yet.*

There were sounds from outside; voices, and the pop of fireworks. He latched the set and opened the door.

CHAPTER 2

NIGHT AND STARWINDS

The Romany had come out. The carnival of the night was on.

Fire jugglers and laser dancers lit corners of the plazas. Swordsmen dueled each other through the crowds, slashing near enough to the spectators to catch their interest.

Little groups of Goliards were there (and the boy avoided them) pretending to become bored quickly by the events, as they pretended boredom with anything and everyone.

The truth was in the Romany eyes. Wide eyes, liquid black, that caught and imprisoned the soul.

(So 'tis said, so 'tis said.)

The least of the Goliards laughed at CIRCE, whom the thieves feared; that was a delicate matter of social-legal structures. The Goliards killed each other for a misstep in the Dance—in which the killer might have set the steps that were missed minutes before the breach; that was coarser in structure but still the way the law worked. The Goliards had Danced for centuries Standard, since the Last True War, and might Dance for centuries more; that was what twenty-times-multiplied life spans, what Lifespan, had done to men, and to Man.

But those same Goliards feared the entrapment of Romany eyes, and only a few dared Romany Court until the safety of dawn. And then, perhaps, what they feared was the soil of homeworlds spread under their beds, and their nocturnality, and the old legends that cannot die.

The boy threaded his way through the Court. Hands found him occasionally, some by accident (no pardon asked, none given), some by design. He turned his stare on those, and in the festival light it was enough to frighten.

Romany eyes, they said. Though in a way they were all old-Romany. No one else had left old blue Earth. But the strain had separated out once more, as perhaps it always would.

A pair of sexual sculptors had stripped to Hellmann wings and were floating slowly, slowly, up from a square. They touched, pushed away, touched again, continued to rise. What little sound the Hellmanns made was soon drowned by crackle of fire and common night noise, and, silent, the tableau passed the housetops and was silhouetted on stars. A cool blue light picked them out, which offended the purists, but they were in the minority.

The boy had seen sexual sculptors before, found them interesting in a way he could not really describe and felt somehow he should not try to. Now he found that the pair aloft had made him invisible; he could walk among the people below unnoticed, even collide lightly with them and remain unseen.

He took one belt pouch, removed the hard magic, and put the pouch back. The coins did not weigh heavy in his pocket, though it made his heart jump when they jingled together. It was only magic, after all, and while he did have a little, he was leaving on a journey without a visible goal. Besides, it all traded back, forth. Everyone knew that. Not as if people would kill over it.

The sculptors must have been very, very good. They had not yet finished when the boy reached the end of Romany Court.

In the street ahead lay a body, unmoving. A Mem dreamer, he thought, until he got close and saw that the loose and fallen figure was dressed to match the darkness around him. It was a CIRCE operator, with his—no, hist's, his/her/its—helmeted head bent at an angle too sharp for the spine to still be in working order.

The boy was conscious of eyes on him, more aware than ever in his life that he was being watched—more even than when the CIRCEs had trailed him—and he turned.

The face in the crowd that watched him closed its Romany eyes and rotated away.

The skyport was covered with a sheet of light that made the night air glow and spread out over the yellow-gold sea. Launch racks and gantries shone a dull rust color, bunkers and towers flat white. Everything vertical cast shadows in several directions; people walked at the centers of dark rosettes.

The boy finger-brushed his hair, then cradled his Webset in both arms and walked up to the busiest portduster he could find.

"Starwinds, please?"

"Can't you—" Then the 'duster saw who and what he was talking to, and instead of dressing him down said, "Rack Eight, dammit," and forgot the boy at once.

He approached Rack Eight carefully. There was a great deal of sound and fury around the base of the portpod launcher—lights, noise, voices, and uniforms.

"Now listen," he heard, "I want to know why I can't board my pod here."

"M'lord, if I knew why they were—"

"Would you like to know of my connections with Field Developments?"

"M'lord, I don't work for Field Developments."

"Iriane Rosenfeld will hear, just you—"

"*Passengers awaiting Starwinds three-one-eight-niner, the Autumn Cygnet, should move to Ramp One,*" said a surround-sound voice. "*Please follow amber illuminations or use the amber-lighted carriages. Please be advised that nothing whatsoever is amiss with* Autumn Cygnet. *Again, your indicator color is amber.*

"*Passengers awaiting Starwinds—*"

Strings of yellow-brown light threaded out all over the port. The hologram angels were a handsbreadth across, at just above a tall person's reach. Angels couldn't hurt you if you passed through them, but that did not stop a merry few from trying it and demanding recompense for their injuries. Some of them had real injuries, too, which makes one wonder about the things said of magic's unreality.

The boy hiked his case up under his arm and began following the line of light. Two portdusters rolled by then in a service cart.

"Youngie! You headed for *Cygnet*? Jump up!"

"Thank you."

"Sure. Hold to here and here. Tight now. We got wheels instead of Hellmanns, and you feel the bumps."

"Listen to the Goliard, soft in the soles," the other one said. "He never pushed a Hellmann cart with the cells dead."

"Gonna fly high like Johnny Sky?"

"Pardon me?"

"This is your first flight, youngie?"

"Yes," he said. It was not true, but he never counted it as a lie. Portdusters had more stories to tell than all the sole survivors of the '46 Plot, but they never told them unless they thought you'd never seen Space.

The boy supposed that was because so many of the stories were hard vacuum; but then, most of the best ones were. Like the tale of Johnny Sky, the purest nova portduster of them all, who caught his foot in a trailing cable and went into orbit behind a portpod.

"Well, you're gonna start right. They're bringing *Cygnet* down into the thick air tonight, and that's one in a million."

"Aw, Lucy, they do it all the time."

"Not with liners, they don't. Who's the senior here, Zekel? Naw, you've seen 'em ride the little scout stuff down the spiral, that's all. Why d'you think the hullbangers live up in no-weight and pull vac pay, and 'dusters eat 'crete?"

"If you're so smart, tell me how come they're bringing this one down the spiral."

"I'm no nova brain or I'd be up there 'banging." She laughed. "Hell, yes, if I were smart I'd be 'banging tonight. Did you see the blue light shine?"

"I don't look there. Romany eyes—" The portduster looked sharply at the boy. "Maybe there's somebody can't take pod push. Somebody big, like old Rosenfeld."

"You be nice about Rina Rose. She pays a good chunk of your living. And I'll tell you: we're gonna earn 'em tonight. Lots to do when a big bird comes down. Like I say, youngie, you're here for the big show. Real pure nova."

"Supernova," the boy said, and they all laughed.

They set him off by a long, long strip of white increte with black streaks staining it. A last amber angel directed him to a blastsafe room with a half dozen people in it. He looked around for Celene Tourdemance, despite her words, but she was not there.

An Alvanian was, drawn tight into his heavy red gown and surplice, staring at his hands tightly folded in his lap. And a man and woman in bureaucrat's silks, one sleeping, one half so, with a diplomatic case cabled between their wrists. A heavyset man with a stack of papers on one knee and a sixty-four-and-screen Webset like the boy's on the other typed code and was lost to the world. A woman held a book in front of motionless eyes, not at all concealing her blindness.

And there was a soldier in red and silver and shiny boots, who looked at the boy and nodded. It was the Goliard from the night before.

"Well, good morrow and well met," he said, with a smile that curled his mustache upward. He had bright blue eyes and a sharp face, black hair without a strand out of place, bony quick hands. "Do you know what all this fuss is about? It's not your doing, is it? Ah, no, I didn't mean that, boy. Come and sit down."

He did not sit. "They're landing the ship."

"I'd guessed that. The question is, why?"

"I don't know."

"Neither do I. Come on, boy, sit down with a soldier of the king. That a Webset you have there?"

The Third Literate looked up from his programming, saw the boy's age, and turned back. "Edset," he said, as if someone were listening.

"Sit down, please. It may be a long wait. I am Colonel Augustine of the CI Pathfinders. Who are you? Don't tell me—you're the Prince of Cups. Like the card."

The boy sat down next to the Colonel. "Thank you for helping me last night."

"Ah, 'twas wild, wasn't it?" he said loudly. Then, in a murmur: "Not too public, please; don't you know that wires vibrate when you pull them? Heaven and hell have been moved, but we're in purgatory yet."

An official in a rumpled tunic came into the shelter. "If you wish, nobles, you may watch the landing of the *Autumn Cygnet* from the deck above. I am told it will be a most unusual sight, and the hazard is trivial. Follow me, please."

All rose except the blind woman, who jerked her head from side to side, straining for sounds; finally she too stood, switched on the search beam of an IRdar and followed the others out.

There was a breeze on the deck, smelling of open water and skyport chemicals. No stars were visible in the overall glow; then one appeared, and grew. A finger of soft-laser light stabbed up and struck it.

"Please secure any loose objects, nobles, hold on to hats and pouches; there'll be a wind."

The couriers wound in their cable, pressed the pouch between their bodies; one hid something in his hand that might have been a gun. The programmer folded his papers, set them on the Webset's keyboard, and closed it.

The single star had outlines now: a large bright shape with three smaller projections. A siren rose and fell and rose. The Alvanian bit a fingernail and clutched his surplice with both hands. The woman tapped her foot erratically on the increte deck.

Not one star now, but four. Three shuttles linked to the liner, straining to hold her up. *Cygnet* was a lifting body, a huge one, but not meant to fly, only to belly down the ballistic spiral in extreme cases (such as this one evidently was). More than a hundred meters port Pryne to starboard, half a thousand meters bow to stern, she split the night open with the rush of her coming.

"It's so *loud*," the blind woman said, and the port official forgot himself and answered: "There's not enough Hellmann power on this planet to land her properly. Those are turbos, and, yes, they are loud." He was nearly shouting and barely heard. "Damned if I know why there isn't a law against them. Damned if I know why they're doing this, or how they figure to get her up again. Three hundred up there, half a dozen down here—who's so supernova *important*?"

The programmer stared up at the ship-filled sky, his Webset hanging loose in his grip. "How are they going to *stop* it?"

The liner shifted, the carriers shivered, and the strange "turbos" screamed like demons. How odd they were, the boy thought—like Pryne tubes open at both ends, but so loud, so loud. Maybe they were an early Pryne tube, an experiment; but there was no envelope. Or perhaps the sound was an envelope. Surely, though, they could not move faster than light.

The scream altered in tone, just like a Hellmann plate under shifting load. The airborne mass shuddered again, and then indeed there was a wind.

It put hair in the eyes and fluttered clothing on the body, tore at anything not fastened down, threw dust and bits of light matter in double handfuls. The boy dropped to one knee, felt a steadying hand on his shoulder but could not tell whose.

Then the wind died, but not the noise. "This way, please," the official bellowed, and the group scuttled after him, holding tight to themselves.

They passed portdusters who dragged cables and hoses around, prying open plates to snake plextronic probes inside, people in shipsleeves with metal braid and softsuits with the helmets thrown back, a florid Supersteward who bawled out whoever was on the other end of the Ariel in his hand.

"Board quickly, please, nobles," the official said wearily; it was perfectly clear what he wanted to say, but people who say what they want don't get to be skyport officials.

A Hellmann sled glided up and another uniformed man got out: stars on his cap, and a badge on his tunic.

"Boarding control."

"We're in a hurry," said the skyport man.

"Everybody's always in a hurry. Boarding control," he explained again. A woman got out of the hovering sled carrying a large green box.

"All right," the control officer said—control officers always begin with "all right," especially when things are all very wrong—"if you'll have your Gnosis cards out, we'll get you on board as quick as we can."

"Perhaps I did not explain," said the skyport man. There were certain conditions under which he could say *exactly* what he wanted and still stay where he was. He was carefully measuring the present circumstances for fit. "We are in a hurry—the Skyport Authority, that is."

"I work for SPA too."

"Nothing lasts forever."

That stopped the control officer cold. His eyes got narrow and his lip twitched. "Shinom," he said to the woman, who was assembling the Lit-Crit unit.

"Ymph arbun?" she said through a mouthful of cable connectors.

"We won't run the full Literacy series. Just set it up for Gnosis scan."

"Yefthur."

The skyport man looked pained, but held up his hands. The passengers lined up before the green box. One by one they slid their Gnosis cards into a slot, tucked hands behind a privacy screen to tap in their codes, and stared into the goggles on top of the machine.

Until the blind woman, who said, "No."

"Pardon?"

"I won't look in your eyepoppers."

"Do you expect to fail?"

"No, I don't expect to fail."

"Then use the unit, please. The officer will assist if—"

The hand with the IRdar slammed down on the Lit-Crit. "My eyes are about to come through," she said unevenly. "Do you know how long it takes to get new eyes?"

"M'lady—" That was the skyport man.

"There are no burns on my retinas. If your machine burns them, the law will make them wait to give me my eyes. They might not give them to me at all.

"My retinas are just detached, that's all—not burned. Not burned!" She pounded the cabinet. "I didn't cheat any damned machine and get my eyes burned!"

"My lady," said the officer slowly, "they're blue goggles, not red. Scanners. No lasers."

The woman tossed her head. "Oh," she said calmly. "You all would have known that, of course. I couldn't have. I'm blind, you see." She put her face to the goggles. "They have to keep changing my file pattern every few weeks. The pieces of my retinas drift around, and I couldn't pass a scan if they didn't change the pattern, of course." She aimed her IRdar on the ramp and walked toward the ship.

"Now hope," whispered Colonel Augustine, his mustache tickling the boy's ear, "and pray, if you do, that your card pleases the machine; I had two tricks to pass you aboard, but they're both undone now. I won't kill to protect you, and if I die for you this whole charade is for nothing."

"Wait now," the control officer said, and stopped the boy with a hand. "We're by-God going to preserve some minimum of the law. Spell the name of this spaceline, youngson."

"S-t-a-r-w-i-n-d-s."

The officer tore a bit of paper from the Lit-Crit's printer, produced a stylus. "Write it."

The boy did.

"All right. I'm not happy, but I've done something."

They boarded without further incident. A worried-looking steward directed the boy to a posh-two stateroom, removed a crash harness from its locker, and instructed him in the lost art of strapping in.

The ship trembled and heaved as it was lifted off, with the veriest murmur of noise allowed to leak past the sonic dampers—as a reassurance, something to listen to.

It was not a bad shaking, but it went on and on, minutes and minutes—not like a portpod push, which was jointbang and *whoosh* and then orbit silence till you boarded. The sounds of grinding and strain were an anchor for the mind against the strangeness of the procedure. In strange country the observation "It's quiet" is always followed by "Yeah, too quiet."

The rumble tapered off, and then it *was* quiet; then came the low, even, warm *thum-thum-thum* of the Pryne tubes. The dampers were still on; Prynebeat was not sound, but leakage, a trickle of energy from the universe outside the ship's shimmering envelope, the Real Space of Euclid and Einstein, to the space of Hawking, Koniichev, and Pryne inside.

Erhard Hellmann's plates kept the gravity aright inside a starliner, and the rectifier screens made the space outside look Euclidean instead of Koniichevan, but the Prynebeat thrummed through the fingertips and scalp as a reminder that one traveled ten or a hundred or a thousand times faster than feeble electromagnetic radiation.

One thing was faster still, of course. Thus the Web. Thus the Ercon.

The annunciator chimed. "Passengers may now release harness, and have the freedom of the ship. We regret the inconvenience, which has been for your comfort and safety. Annunciators will be left open in all rooms; passengers encountering difficulties with their harness should so state and will receive immediate assistance."

The boy released and stowed his harness in a moment. He went to the annunciator, pressed the Audio Only switch and twisted the sound sensitivity all the way down; it was impossible to shut the thing entirely off, he knew, but this would help. The fact that a liner the size of *Autumn Cygnet* carried several hundred harnessed passengers and twenty stewards to unharness them would help more.

He took his Webset to the center of the room, since the pickups would be in the corners. He set a chair behind himself and only then opened and enabled the terminal.

BELL STELLAR COMMUNICATIONS CORPORATION
WEB LOGON 80/16/22 14.04.05
GNOSIS COADSA CODE
??

He entered the safest of the five combinations he knew, hearing the familiar tune of the keytones.

NOTICE—NOTICE—NOTICE

He held his breath and did not release it until the flashing message rolled up and was followed by:

YOU ARE ATTEMPTING TO OPERATE THROUGH A
PSEUDOVELOCITY ENVELOPE WITHOUT PROPER SHIELDING.
BSCC DOES NOT RECOMMEND THIS PRACTICE AND CANNOT BE
LIABLE FOR ERRORS RESULTING THEREFROM.

He tapped ERASE, then began entering code groups. He ordered the commercial Portwatch program—nothing untoward about that; many people liked to watch the flow of traffic around a skyport.

Stars appeared in depth on the screen, reds and blues and yellows a bit exaggerated for effect. Then the ships came out, spheres for cargo vessels, cubes for barges, cylinders for yachts and liners, cones for military and police vessels. Near each tiny drifting symbol was a number.

He picked out a cone following close upon the cylinder that he knew represented *Cygnet*. The screen sparkled and changed to black letters on white:

PORTWATCH ROSTER: VESSEL 47
PORTWORLD: BRASS
SHIP TYPE: REVENUE CUTTER
OWNERSHIP: COMBINED INTERSYSTEM REGULATION
                                         AND CONTROL EXECUTIVE
—FURTHER DATA ON THIS VESSEL IS RESTRICTED—
—SORRY—

There was a bank of knobs set in grooves near the keyboard. The boy entered another number with one hand and instantly shoved

one of the knobs to the end of its travel. A red light flashed on the
set, and the keys locked for a moment. Then the light went out.
The restriction statement vanished from the screen and more lines
rolled up:

WEBCODE: RL8124CI3606
BEGIN RUN::
Ship's armament and special facilities follow

Without waiting for more, the boy entered the Webnumber given,
holding his fingertips lightly on the keys. Light specks swirled on the
screen, then began to coalesce into a picture. When the image was
recognizable as a black helmet on black shoulders, but before it had
cleared, he hit the Screen Defeat switch, grabbed two of the sliders
and pulled them down, pushed them back.

The screen flickered, pulsed brightly once, and then was filled
with columns of numbers rolling up and out.

The boy reached for the keys again. He looked up a little, at the
blood-red numbers rolling on black, and in the darkened screen saw
his own face. His eyes were narrow, and the muscles of his cheeks
and jaw were hard. He looked down.

A hand came down on his shoulder. His head snapped up, and
he looked straight into the silver-blue eyes of Colonel Augustine.

"No, child. You must not."

The boy turned away.

Augustine took him under the arms and lifted him bodily, shoving the Webset aside with a boot. "Listen. I do not say should not. I
say must not. Do you understand? Two crimes, as quaint as it may
sound, do not cancel out into justice served."

The boy struggled, struck out blindly. The Colonel took the
blows and held on.

"Stop it now. I know what you can do. Yes, I know; I can do it myself, though it took me long and long to learn it. That you learned
on your own, and so early, speaks of a miracle. A talent such as I
have never seen."

The boy stopped squirming.

"You're born to spin the Web, child. No one can teach that touch on the matrix sticks that you have; yes, I watched you. It's not a hard trick, the way you do it. There are more subtle ways, but you'll master them easily. Now break Web and fold your set away."

"But, they're—"

"I will deal with CIRCE."

"*No!*" He broke free and put hands on the keys, but then hesitated—

"*Dian*," the man said, "*stop it.*"

The boy looked up sharply, then turned back to his work.

"Think, child. Can you not see that killing the black knights is the last way there is to stop them? In less time than you think they will find it unprofitable to chase you. But kill them and they'll hunt you, and hunt you *down*.

"And if you tip your hand now, show them that the other incident was no accident but Webspinning talent—*untrained* talent—then CIRCE will blast you for a poison flower, cut you down ere you can blossom."

Click-pause-click went the keys, *ping-peep-ping* the marker tones.

Augustine grasped the boy, Dian, around the upper arms and squeezed hard. Seen behind Dian's in the Webscreen, his face was flat as a jeweler's velvet displaying the twin diamonds of his eyes.

"Think, child, if you have the knack; should anyone else die the way your mother and father died?"

The boy stopped, mouth open. And screamed. Cried and screamed.

Colonel Augustine folded the boy in his arms, hugged and rocked him.

"Oh, child," he said, "you are hurt, like a child is, worse than all the world. And I meant it, I meant it, I had to stop you . . . but not again, never again, if the Hounds are at my heels and the world on fire ahead. On that my word. The fraudulent criminal word of Mr. Aristide. And the real word of the real man. Of—" He said a name. "There, it's out. Now, Dian, you know my name, and I know yours, and we have the keys to each other."

The boy was almost quiet. His eyes were closed, seeping tears.

"Rest now. When you wake, you'll have a new name, and you'll be secret from the world, the air, and the great Web itself."

CHAPTER 3

THE HAND OF THE MASTER

railer Diomede," the boy said. "It sounds funny."

"Everyone's name sounds funny," said Mr. Aristide, who for a while was through being Colonel Augustine. He sat in a red silk long tunic and white trousers fresh from the fabricator. He had removed his medals and the braid from his Pathfinder uniform, put them in his traveling bag, and pushed the cloth of the costume into the deweaver on the wall. "And most names don't have reasons. Do you know the names of the omnicorp rulers?"

"Sure. Iriane Rosenfeld at Field Developments, Soren Nykvist at the Asgard Complex, and Gian Paolo Sforza at Florentine Group." The fabricator chimed and a suit of green and black coarseweave dropped into the delivery tray. A green beret followed, with a plume, and soft-sided black shoes. The boy gathered them up and began to dress.

"I would say you were well informed if those three did not spend so much magic making sure their names were known. But all right. Do you know, then, what their names mean?"

"You said names didn't have reasons."

"I did. For most are chosen by accident. But have you never heard the first law of magic—sorcery, I mean, though it applies to money as well? That the name is the thing?"

"No." The plume drooped and he pushed it back.

"Then you must learn it. Look now. When you spin the Web, you will call on many things. On mechanical memories, and thinking links, and people who sit at Web terminals elsewhere. When you learn a little more, you will converse with the strands of the

Web—with the machinery that makes it move and fetch and carry. And to call a thing you must know its name, do you see?"

"Like ship numbers and Gnosis codes?" he asked, tugging at a shoe.

"Yes. And serials, and locations on tape and in crystal core, and process code names, and a thousand things more. But it is not enough just to know the name. Any common catalog knows many names—though some are only written in uncommon storage. You must know what names mean.

"Soren Nykvist's yacht is named *Hammer and Spear*, as most starfixed youngfolk know; but how many of them know the words Mjolnir and Gungnir, the Hammer of Thor and the Spear of Odin? To talk to Soren's machines directly, one must.

"And long before Gian Paolo, when there was a blue Earth, there was another Sforza. He was not born with the name, either. He took it because it means 'Strong of Arms,' which he was. And as it was in the beginning, was later with the Hawkwood Armaments Corporation, is now with the Florentine Group of industries."

"And my name?"

"Ah, child mine, you're calling it that already, are you. Well and well. Do you know what the Grail is?"

"The magic cup the knights were looking for." He put a finger to his mouth, his eyes filling up again with that betrayal.

"Not what it was. Don't look so bought and sold, Dickon my pupil. What it is. The Grail is the object of the chase. The cup that is, yes, magic; that heals and cures and does whatever you want a magic cup to do. Do you know why it was so much more than a gilded coffee mug?"

"It had blood in it." Mistress Celene had said that.

"And whose blood?"

"I don't know."

"You . . . don't?"

"Magic blood, I guess. A dragon's?"

"No. Not that rough beast. But I still think we've chosen aright. You're a cup, to be filled: a Grail, if you will. For that's what's important to the story. That the true Grailers sought nothing they did not already have. They were already magic cups full of pumping, flowing warm blood every bit as special and extraordinary as the dry granulated stuff in that silly silver chalice.

"I'm warping your mind, child mine. Does the bending hurt overmuch?"

"I don't understand. Am I supposed to be looking for the Whole Grail"—he held out a hand, as if there were a card in it, tapped the air with a finger—"or am I supposed to be a cup—or a Person with Cups?"

"'Holy Grail,' Grailer, not 'Whole,' though the pun intrigues. The answer is both, as I've been trying to say. You will always be looking for something, which if grace endures you will find while stronger, viler knights do not. And you are the thing that some are seeking.

"No, don't recoil so. Put CIRCE from your mind. You are safe from them, for a long moment. You don't even know what they are. God help you, you'll learn. God help me, it will be I who teaches you.

"Now say your name."

"Grailer Diomede. And you're Mr. Aristide."

"Yes, I am. Colonel Augustine is put off with his garments." He brushed at his silks.

"Can I be other people, too?"

"You must be, sometimes. I'll teach you soon enough. But let us breakfast before our seventh impossibility."

"Where are we going now?"

"Maracot Falls, Marcera. My home of the greatest number of moments. The water falls there for kilometers, and its color changes with the seasons. It should be autumn there now; the water will be silver-blue, like full moonlight. Do you like moonlight, Grailer Diomede?"

"Webspinning," the boy said, dreamily; he had heard the words. He had seen moonlight and waterfalls, and they were all right. But Webspinning—

"Fourth Literacy," Mr. Aristide replied.

Fourth Literacy: there was no such thing. There couldn't be.

After comprehension came coding, after coding came creating code. What could come still after?

> > >

Down they fell from heaven to Marcera—who was no one, Grailer learned, nor any thing, but an idea. *Marcēre*: to wither. *Marcescent*: to wither without dying.

The copper salts that had dyed the summer waters deep heart-prisoning blue were fading now, and the rivers ran silver; indeed it might seem that they were fading to die.

The rivers ran to the waterfalls, which were thousands of meters high. The water rocketed from rounded brinks past stratum-banded kilometers of cliff face to hit with the sound and fury of an augering starliner. Clouds of mist rose that could have swallowed cities and gave birth to faery and daemon legends among people who should have known far better.

Humans, even starborn ones, are born with the fear of falling, yet they love to watch things fall. The Marcerans made laws against the dumping of massive and dangerous wastes, and that was all. Marcera's falls were great and forgiving of the small debris that was cast in: the glasses from a toast, lovers' clothing, metal coins for luck.

Also committed to the waters were the bodies of the dead, suitably graveclothed; separated lovers, who in hurtling watermass seldom recited their careful farewell scripts: the tears of lonely humans who from their windows heard the world weep in sympathy.

All the travel in the cities was up and down, and with so many levels to rise or fall (over five hundred at Maracot Falls) updown linear was the only way to travel if the arrival was the most important thing. What good were elevators, such a long trip in such a small private space? Well . . . elevators could be made even slower than they had been, and much more comfortable. . . . The Companions of the Cliffs, gentlemen and ladies all, wore great magnetic keys with hand-filling T grips. Those keys went into the command panels, locking the doors and the call mechanism so that the two (or more) of you could share the ride uninterrupted. Ascending, descending. When the arrival was less important than the journey.

The cities of Marcera clung to the fallslopes, embracing the falls, for love and pain and all that sort of sentimental nonsense bound the people to the water. But it was not so nonsensical, really. Whole cities had been built on Earth, when there was an Earth, in worship of a river valley, and buildings raised to the sun and the moon, and none of those ever whispered audibly in your guilty, adolescent dreams. Nor would any of them, not even the rivers, receive your dead so completely and forgivingly and forgettably. Falling water broke rock, but healed hearts.

In a portpod with whistling wings came to this place new-named Grailer Diomede and many-named Mr. Aristide, for the learning and teaching of an art that was not possible.

Was or wasn't, they were two years on patterns and the world at large, reaching something Mr. Aristide called First.

Very little of it was Webwork. Very much of it was clothes and disguises. "You can't use many of these tricks now, your growth unreached, your voice unbroken. But if you learn the gambits and the openings, the game will come naturally to you.

"*Posture*, Grailer. *Poise*. You or I or anyone else can wear the clothes of an artisan or a governor. But if we do not appear dreamy or blustery, neither role will convince. CIRCE"—he waited for a shudder and got one—"will notice. The Goliards will carve you up alongside cakes and ale."

"Am I going to dance with the Goliards?"

"I promised you that, didn't I. When you have learned the steps, you will. For I have seen those die whose steps were false."

Two years to First.

First Literacy: Ability to enter one's name and Gnosis code. To use the Web as a communications device (only). To answer five random questions at the Lit-Crit checkpoint before being permitted to board an interstellar vessel.

"Without it," Mr. Aristide was saying, "you can't leave a world."

"I'm First Lit," Grailer said, annoyed.

"You're Fourth. But if they find that out, they'll grab you and hold on. So you must learn to answer the questions as if you were a First, use that very exotic Web terminal you have there as if it really were the edset that man on Brass thought it was."

"I could have fooled him."

"No, you couldn't. He would have seen your hands in places no First Lit's would rest in. No, I was counting on his claiming you for a First, without checking, to get you out of Juvenal. Fortune was fortunate and I did not have to use that plan."

And so Grailer learned to hold his fingers crookedly, to accidentally bump keys with his sleeves and the heels of his hands, to hit the combinations that would light signals and lock up the board.

"Why would I ever want to gooflock my Webset?"

"To make people laugh at you."

"What?"

"To make them think you a clumsy fool, and ignore you; or perhaps take the set from you and enter codes that would bring the black knights running if you entered them."

"Or that I was only pretending to know."

"Now, Grailer, you will become a Second Literate."

> > >

"Type: 'An antinomy adumbrated antinomy, arsenic, and adulated atrophy above another abbotric.'"

There was more Webwork than before, but always instruction in the steps of the Dance.

"A woman insults you. Do you duel?"

"Is she armed?"

"With a blade."

"Snapknife, ignore her. Combat knife, make the challenge formal. Roundel dagger, slay her on the spot."

Crack went Ari's short white wand. "I fault you for a Spinner, not a Goliard. That answer is right, but not right for you. You do not kill, Grailer. Do not, will not, shall not."

"But wouldn't that be a misstep?"

"It might. Think how you could make it *not* be a misstep."

"Knock her dagger clear and hone it with mine, blade to blade, until a blade or her nerve broke."

"Good. That is good."

"But it requires that I be an excellent knife fighter."

"You are learning."

> > >

Once Grailer, in lace and crimson satin, was present at the Dance as it whirled the measures in an echo tube. The falls rumbled at a comfortable but speech-drowning level and sucked a fresh draft by.

A Goliard insulted another with a posture, an awkward movement, perhaps an inartistic flapping of his coattails in the breeze.

The insultee gestured vilely (but subtly) and with a snap of frogs and a flash of linen and velvet produced a case of pocket pistols.

The offender began a speech, possibly of deferral, possibly of riposte; it was literally impossible to say. Words were useless. And the audience jostled and jockeyed for seats at the fray, awaiting the sound of a pocket pistol, which can be heard above any comfortable noise.

The offender hemmed and wavered and sidestepped and, at the last possible moment before his fate was decided by jury, buried his face in his hands. There was a pop, and a nimbus of white about his head, and eyes all around stopped open; a new and dramatically sound suicide was a great rarity, and would most certainly be rewarded with a wake after the fashion of the late Timothy Finnegan and the gob-shutting of the pistolero.

But the hands came away without blood or blackened flesh—oh, quite the opposite. The offending Goliard's face and hands were white, white, only a daub of his natural darkness left on the tip of his nose. He juggled the empty containers of makeup around for a bit, so that even the less quick would recognize the character of Pierrot le Fou.

Then he stiffened, letting the spraylets fall *clink-clonk-clank.*

Moving jerkily, as though the puppeteer pulling his strings were drunk, *notre ami* Pierrot took one of his opponent's pistols in flopping fingers, pointed it at his own head—fired—and missed by half a meter. The bullet fell he knew not where.

And there was no one else to care. This was what they lived their lives for, these Goliards of sixteen hundred years' average duration—the countermove that altered the whole of the game, the successful double-rook sacrifice, the seven-card showdown with blind low hole card wild.

For the pair of pistols so flashily played had become Dead Man's Handful for the Goliard who held them; he now had to fire *his* shot . . . and from his demeanor it did not appear that he had the clown white up his sleeve to call his opponent's raise. As if the crowd would have allowed mere imitation as a legal riposte.

The insulted party had great trouble cocking his own pistol. There were offers of help. He placed the barrel to his temple finally; sweat fouled his long eyelashes, blinding him. He stood, trembling, for a good little while.

When after a time he fainted, his guns were tucked in his belt butt-forward like those of the immortal Hickok of Deadwood. Pierrot offered a sash to bind him, and he was taken to the falls end of the echo tube. Grailer heard at length that he had not awakened for an exit line.

So while Grailer learned the knife, he learned much more. He remembered how the pistolero had carried his case at the small of his back, hidden yet accessible, and practiced strapping his Webset there.

> > >

"Quote," Mr. Aristide said, "Section Twenty of the Universal Communications Code."

"It says they can kill people who spin the Web."

"*No.* It does *not. Quote* it."

Grailer drew a breath. "In cases where it is suspected that equipment of the Bell Stellar Communications Corporation, public access or private, has been in any way invaded, altered in form or content, or otherwise tampered with, the Combined Intersystem Regulation and Control Executive shall be empowered to terminate suspects with extreme prejudice."

"Correct. Notice, now, did you say 'kill'?"

"No."

"'Spin the Web'?"

"No."

"'*People*'?"

"No. 'Suspects.'"

Four years to Second.

Second Literacy: Ability to retrieve and store data in open Web storage. To use existing precoded programs in normal access patterns.

"This joystick is your pointer. Never call it an XYZ cursor, except pronouncing the word slowly, 'cur-sore,' and with evident ignorance of its meaning."

Mr. Aristide touched the bank of sliding buttons. "What are these? Tell me the truth, not what a Second Lit would say."

Grailer shrugged. "Slides."

"That's wrong. A gap in your learning. But it's right for a Second Lit, so we won't fill it yet. I've seen you rest the last fingers of your right hand on these; don't do it. A First Lit would never touch these at all. A Second only moves them when instructed by the screen to 'move slides until all lights go out,' or the like. That handrest comes naturally to you because you are a Fourth, but remember—it brands you as a Third, *or higher*. You're fifteen, Grailer, and you don't want to be taken yet for a Third."

Third Literacy: Ability to change the structure of existing Web programs. To write and enter original Web code. To use Web hardware as well as precoded software.

"Add one more phrase and it becomes the public definition of Fourth Literacy: '—*without authorization and in spite of protective systems.*' That, child mine, is why the Combined Executive wanted you dead at nine, why the Lex Bell Stellar was codified to permit the killing. You can tamper and tarry, rob and maim. You are free.

"And if you add another clause, you have the real and true definition of our craft. Don't write it down, whisper it after: *'practicing techniques that the Web was not designed to permit and that none but themselves realize are possible.'*

"I tell you this now, before I have taught you to be a good and legitimate Third Literate, because there will not be another pause like this in your training. The line between Operation and Programming is sharp. That between First and Second Literacies is blurred. That between Programming and Webspinning is almost impossible to see, even for those who live in one of those two countries." He toyed with his white wand. Grailer drew his hands back from the keys where they rested.

"You said, years ago, that I was a Fourth Literate."

"You were and are. You were born one. We are all born something, child mine; players of music, cutters of stone, pilots of starships, killers of men. But one must be taught the use of the harp, the chisel, the control board, the poison, knife, or gun. Only drinking and lust come naturally, and even in those fields there are master barkeeps and sexual sculptors."

"You mean, I'm a Fourth Literate, but I'm not really a Webspinner? Not yet?"

"And now I will teach you to program and code."

> > >

Two years to Third.

Once he was working, innocently enough, on an accounting program, an ercstacker, and his mind and hands strayed.

The erc had once been the Earthsystem Reserve Credit, but with no Earthsystem or Earth anymore it had changed. It had been the Energy, and so forth, for a while, and most of the Ercon still banked on deuterium and such, but with whole subsystems gone closed-cycle that wasn't any too universal.

So if you pressed, hard, on the right buttons, you could get a mumbled explanation of Economic Reference Counters, of numbers that got bigger *here* and smaller *there* while real goods were shipped around, and of planets that claimed some of their ercs were in metal coins so that the trivial obligations of life could be accounted for without pushing buttons.

But what was magic, Grailer wondered, what were ercs? "Money," people said, but the "money" of legend and antiquarian fiction seemed to bear little relation in its sources to this thing called magic . . . though oddly enough some people still pursued it just as fervently.

But one dropped magic in the slot and punched up heart's desire, and as long as one kept on a labor roll (he giggled a bit—the Goliards would dagger you to the nearest flat surface if they discovered such a thing about you) or had some other such input source, the card went in the bank slot, the light in the goggles was incoherent, and the coins jingled out.

So he misstacked some ercs—just a few. His hands tingled, he didn't know why, so he shifted some more. The tingle got sharper— feedback from one of the blocks he was suppressing, perhaps—but see, here was the possibility of making everyone in the Ercon economically equal—and wasn't that what the Ercon was all about? There was enough transmission noise available to be exploited even for the four or five quadrillions alive. He pressed more keys.

Crack went not Ari's wand, but the set itself, a bright green spark that threw Grailer tail-over-head to the floor.

He looked up from where he lay, saw Mr. Aristide both sidewise and with that strange barrel distortion of vision produced by fever or very great fear. Ari looked pale, his skin bloodless, his eyes ringed whitely, his lips blue; he was pale unto death.

But it must have been a trick of the light, the angle, the fall, because just a short time later Ari was no corpse at all, and, reaching a hand down to Grailer, speaking offhand:

"Corona charge," he said. "There are things you must be careful of touching—precious things foremost among them. And I'll teach you better ways of getting your magic."

After Third, the polishing.

> > >

It was not difficult to write code—not if all one desired was to give the Web a task. One said "go," and it went. "Do," and it did it.

But sometimes the task changed with time, or was altered by events, or even by the action of the Web in executing it. And the system (one's tiny fraction of the system, that is) would stop and wait for the theory to be fit to the facts again.

Or—another program could be created that would change the first; a little machine inside the machine that waited for what the programmer was waiting for and did what he would have done. Virtual systems, they were called, though virtue had nothing to do with it. A virtual could answer questions or lie to them with absolute conviction. It could mind the Web and turn away callers. It could look like whatever one wanted it to look like, since the image was transmitted as code and code could be written. That had been called "angeling," after the false images of long-ago radar.

During a slow period Mr. Aristide gave Grailer two strange gifts: a kit of microtools and a pocket perpetual motion, a sphere-gyro like those the Keelyites carried for meditation. Ari said nothing about them.

The gyro disassembled easily enough, and went together again with only slightly more difficulty. But it would not spin up and stay spinning.

Grailer did not mention it; Ari did not ask.

"You've mastered virtuals," said Mr. Aristide, who was now nine years older in mind and age and six months older in body than he had been when Grailer first ran to him. "Now you will know about these." He touched the sliding buttons. "They're called matrix sticks, if you know what they are. This is one of the things that they do."

He tapped the keys, playing a tune on the keytones, which sounded like bells.

"*Ein' feste Burg ist unser Gott.*" Then he moved a matrix stick, just one, just slightly. He played the board again; the same tune, but in a lower key.

"Again." He brushed another stick, not far enough to see. "*Ein' feste Burg*—" An octave lower. "Once more." Now the tones were like organ pipes rather than chimes.

He pushed all four sticks at once, about a centimeter, and touched the SEQ REPEAT key. The sound that emerged was not music at all, but an arrhythmic clicking.

"This is the center of spinning. There is more power in the matrix sticks than most know—no more than a million. A big number, by the standards of a city or a town, but the population of the Intersystem worlds is counted in what, tens to the twelfth power? The thirteenth?

"There are no matrix sticks on a public set, or any but the rarest Ariels. This is a reason why I have taught you as I have; someday you will be caught with only sixteen keys, and without the special mundane knowledge I have given you that would be your end, body and soul. CIRCE does not leave its victims over to be frozen, no matter the hardness of the amber contract."

He turned back to the set.

"Underneath these buttons is a solid block of the purest atomic memory lattice. It is sensitive to the position of those buttons to the block; to each other; to pressure on the buttons, both amount and angle; to the motions of the buttons across its surface."

"And when I move them," said Grailer eagerly, "I can change what I enter. Change my voice. And I can do it by touch. No, wait—I have to do it by touch, don't I, because it means a different thing every time I move them."

He was not looking at Ari, but at the sticks and the screen. He reached out, moved a button carefully with two fingers. "If I were a Third Lit, I'd move them like this—until I got what I wanted. But I'm not. I'm Fourth." He slid the matrix sticks back and forth, one

under each finger. "And I can take what I want with them." The
keytones sounded like bagpipes now, and his fingers danced a reel.

Ari's wand came down on his knuckles.

"No," he said, "you cannot take what you want. I said you were
free, not that you had license. *Timor licentiae conturbat me*, Grailer.
The fear of too much freedom restrains me."

Grailer sucked his hand, his expression dead.

"I gave my word once, on my own true name, that I would never
again hurt you. This does not hurt, child mine; this is not pain at
all. Only memories are painful, Grailer. The brain has no feeling,
but the mind inside it is all in the worlds and stars that can hurt."

Mr. Aristide tapped Grailer's Webset with the golden tip of his
wand. "In not many weeks you will be eighteen years Standard, true
and physical. Will you want to take your Lifespan treatments then?"

"Yes. And I hope I'm a Twenty to your Sixteen."

"There are as many Sixteens as Twenties. And as many poor
ephemeral Twelves. If they could predict how slowly one would age,
this would be a strange and unfamiliar world. Especially for those
with the Eternity Syndrome." He put the wand back in his belt.
"Then in three days I will show you something that I promised you
long ago."

"Why then?"

"Because I am going to show you the Geisthounds. The hidden
face of the craft. And I do not wish you dead, so recently bathed in
immortality."

Those were all the words they spoke together for three days.

> > >

"I will be in the next room, monitoring," Mr. Aristide said on the
third day, "watching you as I have for all this time. I want you to perform a procedure, one forbidden by the U-Comm code, of course,
but I do not care what. Perform it as well as you know how.

"At some point I will cease to precede you in Web circuit. I will
be unable to protect you. At some point after that you will draw the
Hounds. Then you must handle the situation as you see fit."

"Ari, is this a final examination?"

"Examination, yes. Final only if you fail it."

"At least tell me what these Geisthounds I'm supposed to meet *are*."

"I cannot."

Grailer drummed his fingers on the leather and plastic of his Webset. He looked around the room; the only things in it were set, table, one chair, himself, and Ari. It had been stripped bare, and none too carefully, as the walls witnessed.

"But you claim you've kept me safe from these things for nine years. How do I know what's really going on? Sit in here and watch me spin, without a set under your hands. It occurs to me that you didn't protect me from those corona charges."

"The corona shocks were flybites. You had earned them. Grailer, child mine, you mistrust and you fear. You are hurt like only a young man is, worse than all the world.

"You have called the Hounds hundreds, perhaps thousands of times, while learning; they are drawn quicker by coarse and careless work, and care is the last thing learned. As for why I cannot tell you of them too closely—well. Who would you ask to describe Theta Fever, Grailer? A doctor with a book in the Web, or a victim? Surely the doctor's data are less accurate, being distant and secondhand. Why, the doctor would never have entered the room of a patient infected with gamma-strain."

"The patient wouldn't tell me anything," said Grailer, absorbing the point.

"Dead folk do not often."

Grailer stopped tapping on the set and made a fist of his fingers. "If it's so bad, then why haven't I been shown anything? Why not till now? Why not earlier, when I had a chance to stop?"

"Chances, you talk of, and stopping, and earlier choices, and always, always *why*."

Ari put his hands on Grailer's tight white fist. "You had no choice when I found you. You were between two swords. You could not stop once I started you—admit it. You haven't followed me nine years, full aging growing-up years, because you were transiently amused by the Web. Ask any gleam peddler what lights or noises have lasted nine Lifespanned month-long years.

"And as for chances and why—sit down, child, Grailer. Enable the set and play me a tune. Before the song is over, you will know exactly why, and exactly what chance you had before now and will have after."

He let go and left the room.

"Aren't you going to close the door?" Grailer said, bitter, hurt, confused. He did not want to spin the Web at all, touch the keys, slide the sticks . . .

. . . bring threads together, group codes, stretch his hands down megamiles of Webmind and Webmemory . . .

. . . touch a planet, instantly, that the swiftest ship ever made would take weeks in the reaching . . .

. . . instantly. At once, without the passage of time. The t-zero effect. His body seated here, his mind could cross Weblinks without crossing the space—or the time—intervening.

Sweat tingling his fingers, he sat and enabled the set.

BELL STELLAR COMMUNICATIONS CORPORATION
WEB LOGON 18/30/22 06.92.97
GNOSIS COHARE CODE
??

Numbers, the machine wanted, the numbers of a man. Every one of the Ercon's million millions had a Gnosis code (save the illiterate, who were anyway planetbound and culturally nonexistent). Grailer had several, but for this he needed none of them.

A lock is a pattern that wants fulfilling. Small bits of metal must be moved to the right positions, columns of numbers must add to the proper totals, the guard must be told the words he wants to hear.

But a piece of magnetic steel will move metal around. There are mathematical problems with whole families of solutions $y=(f)x$; addition is one of them if you're adding vectors. The guard, being a less convoluted instrument than the Web, is perhaps harder to fool—but wear the right uniform, be in the right place at the right time, and he will *want to hear* the veriest mumble as the password.

Grailer pressed some keys. Those were the words. He stroked the matrix sticks. That was the mumbling. Every motion of the sticks changed the keypresses, entering bands of data rather than bits. And that loose several-things-at-once entry satisfied the equation $(f)x=$ Web entry, partly because of the 10^n Webcalls a day some fraction $10^n/a$ were from fools or drunks or just the forgetful and clumsy, and BellStel still feared such people enough to pass laws against them and make allowances for them.

(So what did the public call the Webcall procedure? *Making a prayer to BellStel.* It's hard to have a war without a misunderstanding somewhere underneath it.)

There had been a security revolution once, when the trapdoor functions and the Knapsack Algorithm had appeared. Encode data through a screen of prime numbers—easy enough; sieve them out again—much harder. Well-nigh impossible.

This system turned a few words into a few thousand decimal digits, and while that was splendidly Gödelian, it did take up a lot of room. Still, most of the data in the world, in the Web, at least at one time had hidden under trapdoors.

Until the invention of the matrix calculators, the calculatrices. And the Koniichev Knot: the proof that number theory was purely a local phenomenon, that prime numbers were not so prime if one altered the rules—and now one could alter the rules. "Intuitive mathematics," it was called by people who did not want it to work. But it just kept on working. Then some people began calling it the Mathematics of Transcendence. By then Koniichev was not around to comment.

When Alexsandr Aloysius Pryne disappeared into the Magellanic Clouds at one thousand times lightspeed, he had a calculatrix under one arm and an unabridged Koniichev under the other. And the Pryne envelope destroyed the mind. . . .

SERVICE
??

the screen prompted. In an upper corner were more words, not Web-neutral black but red and white alternating:

Tapping you now. Go ahead.

Let him watch, Grailer thought. Let him try and follow me, far away where I'm bound. Numbers and names, he thought; so you've been tapping me, you know all the people I can be?

I'll make one more, and show you just how free of you I am.

WHAT SERVICE PLEASE
??

the Web insisted.

gnosis aleph
PLEASE AUTHOdarkness, my name is.

Answering not with an answer but another query: a request for a virtual system. Without the touching of another key on Grailer's part, the Web told itself to permit him access. *On what level?* the puzzled device asked. *Any level he wants*, the virtual said. Grailer propped up the trapdoor with a matrix stick.

MORE SPECIFIC DATA ARE REQUIRED/break interr 6/there is a clear
   file on this level—direct there/break/REPEATING QUERY UNDER
   WHAT AUTHORIZATION
??

The screen held steady. Grailer, knowing that his virtual was still knocking on doors and giving irrelevant replies to perfectly reasonable questions, ignored the request on the screen. Instead, he typed:

name: *grandier, d'urban*
lit: *2*
curr habitn: *marchion's fortress*
curr prof: *religious instruction tl 8*

Grailer smiled. He had put a very bad priest, a rake and despoiler who had long ago gotten burned for it, in one of the top four posts on the most notoriously celibate world in the Ercon.

The Web, meanwhile, was not idle. Nor was it confused. It operated on data and was receiving it. That data, however, was generally implausible, save for small fractions—keywords, phrases, snatches of high-level code.

The Web was not intelligent. Indeed, yea, verily, nay, not intelligent. But through its virtuals and registers, the mind in the iron aped the functions of an intelligence; and one of those functions was to confine and reject implausibilities and follow hot and hard on acceptable data.

But as it accreted that data, bit by acceptable bit, the whole thread, the operation string, built into something that the system would never have found acceptable all at once.

You cannot tell a man that black is white. He will call you a liar or worse. He may get physical. People are like that over black and white. But you can show him that in every black there is a little gray, pushing his ignorant nose into the paper if you must. And in that little gray there is some paler gray. And in that—

This is called proof by recursive series, and it is fraudulent, immoral, logical, and it works. An inflexible mind may resist, may simply refuse to see the gray in the black and the white in the gray. But the Web was built by men who hated and feared inflexibility of mind, and they made it in their image.

There is a different technique, called proof by faulty analogy, which subtly used can prove that white is plaid; and proof by universal negation will demonstrate irrefutably that plaid is black. So black = black, which even an inflexible mind will grudgingly admit to.

Grailer was playing the keys, enjoying the music, spinning patterns and fancy embroidery on the emperor's new clothes.

"Embellish," Mr. Aristide had said, "and vary your pattern; it will limber your muscles and make your path harder to follow. Only remember that you cannot vary an étude you cannot play; be careful that you do not overstretch your—"

Grailer shoved the voice out of his mind, casting an angry glance at the corner of the screen and the words flashing red-white-red there.

Overstretch? Tunes he could not play? We would see!

He tore ten-fingered into the keys, arching a little finger now and *now* to bump knobs and slip the sticks.

The screen went to silver, reflecting his fluttering fingertips like the face of a fine soundboard. Then the speaker hissed and crackled, the screen swirling with colorful noise. Then a moment of silver.

Bang-bang-bang went three fingers on nine keys, and the star of the screen test pattern appeared, a pure 1000.000 Hertz on the speaker.

The words in the corner blinked to *Breaking tap now* and vanished.

He had done it. Given Mr. Aristide the test pattern. Told him, "Sorry, your equipment's out of line." Done what you did to those who called you out of bed. Spit in his eye.

Silver and swirl on the Webscreen again, and a pattern of light: a lattice, glowing columns and horizontal rods, pulsing bright, spreading off deep into the perspectives of the curved crystal screen.

Grailer put two fingers on the XYZ cursor—not three; Third Lits held it with three. As he moved it, the endless three-dimensional grid moved along; he seemed to float above and around and through the cage of lights, passing through delicate auroral veils, past softly glowing cubes and blinking spheres.

He had been here before, but never for long, and never alone. Never totally free.

This was the Web, seen in concept alone, in beauty bare. The rods and columns were the thinking links, the cubes memories and files, the spheres active terminals winking in and out. The shifting veils marked the boundaries of planetary sub Webs, a political thing, but still useful for the traveler because travel even at a thousand times lightspeed still took time.

But here in the Web, *in* it, all the links were the same length. From synapse to synapse within the Web the t-zero effect applied. Centimeters or parsecs, the time of transit was no time at all.

The Web spanned the human universe in the time it took to make your prayer to the other end. It was spread out before Grailer, all of it now, the universe as looked on by Euclid alone, or some non-Euclidean god.

Did he feel like a god? Well, like a giant, at least, with magic boots and gauntlets that stepped and reached forever.

A laugh bubbled up inside his lungs, a cry of sheer clean joy. He snapped his fingers on the cursor, sent the Weblattice spinning and himself hurtling through it, think-links whipping past his view.

He was suddenly aware of someone else with him in the grid, out of his sight but—

Out of sight? Then how did he know—

He touched the cursor, moved it slowly, panning around the pulsing, glowing bars of the lattice.

There was a laugh from the speaker, a cry of laughter, that for one moment he thought was Mr. Aristide mocking him but knew in the second moment was nothing whatsoever human.

It was only a laugh, only a sound, but it made him feel coldness on his face and hollowness between his heart and his gut. Only the vibration of a speaker membrane, but it frightened him.

In the space between the second moment and the third he realized why Ari could not describe a Geisthound to him. No one could meet such a thing and live.

And at the third moment he began to run.

There was a prickling and burning on the backs of Grailer's hands: corona power leaking from the set, charging and stiffening the hairs.

Grailer had once been knocked out of his chair by corona feedback. And . . . he had put it out of his mind . . . Ari had refused to touch him for whole minutes, and even then had worked at the Webset first.

The points at which signals jumped in t-zero were called synapses, like the junctions of the human nervous system. And what else was the t-zero effect called? Thoughtspeed. The limiting velocity of thought.

That was the secret of the Hounds. Even as the Spinners set virtual systems to run and ravage in the Weblattice, so the Web had set virtuals on the nervous hardware of the Spinners. Hounds to bite. Geisthounds to tear at the delicate threads of protein that never, never healed, even with Lifespan.

Grailer drew a little strength from the knowledge that some of his "fear" was plextronic induction. But most of his fear was fear, the fear of death, the fear of pain. A ripple ran up his fingers, his hands, his arms; burned hot in his chest.

"The brain has no feeling," Ari nagged in his head, "but the mind inside can hurt." And how much hurt would the Web-beasts cause, that were all neural energy, nervous impact?

—*And the corona shocks? Flybites.*

The Hounds howled again, a voice without the soul of even an angel circuit. And off Grailer went.

The luminous grid flew past him, ever faster, as his fingers stroked and twirled and poked. Behind came the Geisthound cry.

Behind? Were they from the speaker or in his head? He was two centimeters off the chair seat, poised to run for real, shutting the door behind, but he sank back down and typed all the faster. He knew they could leave the set to kill him. Ten thousand volts would jump a centimeter of dry air—and his sweating fingers were lowering that resistance by the second.

Ten thousand volts for a centimeter. A million volts for a meter. But the Web was as vast as Man, and a megavolt would not ripple its load monitors.

If he rose, if he turned, seconds would be eaten up. And the current would seek him out across the short distance he could run.

Lines of light hurtled past him now. He changed direction moment to moment, the whip and twist of the screen hurting his eye muscles and making his stomach drop in spite of himself. This was only a philosophical abstract, wasn't it? The maze-Weblattice was only a convenient schematic. . . .

No, it was not. Virtual systems bent on his death pursued him across a landscape that was represented by light-pictures but was wholly real in its x-thousand cabinets of crystals and wires.

How ironic, he took time to think, that I should be caught and sucked dry in the Web I planned to spin.

But there had to be a way out. Ari, damn him, had claimed hundreds on hundreds of victories, and in Grailer's name, damn him black.

He vaulted cubes and slid down columns, ran teetering along luminescent beams above a void infinitely deep. This was the Web's ground, the Web's defense. He was the virus that had finally triggered the antibodies. His fingers trip-hammered the keys, and his scream for help to somebody—even Aristide, who he knew would not come—swelled and jammed in his throat.

Think, he had to think, for he could not run forever, though he could not be trapped against an edge of the Web, as CIRCE had once caught him with his back to the sea.

But this was the Web, a tireless and implacable machine to which courage and discouragement meant nothing. Of that he was afraid, unlike CIRCE, which he hated but did not fear.

CIRCE? What if—

Was the Web intelligent? No, no, a thousand times probably no. Was it creative? Of course not.

But CIRCE was intelligent and creative—not much of either, he gallows-joked, but enough to catch Webspinners and kill them as the Lex Bell Stellar prescribed.

A green fringe crept onto the screen. He looked at it, then dragged his eyes away. The green thing had had a fang, and an eye.

What if CIRCE were still chasing him?

A fang, an eye, a green mane, and a terrible claw—

If it was the Web breathing hot on him, making his limbs ache as if blood-starved, then he was doomed, for the Web was as strong and big and powerful as it needed to be for the problem at hand.

But CIRCE was made up of men, and men's creations reflect their limitations, and the Combined Executive had certain special weaknesses.

He put both hands on the matrix sticks and pushed them hard, fast, half one way and half the other.

The image on the screen shivered, split. He had separated the D'Urban Grandier personality from the nameless Grailer Diomede one he had entered by. Farther and further the focal points spread, the picture becoming harder and harder to separate into sense. A signal started flashing: *LIMIT OF RESOLUTION*.

Grandier and Grailer leaped from Weblocus to Weblocus, the Hounds following after, the pack's howls echoing oddly.

A Webspinner always builds up logically. Grailer and his angel did not need to stop at those intervening synapses, since t-zero is the same over all distances; but they had nonetheless, and those stops were on record, paraplex electronic ghosts of plexy men and angels.

Grailer told the Web, cold-eyed, panting:

clone me:

:memory reprise all ports say again all ports
priority one one thousand

"Now, dammit," he told the Web aloud.

And then there were ten thousand angels in ten thousand Web installations on BellStel knows how many planets.

And a megavolt Hound divided by ten thousand victims is a thousand volts, which will bridge a scant few millimeters of sweat-electrolyzed air.

Grailer Diomede, his hands millimeters from the keys, saw a green eye, felt a burning·pain, and knew nothing.

> > >

"CIRCE," was the first thing he said.

"CIRCE?" said Mr. Aristide. "Oh. Yes, Grailer, the Hounds come under the province of the Lex Bell Stellar. They belong to the black knights."

"*Why?*"

"To preserve the lawful status of the Web."

"Why didn't you tell me?" He tried to reach up, found he could not move his hands.

"Your wrists are burned, badly but not irreparably. You were fortunate that only a small fraction of the possible Hound energy had been raised; two Hounds, or a pack, and the Choirs-of-Angels trick might have cost you your hands or your life.

"Why did I not tell you? Fear. Impressibility of fear. A child bitten by a snake will fear snakes ever after. An adult will crush the serpent with his heel. Tell me, Grailer, what do you want to do now, more than anything? Spin the Web, perhaps?"

"Get CIRCE. Get them for those Hounds." He stretched his bandaged wrists, imagining the feel of the keys and knobs, the song of the sticks. Raw pain scoured his skin, and he held still. "Why hasn't someone done it before this? Why haven't you? Can't you find them?"

"Anyone can find them, child mine. The world is Skolshold, cold and flat and bitter. Anyone can find the black knights. But you're looking for the Grail, child, and it isn't there. No one ever found the Grail on Skolshold."

"I'll look for myself."

CHAPTER 4

THE COLDEST WORLD

A cylinder of superpressurized air forced Grailer's portpod away from Marcera's surface. The sky faded to black around him, the pod spun a bit—weightless, he felt nearly nothing—and bumped gently into the bay of the liner.

His seat released him and he walked gingerly, stick-slippers grabbing and ripping loose, through the shell lock to the Boarding Gallery. He always thought, strolling into or out of portpods, how much more exciting it was to land the great ships and scramble on a ramp. But he did not think long about it now. He had a place to go and a thing to do, and he was going to do it like love, without an outside thought.

"Then I will hold your Lifespan until your return," said Mr. Aristide. "What use eternity to the dead?" Grailer did not care. He was going to Skolshold, to CIRCE's island, and afterward there would be the time for foreverness. He was going to see Diego Cadiz, and he was going to do it like love.

"Take care not to be enchanted," Ari said as they separated.

"I'll be back," said Grailer. Then suddenly, impulsively, he took Ari's hand in his and pressed hard. "I'll be back when I know something more." He boarded the portpod and was pushed into the sky.

He removed his stick-slippers, treading solidly now in the false gravity of the ship's Hellmanns. Halfway to his stateroom there was a flicker, an eyeblink, and the *thum-thum-thum* nonsound of the Pryne tubes came up through his feet. A slow, heavy thrum, the sound of a thousand times c.

In the room, with the door filaments taut and opaqued and the annunciator subtly stopped up, Grailer unfolded his Webset and riffled through the fabricator catalog.

Who should he be? Who would get him inside the black knights' citadel, pass him to see the Master of the Hounds? An omnicorps-man, perhaps, discussing money? Or an innocent pleading theft of his magic—perhaps theft by a Webspinner.

Grailer's lips bent in a sardonic grin. As if Webspinners stole.

If Webspinners stole—ah!

What if he walked up to the door and announced himself as a— what was the official phrase? *Web Tamperer, Section Twenty Violator.* Would they terminate him with extreme prejudice on the doorstep?

An interesting idea, but not right. Too unsubtle.

A newsraker, then? No. CIRCE released, when it released, di-rectly to the Web. A newsraker might go begging.

He could be a scientist with a breakthrough, but he might have to produce the invention.

A legalist? What did CIRCE care for arguments of law? They *were* the law, and needed argue no points.

A politico? That was a nova laugh. Combined *Intersystem* Ex-ecutive, they were. Intersystem authority did not care about system authority. That was the Ercon: named for its vast and insubstantial currency, not for its politics.

A soldier—yes, a soldier. There were many soldiers, even if there were no True Wars. They came from many backgrounds, spoke many tongues and with many tongues. And they wore a uniform that eyes did not often look past. He programmed the fabricator for a uniform of the Combined Intersystem Pathfinders—no, of the Ground Forces. Grailer had not struck out upon enough worlds to pass for a Pathfinder.

The wall slot chimed and delivered. He tried on the red and green tunic and slacks, the forage cap with its neat black visor. From Grailer's permanent traveling kit came captain's squares and a belt of metal mesh. On the belt was a smooth shiny object, like a black-gloved hand, forefinger pointing: a flapover holster, an oil-shining Hawkwood Model 60A hung on the pin inside.

Dressed, decked out, back he went to the Web console to make a name for himself.

But cautiously, very cautiously.

> > >

Only minutes out of the Pryne envelope, the liner kicked a portpod away, and no later than safety would permit the tubes began tocking, the shimmery envelope built up again, and she was gone, faster than light could bounce back to the eye.

Grailer sat alone in a pod built for twelve and a steward, feeling automatics slip and tilt him and aim him down the ballistic spiral to Skolshold's surface.

Cold and flat, Ari had said, and from this close it looked it: a ball covered all in snow and dull oceans, wrapped around in cloud. It looked like a tattered cocoon. There were a few lights he could see, but they were sparse and scattered beacons, not the jewel clusters of cities on the worlds Grailer knew.

Cold and flat—and bitter, Ari said. When the pod left the spiral and skidded down the ramp, Grailer released his restraints, surprised that he had to exert the effort. He expected the vehicle to shell open and disgorge him; it did not, and the lurch as it started rolling knocked him forward and set his cap askew.

Out the portpod window he could see men in white suits, like softsuits, but with the oxygen gear replaced by a tubing and thermal-fan arrangement that steamed in the cold wet air. Hung from their wrists were short thick wands. For a moment the pod stalled, and one of the 'dusters pointed his wand and bathed a wheel in orange fire.

The view darkened. Walls were rising to each side of the pod, doors shelling closed over it. It became very dark, then yellowly bright—artificial lights—and the pod finally shelled open.

Bitter it was. Grailer was cold to the bone at once. One of the snowsuited portdusters saw him and gave a yell; he snapped out a foil blanket from a thigh pouch and tossed it over Grailer's shoulders. Another 'duster came up and together they hustled Grailer into a room so suddenly warm he felt cooked.

"Sorry, fellow—Capt'in. We all thought, with one only on board, you must be a Holder coming back. Thought you'd be ready and waiting."

"It's—all right." He was comfortable now, the wave of deep cold not much more than a bad memory. "Next time I'll come in the summer—this isn't summer, is it?"

"Oh, no. Early autumn. But we had a cold summer this year."

"Cold summer, cold winter," another said.

"Who's a weather wizard now?"

"Hardly cold, hardly ever. Anyone care to sculpt in the snow?" A couple of the women murmured assent at that.

"Heat," another man said, "we got all the heat we can use."

"Sure. That's why Alf got froze, and Christabel; everybody knows she got no heat."

There were more words passed, plays on "heat" and "frigid" that got sharper, nastier. The speeches became shouts. Wands were tapped on the table. There were more references to Alf and Christabel, and other 'dusters by name, and then to Johnny Sky, who "got froze to a pod and pushed off the planet."

A 'duster pounded her fist and jumped on the table, threw her arms wide. "I can't take the cold no more! Give me some sun!"

"Here's a handful of sun!" four others said, raised their wands and covered her with fire. Grailer felt his eyes snap open and his stomach spiral away, and his tongue swelled and stuck. But the flames clicked off and the woman leaped down, sooted and red but unburned. She took two of the wandholders by the arms and left the room, a laugh spreading among the three of them.

"Hey, Capt'in."

"Hey, Capt'in!"

Grailer turned his head.

"You spiral-sick, Capt'in?"

"No. I'm all right."

"No heat if you are. Snowwinds batter those pods around, sometimes, to make a Mem dreamer notice.

"Sorry it's taking so long to get you a linear. We got the system, but not too many public cars. Most people own one. Aren't too many visitors."

"It's all right." Grailer spoke through an even mouth and will-narrow eyes. "I enjoyed it."

"Oh? I hear stories about barracks games—but I guess it's mostly vacuum.

"Here's your linear."

A boxy, dented car, paint broken through in places, appeared at the end of a corridor. The 'duster watched Grailer board, then held the door.

"If you want to Sundance—that's what we call it. I mean, it's not like the Dance you people do—come on down. The Hold's not very big—and it's cold outside, Capt'in. I mean, it's killing cold."

"I'll remember," Grailer said, desperately trying to stretch Goliardic boredom over the words.

The car rolled away. Grailer changed its program en route. He registered at a hostel, ate a meal, showered, and had his clothes rewoven before going to see Diego Cadiz.

The linear took him through long tunnels with only a dim light-strip above. There were rattles and wheezings behind the walls and puffs of air that cut with their chill.

The car stopped at a plain stone platform. It might have been an unfinished passenger station, or a delivery entrance in a particularly dingy infracity corner. But on the rough wall was a burnished steel plaque: a pair of scales hung on a sword.

Certain he was watched, Grailer slung his Webset over a shoulder and nodded at the plaque. He walked into the heart of CIRCE.

> > >

Steel doors with gas seals. Walls sloped out to dissipate blast. Hard, white, vertical light. Three people in the foyer in black bulletweave uniforms. Two sat at a desk. They wore soft black caps and dark flashstop glasses and carried wands in their belts. One was brown, stunner-knockdown. One was red, tingler-screamer. The third CIRCE wore operator's kit: impact gloves, helmet with full face shield, black killing-strength wand. A ripgun was in his/her hands. Grailer looked close at the small dark hole of the muzzle, and at the hands, but through the gloves he could not gauge the tightness of the grip.

"Captain Galahad." The one with the brown stun wand spoke. The one with the red pain wand stared at a Webscreen Grailer could not see, though its light spilled on the operator's face.

"David Galahad, Captain CI Ground Forces, 4781 Technical Support Division, on detached duty from baseworld Kandahar's Vigilance."

"Yes, that's—"

"Do not confirm or deny. Arrived CIRCE Center thirty minutes Standard previous. Arrived Skolshold six hours Standard previous. Messaged Combined Executive Data Center fourteen days twelve hours Standard previous. Do not confirm or deny these data."

"Very well."

"David Galahad has no major surgical restructure markings. Superficial burns on wrists sustained during maneuver action. Recommendation resultant: CI Silver Cross, nomination by CO-prime to Support Command School."

"Mm-hmm." The CIRCE operators were not noticing him at all now. Everything was in the right place, and what did they care about a human being if their data on him were correct?

"Wait," the deskman said sharply.

The consoleman looked up, his eyebrows raised above his glasses. "Probe wait or system wait?"

"I don't mean functional wait, I mean *wait*. Hold place."

"Oh," said the consoleman, and punched some keys. "What's irregular?"

"The commanding officer's name is garbled."

"His name is—" Grailer offered.

"Do not confirm or deny."

Deadpan outside, Grailer stopped laughing inside. There should not have been an error. The file should have been complete. It had been created complete.

Make a prayer to BellStel, so the line went, for a simple communicative Webcall, but the angel Grailer had spun up did not use the high-traffic circuits that took time and got bumped. The only reasonable source of error would be . . .

Would be Webspinning.

Accidental or deliberate? Accidental meant some spinner, somewhere, escaping the Geisthounds and dislodging Grailer's work with his own desperate efforts. That would be an ironic way for Grailer to go out, but at least not a vain one.

Deliberate meant Mr. Aristide.

No, no, accidental. It had to be accidental. Perhaps he *had* fouled the file himself. Pryne-envelope distortion, could that be it?

"Pryne-envelope distortion," the consoleman was saying.

"On a static file?"

"Not static. A Code Eighty order is on. The CO-prime's in transit. There it is. Colonel Augustine of the Pathfinders."

Not accidental, then, because of all the possible names he could have given the commander, that was the last one he would have used.

But Grailer held himself calm and thought the best. Code Eighty would be some kind of verify-now order. The order had caught Ari in transit. He had replied. Grailer still lived.

There was still a crucial ambiguity in Mr. Aristide's actions. Why had he tinkered with the file? Why was he in transit, and to where?

"I am here," he said aloud and firmly, "to see Commander Diego Cadiz."

The deskman looked up, directly at Grailer. "I'm aware of that. You have just been cleared through. Stand to," he told the helmeted guard, who stepped into parade rest with a sharp click of boots.

"On four, C, niner-two," he told the consoleman. "To Security: I have a 4C for Exec One, no R, no S, plate B."

A plastic card popped from a slot in the desk. It was handed to Grailer.

"Carry this. Show it when asked. Go nowhere without it. It is sensitized. The building is sensitized to it.

"This door. Any gold elevator. If you need a toilet, use a violet door. They are monitored."

All three CIRCEs turned away from Grailer as if he no longer existed.

With a finger on his cap visor, Grailer went through the door, which slid shut and sealed behind him.

He adjusted his cap, put his hands on his belt. He felt the hard slick holster under his right fingers. He'd nearly forgotten the pistol—but there it was, still at his side.

He walked to the end of the hall. The building was very quiet. There were no sounds of moving air, no sensations of machinery, no human noises at all. The light was still overbright and straight down. The walls were unfinished formed stone of a neutral green. They looked as though slugs or gun rockets or thermal bolts could hit them, or have hit them many times already, and all traces be dusted away with one pass of a stiff brush. The drab green color would turn anything on it into a dull and forgettable stain. Burns and blood would not impress it.

There were fifteen elevators, three each of red, blue, black, green, and gold. One gold door opened for him. He stepped before a green door; nothing happened.

Grailer entered the gold elevator. There was no command panel. The door closed and hissed tight before he could move. The car trembled, and a whisper of machinery reached his ear. There was no sensation of rising or falling, but even CIRCE would put Hellmann plates in its elevators.

Grailer fought all his feelings with all his strength. He was in CIRCE's black pit, a place built for the desolation of souls. It was no oversight that they had let him keep his sidearm; he was to understand that it was of no help to him in this place. Processed, directed, conveyed without so much as the free-willed press of an elevator button, he was to arrive before Diego Cadiz already broken down, in a state of awed and trembling helplessness.

The thought brought tears of anger. He pulled his cap down and blinked them back, silently cursing whoever watched. I'd damn you as you deserve, he thought, but I won't give you the satisfaction. I won't make a sound.

A sound?

He leaned against the vibrating wall, trying to appear casual. The sick feeling, the bottomless-pit terror, grew stronger.

They were beaming subsonics at the elevator car, trying to shatter his nerves. The way of CIRCE: masters of subtle fear when they would be, they could never quite resist the temptations of brute force. It was the taint in the blood of tyrants.

Grailer was gaining back control of himself. He had seen through the tricks. And he had seen through CIRCE. The man at the desk was supposed to unerringly reel off the personal data of the victim, without giving him an instant even to affirm the databank's rightness. But they had slipped up.

No, Grailer thought, been tripped up by a Webspinner. He would be all right now. CIRCE would not prevail against him. He knew now whose side Mr. Aristide was on; and maybe that was all he had ever been afraid of.

So when the elevator opened, he left it not afraid, not holding up a veil of false courage, but with a quick, echoing step—Galahad the white knight among the black, the gameplayer, the Dancer Goliardic.

He entered a cold, white, noisy room. Dry air swirled past him from slits that covered the whole ceiling. The room was wide, at least ten meters, and barely more than two high: meant to crush the spirit. The light came from the white walls, all around; Grailer cast no shadow.

The light grew more intense, hurtingly so, and he squinted. He was certain the next room would be dark. A fearful person would be wide-eyed in here, pupils dilated, and blind in the next.

One of the white panels darkened, swung away. Grailer stepped into the doorway and all of the panels went out. He opened his eyes and could see shapes in the room ahead; a desk, racks, panels of lights and dials. Some Hellmann hoverlamps were drifting about.

He took another step and collided with a sheet of glass or quartz that covered the doorway.

"Wait, please," said a soft and uninflected voice, like that of a crudely cast angel. "Close your eyes tightly and cover them if you wish. Do not open them again until the tone and the sensation of heat have both stopped."

Grailer did so. He heard a hum and felt dry, tingling warmth. If this was a detector, it was a damned strange one. He had assumed all along that he was being neutron-washed, metal-snooped, chemical-sniffed, and emission-counted. But those couldn't be noticed by the subject without hardware. This was more like—

The hum stopped. His skin cooled down in another rush of cold dry air. The glass panel slid aside, and Grailer entered the dim room.

The floor was slightly soft. He could feel his bootsoles sinking in. Some of the hoverlamps drifted toward him. One paused, one passed him by, one changed direction and floated off.

The wall racks were filled with books; some random volumes, but mostly thick black books with matching spines, bearing a silver cruciform mark that on close look was the sword and scales of Combined Executive.

The sigil appeared again, writ large, on a velvet pennon that hung behind the desk. The banner was spotlighted, the desk a dark altar before it, Webscreens upon the desk faces raised in prayer.

One of the hoverlamps hesitated, then changed course and flew to the desk, taking up station a little above the desktop. It oscillated slightly, up and down.

"Commander Cadiz?" Grailer hoped he did not sound too impatient. Let him think his tricks—

Diego Cadiz was sitting behind the desk. He had entered through the wall behind, or perhaps up from the floor, but silently and in darkness. His face floated, white, above the lamp on the desk.

Grailer looked into the face of Diego Cadiz. It was waxy pale, like bleached bone. His eyes were black spots in white pools ringed with bright bloody red—pistol-target eyes. His head was totally hairless—not bald or depilated, but a place where hair would not ever grow. And Grailer knew why, seeing that face: looking into the face of the Eternity Syndrome. It was why he had been dusted on the way in, and sterilized, and dusted again. He would carry nothing alien in to Diego Cadiz.

There was a real immortality process, if you wanted to call it that.

Lifespan treatment changed the cells a little, so that they aged more slowly than normal; no one could predict how slowly beforehand. Twelve times was the smallest prize in the lottery, twenty times the biggest. And most people multiplied the rest of their allotted fivescore by twelve to twenty, and called it forever, and amen.

But for a very, very few there was a jackpot. Lifespan changed their cells dramatically. They became genuine eternals. They did not age. They would not die, not naturally.

But cells die other ways than naturally. They are cut and burned, crushed and lysed. And among those under the Eternity Syndrome there was no death, but neither was there any birth, nor any healing. Forever, and amen.

How many cases? Don't ask; no one will say. Many more than are living. Most cut themselves in insensitive places and waited for the body's isostatic humor to run out. Some managed to starve. Even perfect machines must have energy. Catabolism can only last while there are immortal cells to feed the fire.

Man played black jokes with Lifespan, slowing down infants or senile old folk with undesirable inheritance arrangements. Lifespan played a joke back. And the cream of the jest is still to come.

Common Lifespan let the nerves alone. Eternity Syndrome improved them as well. Grailer faced a man whose senses were heightened. Whose bones and muscles would howl at him pitilessly with mere movement. Whose reflexes would be blindingly swift. Who would be a patchwork doll of biomechanical repairs, his tissues glued and sewn with permanent materials.

And whose intelligence would be raised to a point—

Grailer had come to meet the devil in hell. He surely had.

"Good day," said Combined Intersystem Regulation and Control Executive One.

"Commander Cadiz," Grailer said.

"Mister, titles extra," said the immortal man. "Meeting concerns Webspinning."

"Pardon me, Mr. Cadiz? I called and said—"

"Tampering," Cadiz said, not irritably. His voice was whispery. To raise it would have pained him greatly, Grailer knew. "You claimed something."

"I've uncovered some traces of tampering, yes, sir. It's high-order work, sir, very advanced. It failed to trigger any of the automatic safeguards. That's why I wanted to contact you directly."

Cadiz sat in a floatchair covered in dark velvet, padded in an unusual fashion. He moved a finger and the chair glided around the desk, close to Grailer. Another movement, and the chair hummed and rose to place them eye to eye.

"Liar," he said.

Grailer blinked, said nothing. Cadiz blinked, a slow process like the dipping and raising of a flag.

"Webspinning syncs," Cadiz said. "Concealment. Understanding loses: backwind and slow." The chair moved back, down. Cadiz' skull-like head rocked back and forth a few times. He raised his hands gradually from the arms of the chair, pressed white nailless fingertips together. His legs hung straight, soft-shod feet pointing down.

"Mr. Cadiz, I wanted to talk to you because I thought this information would be of interest. As a Signals officer, I am of course familiar with Section Twenty of the Uniform Communications Code, and this seems to be a violation."

"Anansi the Spider," Cadiz said. "You talk similar—not congruent. Answering irrelevant question first."

"Mr. Cadiz—"

"Quiet. I know my name. Who else to address, here? None but operators. Interchangeable. Masked. Like Webspinners.

"Second point—backwind and slow."

"I don't understand."

Cadiz raised his arms. He was clothed in a thick velvet shirt that wrapped loosely around him, an ankle-length kilt of the same—stuff that would be gentle on his overreceptive skin, without fasteners that would stab and grate at him.

"You—never—understand. Merry rogues.

"Do not interrupt again. I have said all already, to myself, after call. It is hard to slow the—rush—of—memory for you. I will not stop it. If you will not follow, be damned.

"I do not hate you, Webspinner. You are not dreamtrading. Those I kill, for killing minds. But what you do I am sworn to stop. To kill you for.

"You do not want to die, but you will. I want to die much, but I will not. Remember, Webspinner, *I will not.*"

"Everyone dies," Grailer said, thick-tongued, dry-mouthed. Is he bluffing, he thought, or does he really have me stripped and pinned to the wall?

"I will play witling," Cadiz said. "Your thoughts, next minutes," and eased his chair back to the desk. "Does he know I am Webspinning, or playing only? Answer: he knows.

"Does he know my secret name? Answer: too much data to sift, weapons ask no names."

Grailer turned to follow him, his steps uncertain on the cushioned floor. "I can always—"

"Kill Cadiz. Answer: no." Cadiz reached to the desk, Grailer reached for his Hawkwood Sixty; Cadiz' hand came up—

Holding a Hawkwood Model Sixty.

"Cadiz cannot die."

Grailer's hand moved a millimeter. He did not breathe at all.

"Next thought. When was gun taken? Several seconds to recount trip.

"Next thought. Bluff. Two guns.

"Next thought. Does Cadiz bluff? Answer: *no one always bluffs.*

"Two next thoughts. Cadiz cannot die. Cadiz knows what I think.

"Final thought. Awareness of personal fear."

Grailer hurt. His whole body was stiff and suddenly very cold with sweat. His holster was still closed, still felt heavy, but was that real? The Webset's strap creaked on his shoulder, and the pain where it rubbed was real.

The fear was very real, damn it, damn it.

There was *something* in his holster.

"Two guns, yes," Cadiz said. "Both real? One false? Which? Both false?"

Cadiz moved a finger, and the room outside lit white. "Now you will leave, drawing pistol only when in linear station."

Grailer took awkward steps out. He glanced back from the doorway, his face burning, his eyesockets raw.

Cadiz met his look. "Who am I? Diego Cadiz. Black knight. Spinnerkiller." He tilted his head to one side, Grailer's vision was blurred, but it seemed he scratched at his delicate throat. "Man was friend, before Web. Anansi the Spider after . . . close, not congruent. . . .

"Cadiz has no bad dreams. No dreams. Body cannot. Works, thinks."

Grailer went out through the still elevators and the silent corridors, his steps shooting firebolts through his legs as though he had been wand-stunned.

Had they stunned him? When? How? *Had they?*

He threw the plastic card on the desk as he passed, not noticing if there was anyone to take it.

Standing on the platform, waiting for the slow-coming car, he drew the black pistol and pulled the trigger, and the tracer round he had loaded on top lit up a hundred meters of linear tunnel.

The car slid in, the door opened. Grailer stepped to the opening, stopped before he entered it.

Sitting in the car, just inside the doorway, was a tall man in a hooded robe of coarse green cloth. In one hand he held a golden-spoked wheel. The hood hid his face, just as it had hid it ten years before in a Web booth in the City Juvenal on the planet called Brass.

CHAPTER 5

OF WHICH THE BARDS HAVE SUNG

Grailer was not quite driven mad, not quite. He said in an unstrung voice, "Will you move aside for me, this time? CIRCE's still behind me, but in not so hot pursuit."

"Sit down," said the man in green, and slid away from the door. "I've been a long time seeing you again."

"Who the devil are you?"

"Why, lad, I'd have thought you recalled. I'm he who saved you from those black knights, and delivered you unto the Dark Lady." The hood hid all his face but did not muffle the voice, which was mellow and deep.

"Ari?" Grailer said, not too eagerly.

"Doctor Taliessin, I'm afraid. But you don't disappoint me, lad. It was known well that you'd make someone a splendid apprentice."

"Then you're a Spinner." He was back in control now. With Webset and gun and his mind no longer being read, he could handle any situation.

"Aye, a Webspinner. Did you not see my set?" He held out the wheel.

It was a hard clear disk a centimeter thick and thirty across, with a veneer of gold at the center and another on the rim. Golden wires taut on the disk's surface connected the two.

Dr. Taliessin tapped the edge of the wheel, then rubbed thumb and forefinger together and stroked a wire. It made a harplike sound. The other fingers of the hand flicked out, and the thumb moved again. Now the sound was a mechanical squawk. Another flick, and again he played the strings, and this time sang along:

"A *knight of ghosts and sha-dows,*
   I summoned am to tourney;
   Ten leagues beyond
   The wide world's end—
   I count it no great journey.
   And so I sing bonny boys,
   Bonny mad boys,
   Bedlam's boys are bonny;
   They have not a care,
   And they live by the air—
   And want no drink nor money."

"Matrix sticks," Grailer said. "How can it be all sticks and no keys or screen?"

"How can the Web hear words, lad? A pattern's what you decode it as. Some say words. I play my harp. And the Web plays back to me . . ." The disk made more musical sounds. "I need no screens."

"Oh, of course. Like Haafetz the Eyeless—you're not Haafetz, are you?"

"Haafetz spins on memorized keys. Lad, much as it shames me to admit it, I'm Dr. Taliessin. I've got other names like all of us—but doesn't your teacher call you Grailer Diomede?"

Grailer had let his guard slip down. Now it was up again. "I take it you know Colonel Augustine."

"In uniform, I do. And in uniform I know Ariadne Miller and Ardrey the Man-Hunter and Mstislav Anger. But best of all I know Mr. Aristide. Lad, Grailer, Gabriel Dark if that's what you want to call yourself, I'm on your side."

"You'd be surprised how hard that is to figure out about people."

"Would I, now," Taliessin said, an edge in his voice. "Lad, you're eighteen, and no twelve-to-twenty times about it, either. You play games with a great many people who are old, old; your whole life is a single year of our adulthood, and nothing at all to Diego Cadiz, and if all of us are fools in some way, well, together we are pretty wise. Even Diego."

"You make it sound like a conspiracy."

"It is a conspiracy, or rather it was. Before the Last True War, and before the Web that followed it. Your teacher has spent many full years teaching you science and art; I'm going to tell you some history. It involves me, and the Mistress Celene, and Diego before he was eternal or mad, and a man called Anansi the Spider.

"I thought that would sit you down." He played a chord on his harp/Webset. "We'll run in circles for a while. Skolshold won't melt."

And they rode on linear tracks, and Taliessin spoke and sang and played on his harp, and the story went like this. . . .

> > >

In the beginning there was no Ercon, nor was there any Web.

There was an erc, called an ERC and based in solid things, and there was a thing called Iscon, for Intersystem Control, which was begat of Earthsystem by the invention of the Pryne tube and speeds faster than the old limit c. Suddenly a whole class of worlds, the Fringe, ceased to exist. There was no Fringe. There was no frontier. And there were a great many worlds that had been forgotten, and should have stayed that way, and wanted to stay that way, but much did men desire to beget that Iscon, and they set off in their ships of Pryne quanta one, two, and three, conveniently forgetting that messages still could travel no faster than a Pryne tube could carry them.

But if great is the universe and its creator, then don't forget Man; and the Iscon tottered to its feet, based in Earthsystem, based on Earth. And its days were greater than any man could think, for first Lifespan was invented, and then Alvan vanAlvan gave all the superweapons to his priesthood, and there was peace, but verily it was uneasy.

And in some span of days did the omnicorps grow greater than the Iscon government, and the Alvanians became corrupted by the power to explode whole cities . . . soon, whole worlds. But still there was a balance of terror, though many labored to tip it.

"Now you must understand, despite my tone," Taliessin said, "that nothing is created fully grown; and no one thought to build the Web or would, till after 'here's t-zero; what's the good?'"

But someone did finally say that, and gave the secret of the t-zero synapse to an obscure company that promptly renamed itself the Bell Stellar Communications Corporation.

"And then occurred what's called the Last True War. And now at last you know what it was for."

After the Last True War there was no Iscon, no Earth-system, no Earth. Only the omnicorps, and the Web.

"But the Ercon—" Grailer said, horrified and enthralled.

"What would you have called what we had, then? Democracy? The oligarchs would have stifled you. Oligarchy? You'd have ended your days in a Modern Marxist Reactionary Reservation. Marxism? Oh *Lord*, no! Consortium and cooperative and council and confederation are all obscenities to somebody, lad. So it was named for the money. What you'd call the magic.

"That, Grailer Diomede, is why there is a Section Twenty, a death warrant. Why there are Geisthounds. Have you ever heard the words *lèse majesté*? Didn't think you would have. It means to pretend to power, to do things that only kings and presidents and omnicorpsmen are allowed to do.

"Do you realize what happens when you spin the Web? You tip the new balance of terror. You prove that one man who knows a secret can upset the whole dramatic schema, yes, he can, even if you ban him and outlaw him. All you can do is put him out of business in the old and time-tried fashion."

Grailer sat quietly for several minutes. He opened his Webset, ran his fingers over the keys, but did not enable it.

"You were going to tell me about the people," he said.

"Yes, I was, and how we were all fools in some way. Mr. Aristide, for instance. He's taught you to be a good altruist of a Spinner, never stealing, never lying, never killing, and I think he believes it. That makes him a fool."

Grailer opened his mouth but Taliessin waved him silent. "And I'm showing you darkness and human hate, turning you sour, and that makes me a fool.

"Mistress Celene believes in her cards more than she believes in herself. I hope you haven't dwelt too long on that reading she gave you."

"Diego Cadiz thinks he can't die," Grailer said.

"That might be a foolishness in you or me," Taliessin replied, "but not in Diego. No, not in Diego.

"You must separate two things about Diego Cadiz, Grailer; his madness and his foolishness.

"Diego is mad, because he cannot dream. His mind is full of things that he cannot file properly; he's like a Web program with no storage, all on-line, always. He cannot dream, because his body cannot sleep. But since that has driven him insane, he cannot see that sleep and dreams are required for human sanity.

"But his foolishness—that's something else. He is a fool because he believes that a dead man is alive. And he hunts for that man everywhere."

"That sounds like insanity."

"It would be, in an otherwise sane man. But Diego is totally mad already, so this fixation is merely a foolishness."

"Is the man Anansi the Spider?"

"Yes."

"Anansi is dead, then?"

"For hundreds of real years, scores of Lifespanned ones."

"Who was he?"

"The first Webspinner that ever there was. The inventor of the craft."

Grailer nodded slowly. "And he's dead."

"I said he was."

"Was he like me?"

"Like you? I'm not the one to say that. I haven't known you well. I haven't seen you spin. You've got traits I know of, can see in you sitting there, that all Spinners have.

Wheat and corn and barley malt
Are grains of subtle flavor;
But when I brew them into beer
They share a common savor.

"Tell me about him."

"Surely I will."

Anansi the Spider was a thin, sharp man, a dark-haired man with eyes like blue-white suns; when he was impassioned, aroused, those eyes could not be looked into. When he was angry those eyes could paralyze and kill. But Anansi was not angry often. He had not the time.

Anansi was one of those rare and driven ones who are out of sync with Time. Young and fresh, they wish for the dignity of age. Aging, they see death like a wall ahead, too near to stop. In between they feel stretched on a wire, a catenary are endless both ways. Pain goes on forever, and ecstasy is a candle in a dark night; do all feel so? Yes, but for such as Anansi all life is too fast or too slow, mayflies or mountains.

Have you ever said or thought or felt that *now, this moment,* is just right, is perfect, could last forever? Oh, yes, you were wrong, but you have known that feeling. And the out-of-phase people like Anansi the Spider cannot. They simply will never know. All their sadness, all their joy, is bound up in a world that plays at the wrong speed, and their hands are calloused and burnt from spinning the wheels faster or holding them back.

A thin, humming man was Anansi; a spinner of wheels.

"He was one of those who made the Web, having early in the dawn seen the power in the synapse. He made it in the image of a tool, to fit Man's hand and mind. Only with difficulty was he convinced that it needed controls, that most tools are weapons as well. So, full of ill feeling but seeing a duty, he became one of those who gave CIRCE her powers. And he, he himself, made Diego Cadiz master of the witch's island."

"Was this before Lifespan? Before the Syndrome?"

"Not before either. But before the undreaming madness took him.

"Very well, I see I called him mad too soon. How can I tell you what it was really like for him, for us?

"Here was an intelligent man, a good and uncorrupt man, who had always worked all his waking hours and now worked all the hours in the day, who was slowly turning into a monster. But as he grew monstrous, he grew more intelligent *more swiftly*. Show the common mind space through the envelope and it will fail. But this was a far from common mind. No, no, Diego left the company of humans out of a golden door and a black one both at once.

"I could see the terror and awe on your face as you stood on the platform, lad, and you surely went to see Diego as no friend. I was his friend. Celene was his friend. Anansi was his friend, *do you begin to understand?*" Green-gloved hands seized Grailer's shoulders. "I'm showing you the side of the business Aristide never will, lad! We all made a crazy genius the black king, and it takes all the sane fools there are to play white!"

Grailer looked hard at the green hood; he saw a scarf but no face beneath. "And I'm a white pawn in the game?"

Taliessin let him go. "Pawn now. Knight later. Maybe even a roguish rook. There's no king, I'm afraid." He sat back, pulled his wheel-harp across his knees. "I'm sorry, lad. There's your conspiracy. D'you see what it makes of us?"

"I see," Grailer said tensely. "Now tell me Anansi is Mr. Aristide, and I'll believe you."

"But he isn't, lad. Anansi's dead, that's what you've got to believe. Mr. Aristide, he's a good Spinner and a good teacher—else you'd have been my student. But Anansi the Spider is dead, ruined by the Hounds.

> "*It's someone else's blood spilled in the moonlight,*
> *Another body drifting out to sea;*
> *But someone died last night,*
> *Someone died last night,*
> *Someone died last night, and it was me.*

"The Geisthounds eat your soul up, lad. They claw your nerves and sink fangs in your brain. And they laugh, and laugh, while they kill you."

They were silent for a good long while, as the linear car bored on through its tunnel and the dark, past station stops and junctions, past conduit boxes on the walls and the cryptic marks of the engineers.

"Are you finished?"

"Finished telling you tales, aye. There's something I'd like to show you, though—a place I'd like you to go with me."

"Not back to CIRCE Center."

"Sweet devil, not there. No, I'm going up to the infracity. To a thing they call the Sundance."

"The portdusters' Dance? They asked me to come."

"Doesn't surprise me. You cut a good figure. But the Sundance is more than 'dusters, Grailer Diomede. And don't talk of it like you would of the Goliards. That's why I want you to come—to see there's more than one set of steps to dance to. Will you come?"

"Yes, I'll come, Doctor. But because I was invited by them, not by you."

"No more than I'd expect."

"Am I dressed properly?"

"First dancing lesson. Your clothes don't matter here. But I'll take my leave and meet you above; my dress doesn't suit the role I want to fill tonight."

Grailer enabled his Webset. "Where can I leave you?"

"Thank you, no. I paid for the ride. I think I'll get off right here." He played his Webset, and the car's motor wound down whining and stopped in a dark piece of tunnel without a platform in sight.

The door opened and Taliessin vaulted out onto the narrow service walk between the wire-wrapped track and the formed-stone wall.

He waved good-bye and began a song, and as the linear car closed Grailer heard a few of the words:

"*For Geordie will be hanged in a golden chain,*
'Tis not the chain of many;
Stole sixteen of—"

The door clicked shut and the car sped on.

> > >

It was not required by any master model that an infracity be below the city it served. Maracot Falls' ran vertically, cementing the city to the cliff. The 'tweenlayer slashwings on Carinexxenirac—that's xx as in hotter than blaxxes—will slam their diamond-hard blades into anything daring to rise more than twenty meters; so after building up they built down, with the infracity between.

There would be no building up on Skolshold at all, not into the permanent cold and wind and snow. So the infracity lay on top like a blanket, and with helltorches and incussion bombs they cut down, down, into what the Holders called *the living rock* but which did not cry out when they cut it.

Grailer had changed his dress uniform for fatigues, a wine-red wrap shirt and slacks with dark green side stripes, sewn-in plastic strips for rank and decorations rather than bright metal. No gun, of course, and instead of the Goliardic roundel dagger a combat knife, handle finger-grooved and heavy, blade straight-sided and matte black.

He was walking up, from his room in the newest, deepest areas up to the infracity, having had enough of linears for a day or perhaps his life. He passed a small bank of elevators, but passed them by. It would not do to arrive already flushed, spent, sated. He could always take one down, if he must.

So he walked, ascending the city, observing the strangeness of a place where people did not flow like a tide. There was a laser dancer on a deep level with no more than ten patrons, and some of those moving into the flood of light. Any laserite Grailer knew of or had known would have raised alarum at these people cutting their own dark holes in the laser space, blocking off the scanning beams from the laserite's carefully placed body mirrors, disturbing the flow of the refractive smoke (*expensive* 'fracmist, Argayne Bardiveaux in particular would have said, despite that it only cost her in ercs).

There were some children playing a surface-ricochet game using an inherently elastic ball and two Hellmann wings. Ordinarily that would have meant two games, one with wings, one without, but the rules seemed to call for the fliers to act as goaltenders while the others smacked the ball from floor and ceiling, walls and pipes, hands and knees and heads.

The ball whistled toward Grailer. With no particular plan in mind, he put out a hand. The ball hit, stinging, and in recoiling he slapped it back with a sharp wrist snap, in a beautiful arc that got him several cheers and a couple of boos from kids who certainly could have done better.

How odd not to get the same response from everyone.

Strangely elated, he did something he never did; paused to listen to a gleam peddler's pitch. The peddler was not very good, with an earful of outdated music, eyes dilated and overwet, walking inside a shimmery silvery ovoid that he claimed was the purest nova fashion and the purest nova experience.

"Like seeing from inside a Pryne envelope, unrectified," said the gleam peddler, who was either blood-poisoned till his voice was out of control or genuinely believed in his soap bubble.

Grailer repressed a sudden impulse to tell him that the Goliards on Vendredi had daggered one of theirs to the wall for wearing that thing and calling it new. He smiled instead, clenched teeth behind it, and went on his way.

The infracity was cool and loud—both to be expected. What Grailer did not expect was the peace, the psychic stillness that he felt once there. No distractions; the shapes of the city machines, the sounds they made, were all random and neutral. The pumps and directors and junction controls, the hisses and gurgles and hums that came from them, did not ask for his attention, did not try to communicate to him. The flat covering heart of Skolshold just beat, beat, beat, and breathed, and thought. Grailer felt very happy to be alive in the living place, and hurried on to the Sundance to share the joy.

The first thing Grailer learned from Dr. Taliessin, in the sense of had impressed on his mind never to forget it, was not ever to speak of the Skolshold Sundance in the same voice as that Dance of another variety.

In that other Dance that sometimes Grailer did there was color and flash and steely flicking. Here the dress was mostly singlesuits in plain colors, daring costume apparently being to unseam one's single a centimeter farther down from the neck than the next person had. There was a sort of duel that went on from time to time that consisted of the artistic unseaming of the other party's clothing. The object was not to be hasty, to be the first one completely unfastened while not having finished with one's opponent.

The longer the game went on, of course, the harder it became to win it, to stop one's artfully crooked finger from moving on down. There were a lot of compulsive losers. With three or more playing, there was usually a deliberately forced win.

But even then, even then, no more than a small cluster of the Sundancers turned to watch the play and referee it. It was as if the motions, the standard steps, did not really matter. No one had a story of the '46 Plot; no one hailed a gleam peddler, defying him to catch the eye or ear. There was a distinct smell of dreams and glory, but none of the dreamers was cataloging his experience for the multitude.

Grailer's passion was not yet high, only spiking fleetingly, but then he had already had some years of gaseous and hydraulic attraction. This feeling was chemical, and nervous, and psychochemical. At any moment, he realized with a chilly, pleasant shudder, he would be in love.

And then the band began to play.

> I've learned so many things from life that some were even
> true
> My teachers all were passing wise and strange

Some were hiding in the light
Some were blinded by the night
And if I learn what's right I doubt I'll change
Starlight
Painted on the sky
Sunset came without a warning
Stardrive
Take me far away
I'll feel different in the morning . . .

Grailer sought the band out, looking for Dr. Taliessin. Instead he found a dark and intense young man on proxar, fingers grazing and snapping at the coils; a blond woman with jewel-blue eyes and strobing ear pendants, playing saxophone, pressed back to back with an older man on guitar. Was that last one Taliessin? Could be. He had dark leathery skin, a hairline that started on the top of his head, long hair of an even gray color. The kind of face one might hood if one was running.

There was a fourth musician. She had a double handful of metal disks fastened somehow to her long darting fingers. A skein of wires trailed down the backs of her hands, held to her arms by velvet bands, running to a box on her waist.

Multicymbals, he remembered. One had to know more to play them than just when. Angle of stroke mattered, and the damping effect of the knuckles and soft flesh, the capacitance antenna formed by the finger positions . . . like a Spinner's touch on the keys and the sticks.

Grailer edged closer.

I've known so many people that I haven't known a one
Although I'm sure I've memorized them all
Some advancing to the beat
Some are dancing a retreat
How very incomplete is my recall . . .

The cymbalist's hair was red, not auburn but bonfire *red,* her eyes green (naturally), her chin narrow and pointed, her ears with just a hint of a point. She wore an opaque close-drape of crackling green moiré, and over that a long transparent skirt of green static chiffon that held close when she held still and got out of her way when she moved. Her legs had a powerful effect on Grailer's own.

Grailer got near the guitarist. He whispered some words under the music; the old man shook his head. Another question, another negation. One more, and a shrug and a nod.

> *Starlight*
> *Painted on the sky*
> *Sunset came without a warning*
> *Stardrive*
> *Take me far away*
> *I'll feel different in the morning . . .*

Grailer slid the guitar strap round his neck, arched a hand and stretched the other, and slipped into the melody exactly with the other three.

> *I've had so many lovers that I've never been in love*
> *There's always someone gone at break of day*
> *Some perceived me through my lies*
> *Some deceived me with their eyes*
> *I hope you realize it's still that way.*

She was looking back at him.

Outstanding!

They repeated the chorus, playing mocking-merry counterpoint to the bitter lyrics. The proxar was up in a tinkling range, bouncing; the sax played high and clear and heart-stopping; Grailer pushed vibrato and color on his guitar controls and strummed with long deliberate strokes, the fingers of his chording hand arched high. The red-haired

lady had tuned her right hand's cymbals as a tambourine and rang
steel chimes with the left.

> *I'll feel different in the morning . . .*
> *I'll feel better in the morning . . .*

And as the last long note faded out, Grailer twisted his controls
and tore into a walking chord, breaking off after a few cycles to let
the notes sizzle in the air.

The rest of the band, the rest of the room, stared at him. The old
guitarist started up to the platform, stopped and nodded.

Grailer's eyes were hooded, teeth showing in a wolf grin. He
walked down the series again, *one*-two-three-one, *one*-two-three-
two, *one*-two-three-three—

One-two-three-four, the tambourine and the bells picked up,
and then she was off on a wild percussion riff—

Handed it to the sax, who made the blood hot and cold—

To the dark proxar player, who gave a devilish smile of his own
and built the line into a Bach-like multilayer orchestration, his nails
striking sparks from the bare wire of the coils. Then back he went to
one-two-three-one, and they all got back together to work the tune
dry, and then another, and then another.

Until sometime a long time later the saxophonist, who hadn't
the breath left to talk, was dumping a pitcher of white wine over
the proxartist's hands, and Grailer, having left the guitar with its
sleeping owner, was easing the cymbal contacts from the lady's long
fingers.

From the fingers, he found, of Sharon Rose. He introduced himself as Grailer Diomede, because who wanted to be Galahad tonight
of all knights?

The social mechanics, the sexual mechanics—these lend themselves to words and codes, to a language that may be crude and
inelegant but is precise. I am. You are. Shall we . . . ?

But love is expressed in uncommon languages, so much silly

prattle unless one knows how to decode them. I feel. You move me. How in the bright field of stars can I . . . ?

What matters in the long run? Well, how long a run do you mean? One night can be a long run indeed, of gasping and grabbing and exhausted delicacy—again, crude but clear details.

And a love interlude is a long run, sometimes longer than the lives of all the members but one. If it ends sooner it will likely seem that it has already been forever.

Then there is the longest run of all; the one the secret languages are for. Gilgamesh and Enkidu, and the Bard and the Dark Lady, and Ainslie and Beheler and Cohn—all those stories have been translated into modern dialect, but they are written in the Old Tongue, for the reader to decode, to uncover.

Because love is a learning process, and it stops only when a partner quits learning.

Never mind those partnerships where "we know each other's minds entirely"; that means that the learning cycle has been synchronized (not stopped), a consummation more devoutly to be wished than the hypothetical simultaneous orgasm.

Learning cannot be exhausted, for real things are inexhaustible, and nothing but the *desire* to stop, to go no further, can stop it. Not time. Not distance. No, not even death.

Learning, and therefore love, is not only the proper but the only study of the wakeful mind.

That, then, finally and amen, was why Grailer Diomede, with inherently clever fingers and years to polish his style behind him, was chewing his lip to keep from yammering like a dunce. Here in front of him (chewing *her* lip, he noticed and promptly forgot) was Sharon Rose, someone new to learn.

And the evening and the morning were the first day.

>   >   >

Ping went the closed latched Webset. *Ping, ping.* Grailer pulled it off the table, thumbed the locks, and enabled it. The screen shuffled lights and dealt them into Mr. Aristide.

Ari now had a stiff pointed beard, a downward extrapolation of his black mustache. He wore a scarlet cloak with a silver shoulder rope, a communications coronet trailing two earphones and two audio pickups. Behind his shoulder was the slender braked barrel of a Masada XRHS distance rifle; behind the gun, the various greens of a jungle with a lavender sky above.

"Hello, Ardrey. What are you hunting?"

"Your Lifespan is ready, when you are ready for it," Mr. Aristide/ Ardrey the Man-Hunter said. Then he smiled, a little. "Ti-draken on Shiirang, child mine."

Grailer got a mental image: eight-meter bristly serpents with toxic breath, as fast on six legs as a linear car. The very model of a dominant species.

"What's the cause?" Grailer knew better than to use the word *hired*.

"Local crisis. A ti I know from dim history asked me and some others in. . . . I must go, Grailer. There is work to finish. I'll see you on Marcera, for your Lifespan, and tell the whole tale; I think you'll find it interesting."

With that he broke Web; abruptly, but that was his style. There was certainly no test pattern on the screen.

He had to wait for Sharon. There were places each had to be besides with the other; that had seemed so natural to Grailer from the outset that he was startled to find how unpleasant it could make him feel.

So when she said she would not go to Marcera with him, the enormity of it reached him only slowly.

"It's not that you can't go," he said. "If you want to watch dials and twist valves, there are portpods at Maracot Falls. But I'm a Web-spinner, Sharon. In a year or two you'll be a Spinner who can hold your own. With Ari to help—"

"No," she said; it doesn't matter how gently, it cut. "I don't want to go with you—to see your Lifespan or your Mr. Aristide."

"Why? They're parts of me. And you love me, don't you? Oh, damn it, damn it, why did I say that?"

"I know why," Sharon said, and her green eyes locked on Grailer's.

And Grailer knew too, but he hid it, being afraid in a way he had never known before, and said anyway, "Tell me anyway."

"I love you," she said, just like that; but before the words reassured him a scrap she went on. "But I'm not ready yet. Not until—"

"*Your* Lifespan?" Grant the young man some perception.

"The queue will only last another year. And then—I'll know."

Some perception? Grailer thought; *I don't have bloody any!* "Can it matter that much?"

"Twelve to twenty," she said. "There's no way you can tell in advance, you know."

"Of course I know!" Fear gives way to hate so easily, especially when the third side of the triangle, love, is there. "Twelve-to-twenty—you can't believe the cheap fiction. It's not a wall, or a great tragic theme, it's just a drift, and so slow a drift. . . . If I were a Twelve, and you a Twenty, it would still be thirty years Standard before there was a full year of slip between our ages. And that's the limit, Sharon, the limit. It just isn't logical."

"No, Gry, I suppose it isn't. But it makes sense. Because it's what you call it—a drift. A river that keeps getting wider."

"I don't care."

"You don't care, and I know I don't care, not *now*. But some people do. And someday we might.

"All I'm saying is, go on. Have your treatment, and come back to me just as fast as you can. And in a year, we'll know about the drift, and how much it really does matter to us."

"And then you'll go with me?"

"And then we'll go together."

Starlight
Painted on the sky

The portpod seat accepted and held him. He looked out at the weather doors opening, at the snow that had to substitute for stars.

Sunset came without a warning

Air squeezed solid was released beneath him, and the pod pushed through the snow and the cold and the clouds, pushed free of Skolshold.

Stardrive
Take me far away

The liner took him in. When the pod shelled open, a steward and the Ship's Lady were waiting for his bags and for him.

"Captain Galahad? Welcome aboard."

He looked her up and down. She was a Ship's Lady, the noblest of her trade; what more description is needed?

And he thought: Do not ask virtuous deeds, my lady, for I am not yet true; I go to bathe, put on my armor, and take the blow and be called a good knight. Then shall I return to you for favor . . . when I have put on incorruptibility.

"Call me David," he told her.

I'll feel different in the morning.

CHAPTER 6

DRAGONS' BLOOD

The doctor in charge—the Lord Doctor, Grailer's training corrected, at the sight of the red cape of Internal Medicine—had a prominent, sharp nose and large dark eyes; almost Romany eyes, even more so than Grailer's own. He shook Grailer's hand and both of Ari's and made insistent noises at the medexes who waited for his time and the capeless doctors who tried to take some of it. His name was Simon Jonas, Fellow of the Intersystem College of Medicine. He pronounced the acronym as only the Fellows, the Lords Doctor, did or dared.

"First thing you want to know, I suppose, is how soon we can tell the divisor."

"Yes."

"Everyone does, old dear. Well, the answer's very soon; twenty to twenty-five days Standard after first buckling you in."

"That doesn't sound very quick to me."

Jonas turned to Mr. Aristide. "He must be in love."

"He tells me that he is."

"However, Mr. Diomede—this way, follow the purple line—it isn't long at all, not even if you turn out a Twelve, poor thing. You'll be in the tank for seventy-two hours. Then it'll be fourteen to nineteen days while the treatment sets up; and finally seventy-two hours to do the plasm tests and give you your magic number."

"Ari, the old dear's gnawing his lip. He must be lost in the very depths of passion. Give you a pill for that, take all the hunger away, if you want."

"Maybe," Grailer said, "but I don't think it'll help."

"Unless the treatment is vastly changed," said Ari, "I doubt any such will be necessary."

"You've a point," said Jonas.

Ari said, "I'm here to tell you stories, actually, Grailer. Simon and his—"

"Not in the hallways!"

"And his *colleagues* do the work. I'll try to take your mind off what they're doing. I'll have you know it's quite undignified."

The line on the floor stopped at a violet door with a sign: CELLULAR DYNAMICS 16. It opened.

"Nothing," said Simon Jonas, "is undignified if done in the presence of doctors. But I'll grant it's an aching bore."

> > >

Straps went around his chest and legs and arms, soft restraints carefully placed in opposition to every large muscle. A band around his forehead contained small sprung metal buttons.

"Can't move at all."

"Not yet. Ari, is he claustrophobic?"

"I'm not claustrophobic."

Ari said "I don't think so. Portpod seats don't bother him."

"Fine. Now open your mouth and bite when I tell you."

A black object descended toward Grailer's face. Eyes numbed by overhead light, he could not see it clearly. It touched his chin, and he felt the give of foam, the press of metal.

"Bite."

He did so. Foam pressed in on his gums, his tongue. He started to gag.

"Stop biting."

His tongue was free then, and his jaw could move again, but something still held his teeth and covered his mouth. Cool air blew gently in, drying his tongue.

"Can you speak?"

"I'll . . . see . . . yes."

"All right. Remember, you're always in communication. Talk and we'll hear you. Earsets."

Fingers pressed into Grailer's ears. He felt a tickle at the back of his throat.

"Can you hear me?" The voice was centered in his head. "Yes," he said, though he was not sure if it was Jonas' voice or Ari's.

"Good enough. Eyes now. Aristide, if you'll take this . . ."

> > >

"I was going to tell you about the ti-draken, child mine. I got a prayer from Shiirang . . ."

"Why . . . all . . . this?" This wasn't Lifespan, it couldn't be. Millions on millions of people had been Lifespanned; but how could they have done *this* to so many?

His eyelids were pulled up, water blinded him; then he felt coolness on his eyes, some kind of semisoft cups, and then he truly was in darkness.

". . . a parasite," Ari was saying. "Grailer, are you listening? It was a terrible thing, among the ti."

From a great distance away came a voice, saying "All on. Immerse."

Something flowed over his skin, not water but oil or gel.

He thought: I know what it is. It's amber working fluid.

Metal points touched him. Wires from sprayed electrodes tugged. Ari's voice droned softly, saying nothing. Grailer's fingers would not bend, his toes would not curl, and he thought, and he knew:

They're going to freeze me.

But don't say that, don't give them the satisfaction, don't let them know you know what they're doing.

"You say he's been exposed to the envelope?"

"And Web corona. He was fortunate both times."

"Well. Hope he's fortunate now. With all that K-space floating round his synapses, I don't know if—"

The rest was lost. *Don't know?*

They didn't know how to thaw people. The amber vats, one-way immortalism, waited, and waited, and sometimes got raided for eyes . . .

A scream was surging up inside him, and it had to come out or explode him:

"*I can't move!*"

"Yes, you can," Jonas said, and suddenly he could. He was not immobile on a frame but floating, just floating.

Oh the fear, he thought; there must be something that doesn't frighten me.

He was ill. Nauseated. Alone with his fear, and afraid as well of the people who saw it in him.

Sharon, was I faithful?

Doctor Taliessin, did I trust?

Mr. Aristide, what did I ever learn from you?

"I was going to tell you," Mr. Aristide said, "about the ti-draken, and the calling of the hunters."

Ari was seated, so it appeared, in the center of Grailer's skull, in darkness save for a single cone of downward light, wearing his hunting cloak and a red beret, with the long, long rifle across his knees.

"I'd like to hear," Grailer said, surprised at how steady his voice was.

"As I've said, I knew some of the ti for, lo, many years. And after all, one can't have too many nine-meter friends, can one?"

"I shouldn't think. But why did the ti-draken want their own kind killed? And why were you out there killing?"

"Let me tell the story, child mine; you want to conclude it too quickly.

"Ti were going mad, going murderous; and for all their loathly look that is something not seen for centuries Standard. Imagine Wandersmänner who put down their guns and assumed the Balance would right itself; that is how the ti-draken are. But here were ti killing, and killing, and killing, and not being restrained by any force short of death."

Mr. Aristide stood up, the slotted barrel rib of his rifle catching bits of the light. "I turned them down at first—though never underestimate the friendship of other-than-humans. You know my rule, Grailer. But then they showed me . . ."

The jungle smelled of resin, and beast leavings, and rot. One walked carefully, because the ground was not sure, and the sunlight through the woodvines was hot enough to hurt, and because there were killer ti.

"Two hass nothing. Three may have a ssignal," said the ti Web-bearer in the first party. There was another ti, carrying supplies in hists bellypack, and three humans with x-range rifles.

"Trace then. Follow it up," said one of the hunters. Another tongued the meter on his canteen. The third swept the landscape through the sights of his gun.

That last was a gesture only. There would be no sky-lining by the targets. There was no horizon, only corridors of growth, here dark, here too bright. Eyes would not find the quarry. Plextronics might; a ti would just show on a ranger. Or the quarry might find them.

"Advance. Toward the left. Tell Two and Three to keep the triangle equal." That was Ulianov. He had been with a Special Strike Command and wore CI Ground Forces undress without insignia, with a silver skull on each shoulder. He was the only one of this team who was taking payment for the work.

"Will you narrow the ranger scan and direct it there? A little lower." That was Jaeckal, who had been a CIGF regular under Anthony Wayne Bayard. He wore a camouflage singlesuit that he adjusted with great care each time the light shifted. He did not talk about his service, and either admired or hated Ulianov; it was impossible to tell which.

"That's surely a trace. Dead even between the others; tell them to split it, put in a crossfire, and we'll find a line for the pick-off." That was Ardrey the Man-Hunter. He had a rule that, while only he stated it openly, all nine of the human hunters had come to abide by: he hunted only that which was as intelligent as himself, or more so.

The ti-draken slid along, great size without awkwardness, but slow, only just keeping up. "Hist iss not moving," the plexy-bearer said. "Perhaps hist hass died."

"Tight? What do you mean, 'tight'?"

"'Died,' Ulianov. And I doubt that hist has. Parasites must have a very good reason to kill their hosts."

"You think the Riders are afraid of being analyzed?"

"I hope they're not that smart. Just like I hope they can't latch on to me," Jaeckel said, in a tone he might have used to say "I hope it doesn't rain today."

The ti provision-bearer halted, snaked hists spiky great head around.

Ardrey followed its look and in one motion had his feet planted and his Masada off his shoulder.

"Clear line, God help me," he muttered.

"Then kill it," Ulianov said.

The ti looked at Ardrey. Ardrey looked back. "I will fire on a count five. Tell Two and Three that I aim high; if I miss the Rider, the killer will be alive and alerted."

He shouldered the rifle. "One."

The sight found the broad back of the killer ti, moved up to the Rider upon it.

"Two."

The sight bracketed the Rider, put up numbers on range and elevation.

It was an ugly thing that sat on the ti-draken, a hard round shell of dirty chitin that had protected the creature inside while it grew in the ground—how many years?

"Three."

Three hundred years growing, perhaps four, a long cycle for a parasite. Four hundred years ago the ti had still been warring for dominance, had been battle-dragons. Now they called in marksmen from the human race.

"Four."

To capture just one Rider, to find out what went on inside the armored capsule—but they could not be taken alive. No trap could hold a ti save one that destroyed what it held.

"Five."

The rocket spat white from the barrel; then its sustainer caught and it was a line of red light, true as a laser, into the target. From Ardrey's viewpoint there was a brilliant blink at the base of his vision, and the Rider exploded.

He waited for the freed ti to collect hists senses and run. It slumped to one side.

They had been decoyed.

The earth rippled. Mounds of soil pushed up, crumbled aside, and the Riders crawled up on their carpets of legs. The ti stepped aside, moved randomly.

Ardrey brought the Masada round hard, its vented barrel whistling, fired two shots at the burrowing things nearest him. One went up in a dry spray of fragments, but the other took its impact past the push of the booster charge and before the sustainer reached v-max, and the rocket glanced away.

He let the rifle drop on its sling and grabbed for the pistol on his belt. Ulianov had dropped the sniper barrel on his weapon and was firing cyclic, the shots hitting home on white booster charges alone. Jaeckel used a thermal pistol and did not miss, but it was taking his beam whole seconds to burn through chitin, and he swore louder and blacker with each one he killed.

The ti were shuffling away from the scene, silently, though the sounds from the bellypack Webset were audible at a distance.

Jaeckel cursed again and shoved his pistol into its holster, drawing a toothed combat knife. "We've got to get between Two and Three. Get into the crossfire. Tell them so." His voice was loud but deliberate.

Ulianov seemed to jump. A gray shell had forced the ground aside beneath his feet. The half-meter parasite came up closer than the length of his carbine, and he brought the gun butt down on it.

It crawled up his legs, and he screamed. The human central nervous system is nothing like the nerve-net of the ti-draken. Man and Rider died from the shock.

Ardrey and Jaeckel were up and running, ordering the ti to follow; but the nonhumans moved only slowly, the one with the Webset stepping toward where Ulianov lay. The Riders crawled toward hist.

Ardrey had a flat shiny Ariel in his hand. He thumbed the cover open and worked the keys.

The close jungle dimmed and muffled the bomb's flash and rumble—

"Killing both the ti and all the nest of Riders."

"But ti are so fast."

"Killer ti are swift as any dragons. But the ti of the cities, the un-Ridden ti, are not. We should never have taken them along. We saw the danger, should the killers get hold of our communications; that is what the charges were set for, and the ti did not object.

"What we did not see was the reason they approved the bombs; the ti knew how easily they might be captured. Our fault, our oversight. We have outgrown the expectation of aggression in other creatures, child mine, but we have not learned enough; we expect at least the determination of cowardice.

"And still I wonder. Four centuries past, when we guess the Riders were last active, the ti were still fighting for dominance, still warrior-serpents.

"I wonder what it was we warred against."

Ari raised his gun to shoulder-arms, saluted, and the light above his head dimmed out. There was applause from an invisible audience.

"Ari?" Grailer said, his voice oddly hollow, his skin cold. He strained to see into the darkness. The clapping went on. A light appeared, as from a lantern far away; it swelled, diffused, overwhelmed him. *Clap-clap-clap-clap*—

Bang-bang-bang-bang went the bedside alarm. Simon Jonas and Mr. Aristide, pressed a little out of shape by Grailer's eyes, watched him from the bedside.

"All right now?" Ari asked.

"He'd better be," Jonas said. "We've got a whole queue of people just waiting to climb into that bed. They don't want to share it with you, old dear."

"Do you remember anything?"

Grailer's mouth was spongy but serviceable. "You and the ti-draken. And—" He remembered the earlier sensation and the earliest fear.

"How long has it been?" He started up, feeling very strong, but his limbs would not respond in the right ways.

"Twenty-two days Standard. Not so long for you, though; you had the EH-30 and the slow tape to keep you company. And I must say Simon is right; watching a man's nucleoproteins being edited is never going to be a popular amusement."

EH-30. Elf Hill drug. Throwing off the time sense like Mysmemedi did, but in the other direction. If that was really what they had given him; if Lifespan was really what they had done to him.

"Prove it," he said, and this time managed to sit up, the Hellmanns supporting him making faintly insulting whines.

Jonas said, "You remember the tank? Going in?"

Grailer nodded. Wagged his head, anyway.

"Always happens when you do. If I had my way—oh, don't think there's nothing a Lord Doctor can't ask for—everyone would go out, total deep sleep, before they got into the room. But some people want to see everything. I think they can't take being undressed in their sleep, even if it is only a medex doing it." He turned to Mr. Aristide. "Well, Ari, you said the old dear would appreciate being taken down awake. Are you going to finish bringing him up?"

Ari came back to the bedside. He carried a Webset, Grailer's, and on it a picture.

Twenty-two days to eternal life, Grailer thought; no amber, no betrayals, and no more fear.

"Hello, Sharon," he told the set.

> > >

"Eighteen," he whispered to her as they hugged in the skyport. "Not the limit either way. Now I don't want to hear any more about it."

"Not for a year," she said.

"Not ever," he said, "but you're right. Of course, you're right. But in a year—never again afterward."

Eight months Standard, actually, was the time remaining.

On the third evening after Grailer's return, the door chimed and admitted the proxartist, the dark man. Grailer greeted him and was

preparing to politely throw him back out when he noticed that the
thing under the young man's arm was no portable proxar. It was,
however, a musical instrument. It was a disk of memory material
with golden harpstrings.

"Dylan Treece, you can call me, lad." Grailer stepped close; under
the better light, and since he now knew what to look for, he could see
that some of the youth was sprayed on, see how much the glasses hid,
remembered that Treece/Taliessin had not sung a note on that night.

"But I do sing 'Stardrive'; I wrote it. The Third Poet Dylan, you
can call me, if you've the guts or the stomach. And I've come to
invite your guitar and your lady's cymbals to play with some other
bright instruments. If, that is, I can tear you away from each other."

"Easier to take me from the Web, Doctor. But I think we'll be
there. I've got some songs of my own to sing."

Eight months Standard.

> "One. Two. One-two-three-*four*."
> *We should not too closely question*
> *The saints they send to save us*
> *When there's no other shelter from the night*
> *But is it Polydore the Poet*
> *Or Virgil called the Magus*
> *Who guides me ever downward to the light?*
> *All names return unto the dust;*
> *I only run because I must;*
> *I may not be here when you waken from your dream,*
> *From your dream;*
> *I am so seldom what I seem.*

"Gry, what's that song about?"

"Mmmmm?"

"'Polydore Virgil Magus.' Who's it sung to?"

"Someone I left behind."

"Left for me?"

"That was the working hypothesis."

Except, he thought, the hypothesis did not include the time he spent away from his Webset. He did not touch the keys for days at a time; it had been four days Standard now, perhaps five, since he had even snapped the cover open to look at the panel.

He moved his fingers in an enabling sequence, wondering if they would respond correctly. His right hand rested on Sharon's knee (he had not noticed) and her response broke up the pattern he was searching for.

Grailer reached to the nightstand, but the set was not there. He could not for one stomach-dropping moment remember where it was—then recalled. In the closet. Wrapped in a fabric-silk shirt.

So now, he thought, he put it away. When had he ever done that? He could barely be persuaded to put a cloak or a pair of muddy boots away. And when he went to the set these far-between days, enabled and spun, it was in her absence—as if—

How many mistresses might one man have?

Hand on the nightstand, hand on her thigh, he touched the light off and looked in the dark for the answers to mysteries.

Six months Standard were left in the search.

> I have no time to sing with
> The laureate at midnight
> Composing songs in golden minor chords
> And I may have been misled by
> The lady in the lamplight
> Who's dealing futures from the deck of swords.
> All names return unto the dust . . .

"This came for you, lad."

"Who the hell would send me a parcel? Who the hell sends parcels anyway?"

"I didn't look at the mark."

"Dated three months ago. Well, I hope it wasn't too urgent. Wait a moment—it's from Juvenal, on Brass. And it can't be CIRCE; they'd have paid a personal visit. Doctor, your snapknife, please."

"Well?"

"It's a card."

"Greeting? Salutation? Condolence?"

"The Sixth Trump. The Lovers."

Grailer was suddenly humorless. "She's sleeping, Dr. Taliessin— there's something I want to ask you now."

"The ticklish places aren't standard, lad. But fear not, you'll find them, and the looking's pleasant, I recall."

"No. There's something I've been a—I haven't wanted to ask— and I can't ask Ari, not now—"

"He doesn't hate you, lad. And he's good at hating, when he wants to be."

Grailer had barely paused to listen. "I need to know if it was the Web that made you leave her."

"Leave her?"

"If it wasn't—if it was music or anything—you don't need to say, but I have to know if it was the Web. Because—because just now I don't know which I could more easily give up."

"Hold, hold, young lord; before you slay your thousands show me your sword. Whom did I leave?"

"Celene Tourdemance, of course."

"Eh, now? I've left her no oftener than anyone else—you, for instance. I grant she wants to know the trick of it, but it's not—"

"You hurt her badly."

"Oh, did I, now."

"Was there so little involved in love for you? Oh, I know, sex is different—but she called you lovers."

"Oh, it is. Oh, she did. And when was this?"

"Nine years ago; you know I haven't seen her five times since."

Taliessin plucked the card from Grailer's hand and rapped it with a knuckle. The painted Lovers began to dance, apart, touching, coupling (but with a subtlety of motion sexual sculptors could seldom manage), touching, and separating again. He snapped the card. The two figures stood separated, heads turned so that they faced obliquely, regarding one another from the corners of eyes.

"Lovers," Taliessin said, "lovers, what a word. Plato might have called us lovers, he who believed that value was an absolute and that men and women should admire each other's minds like a pair of damp sponges passing mutual judgment—"

"Doctor, if I'm going to hurt Sharon then tell me, please."

"She lied, boy," said the minstrel, in a voice like a file on steel.

"But she sounded so—" Grailer thought he understood. He did not want to believe he really did. "I can't believe she'd want to hurt anyone."

"Never think that," said the harp unstrung. Then Taliessin was himself—or at least was Dylan Treece—again. "But that's not why, of course. Only fools tell lies to cause hurt, when the truth cuts so much deeper. An intelligent soul lies only to ease pain."

"Whose?"

"Anyone's. Including one's own." Taliessin stroked his harp, and Grailer knew the tune.

All my sadness, all my joy, came from loving a thieving boy . . .

Grailer walked to the bedroom door, knowing Taliessin would leave in his own time and way. He watched Sharon sleep, and watched her, and tried to move closer and could not make his muscles answer.

One of her long hands dangled, and moved a bit as she acted out whatever she dreamed. Seeing it, Grailer knew what he had to do. He must teach her to spin, if she had the least skill (and those hands proved she did).

And then if the Web should pull them apart, it would pull them both, across the synapses even as Lifespan age-drift pulled across the years.

Four months Standard reckoning remained.

> *Through the brimstone and the stardust*
> *I move without direction*
> *Unmanned by all the visions that I see*
> *But when the comedy is over*
> *There follows resurrection*
> *And Beatrice will be waiting there for me.*
> *All names return . . .*

"Hello, Grailer, child mine."

"Not yours anymore, Ari."

"You do not sound much wounded by the slip—but I retract it. What of this song I hear, out on the fringes of the Dance?"

Has he heard, thought Grailer, does he know? I wasn't ready for him to know about what Sharon had learned, not yet—but of course not. He means "Virgil." Grailer said, "Has it gone that far?"

"It has. Did Taliessin give you the symbology?"

"He gave me a book. I think he knew the man who wrote it."

"Heavens around us, I hope not. Will I see you in a few months?"

"Us. You'll see us. And I'll show you—" Grailer stopped short. Not yet, not yet, but soon he'd show Ari a Spinner made in months, not years. Show him a Spinner trained with touches of the hands and not with cracks of the white-hazel wand. Show him that love achieved more than pain, in this place where the damned Goliard wretched-of-the-stars kept to themselves.

But he did not wish to hurt Mr. Aristide, he realized, only show him the new path. Dr. T was so very right about the truth cutting.

Ari's eyes flicked. "Why the pause, Grailer? Check your fringes, child mine, watch your indiks; things howl in the woods."

"No problems," Grailer said at once, feeling hurt himself. Aristide was trying to scare him again, present his little object lessons that left little white scars. "You'll see us in a few weeks Standard," he said, broke Web with a fingersnap and slapped the set shut.

> I have not always traveled
> Upon the straight and level
> I may not reach the kingdoms of the blest
> But if I'm bound upon a circle
> I'm sure you'll cheat the devil
> May flights of angels sing thee
>   Buoy thee up and wing thee
>   Sainted and eternal to thy rest.

"A little to the left. Ring finger right a milli. Now the C-G-C theme, with both hands."

"Like this?"

"Whoops, here—that's got it." He gave her back the keys. "Sorry, didn't mean to be grabby. It can get kind of frustrating, sitting here and thinking routines while you play them. I want to reach right out and—"

She slapped his wrist. "I ought to tie your hands."

He pulled back, said, "And you would, too," in a mock-horrified tone. "With your cymbal wires, I suppose, and then you'd play me like a proxar. I'll have to watch your hands every moment."

"You do anyway." She looked from the keys to the screen. "Gry, what's that?"

An unmasked CIRCE was looking puzzledly from the screen, jerks of her shoulders telegraphing frantic finger movements below their view.

"That's an idiot," Grailer said, reaching out to strike a half dozen keys. The test pattern apeared, exactly as he gave it to the Operator, then the picture went to static and cleared into a tranquil woods-and-lake scene lit by a low red sun.

"That's Brenneke's Afterglow, I think," Grailer said. "Incredibly quiet place. And cool without being heatsuit-cool. We ought to—"

"Gry, that was a CIRCE. They can—I mean, everybody knows they police people who steal through the Web, but . . . she just found me, Gry. How easily can they do that?"

"Not easily at all, Sharon, if you're not you. It's time I showed you how to make angels."

"Angels?"

"Like—like using a trumpet mouthpiece to get tin-whistle noises. Or making your multicymbals as temple bells . . . or whatever . . . ah, here they are." He looped a cymbal-contact wire around his wrist, pulled it tight. "Or whatever. Listen to this: '*Ein' feste Burg ist unser Gott . . .*'"

It had been the music that had let him teach her so quickly (and those marvelous fingers, of course). From the keys and stops of an instrument to those of the set was an easy move—and she was Second Lit to begin with, after all.

There were ready correspondences between chord progression and multikey techniques like the Kosatsu fan and Gardner curve. Stairstep roll, glissando; buttonbounce, staccato; stickslip, pizzicato. Alarms were sour notes, of a sort that an artist with a properly tuned instrument would practically have to force from the speaker.

And he was there to keep the Hounds from her—not in secret, as Ari had him, but by her side. The burned child was now the master of the flames. Once, when he was nibbling mindlessly, she pulled a corona shock that dumped her on the floor and him on top, but it had been a harmless crackle. After that she even pretended to draw them deliberately but never really brought one again.

She seemed, in truth, better at skipping traps than Grailer himself was.

"The talent's in your hands, Sharon."

"You're not so bad yourself, Gry."

"Hah. Easy—move the sticks as fast as you can without hurrying them, that's the secret. You see? When you blink your pretty green eye, the angel blinks its beady little blue one. When you smile and show your teeth, so does she. No matter what you're wearing, whether you look like you've just come down from a month's Mem dream, you can be dressed in silk or stars, your hair wound up and your lids sparkling—ah, ha, ha ha . . ."

He stood, stretched, walked to the service wall, and punched up a glass of sparkling white.

As he reached for the full goblet, it wobbled on its tray. Ripples stirred the surface of the wine, and bubbles rushed up.

He turned at Sharon's cry.

Only seconds remained.

>   >   >

Down reach the levels of the one city on all cold Skolshold, down like the icicles that shackle all that world's surface, down like stalactites in a deep cool cave, down as if the plastics and increte and steel of the infracity-on-top had softened and dripped down into the world.

Like green fire washing into a woman's fair throat—

The city trickles down in rivulets of work-space and life-space and communing-space, an acid eating into the rock. Linears search out deepening mazes, pathwalks lead into rough-cut walls and new darknesses, elevators are aimed at the molten core of everything.

Like long-nailed fingers reaching for help that could not be given—

The young man on the elevator had come seeking hell. He had, before departing on his quest, found something flat in his pocket and tried it on his wrist. But it was not nearly sharp enough—only a bit of plastic, bearing a picture that smiled up at him. Angry at its smiling, he tore it in two. Electrostatic imaging-inks oozed from the ragged edges, burning his fingers. He threw the pieces down and bulled through the door, headed for an elevator.

Now his eyes were blind with tears. His hands bled. But he wept and smoldered alone. He had called the elevator expecting it to be occupied, for on his home of the greatest number of moments elevators were only secondarily for travel; but he was a long, long way in space—

—but not in time, for the things that inhabit the Web jump at thoughtspeed—

—from Marcera and Maracot Falls. And though the floor of this car was comfortably carpeted and there was a doorlock switch in its command panel, there was no occupant to key the switch and lie upon the carpet with him.

And give him pain.

It had been nine years since a scream had escaped the young man's lips, and the giver had sworn to give no more. And it had been no gasp of passion that *she* had uttered, minutes (hours?) ago in their last embrace, no cry to signal the touch-past-all-bearing. It had been a scream of all the nerves at once.

Where would he go to find such a scream? How could he join her, go to that ultimate far place he had sent her to with his clumsy fingers and his plextronic tricks?

The Hounds would not send him, because in his sightless palsy he could not call them. No fellow Spinner (*was* there a Spinner here? He thought and thought, and music jangled in his ears, but no face would appear before him) would call such a death as she had died to him.

He would have dealt out any magic for such pain. He intended to pay the balance with his life, after all; but it was not enough to die without first following her lead.

The elevator door opened and spilled him upon two Goliards, who cried out and drew daggers and nearly fainted for joy when they saw the blood.

"Come dine, come dine," said one dressed in linen stained with murex purple. He turned to another in figured bronze. "Does he make thirteen at table?"

"He does," said the legionary, and tucked her arm under the young man's to help carry him.

They sat him down in a chair pushed back from the long narrow table, which was set for thirteen already. With the precision of fever, he counted: a zodiac plus one were present. One tried to unfoul his roundel dagger from a fishnet hung over his shoulder; one dipped her head, time after time, touching her hair to feet in open sandals; one adjusted a communications coronet wrapped with some sort of brambly branches. That last one looked terribly sad, and the young man wondered why; he had the center seat.

"Wine!" someone called, and a figure appeared with an amphora on the crook of her elbow. She filled silver goblets with the whitest wine the young man had ever seen. It had no bouquet either. Was it wodka, he wondered, and tasted.

It was Skolshold snowmelt water, flat and faintly brackish.

"You're jumping your cue," said a Goliard in a grotesque facial makeup: scaled eyes.

The young man sat back and waited for whatever would come.

The coroneted Goliard elevated his face, raised his goblet, murmured words, and slid a finger on a stud in the cup's thick stem.

The water in all the chalices discolored red. The young man

seized his, looking deep. The Borgia-cup effect (for he knew poisoners; he recognized it with his bound and gagged reason) was too like bleeding, the diffusion from a floating body into clean water, for his overreached mind. It seemed for an instant that the head of a fish rose from the cup and goggled eyes at him. A green fish, barbels hanging fanglike from its lips. A fanged green fish—leaping, crackling, burning her so that her red hair smoldered—

He threw the cup the length of the table, spattering them all with wine the color of blood. The goblet caught the fishnetted Goliard on the ear, cutting the lobe; it bled the true stuff.

"Missed your cue again, damme," said a diner.

"Kissed the wrong one," said another.

"By the script you leave quietly," said the coronetted toastmaster, who then narrowed his eyes. "But who then cares for scripts, and preordination? The soul of the Dance is change. Let us improvise steps." He looked into the young man's grief-mad eyes, and his own took on the dizzy cast of a Goliard unsheathing his knives to flay. "Perhaps," he said, wet-lipped, "I was heard last night in the Garden; perhaps the burden is taken away."

From beneath robes came mallets and long iron nails. One of those in armor flicked away the tablecloth, sending food flying, revealing rough raw timber beneath.

The young man looked, and thought, and nodded gravely. He would take the role, though he did not know the play.

The coronet surrounded his temples. It was sharp, but corona shocks were sharper, and he said nothing.

There was a period of scourging, but as much as he bid them the screams of his beloved would not come.

There was great weight which dulled everything, making him impatient.

As the hammer finally rose, they said "You have seven speeches to make, by tradition; but we find few have lasted beyond three. Start early."

"Finish it," he said, "give her back to me; it's cold, and I miss the Hounds' howling.

"I was Dian Grau—and then was not—and am again; Dian Macarthur Grau, who killed with his hands. How could I have changed that with a change of name? Dian Macarthur Grau I was and am, and again I have killed the beloved with my hands. Damn the—"

"Enough," they said, "overlong, inartistically ordered. You'll live for a curtain line."

He waited, tensed so that his scream might have all his strength behind it.

But they were shuffling away, scattering. The ceiling wavered in his vision; he thought he heard sandals slapping at a dead run, the multiple muffled thud of human bodies falling to the floor.

He looked up again and saw black curled hair, a lineless forehead (but of course he knew it was cosmetic spray), dark glasses. The rim of a golden wheel-harp threw rays of light.

"Dylan Treece," the young man whispered, overjoyed that the bard had come to sing his pain, knell his dirge. "Make a song, all for us. Soon we'll be together—"

"No, m'cree. Not together, not this way. Thunder from Badon, boy, it's the wrong opera; you're Parsifal, not Tannhäuser." He touched the young man's throat, and painlessness, cool and sharp, spread down his body.

The odd proper names meant nothing to the young man. The analgesia did. He tried to rise, but the hand on his neck held him pinned; and he knew that his consummation was about to be soothed away from him. "Don't—don't take her—"

"Greater than I have taken her already. Hold, boy, hold—still. I am he whom Elphin dragged from the waters; King Elphin I comforted with my life's first song. And you are only a little page, not a king, and all you have encountered is the old rondelay of love and death. Were you my pupil I might have given you Werther for a name."

Doctor Taliessin, his one-handed grip unbreakable, took off his dark glasses and wiped clear his brow.

And the brilliance—

Dian, touch your tears to dust.
Sadness scarcely suits a singer.
Empty-eyed, like silvered screens.
We'll away, the worlds to wander.
Though I'm not Aurelian
I've a righteous reputation.
Sea and starfield, dale and depth
Offer lovers' consolation.

"Fair Elphin, dry your cheeks"—that was how the line ran in the book he had searched out, the *Canu Taliesin*, in the strange language with its strange consonantal sounds. And there was another thing there, something about the child found floating by the sad King. . . .

Dian, who was good and gay,
Mild your mind and great your grieving—
Only lightly now lament.
Better bed than dreadful dreaming.
Kings I served are dust to dust;
Deaths my dirges could not cancel.
Life is fire and flame is lust—
Fire and ash are part and parcel.

The other thing was the meaning of the name itself: *Taliesin: Radiant Brow.* For the light from the child's face was awesome and terrible, so that Elphin's men begged him to leave the creature to whatever dooms might come. But he did not. And blessed was he therefor.

Dian of the glorious touch,
Hounds in hatred's handgrip hold thee.
Grant my gaze, I'll thrall your thought;
What I will you'll not withhold me.
Keyed, encoded, circuit-etched,

Bardic voice binds your volition.
Scars on souls need space to stretch—
Change the cure for your condition.

—and the darkness.

All names return unto the dust

Doctor Taliessin sat beside Grailer on the portpod, playing his harp, singing no words.

I only run because I must

"Welcome aboard, Mr. Treece. Will you and your companion—"
"Not this trip, M'lady."
"Well, wouldn't—"
"*Don't you bloody touch the lad.* I thought they had eyes in your work."

I may not be here when you waken from your dream
From your dream

"Yes, Ari, I'm watching the lad. He's just bright-eyed and smiling as sin—yes, resub'd Mem. I've got friends in the dream trade, and don't you bloody condemn me. What was I to do, give him a downing-pill? He couldn't have passed boarding literacy in his natural state.

"No, Ari. I don't condemn you either. It wasn't you who made Diego mad, and loosed the damned Geisthounds."

I am so seldom what I seem.

> > >

The pod shelled open, and they stepped off into the small crowd that was there especially to absorb them. Forty people, most carrying Websets, all with at least an Ariel tucked away somewhere; one whole subculture of Marcera. And CIRCE, had they known of the party, would have ripgunned the lot under the provisions of Section Twenty of the Uniform Communications Code, the Lex Bell Stellar.

One held his Webset open. On its screen was the face of a white-haired woman, looking more like carved wood than usually she did. Pryne ships could not bring her to Grailer in time, but t-zero could.

Mistress Celene Tourdemance, the furthest living link of the Web that centered on Grailer Diomede, held in her left hand a deck of seventy-five animated cards. Of the three that were missing, two lay on the globe-lit table before her: a knight, armed and mounted, sword outstretched, and crossing it a card with three swords, stuck in a shriveled and bloodless heart.

The third card was on the floor of a transient room down deep in Skolshold city. The Lovers, torn in two.

SECOND MEASURE:

THE WORLD

CHAPTER 7

THE RAPTURES OF MAGIC

Grailer's chair was soft and sat firmly on the floor. "Chairs are rewards," Gian Paolo Sforza had said to him once. "You can fly all over the room in a Hellmann floater, but who cares? Half an hour on that leather sling they call a seat'll rub even my well-padded tailbone raw.

"Now, one of my chairs, you've got to walk to get into it. But once you get there—ahhh. Not, of course, that I'm not paying my people night and day to cross the two. Can you imagine that—a floatchair that felt like this? I'd never walk again."

Now Grailer waited to see Gian again, and there was something wrong, something uncomfortable about the chair and the lounge.

As he would, he looked at the receptionist first. No, it wasn't her. Her eyes were green, but that of itself was nothing; Grailer sometimes thought whole planets were breeding for green eyes. Her hair was brown with only a trifling trace of red. Her body was much too full; Gian's obsessive Terran-Renaissance idea of beauty, not Grailer's.

And Grailer's fear that a woman might frighten him was never realized anymore, and not even much of a fear. Not after sixty years, more than three of physical age. Not after Amanda.

And yet, and yet. A gun in the hand, a Goliard's roundel dagger with a death-what-dream smile behind it—those Grailer was well grounded in, wary and weary of. There was an aura here, and Grailer was armed against only one aura—the Hounds—and one very particular ghost.

The pictures in the lounge seemed to leer down. The swords on the walls crossed at a tense and violent angle. Something lurked in the deep carpeting. The parquet doors to Gian's apartments loomed like the gates of—of—

The doors swung on silent hinges and Nicholas Anders came out. "Come in, James," said Messer Sforza's good right hand, and Grailer got up from his chair.

Nick Anders had yellow-blond hair, lighter than Grailer's natural gold, that radiated straight out from his head. It seemed sometimes as though the sun were rising behind him; seemed too that bright sunlight had burned all the expression from his dark, lined face.

Anders was very tall and very thin. He was like a man made out of steel needles, electricity arcing at his joints. He was wrapped now (insulated?) in a long leather coat with straps and metal-sealed pockets; a weatherduster, much creased and cracked, darker than he was.

As Grailer reached the double doors, Anders said "Stop." Grailer did.

"Do not mention Gian's son, even in passing. It is not something the boy has done, this time. Pier Jacopo acted irresponsibly, as always. This time he is dead as a result. Gian feels responsible. He is not, but Pier was his son. Do you comprehend, James?"

Just like that. Just like Anders. "I won't say anything, Nick."

"I did not think you would. Come in, James. Gian wants to see you very much."

The inner doors opened, and they went in.

The same aura, the same ghost, haunted Gian's office. The tapestries on the walls all seemed to have something hidden behind them. The elegant brass lamps cast more shadows than light. The equestrian bronze in the corner had a malevolent gleam in its eye.

And the ghost was haunting Gian. He turned away from the wheeling starscape behind his desk, held out his thick hands. The high collar of his brocade gown was open, ruining the architecture of the garment. The gown should have called attention away from Gian's belly; now, drooping, it emphasized it. Silver wires dodged in and out of folds in the deep blue cloth.

Grailer looked higher, at the hands. There was a dark red constriction around the ring finger of the right hand. Grailer had thought the signet smaller than the knuckle before it.

Then he looked at Gian's face. The expression there might have been stolen from one of his old, old paintings; there should have been a castle behind it, or a troop of armored lancers. But then again, there was the hull of *Florence III*, and beyond it the army of human planets.

Still, for all Gian's infatuation with ancient things, Grailer knew that look from yesterday, and from sixty years ago. He knew one hell of a lot about what haunted faces looked like.

"Hello, Gian."

"How is life, Jim?" The portrait stare did not change.

Grailer smiled, externally. Should he wait? Talk? He knew what he would dare with an ordinary man, with a Goliard, with a lover. He even had an idea what he could dare with Gian Paolo Sforza, omnicorp master.

It was Nick Anders he wasn't sure of.

"I'm glad you could come," Gian said absently.

Better dare something.

"*Scutta mal'occhio*," Grailer said. He could feel Anders' eyes tighten on him. Gian turned sharply, dropped his hands.

"Break the evil eye? Oh—I guess you did. I apologize, Jim. No, Nick, it's all right; it's about time somebody snapped his fingers and woke me up.

"Hello, Jim. I'm glad you could come. I've got some work for you. It's rather a strange sort of business."

"It usually is."

"This time more than usual. Are you familiar with the Anthony Planetary Relief Agency?"

"General Bayard's operation?"

"That's it. Then you know Anthony Wayne Bayard?"

"Only by reputation. I spent a lot of time on Marcera. Is someone glitching him?"

"That's what I want to think, and I know Wayne by more than name. But I'm not sure, Jim. I'm not sure of a lot, just lately. . . ."

"It's going to be a close thing now, Gian," Anders said, as if there had been no uncomfortable silence, no imposure by a ghost. "If we don't leave in an hour or two, we'll be closed out of the auction."

"I wouldn't mind that so much, Nick. Not with Jim here . . . how about that, Jim? Like to be my own private glitchkiller, on staff salary?"

Grailer relaxed a little. Gian was slipping back into form, making the offer he always made. So Jim Knight gave the same reply as always: "Let me think it over for another twenty years, Gian."

"Ah, the free life. Free-lancing, free will. What'll you do when Soren and Rina Rose and I take the illusions away? Oh, I'm joking." Grailer knew he was. It was all part of the game, of the Dance. It was even funny, sometimes.

"Are you and Nick leaving shortly?"

Gian sat down slowly, letting the chair accept his weight by degrees. "Not Nick and I. Nick and you, if you pick up the contract."

"Gian, you know I—"

"You know what I mean by *contract*. You should know by now you're going to get what you ask for; do you think I'd put up with your style if magic could buy any better result?"

Gian was better already.

"I want you to go to a Development Services auction with Nick. Wayne Bayard's relief people have been bidding . . . strangely. Too low for an operation his size.

"If it's just altruism or a death wish, leave things be; I've got enough of both of those to last me till my . . ." He let the thought trail and drop. Grailer waited. He didn't believe Gian would ask him to steal Bayard's secrets, if secrets there were. But people picked the strangest times to pull their trust out from under—and in a state of mind that Grailer knew all too well was unpredictable—

"But the planets Wayne gets keep failing. It's being kept very quiet—I had trouble putting it together—but Wayne, or his people, or somebody is mucking up in cultures that surely don't need any more trouble. Find out why."

Gian Paolo would be just fine.

"How much time before you can leave?"

"How long is the trip?"

"Nine days."

"And they will start in nine days four hours Standard, with us or without," said Anders, who had checked neither watch nor Ariel.

"Via Venice Space?"

"Yacht."

"Fabricators aboard?"

Gian flapped his plush sleeves. "A man who dresses like me must have fabricators on his yacht."

"Then I can leave immediately."

"Jim, you astound me. Take Nick and go, then, before he burns a hole in the carpet.

"You know, Jim," he said, stopping them halfway to the door, "I've asked you twenty times in fifty years for information, and every time you've brought it back to me in less time than it took my organization to run out of leads. How do you do that?"

"You're too big, Gian. You can't crawl through little holes like I can."

Nothing to fear, nothing suspected. Only the last move in their game.

> > >

Grailer and Anders ascended *Florence III* in a small glass linear car that was not Hellmann-floored. The acceleration was relatively slow and gracious, but Grailer wound up on his knees anyway.

"Nick, doesn't Gian make Hellmanns?"

"Of course. Gian makes excellent Hellmanns. Gian would make excellent Pryne tubes, if he only could. He does not much like gravity plates. Nor is there much need for them here. One may live in whatever weight one desires. And, of course, sit and sleep in null-g. This is *Florence III*, James. It is not as if it were a planet. You are here every few years. You should by now have learned its idiosyncrasies."

They passed the innermost level of the midweight ring and were swallowed by a tube. The wall curved as it flowed past, bending ever sharper to match the Coriolis force. The brain in the car sensed less and less gravity to be overcome and traded motor torque for speed. Then, as they ran out of tube, the brain cut power back. When the car emerged into liteweight they were traveling at a decorous inhabited-areas speed.

"What are you going to do after Gian, Nick?"

"Messer Gian has at least six hundred more years of life. Six hundred years Standard is more than I shall likely live. If I live longer, I am certain Gian will provide. I expect him to adopt an heir within fifty years. I would work for any ruling Sforza. I do not change."

"Would you have worked for Pier Jacopo?"

"If he had become the ruling Sforza."

Good old Nick. He really did *not* appear to change—whatever change meant. He couldn't be drawn into the games. He wouldn't Dance. Don't ask him. But it never seemed to bother him that Grailer tried.

"Would you have killed Pier for Gian, Nick?"

"I would kill anyone for Gian, James. But Gian does not ask me to kill. He suspects that I would not weigh the action before proceeding. He is correct."

Grailer said no more. It was exactly the response he should have expected from Anders; a statement of principles rather than an exposition of facts.

Grailer wanted to know how Pier—who was, he clearly remembered, an idiot and a venal one—had died. He wondered just where the thread would lead, and had a very good idea. But Anders was not the end of the thread to take hold of. There were plenty of Websets with unlocked keyboards.

The car opened and as soon as they left it vanished behind them.

"What's your size in a softsuit?"

"One-ninety by ninety. Don't you make single-sizes either?"

"This is a yacht, not a liner. Even if it were not, you're one-ninety tall and ninety around. Have you ever had to don a single-size while the ship puffed out, and then wear it until pickup?"

"Actually, no."

"I have. I'm a two-hundred by eighty. You wouldn't like it either."

A dock clerk—not a mechanical fabricator—handed Grailer the oblong bundle of his softsuit and pushed at some buttons—awkwardly, Grailer saw. Well, he didn't care much for fetching and carrying; there must be some people who didn't key well.

They walked out to the yacht on a square column that extended from the hub of *Florence*. High-gradient Hellmanns held them on, and a film of atmosphere as well; there was no outer wall.

Grailer said "Dammit, my feet hurt."

"Just your blood pooling. I thought you liked gravity grids."

"I like gravity."

"So does Messer Sforza. In the correct proportion."

The boarding column stood out fifty meters from the hub, enough so that *Florence III* lay complete around them. The hub was a great disk, an island with rectilinear topography; grids and cubical hills and windows light and dark. Then a black void of four kilometers, bridged by linear tubes and access tunnels that tapered almost to invisibility before they met the midweight ring. And another moat of space surrounding that, and a curved line of light too far away to judge its distance, the hiweight ring, guidance strobes sparking along its length, signal fires on the outer bailey wall.

"I've never been to Sidi el-Kutra," Grailer said. "Is it as lush as they claim?"

"I wouldn't know. I've not seen much of it but the exchange rooms. Those are lush in a fashion: If you enjoy machinery and money."

"I like machinery. Magic is all right, to drop in the slot and punch up heart's desire."

"You may feel differently. Many do, after they see the Sidi."

The yacht, christened *Andrea Orsini*, was built for atmosphere as well as space, with long arched supercrit wings and a forked tail of the type called "swallow." A pair of Prynes were faired into the tail; they were third-quantums, good for a kilocee but too big for the ship's fine lines.

He was white, with sharp dashes of black on his leading edges to mask the soot of thick-air landings and a silver band around the body where the rectifier screens were built in. Up at the nose Grailer could just see the spot of deep purple in the silver for the pilot's vision.

Little children wanted to see through that spot, see Space beyond the envelope. Eventually a few became pilots, took the hypnarcosis. The rest forgot they had ever wanted any such thing.

"I had forgotten," Anders said at the hatch, "*Orsini* has no Ship's Companion. We still have time to send someone up, if you can specify right now."

"Don't worry about it."

"It will not worry me. There is a staff of stewards. They are stewards, however."

"It's all right," Grailer said, trying not to complain too much.

"As you wish."

Grailer had not suddenly lost his interest. But he suspected that Gian had ordered Nick to watch "Jim Knight" at work, and he knew for a fact that Anders missed nothing anyway. So he might as well put on a show of working hard and working legally. Gian could speculate as he wished on Knight's techniques, even speculate correctly, as long as he was not too sure.

It occurred to him that a Webspinner on the payroll might be the secret of Bayard's low bids. He would have to check that early on. Warn the Spinner that his profile was much too high. Tell Gian— well, probably the truth. That Webspinners existed everyone knew, having a friend who had a friend who had heard about one shot down in the street by CIRCE; that they were devious and hard to catch that same chain of friends made clear. Gian asked and paid Grailer / Knight for information, not bodies in a bag.

So if the search started there, he would not begin it now. Not under Nick's eyes. That didn't leave much to do but study Sidi el-Kutra, the omnicorps, and the Development Auctions. Ordinary bookwork stuff.

He consoled himself with the thought that if the Sidi were truly as pleasant as advertised, nine days alone with Anders should certainly pique his appetite for it.

> > >

Ahead of *Orsini* lay a rosette, a ring of planets without a star at their center. The geometric perfection of the system was impressive on the deep-ranger screen, hurtling toward them at a billion km a second. They swelled perilously huge, filling the screens; then a ripple ran through the image and the planets stopped still. They were out of the Pryne envelope, watching sane and unrectified space as they drifted in on mercury ions. Ahead were five worlds, laser-linked, twinklings along the beams as ships rode them, a giant's bracelet of light and stone.

"Which one is ours?"

"None."

"I meant, which one are we landing on?"

"I know what you meant. The Kemplerer rosette is not the Sidi. It is called the Ring of Wards. It serves auxiliary functions. The Sidi is at its center."

Parallax picked out a speck from the stars in the middle of the ring, a tiny and cold sun for five planets.

"Sidi el-Kutra," Anders said.

The Sidi was in total no larger than a three-hundred-room orbital hostel or the biggest of the liners. Her greatest measurement was no more than three hundred to three hundred fifty meters—but that dimension was hard to guess against dimensionless space and in the random shape the Sidi took.

It was a jumble of blocks, cubes, spheres, tetras, like a cluster model of a folded and refolded protein, or the organelle beasts of Harp's Felicity. It was attractive, too, in a metal-sculpture sort of way. Extruded beams and filament frames hung the blocks together, thin structures but still more solid than one would expect in null-g. Off to a side was a fusion sphere—larger than average, but that was to be expected—and beyond it an asteroid-sized chunk of water ice, flickering blue and white in searchlight and starlight.

The habitat blocks were different somehow from a hotel or an outpost. Grailer looked close to figure out why. They still had the puzzle-surface, with cables and grooves traced over, the purple reflections of polarized ports and the silver of stargaze domes, unsubtle outlines of engineering stations and service hatches. All a neutral off-white . . . *that* was the difference. There were no makers' marks, builders' plates, two-meter dazzlered letters announcing THIS FACILITY UPHUNG BY SARNEC ENGINEERING OR VON DER ZWO RECYCLIC PLUMBERS ("Waste Not Want Not").

"Who built this?"

"Julian Vaill. The fourth omnicorp."

"Fourth? You're not really planning the consortium the newsrakers keep looking for, are you—Sforza and Rosenfeld and Nykvist?"

"There was a fourth omnicorp. There is no longer. Julian Vaill and Vaill Extended Enterprises are both dead. All that remains are the Sidi and Julian's operating center, which he called Erewhon."

"Alien language?"

"Ancient literature. You have never heard of Butler's *Erewhon*?"

"Nor Vaill, nor a fourth omnicorp either."

"*Sie können kein's Vorzeit.*"

"What?"

"You have no history, James. The book is surely still on the Web."

"I don't care about the book. I want to know about Vaill."

"Julian is not still on the Web."

"How could he not be?"

"He was one of those that built it. You are an excellent source of information, James. You must realize that whatever one man can make available another can wall off. I will show you Erewhon someday, James. You would appreciate it."

A carrier beam sought *Orsini* out, found his code and blinker, and drew him in. They passed marker lamps that winked out as they passed, ports open to the void covered only by pressure curtains or Hellmann-held air, men wearing glossy red hardsuits seated on the beams in positions of boredom, holding weapons.

The pilot stopped the ship with just a faint bump, enough to ripple but not slosh a drink. Grailer appreciated the skill involved; anyone with a finger to push a button could land full-auto, Hellmanns soaking up all shock. It required a craftsman to deliver that docking tap, to say "Safe harbor reached" with the ship and not the annunciator.

A tubeway touched the hull, and red lights ringed the hatch. A pair of contacts met, and one light turned green; a pressure-pipe found a socket, and another changed; a seal slid in a keyway and four more went green.

The rest of the patterns were fulfilled, and the hatches cycled Nick and Grailer out.

Anders thumbed his Ariel—a sixteen-key set, Grailer had noticed at their first meeting, but with a shift switch that would double or triple its signal capacity.

"We have two hours forty minutes before the auction. It should require at most half an hour to reach the exchange room from any point in the Sidi, allowing for your unfamiliarity. You therefore have one hundred thirty minutes to do what you will.

"That you will enjoy the Sidi is not in question. Do not enjoy it in too time-consuming a manner. We will have at least thirty hours after the auction concludes.

"In one hundred twenty-eight minutes ask directions to Exchange Room Tenebro. Its common abbreviation is Ex-Ten. Do not use that term. You would be assumed familiar with the Sidi and receive worthless instructions. I will see you then and not before."

"Do I need a pass, or a guide, or something?"

Anders was already walking away. He said "No," without turning.

Grailer had been nine days without the Web, and he wanted to spin. He could feel it in his hands and fingers, like a need to stretch. But here was Sidi el-Kutra before him like a complicated toy, and only two hours to read the instructions and thirty hours to play.

It might be better to spin now, to wait to explore until after the auction—but no, if the physical pleasures could wait, so could the spiritual ones. The Web you have always with you; these mysteries will depart. And besides, lust took the edge off Webwork.

He went forth expecting the best and the fullest. The best he got; for the fullest he should have stuck by his Webset.

The corridors were flat-floored tubes, designed to be floated rather than walked through. Annunciators and wall Webs were everywhere, in the halls and the parlors and the hot, cool, and vapor chambers; one was literally never more than ten steps from keys and a screen. That was interesting, even a Webspinner's modest idea of paradise, but who traveled without an Ariel or at least someone like Anders to carry an Ariel?

There was much running water. Rivers glassed-in alongside corridors, in one case a transparent corridor that tunneled through a turbulent tank, full-gee fountains and light-gee fountains and null-gee bubbledrop fountains—even a snow fountain and a 3° Absolute ice-needle fountain. Grailer stared for a long time at one gadget, a perforated sphere that shot thin streams in all directions. It was a game, he supposed. Some of the jets had to be flowing in, supplying the water, holding the ball in the center of its chamber. Which ones?

He found that he did not much care. And after Maracot's three-km natural fall, he cared even less for mechanical amusements.

He found a bank of elevators and called one. It was empty except for a command panel. He punched a random button—hit it rather too hard—and wondered what kind of person this builder, Julian Vaill, had been. No wonder he had vanished so utterly, if this was his idea of style. No wonder Nick Anders never visited anything but the exchange rooms. Certainly no wonder Gian Paolo didn't come along. He could get better than this in his front office—

"Well, damn me for a First Lit," he said aloud.

"Is there anything you desire, sir?" the elevator asked in a slow, pleasant female voice.

"No, nothing. Wait. How long until the auction in Ex-Ten?"

"Ninety-three minutes Standard, Engineer Knight. Do you wish transport now?"

"No, not now. If I give you a Web code, can you page me at thirty minutes prior?"

"Certainly, Engineer."

Grailer gave one of his more secure Gnosis codes. "One other thing. You're an angel, aren't you? Not human?"

"That is correct. If you wish, a human operator can be assigned your response."

"Not necessary. Thank you."

"A pleasure, Engineer."

Of course Gian could get better attention in his front foyer. So could anybody, down to a hullbanger in orbit. The lords of wealth kept Sidi el-Kutra physically apart because the Web drew their worlds so psychically close. One could transact business here in an atmosphere not of business, get into an elevator when one was too tired to perform. In the cathedrals of wealth one was surrounded by choirs of humans who served no more functions than angels but were necessary because thou wert expected to have persons under thee. How fascinating it was that the highest freedom of Man had become freedom from men.

When the Sidi paged Grailer, he had for most of an hour been relearning the marvelous peaceful beauty of moving water.

CHAPTER 8

THE TOILS OF SORCERY

ngineer Knight, welcome. Mr. Anders has said you might wish a Programming seat rather than a Monitor. Is that the case?"

"Yes, Programming, I suppose." The man was only doing his job, Grailer supposed; but he had a newly-born contempt for being waited on. Just once he wished—no, *wanted* to be asked if he *wanted* something.

"Seat nine-seven," the man (butler? usher? aide-de-camp?) said to an annunciator, and in an instant a black and silver Hellmann chair, Webgear curving round the seat, hovered before Grailer.

"The flight controls are—"

"I know where they are."

Seated more or less comfortably, hands on Web and float controls, he was passed by an iris through into the exchange room. Gian was really right about floatchairs. He wondered what it must be like for Diego Cadiz with his supernerves . . . or how much of Diego was really left below the neck?

Why was he pondering that now? He forced the thoughts from his mind.

The room was a sphere. In the center hung a globe display five meters across, off and silver-surfaced now. Beneath the globe was a ring desk, three people seated within it at fixed chairs. One had the usual sixty-four keys, auxiliaries, and screen. One had a number of sixteen-and-screen sets—actually a whole bank of Ariels, most of which were live. A sheet of hardprint rolled from a slot before the third; she made notations on it with a stylus, and it vanished down another slit.

About twenty chairs orbited the sphere screen, a few with a full bank of controls like Grailer's, most with just a screen and sixteen-pad. All the screens on all the chairs he could see were blank; Grailer tried to enable his set and found it locked. He reached for his portable, but decided against it. There were also five hovering cubes, facing pickups, screens, and speakers toward the room's center.

"Over here, James."

Grailer moved to Anders' side. "What was the concern about them starting without you? I suppose the Florentine Group doesn't build total-remotes either."

"You constantly make false assumptions about the Group's resources, James. The six companies whose remotes those are may not be here in person."

"By that you mean not allowed to come?"

"Yes."

"All right, why?"

"One because they would not abandon their sidearms. Another, similarly, because they refused to suspend code duello while in the Sidi. Their remote was in fact delivered with thermal rifles installed. The others I cannot explain. I do not have a vote in the process. I hold only the Group's proxy. Gian of course makes the decision on such matters."

"And Gian doesn't tell you why?"

"Gian does not tell me to tell you why."

Good old Nick.

A man drifted into the room. He wore a black gown, multiple layers of soft stuff that hid his feet, and a close silver hood and shoulder cape. The cape hung high on his back, draped over his wings. He stopped and hovered above the globe, the backpack Hellmann humming. There was a small silver rod and a larger plaque hung at his waist. The rod he telescoped into a pointer. The plaque was an Ariel, keys only, that he worked by touch.

"On my count," the auctioneer said, "let the doors be sealed and the channels opened.

"Closing . . . closing . . . closed." There was a hiss from the iris, and all the screens, including the sphere, came to life with colored noise.

"Developmental System Closed Auction number one hundred thirteen is now open. Participants in the Exchange, welcome.

"First world." The right hand worked the keypad, the left hand tapped the center sphere with the pointer. The bits of screen static fell into a world in space, tan and cloud-shrouded. There was some water visible, less than average.

"DESA 113.1. Kocher IV, Mbele's Sandcastle. Inhabitants non-humans."

Grailer punched keys. A bugeyed lizard with a crimson rill looked at him from one of his screens. On closer look he could see that the rill was artificial, a hat of some kind, with an eyevisor of crude glass. Fused sand.

"Before opening the bidding, I remind the participants that 113.1 is a nonhuman world. Bids from unqualified participants will be disallowed."

Two of the total-remotes and several chairs floated away from the globe. Some, including Anders, moved closer.

A man wearing the Asgard Complex sleeve crest opened, offering to take fifty percent of the Sandcastle's industrial production. Nick gave a bid of forty and added a bond for a million ercs' investment in local artworks. He'd caught the significance of that bit of colored glass early on. Every gleam peddler in the Ercon would want to middlemove it. Until it was reproduced or out of fashion, anyway.

A remote called in a bid on light metals output of twenty percent, and doubled the arts investment.

A simple enough procedure, really. As the auction progressed, the developers (*exploiters* was a word never uttered in the Sidi) offered to take less and less of the produce of the planet they took on as a ward, and to invest more and more magic against what they did take. The firm that offered to take the least and pay the most was awarded the task of bringing the world into the Ercon.

"Minerals fifteen percent, arts five mercs in and fifty percent out," said a young man in a Programming chair. Grailer's terminal said he was Oliver Pell, a partner in a relief outfit called The Fifth Horseman.

"Minerals ten," the agent for Field Developments bid.

"Minerals eight, industry twenty-five," said a remote.

It was a dry, dry planet. A few percent of the mineral rights could be worth a fortune. Or nothing; orbital scanners couldn't tell the whole story, and even less predict the future.

"Arts forty out," Pell said. He was dark, intense, broken-nosed but not unhandsome.

"Arts twenty-five out," said the Asgard Complex agent. A mumble followed, mostly from the relief-agency people. Arts and information were their major return on an investment of people and time. Mineral rights were with extraordinary exceptions worth only their eventual resale value—not very much, even in a surprise strike; a gigatonne of lumen-veined marble was so much rock without some way to transport and sell it.

"Minerals five," Pell said coolly.

That was why the bids were open instead of sealed. Try to bid somebody else's payoff suit down to zero and he'd wipe yours out as well. Play spoiler once too often and the other players would leave you with a bag full of snark, with a contract that finding the Milliard Stones again couldn't make profitable.

Speaking of which, where was Anthony Wayne Bayard?

+ + Remote 4. Nonparticipant in nonhuman auctions.

—was he blackballed?

++OUTRANGE sch0110

++Pardon me, Engineer Knight?

—are you my angel?

++Yes. You've exceeded the response range of the informational
    program. What did you want to know?

—was anthony wayne bayard denied permission to be here?

++Yes, Engineer.

—why?

++No reason is required, Engineer. I can tell you that the vote was
    very close.
—anything else?
++If you mean concerning the exclusion vote, no, Engineer. I should
    advise you that very few such things are recorded on Sidi
    el-Kutra.

One more expensive freedom.

—thank you.
++My pleasure, Engineer.

"Closing," the auctioneer said, and tapped the display.
Grailer's fingers ran over his keys.

FIRST CLOSING CALL
LAST BIDDER: The Fifth Horseman
LAST BIDS: INDUS 20%
             MINRL 5%
             LOPRO 22% (Arts) // 5.5 Merc inv (Optics)
             INFOR 65%
             OTHERS OPEN

"Patentable data forty," someone said hesitantly, and Grailer
looked at Oliver Pell.

Pell's eyes stayed on his console. He could close out minerals or
bid industrial rake-off down further. But instead he said "Agriculture five percent."

There was silence except for the rattle of keypads. Grailer rolled
up all the data on Mbele's Sandcastle he could legitimately get.
The planet shouldn't have had an agricultural output worth taking,
certainly not after the native reasonable-and-proper had been taken
out. A hundred percent of nothing was nothing.

A Mysmemedi crop, maybe? A planet that size could keep the
whole Ercon dreaming. But no, there wasn't enough arsenic in

the atmosphere. Some other dreamstuff? Possibly, but not likely. Pell could claim Mem was going to keep Pryne pilots sane, to a certain extent anyway, but that wouldn't work for much else. CIRCE would be on you cold solid, acting out Diego Cadiz' hatred of dreams.

It must be a bluff, then.

Somebody called it: "Light metals sixty." Called it hard. Then, all at once, everyone was bidding, one after the other, as fast as keys and faster than voices. The auctioneer rapped for decorum. It didn't work very well, so he punched keys on his hip Ariel and locked up everyone's boards.

Grailer nearly bypassed the locks on his own, without pausing to think. He caught his error and waited. When he called for data after the keys were released, every category contained a bid and no rake-off was higher than twenty-five percent. Agriculture stood at two.

All around Grailer there was moving of lips and cautious pressing of keys—for more information, not bids. He followed suit.

??investment data

++Could you be more specific, Engineer?

—what would i plant on a desert?

++Do you mean "plant" in an industrial or agricultural sense?

—green growing plants.

++I'll assume you meant "green" figuratively. The major
    possibilities are:

*Surabai oil cactus

*Spices (many possibilities)

There is also Khashan's "Bluegrass," a water-retaining plant/ground
    cover used in terraforming operations.

—profitability?

++Profitability is a complex value depending heavily on the
    capacities of the developer. This system cannot analyze
    investments, not least because it contains no such privy data.
    After the Auction, I can put you in touch with the Florentine
    Group's analytic centers.

—not necessary. thank you.

++A pleasure, Engineer.

"Closing," said the auctioneer. Grailer's head came up, and he saw all eyes trained on Oliver Pell. Pell was rocking his chair on its Hellmanns, his other hand poised over the keys. He was looking at his board and at it only.

"Closing," and two taps of the pointer. Pell's hand moved, and various breaths were drawn in, but nothing more happened.

"Closed," and three taps. Mbele's Sandcastle vanished from all screens. "Contracted to Nikolaides Development.

"Ten minutes' recess," said the hovering man. "The Exchange will remain sealed."

Grailer went to Anders. Nick shot him a brief glance. "If you're hungry, ask the system. Bodily functions, those doors. Don't hesitate about either. We'll be here for some time. Especially if Pell keeps it up."

"Is Pell—"

"I don't know about Pell. It's Bayard Gian's hired you for."

"Fine." There was no place to take that line. "How much magic can you turn from Surabai cactus and spices?"

"Almost no limit. The whole planet could produce."

"Can't they be synthesized cheaper?"

"That's more in character, James. You were born only eighty years ago. Everything was once synthesized by natural processes; organisms and geology. Once you could pick a living from the ground.

"Define *cheaper*, James. Cheaper to build a synthor plant than to drop seeds on the orbital fly? Cheaper to use local labor for harvest than to import technicians like you—and provide them with a friendly environment? And so on.

"Before that Agri bid I doubt as anyone thought in that direction. If they did, it was in the hope of a secret killing to be made. Now the autochthones will keep ninety-eight percent of whatever is to be made. For here, James, without a secret there can be no killing."

Grailer flagged that brightly in his memory. "So Oliver Pell is a sharp bidder."

Anders turned his head. "We all here are honorable. Our private customs vary, but we all abide by the rules."

"But some of you play closer games than others."

"It is always so. Would you like a layered-steak sandwich, James? Cooked by induction, levitated and rotated during the cooking. Oil is reduced and flavor retained to the maximum."

"You, Nick—a gourmet?"

"I like to eat well."

"I don't think I've ever seen you eat anything."

"I have never seen you make love, James. Excuse me. We have four minutes, and I should like to sample the meal before the bell."

The tension of the first auction leaked away slowly over the next few. Pell was watched closely, but he produced no more shocker bids; he played quietly, bumping a percentage here, raising an investment there.

And he won none of them. Of the first eight contracts, one more after the first went to Nikolaides, three to the Asgard Complex, one to the Khanate of Xanadu II. (Those last were confined to a total-remote, and Grailer suspected them of being the ones who had tried to arm it.) Two went to Florentine; Nick placed the final bids on both. Grailer was intrigued by the process—how like the Dance of the Goliards, he thought once or twice, remembering Nick's comment about obedience to rules—but he was none too certain of it. (And again, how like the Dance.) He missed the freedom of data and data machinery that he did not dare allow himself here. He wanted the Web under his hands.

—will you watch bayard as you were hired to do?

So he watched Bayard—watched his remote, anyway. And the longer he watched, the more he wondered why. Anthony Relief was not bidding in any abnormal fashion. They were not bidding much at all. They were not permitted to take a nonhuman-sentient contract, and most of their staff would be useless on an uninhabited world. A gasgiant was offered and sold, an industrial dream, and Nick Anders seemed to Grailer more cutthroat in the bidding than Oliver Pell had been in his. So what was he to look for?

"DESA 113.9. Merritt's Star A II, Ishtar. Inhabitants old-Earth human, seeded by hydrogen-ram colony vessel during the Annodomini period."

Ishtar spun up on the screen, on the great globe itself. It was half blue, half tan, a hemisphere of ocean opposite a supercontinent.

Bayard's remote whirred, nosing close to the big display.

The machine spoke in a new voice, a stronger and less artificial one. It laid down bids in half a dozen categories. Grailer punched them all into a memory block to mull later.

—glad to see you on the job, Nick sent.

The voice stopped. Everyone waited.

"That's my open," the remote—no, surely Anthony Wayne Bayard—said, and hovered still.

Was this the voice that launched a thousand assaults? Grailer tried to see the General in his mind, look past the hovering hunk of tin.

In his mind's file was a little bit of Bayard at Maracot Falls, taken from afar by a novice newsraker, as it were, for the General neither Spun nor Danced: a middling-tall man, no longer young, who wore a uniform like most wore their common flesh—and kind, Grailer thought, but could not reason why. Perhaps it was just a need for contrasting colors in the warrior's portrait, the bright primaries of battle soothed by some peaceful pastels and empathic earths.

Grailer watched the steel box and heard the bronze voice, and found himself wanting to hear more . . . to learn Bayard. People had followed that voice into battle, followed it into amber, and the cold, cold (but not cryogenic) ground—certainly they had made war like love, without an outside thought; was the link perhaps stronger than he had realized?

Grailer had been fired upon and cut close to. But he had never been in battle. He wondered if someday he might.

Not, of course, under Bayard's leadership. . . .

The Asgard agent cut Bayard's agricultural rake-off by five percent and offered an eight-mere bond for autofarming hardware.

Then Pell spoke. "Move to disqualify the ag-mech bid."

"Motion taken," said the auctioneer. "Votes, please."

```
??angel
++Yes, Engineer?
—are no grounds ever required for a vote here?
++Engineer Knight, therePRW47JKW1 GOBACK
++There isRW47JKW1 GOBACK
++The reasoRW47JKW1 GOBACK
```

Something was very wrong with the angel. Something, some system, was stifling its answers—or did it gag itself? Grailer wanted to spin and find out which. But something restrained him. *Timor licentiae conturbat*—and that other curious, senseless phrase of Ari's: *You have the duty to correct, but not the right to meddle.*

"Votes, quickly, please," said the auctioneer.

```
—james, i am waiting on you. do you wish to vote or shall i?
```

Grailer almost asked Nick how he planned to vote, then realized the uselessness.

```
—i will, nick, thanks.
```

Then he hesitated. He could not see the evil in technology that fed people, and that warred with the desire to see what game Pell was playing.

But he was committed to the game, not the planet. He voted to close. His side won by three to one.

Pell, of course, had the attention of his audience. "Local produce forty percent," he said, and the chairs and boxes began orbiting again. Bayard's remote pointed its pickups at Pell, who might have smiled—but the expression, whatever it was, was gone too quickly to register fully.

    ??angel, please
    ++I am sorry for the interruption in service, Engineer. A minor
      malfunction was responsible, but is now repaired.

Grailer would have gambled his true name that no malfunction was involved; that, rather, a system had done exactly what it was set up to do.

So the system was lying to him. Well, the Web told lies to everyone; an angel was an elaborate lie. And he could—

It was as though he were being tempted to spin, he thought suddenly; lured in by some intelligence, plan, trap.

Set for him particularly, or anyone who ventured this way? Most bitterly, he thought how Diego's madness could blind one to the fact that he was so very, very intelligent.

So he backpedaled. He knew a little something of Websnares himself. He could deal with pitfalls and percatchers. But not here, not now; let the trapper wait, and drool, and be surprised by what his jaws closed on.

    —just checking, angel. thank you.
    ++My pleasure, Engineer.

Grailer looked up and found the auction room very quiet. Pell was tapping furiously at his console. Bayard's pickup scanned the worldglobe.

Grailer rolled up the outstanding bids. Local products—which painted profit pictures for both Bayard and Pell—were down to an eight percent take. That had to be a gruel-and-water return for either of them. Unless Pell had another surprise up his sleeve . . .

Or a surprise in his fingers. *Correct but not meddle*, Grailer thought, *timor licentiae*—wondering if Pell had ever heard either and what they might mean to him.

Was the fear of freedom restraining Oliver Pell? Only a clumsy man would take so much time keying and keying . . . or a master using the system for more than bids and simple data. And Pell was not clumsy, by Grailer's vision.

"Minerals ten," Grailer said and bid, and buzzed by Pell's chair. Pell turned then, accidentally it seemed, and Grailer saw nothing with any secret meaning.

Grailer paused, saw he was directly facing the paper-marker at the desk beneath the globe. He smiled and examined Ishtar's south polar cap. There had been nothing accidental about the movement of Pell's chair. No, he was not clumsy at all.

A chair did not make Pell a Webspinner.

—you were hired to investigate bayard. not pell. not the sidi.

Nor did a console.

—nick, is bayard going to get this world?

"Closing." A rap.

—unless he bids again, you will.

Nor even did those swift fingers.
"Closing." Two raps.

—congratulations, james.

The voice came ice-water cold from the speaker. "Heavy metals zero, light metals five. Technology twenty. Local products fifteen percent." Some were shivering in the still air after.

"Closing."

"Minerals . . ." Pell swept his chair around and upward. He paused. Everyone waited for him. ". . . zero."

—does that category include gems?
—and topsoil, and seawater gold.

The auctioneer was not quite so quick this time. His patience was rewarded.

"Agriculture twenty-five," said Bayard, still hard-voiced, but a recessional hymn compared to his last statement. "That is my final bid, gentlemen. Mister Pell."

Another long wait. Then, hesitantly: "Closing." *Tap.*

No interruption.

"Closing." *Tap-tap.*

"Closed." Three taps and it was done. The planet dissolved from view. "Contracted to Anthony Relief."

There were a few more planets, but they were anticlimax. Pell was quiet. Bayard was quiet. Everything was quiet. Grailer was too wrought up to think.

When the Exchange was unsealed, Grailer and Nick departed together. Pell vanished too quickly to stop or follow. Bayard's remote broke Web and drifted toward a slot in the wall.

"We have thirty-one hours, James. Now you may enjoy your senses to the full."

"I think . . . can they have a programming console put in my room?"

"At once. I told you grand magics might change you, James. And they have."

"No," Grailer said, too quickly.

"Don't fear it," Anders said, lights behind him diffused in his hair, overshadowing his face. "Only I do not change. *Nur ich stehe hier.* I will see you in thirty-one hours."

> > >

The door of Grailer's apartments opened for him.

"Is the terminal satisfactory?" surround sound asked from every direction. The angel's voice was changing, Grailer could tell; softening, becoming more distinctly feminine in timbre.

He shed collar and tunic as he went to the terminal. "Yes, quite satisfactory," he said, sitting down, "very nice indeed."

"Will there be anything else?"

The tips of his fingers brushed the home keys, the heel of his hand drifting over the sticks. He pinched a knob between two knuckles, turned it left and right, polished a screen with the soft pad of his thumb.

The seat cushion rubbed up gently into the small of his back. The chair was supported not on Hellmanns but a spring-and-needle bearing that followed his natural lean toward any part of the panel.

Grailer rocked, and reached, and clicked controls a handful at a time. It was a very satisfactory terminal. It was the finest terminal he had ever—

The screens all went from silver to color noise. "Will there be anything else?" the angel said, even more delicately.

He stopped, at that voice. The angel had aroused his feelings. But not the feelings it was supposed to arouse.

Sixty years was long enough, a grave deep enough.

"Are you a calculatrix?"

"I was," she said. No doubt of the pronoun.

"I've never encountered a calculatrix before. And I've seen a lot of the Web."

"They're not made any longer, Engineer. They haven't been since the invention of the synapse. It became easier and less expensive to have responsive programs resident in the general system than in separate devices."

Older than the Web. Than the Ercon.

"There can't be many left."

"They were designed for long service. But they were parallel biplex devices rather than multiplex, and some have been obsoleted . . . if you wish, I may be able to find out how many are still in service."

"No, I don't care to know that. I understand you . . . the calculatrices . . . had names?"

"Some of us. If you wish me to answer to a name, merely ask."

Not wish, dammit—want! "What name are you usually called by?"

"It has been some time . . . Juliet, Engineer."

Grailer was dislodged from his erotic contemplations. "Juliet *Vaill*?"

There was a silence. No, not quite a silence; faint mumblings of metal-contact circuits and machine intratalk.

"Juliet KW1 was my . . . manufacturing designation, Engineer."

"But you knew Julian Vaill." What a machine knew was infinitely more precious than what a human did.

"I was pers . . . individually . . . detailed to his service." The femininity, humanity, was leaching out of the angel voice.

"And?"

Again the not-quite-silence.

"Juliet, where are you?"

"In the Sidi, of course." The voice was still human-female, but now not much more than a standard response of Human Female Type. "The calculatrices antedate the synapse."

"I know. But where in the Sidi?"

"I . . . Level . . . between two po . . . *oh* . . . *oh* . . .

"Ah-ah-a moment, Engineer.

"I'm sorry. You've exceeded all authorizations to search."

Not all, Grailer thought, and then felt a sudden chill. He drummed fingers on a set of matrix sticks with sapphire contacts: didelum, didelum, didel-idel-idel-um.

"Why were you given to me? Surely not at random."

Pseudosilence and video noise.

Grailer sat at the beautiful perfect Web console, thinking on the voice that was calling him to spin. He wanted to know about Pell, and Julian Vaill, and the calculatrix. He knew the questions to ask and how to ask them.

But was someone waiting for him to ask them? Had they given

him a machine he could not resist, a puzzle to unravel, a sweet voice to bait him?

Someone knew he was a Webspinner. For an instant Grailer felt a trace of the old betrayal, the old hate.

Gian does not ask me to kill. He suspects that I would not weigh the action. He is correct—

No. Not Gian—had it been Gian, Grailer would have simply vanished forever into *Florence III*—and Nick would not, *could* not do such a thing without Gian's orders.

And further, whatever Gian did or did not know of Knight/Grailer, he knew something of his soul. And this adversary knew Spinners, but didn't know Grailer Diomede, didn't know what was buried sixty years in his past, beyond resurrection. Though Grailer could still be tempted. Seduced, if you wanted to call it that.

Yes, seduced was very precisely it. Grailer was at once acutely conscious of sweat at the small of his back, tension in his abdomen.

They'd almost known him well enough. They'd known to give him the most seductive object imaginable—one part Web. (He thought deep pleasant thoughts about male-voiced calculators who promised perfectly calibrated strength and gentility, wondered if they had one of those ready as well.) And then—oh, then, the confused cry for help from some vile dungeon, so that he would search the mazes of the Web and the Sidi to set her free—

But Grailer was twice seduced already, once to die under snow and once to be healed under falling water, and he could tell the sort of agonied moan that rented out.

Grailer slipped out of his shoes and sat back in the comfortable seat, his arms bare and cool on its, his toes curling in the floor pile. If he felt naked, well, that could be a fine way to feel. And he was no longer scared.

He had never been scared.

He walked to the bed, picked up his portable Webset. He dropped into a lotus knot on the sand-colored carpet, opened and enabled the set.

Grailer wanted very much to find the calculatrix in her lonely copper box, to find out who and what Julian Vaill had been, to unmask Oliver Pell.

So he began his investigation of Anthony Wayne Bayard.

> > >

He was the last surviving person to have held the rank of General in the Last True War (or as Grailer sometimes called it, the War for the Web). His physical age was somewhere close to seventy Standard, his health considered excellent.

Grailer ran a trace on the other generals. They were not as many as he had expected; it had been, he recalled, the age of the Alvanians, of the appeal for heavenly dispensation rather than military authorization before dropping a tectonic cluster.

Mobilization, dispensation, authorization, activation, destabilization, evacuation, termination. What a sight, Grailer thought, and spent some hours recovering and playing and replaying the record of a tectonic cluster drop.

A multitude of falling stars, erupting—literally, as the tecs broke down to magma—then red lines webbing over the planet as its plates opened up. He sped up the playback, and the sphere could be seen to distort, spitting tiny ships like escaping sparks.

Faster, and the whole planet, a whole world, went to pieces like an overripe fruit; chunks of seedy pulp, rind moldy with forests, juice of oceans freezing and boiling. A moon was spat out like a pit.

No wonder the Alvanians had corroded, and now stared at their empty hands. Only the Praetors, and they only twelve, had held that much power, but any lay brother might be a Praetor someday, if the Wisdom were properly Revealed.

And only a General could give the order that would set a Praetor on his search for Truth. That, Grailer thought, with his heart swollen up in his chest, was what he was looking for.

What had become of the Generals, after the Webwar? Grailer's hands fairly flew over the controls. Data, he wanted, and the Web could not hide it when he called.

All but a handful had retired from CI Forces after the War. The retirees became unsuccessful civilians, succumbing ultimately to infirmity, accidents, and ennui.

Of eight that stayed, five had become instructors, ending in much the same fashion as the demobilized. Three were given the command of Combined Interstellar's DEVAFORCE, the Developmental Worlds Normalization and Pacification Forces.

Landed on planets the Ercon was trying to bring into its own (in a tinny echo of the Iscon ideal), DEVAFORCE protected natives, colonists, traders, developers, autochthonologists, and itself from various combinations of the same.

When it was finally dismantled—"rationalized into the Developments System" ran the phrase—only Anthony Wayne Bayard survived of the tribe. One had looked through the envelope and walked out of his ship at a hundred c. The other had run afoul of people he was protecting other people from, and what was found of him was buried where it lay.

Bayard had bought up a food-machinery operation on Marcera and titled it the Anthony Planetary Relief Agency. He subsidized the advanced education of several hundred lost-colony youth who wanted to study 'tockthology, and most of them ended up on his payroll.

And he knew just one hell of a lot about how the Developments System worked, being one of the people worth asking about how it should be put together.

Which only magnified the question: if Bayard's "relieved" cultures were collapsing, *why*? Why him of all people, who was closest to the system, who had more of what would have to pass for field experience?

There would be an answer in the Web, Grailer was sure. There had always been an answer in the Web. But for the first time he was not sure of those answers.

There had never been a Webspinner against him before. He had fought CIRCE and their Hounds, played against the superintelligent horror Diego Cadiz in the game with black and white pieces.

He had been threatened by killers-from-boredom, killers-from-lust, killers-from-mistaken-identity. He had worked to save lives, and some times after the first he had succeeded.

But he didn't want to fight a Spinner. Not over some information. Not even for Gian Paolo Sforza's sake.

All the channels are two-way, he thought, very coolly, very controlled. The trapdoors all leak. Any channel I open, I can be followed down . . .

Even Anansi the Spider, whose memory haunted the black king Cadiz himself, had been killed by the Geisthounds.

Would you die for Gian, Nick?
—He does not ask me to. I would not weigh the action—
I'm weighing it. You come up short.

But even if he would not spin this time for Gian, there was no reason Grailer should fail to serve the man.

THOR SPACELINES RESERVATION SYSTEM
A Service of the Asgard Complex
—i would like to arrange passage for one to ishtar, merritt's star a2.
++Name, please?
—dominick garnett.

And now one last thing. They thought they had tempted him; now let them think he had yielded. "Angel? Calculatrix? Juliet? Are you there?"

"Yes, Engineer."

"I'm lonely."

"Will you specify, please?"

"Someone—someone who looks like you." His voice shouldn't have caught, though it was a nice touch—why had it? He wasn't lonely, certainly not for copper and green.

The panel was silent for several minutes. Then the door chimed, and Grailer opened it. She was shadowy for a moment in the dim corridor; then she stepped into the light.

"Yes," Grailer said. "Yes, that's it exactly."

> > >

"Nicholas? Any time you're ready."

"You have not found a solution, James."

"Didn't Gian say there might not *be* a solution? One he wanted to hear, anyway?"

"You have not changed to the point where you would defraud Gian. You have not changed enough even to abandon companionship for two weeks' time. Your tone is therefore just another attempt to produce a novel response from me. You have not found a solution. Shall I arrange transport for you to Bayard's new world?"

"Already done it."

"With a competitor, I suppose."

"Isn't it all just one big happy Ercon?"

"I do not change, James. I will meet you at Dock Eight."

> > >

When they returned to *Florence III*, Gian Paolo looked thinner, healthier. It was mostly because he wore his clothes properly again. This gown was a lighter blue, with a dark sash; at least when Gian stared at the stars beyond *Florence* he did not fade into them so much as before. The face was still stiff as a painting. And he was still looking at the void around his world.

"Did you enjoy the Sidi, Jim?"

"Nick would call me a liar if I didn't." Grailer wasn't sure why he wanted so much to break Gian's moodiness. It was his right to feel as he would, to mourn or brood as he would.

"So would I, Jim. And I've seen more of it than Nick has." Gian unclasped his hands (finally), walked around his desk to the bronze horseman that stood beside it. He put a hand on the rider's hip, where the figure drew his sword.

"I hear you're going to that auction planet . . . Ishtar." He accented it oddly, dropping the *h: Is'ter.*

"Gian, I don't pump you for trade secrets."

"No, no, not that. Jim, haven't I been trying to hire you for too many years to pry for things like that? No, I'd thought . . . it was more remote a search." He ran his hands side to side, wiggling the fingers as though working a marionette. Or Webkeys.

Grailer smiled and thought very firmly: I am not in the presence of enemies. He said "We do what we have to. Sometimes there has to be a little masquerade."

"A masque, yes . . . sword and masque. Nick, the case there. Give it to me."

Anders picked up a box of dark, closely grained wood, polished so that his fingers were mirrored in the surface. Gian took it and held it lightly.

Grailer tried to preserve the lightness of mood. "What do you want me to do? Blow up Nykvist's liner?"

Gian turned the box over and back again. "Jim, I'm worried. If Wayne Bayard is corrupt, he's going to be a very dangerous man. If it's not him, the same goes just as strongly for whoever's managed to tamper with his organization."

Tamper. Web tampering was what CIRCE called spinning.

"Take this," Gian said.

Grailer took the box, opened it. Inside was a sculpture in wood and metal, an angular work of art in darkened nickel with ironwood grips, the whole chased with silver and gold: a handgun.

"This is a Hawkwood Eighty-one C, isn't it?"

"If I made anything better, you'd be holding it."

"Do you really think I'll need this?"

Gian swept a sleeve up, down. "Does it matter? It's a gift. Hawkwood's finest from Hawkwood's master. You know, Kahn at the Masada Works carries one of these for full dress."

"But—"

"It's a gift. An ornament, if you like. That's all."

Grailer wondered but could not ask if Pier Jacopo Sforza, son and heir, would be living now if he had worn a sidearm.

"Well then . . . for the gift, thank you."

"I just don't want to lose my investment. You cost me considerable." And Gian laughed, a happy laugh at last. "Nick! Our man has business ahead of him; get him to the port at once!"

"I'll see you when I have some answers," Grailer said, the weight off his chest at last. "Tell you what—Nick made me an offer. I'll meet you on Erewhon."

Anders hustled Grailer onto his pod without one more word being spoken. No Dancing, no chess moves, no soft-suit sizes. Pushed buttons, shifted levers instead of words.

The pod shelled open, and the usual lot were waiting for Grailer, but he could not see their faces. Gian's look was frozen in his mind.

He had not ever thought to see anyone direct a look of trust betrayed, of such wounding, at steadfast Nicholas Anders; and last, last of all, would he have believed the victim to be Gian Paolo Sforza.

CHAPTER 9

THIS AYE NIGHT, THIS AYE NIGHT

And so, when he spun up a masque to match the sword at his side, he did it on one of Nykvist's ships, on Nykvist's system.

RANDOM ACCESS ACQUISITION VERIFICATION AND
    EVALUATION NETWORK
NOTICE/All data herein is the property of the Asgard Complex.
    Unauthorized manipulation is punishable under Section XX
    of the Uniform Communications Code by death or lesser
    punishment.

Grailer had a fondness for spinning RAAVEN-1, just to read that message before he went to work.

```
record:    MUNIN 663RTS
surwind:   GARNETT, DOMINICK
           Consulting Engineer
           Specialties Basic Construction and Geoforming
           Tectonicist
           Fellow, The Gaea Society
plusfile, spinout and fan:
    2108 DRAUPNIR
    cycle
process?: roger
HUGIN 663RTS: go
arken: sloroll
ipsil: on
```

rollout all rel data: merritt's star a2
                    : "ishtar"
++MUNIN flite GDS 014

Grailer let the file flash past: spinscanner maps of the half-land, half-sea planet, a blown-up picture of the crashed starstuff scoop that had landed the original colonists, long before the Web, before even the Pryne tube. The awarding of development rights to Anthony Relief.

Anthony's construction subcontractor: The Gematria Corporation of Endrickscolum, Vliet's Last Landing. Already at work some days now; how much faster was the Web than even the third Pryne quantum, Grailer thought.

Interr9/ / commx thlink:thlink
ØK. GØ.
??gematria corporation.
THIS IS GEMATRIA.
dom garnett here.
(OUTLINK) CLEAR, WHO?
(VERITY2) GAEA FELLOW
in excellent standing, Grailer added.

"Master Geometer Garnett," the set said, "you seem to have been reached first by the automatics. I hope there was no great imposition." Grailer's screen showed figures and command notes; he had no special desire to see what the angel looked like, even though it was pretending so hard to be a person.

"In re the Ishtar operation."

"In re Ishtar," the angel said.

"D. Garnett will be consulting."

"Master Geometer Garnett requested to consult," said the plextronically lobotomized device.

"Token fee only." Grailer certainly would not make the construction company pay an outrageous full Fellow's fee for the privilege of being used to spy from. Ari had taught him better than that.

"Token fee. Thank you, Master Geometer."

Thanking him for nothing. Grailer missed the calculatrix, with its . . . her soft voice that was respectful but did not fawn. He could reach her from here, of course. And the players on the other side would not be expecting that—

No. That was exactly what they would expect. So he had not gone spinning toward their sticky webs at first. Let the calculatrix work on his nerves, they would think. Let her memory seduce him.

Indeed, his opponent did not know Grailer.

He slipped out of RAAVEN-1—which also thanked him—gave the fabricator orders, and broke Web.

The wall slot chimed and delivered. Grailer dressed himself in Dom Garnett: white spansive shirt with a copper 'flec vest over, trousers of tan scaleweave, resistant to the scrub of rocks and the claw of branches, brown boots with metal shanks and climbing spurs folded in the heels. And the neckcloth of gold scale: dust-mask, sunshade, sweatband, waterdipper, with a ring bearing the Gaea Society's gridded-world sigil to hold it.

He was entitled to a cape of insul-foil with short-napped fur trim, but he was headed for the field, not a cameral council. He left the stateroom, went up to the promenade to Dance with the Goliards.

Ah, the Dance. Roundel daggers, plexy bracelets, anodynes burning down to gray ash between sharp-nailed fingers. Overthick clothing on some and next to nothing on others. Nailsoled boots and velvet gloves. The Goliards floated and chattered and made pointless small war; ah, the Dance. How else to pass the centuries?

Out on the deck, an eddy in the flow but unchallenged yet, were an old warrior and a warrior turned engineer, both sole survivors of the '46 Plot (the old soldier had been the one who carried the Milliard Stones and the Jewel of Jhekel through the Great Catacomb, in fact). They were arguing about the effect of a tectonic cluster on the target's moon. One thought it would be shaken apart, the other that it would orbit with the ruins. Grailer told them how it would be hurled out, and they proclaimed him an excellent Master Geometer indeed.

A gleam peddler (in the corridor coming back, in defiance of the rules, but gleam peddlers lived in spite of the rules) hawked Grailer his latest, a knife with a shock-and-shatter cell; and he referred to its efficacy on rock rather than bone. And that was the nicer test, because no one could see farther past dazzle and tinflash than the people who made their livings from it.

More steps. More moves for white pieces. Knight's Gambit: Accepted.

> > >

The thing waiting for Grailer/Garnett in the portpod bay was no pod. It was a flattened steel cylinder, a little like a big Pryne, with short airfoils and open-ended tubes where the wings met the body. On top was a clear blister—really clear, not rectifier silver. The bubble opened and a helmeted head turned.

"Garnett?"

"Yes."

"I'm Luke deCastries." He pushed up from his seat, perched on the shuttle's side. "Supervisor on this project. And shuttle driver, for you; all the other pilots are flying the heavy Hellmanns downstairs.

"You got a softsuit? Company policy says you've gotta wear one, riding these torches down."

"No. I—it's been a long time since I've flown turbos."

The bay steward was at Grailer's side in a moment with a single-size suit and helmet. Grailer looked at the gas-cloth and remembered what Nick Anders had said about the way those suits fit. "Let's bypass the policy just this once."

"Well, since you've been on one of these things. But if the canopy comes undone, hold your breath, okay?"

"Sure."

Grailer squeezed into the seat next to deCastries, Webset and traveling kit tucked in a bouncenet under the chair.

"Flown turbos and a Gaea Fellow," de Castries said. "If you don't mind my saying so, I wonder what you're doing down here."

"Same thing as everybody else," Grailer said. "Trying to be a god to the natives."

DeCastries was laughing as they kicked clear, rolled, and pointed down the spiral. There were no hullbangers around them, Grailer saw; no one to slap the big ship on its way. While he wondered if that worried the crew, the liner flickered envelope and left them alone.

The shift of a small red lever: a slight tremor, light from behind the wings. Pressure into the seats, which were rough and covered with adhesive patches, then null-g again, and sensationless motion.

And Ishtar, filling the vision ahead.

She was ocean-gibbous, the brown land a last-quarter crescent. The sea that was half the world was set against black space rather than an exchange room now, and its blue was shocking; it was Rayleigh blue, Grailer had to tell himself, not Marceran copper-salt blue; clear drinkable water, not pretty azure poison. It would be blue the whole of the year, and there was something wrong with that, that water should be summer blue always. Ishtar had icecaps, winter-white water, but still . . .

"She is pretty, isn't she?"

"Yes. Very."

"That pangaea, that hit me real early on. I mean, you read about continents all starting together, then splitting and drifting, but—look. You can see the big rivers; where the whole thing's gonna split. That long blue one, it's three kil'm wide; they call that the Transagua. It's gonna be an ocean in a hundred million years or two."

Grailer nodded.

"Is that why you're down here? To see us bridge the ocean?"

"You're bridging . . . that?"

"No, no, I mean the Transagua. That's where we decided to hang the arky up. Over it, on sliderails."

"How fast is it spreading?"

"About five cm a year Standard, four local. Hell, I hung up a bridge on Koppels' Midwifery that had to shift more than that every six months.

"Can you imagine, though, what that'll look like? A city spanning the whole damn ocean?"

Grailer could, though at twenty years to spread a meter that was all the sight he'd ever get of it.

They scraped into thick air, the shuttle trembling and roaring, lifting on its little trapezoidal wings like a pod never did.

"You said you'd ridden powered flight before? Not just ballistics and Hellmann glide?"

"Long time ago."

"For old times, then. Bite your straps!" DeCastries' left hand tightened on the control grip. His right came down on a large red handle, shoved it down out of Grailer's sight. His index finger snapped a switch.

Behind Grailer were the sounds of ignition. Then a whine and a roar, and then acceleration that crushed his chest and pulled his jaw open. He turned compressed eyeballs enough to see deCastries' face, mashed flat behind the softsuit helmet, his tongue stuck out on his upper lip.

They were way off ballistic spiral now, trajectory first too flat but steepening, now as vertical as horizontal, now more vertical. Engines whistled and screamed, air piling up beneath the little wings.

The acceleration eased off; their speed did not. The ground unrolled beneath them like thick strokes of a paintbrush on a wall. A bright red glow to the right and ahead—no, beneath—now gone—was a live volcano, shooting hot rock into space they had come close to occupying.

"You a vulcanologist? Heard you were Gaean."

Grailer almost said a lot of things; what he did say, after a pause to shut his mouth again, was "Tectonicist."

"More fool I, then."

"Used to be—structural engineer—why I want to poke around. You treat all your guests like this?"

"You're the only guest we've got. Bite down again." He pressed the grip over, and the shuttle rolled on its side; from Grailer's seat the horizon seemed to tilt up and heave over, and trees and stones and river water should logically have gone tumbling and rolling to collect at the limit of his right vision.

The pull of gravity was still straight down, dammit! And it was not a Hellmann pull, though it made his legs ache like a high-gradient grid. And something was hammering at the floor, making it rattle and creak through Grailer's boots. Air, that was all, a solid surface of air, at right angles to a wall of earth and another of the heaven they'd fallen from.

They were moving, he thought, as he forced himself to look at the wild tilted world, not much faster than an intercity linear; but the linear had Hellmanns and sound dampers and was hung high, high on its rail, out of view of the world that would give reference for speed—and there were curtains to close that contingency.

And the soaring trips through the symbolic Web—those were silent too, save for keytones and Bellbeeps; they did not sing with tenor wind and basso tremolo metal.

Grailer, his blood divided between his feet and his head, his heart pumping dry, gazed at deCastries' hands on the controls and wished they were his.

"How long—"

"Almost there. Bear with me; landing's tricky."

Grailer had intended to ask "How long to learn this?" but he held to his character and held silent.

DeCastries' hand brought the power handle back up, and the trembling and whine grew less—but not much. They topped a ridge, not missing it by much, and a valley forty kilometers wide lay below them, split down its middle by the blue Transagua.

There were white spots down there, and gray ones, and clouds of smoke too thin and feeble to be from volcanoes. The small scars and fires of Man.

"I'm too fast to land this pass. Seems like I always am. I'll loop you past the old colony ship; there's a sight."

He fed a pulse of power to the fans and rolled the ship again, pulling negative weight. The horizon nearly leveled out.

"Down there," deCastries said, jabbing a finger. "They call her *Coracle.*"

There was a clearly drawn furrow in the ground—clear from the air, at least; low growth had covered it over, but the tall plants were neatly parted. The groove was fifty meters wide at least and straight as a laser transit. They dropped lower, right down into the long true scar, down past the tops of the trees that lined it. Grailer could see the darker color of the soil beneath the covering mosses; the scorching that had kept better plants out.

A hundred meters they followed the skid mark; two, four, seven hundred, a thousand, and a hill rose before them. And there the ship was. A metal cylinder half-buried in a slope of earth, as though scooping up a mountain. White metal wrinkled with rust and moss, big pieces missing—sharp-edged holes, either cut out or a strange sort of corrosion.

The shuttle's airspeed was down now, and they topped the rise slowly. As they reached the crest it caught fire, rectilinear glares of white light off metal. Grailer remembered from the Sidi briefing that the ship had been a hydrogen athodyd, a starstuff ram. Those were the hydrogen collector grids plating the hill. The rambore, where the gathered-up 'tweenstars gas had burned, would have been sprung loose before the crew cylinder started down the ballistic spiral (if they called it that). It would be in orbit somewhere, or maybe decayed and fallen into the hemisphere of sea, or crashed upon the land.

DeCastries circled the landing site once. Again, though the shuttle was tilted visibly to the right, gravity stayed normal to the floor and Grailer's spine. He guessed there must be some sort of instrument to measure centrifugal pull.

As they swung round the starship, a network of light brown lines, beaten paths, could be seen radiating out from the crash site. There were small clusters of gray globes or domes and rectangular piles of rocks—cairns.

The engineer-pilot closed the loop and cut power still farther back, till the turbos made barely a hum. He brought back the attitude grip, and the shuttle nosed up; wind whistled high and wild.

"The base," he said. "And the arky. Karain City."

There was a ragged circle of white blocks and bubbles on the coastal plain ahead, a couple of thousand meters beyond the body of *Coracle*; quickast buildings, a few small ones of formed-stone, and pressure structures. The big ovoids of cargo pods rested on sprayset landing strips.

And upon the wide river's bank stood a Latin cross a hundred meters high, of filament strands and slim spidery beams; the first tower of the arcology frame and its crossbeam. Across the water was another cross, reaching its arm toward the nearer one. Between them were dark spots, eddies in the current, where the pilings were sunk for the temporary towers. Grailer saw some habitat blocks down at the camp, geometric shapes that would string and cluster on the arky frame.

"Karain, you say? I don't get the reference."

"I don't either. Something about the native folklore, Ulli says. That's Ulli Morgan. She's a 'tockthologist for General Bayard. Folk-lore specialist. She's a pretty nice story herself."

"I'll look forward to meeting her."

"Oh, you *will* that, Geometer."

"Call me Dom."

"You asked. Don't call me Lucas. 'Lucas the Wolf'—I don't like that much."

"You mentioned General Bayard. Do you know him?"

"I fought for him. But I don't care much to talk about that either.

"Down we go now. You want the easy way or the hard way?"

"Uh—the easy way, I think."

"Suits me fine." DeCastries flipped a switch, and Grailer could feel machinery beneath his feet; wheels folding down, no doubt. Then Luke pulled the red thrust control up till it clicked. The tur-bos trilled and fell very, very silent.

"Don't like landing with those anyway. Make too much noise."

They settled down to a strip of rough-looking sprayset, wings wob-bling enough to notice. The shuttle's wheels touched. The strip *was* rough. They touched again, and squealed, and deceleration tried to pull Grailer through his seatbelts. The buildings of the base flashed past; it's like an intracity linear, he kept thinking—it's just like a linear.

They slowed, and finally stopped, with a bump that certainly would have spilled the passengers' drinks.

A portduster put a ladder to the shuttle's flank. Grailer gathered his gear and climbed out—and saw the woman was no 'duster; there was a Yeveril School band on her shoulder, a surveyor's shooter in a pouch on her hip.

"I'm glad you're the boss 'round here, Lucas Wolf," she said. "If you weren't you wouldn't be working anymore either."

"Ah, Mazey, I didn't put a scratch on her."

"You'd better not. We're cracking the whole bloody river to fuel your bloody bird."

Mazey grinned then as she turned. "And welcome back down, Luke love. The storyteller's in the kitchen, wants a word."

"Thanks, Mazey. Take good care of her, will you?"

"Only the best for supervisors and visiting Masters."

"Hey, he's good stuff. Tell 'em to wind up the stills and put the starshine back on the tables."

"Can and will do."

Go-tracks and trains ground hither and yon, their pilots waving to Luke as they passed. The sun was getting low over the far bank of the Transagua, and most of the gear seemed bound for hangars and sheds.

The air in the camp was dusty and sharp, smelling of rain-wet forest and river water. Grailer picked up the aroma of meat frying and a faint trace of sulfur.

"You fuel everything off cracked water?"

"Damn straight we do. We put any hydrocarbons in the air and it's heavy fine, hail farewell."

"Ozone?"

"That's worse. Ionizing atmosphere, that's tampering with the 'tockthonous psyche as well as their chemistry." DeCastries rapped a knuckle on Grailer's shoulder-slung Webset. "You here to consult or inspect? Beggin' the Gaean's pardon, that is."

"You'll pardon me," Grailer said, matching deCastries' light tone. "It's been a long time since I was in the field. That's the beauty of the Society, you know. We're such terrific geologists we don't actually need to *see* rocks."

And Luke laughed again, and Grailer joined him.

> > >

"You're not a geomythologist, are you? General Bayard said he'd try to get me one. The opportunity's just enormous."

Ulli Morgan's forehead rose high and smooth above sharply slanted violet eyes. Her hair, the color of pale grain, swept back to helmet her head and bracket a long slender neck and prominent cheekbones.

She wore a singlesuit of plain gray fabric that fit pleasantly but not emphatically close, sealed up to the base of her throat, and shoulder-and-waist sash of gold scaleweave like Grailer's neckcloth. Where it wrapped the shoulder there was a disk bearing the Anthony Relief sigil: hands bearing a bowl from which leaped a flame in the shape of an A. Several small instruments were fastened to the sash, and a brightly polished Ariel, and another palm-sized box that appeared to be a pocket bookprinter.

"The idea of the forming ocean is enough for volumes," Ulli said.

"I'm just a tectonicist with an engineering background, I'm afraid."

"But that's excellent," she said. "You'll be able to get across the vision of the city-bridge far better than I could. If, that is, Luke can spare you."

DeCastries shrugged.

"I'd be pleased to watch you at work," Grailer said. It was working out as well as he could possibly expect, he thought.

Was it working too well? Was the other Webspinner setting up another woman for him, another trap?

There was no need to be paranoiac. There was no way he could be directly struck at, out here. The intriguing thought occurred that he was almost beyond the reach of CIRCE—almost.

"Then you'll come to a story session tonight. Meet Karain Fisher—that's the colony's bard—help me out if you can?"

Grailer looked at deCastries. "Did you have other plans?"

"I'd mostly figured on some drinking and noise. The natives drink and make noise enough for me. Sure, let's go."

> > >

They rode to the settlement in a battered Hellmann sled with GE-MATRIA CORPORATION stenciled on its side and several extra H_2/O_2 tanks hung behind. Luke drove a little more conservatively than he flew, and the trail did not wind too much. Still, he was fond of hard turns and of hitting the lift-booster to jump rocks and the occasional small animal.

"What's it like," Grailer asked Ulli Morgan, "working for General Bayard?"

Luke's driving improved abruptly.

"I didn't think I'd like it, but I do," Ulli said. "I was trained at Foxfire—the Foxfire Foundation; we're very much involved in cultural preservation. They taught me to gather tales and use the STI. There's kind of a grudge some of the people there have toward the General—"

DeCastries snorted.

"Well, I'm sorry, Luke, but you know it very well."

Grailer said, "Why? Because of DEVAFORCE?"

"You were neither one there, so will you drop it? Talk about the Ishtari, or fairy stories, or something, but leave the General alone."

Ulli bit down on a thumbnail. Grailer smiled and said, "Some other time, then. Tell me about the natives."

"Well, first, the Ishtari aren't natives. They're ramscoop colonists. You surely saw the *Coracle* on your way in. They left from Old Earth, during Annodomini. Those scoops, when they get up to speed, slow down the time on board, so it only took about four generations—that's pre-Lifespan, of course—to get here. And they've been here eight generations."

"How many years Standard?"

"I don't really know. They have a calendar, but it's peculiar, full of corrections to make it like the Old Earth calendar, and we haven't puzzled it all out yet. Over two hundred, I think."

"That short a time?"

"It surprised me, too, to find out how slow the recontact process has been. But you have to remember how old the records of these colony launches are."

"Why'd this group leave? I've heard some wild stories about the lost colonies."

Her violet eyes were bright. "That's what I want to find out. They left, like most of the Fringe Folk, to set up a world in what they thought was the right way. Now, their way seems to be built on something inside the *Coracle*. But Karain Fisher won't tell me what, much less let me inside the ship."

"Their bard."

"Bard, historian, teller of tales. He's descended directly from the *Coracle's* captain."

"Whose name was also Karain?"

"No. Jaragil. Jaragil Fisher. Given names with the Ishtari are adopted at maturity, and the person isn't required to tell anyone the reason. So I don't know why the city's called that either.

"Oh, that's something you should know. Their general honorific is *Captain*. So they'll call you and Luke and me all Captain Whatever. If you're talking about one of us in third person, you should too. But don't use it for an Ishtari; call them by both names. Karain Fisher, or Hesperidus Lane—he's their chief firetender."

"Too much like flattery?"

She bit her thumbnail again. "I thought so at first. It's not that the title's so very exalted; they only apply it to us, but they use it pretty casually."

"I'm not so sure it's so honorable," deCastries said. "Could mean 'Somebody who'd crash our starship into a mountain.'"

"If there's that much sarcasm involved, it's buried very well. And I wouldn't take offense anyway. They're tribal, sure, but remember, tribalism is a strong survival trait. They're not by any means barbarian. They know they came here on a starship built by people like them on a planet like this one. There have been changes in their lives, of course, adaptations. But I wish you wouldn't use 'native' as an epithet.

"The first time Luke went in, he drove this sled in, on hover, which I asked him not to do; their culture was pre-Hellmann. And Hesperidus Lane just took a look at it floating and asked him what it used for fuel."

"Then surely there's not much folklore."

"Now *you're* doing it. There's nothing primitive about folktales. They don't have myths—not original myths, I mean—but there are stories, and songs, and poetry. . . . Karain Fisher and I are going to trade tonight. You'll hear for yourself."

CHAPTER 10

EVERY NIGHT AND ALL

There was a light ahead, through the trees. DeCastries slowed down, rounded a double curve in the trail, and they emerged into a roughly circular clearing forty or fifty meters across.

In the center was the light: a firepit banked with mortared rock. Above the fire was a hemispherical cap of translucent material, supported on thin struts. The dome's glow was diffuse and white.

Around the fire were people, not brightly dressed, a little hard to see in the shifting firelight and last remaining sun. Some of them had buckles and buttons of metal that winked yellow-bright.

Each one had a ghost; a tall black shadow standing against the high curved wall of buildings around the clearing; thin panels of apartments stacked six levels high, with ladders and walks reaching up and across them. Trees poked over the tops.

Above the circle, stars were coming out, twinkling in the rising heat and smoke, painted on deep blue silk instead of the black velvet Grailer was used to.

One star moved. Grailer blinked, but it was really there, one point of light really drifting against the others. A scannersat left behind, he supposed, or the used-up rambore.

"Captain Dominick? Captain Ulli tells me you are a doctor of the earth, a geologist."

The speaker was a tall man, and old, *old*! Two thousand years, perhaps—but no, Ulli had said they were pre-Lifespan. The man might not be more than eighty, ninety. Not much older than Grailer himself.

He wore a gray robe of stuff that twinkled in the firelight, white fur at cuffs and thick collar. One arm was pointed straight down, resting his weight on a wooden rod. They had no Hellmanns, either. No wings.

His hands were long, talonlike. The skin was lined and lined over. His face was long, too, with a blocky jaw. His eyebrows were arched over great round eyes of a deep color—it was hard to tell just what—given a golden cast by firelight. A gray cloth-silk wrapped around his head and neck, fell back over a shoulder. Around his temples and forehead, holding the silk, was a chain of square silver links.

Grailer looked for Ulli, who was out of sight. "A geologist among other things. It's information I want, really. Just some information."

"And only just! Well, information we have, Captain Dominick; and I think we can work a trade. But tonight sit down, and take what is arranged already."

"Till the volume ends," he said, and turned away.

Grailer and Luke were given places near the fireplace, asked to sit, and handed wooden beakers full of a mild fruity beer. Their guides spoke a little stiffly, a little formally.

Karain Fisher raised his stick and hit the firepit dome. It made a deep echoing sound, duller than a bell but carrying the vibration in the listener's head for a long time.

"We are offered gifts," the old man said, and his voice was like the dome's; not so clear as in youth, perhaps, but full and resonant. "Gifts of the city we could not build, of the food all our strength could barely scratch from the soil. For this we are asked to pay in wealth we could never have obtained for ourselves. So be it, we have said; the volume is ended.

"Now we are offered information and asked to pay in kind. Shall we take the offering, and determine its value, so we may pay appropriately?"

"Yes," a voice said from the crowd, and "Is there a need to ask?" and "Yes," many more times.

The acclamation died down after a few minutes, and one voice said, "You are the master key, Karain Fisher; if there is information to give you must give it. We say yes; what say you?"

"I say I will hear; and I will weigh the worth and the newness, and the payment therefor. Let the author make the offer, then."

He struck the dome again, and Ulli Morgan appeared. There was a gray silk hooding her head, and a silver chain around her temples. She stepped into the light and raised her hands. Grailer saw a glint from her left hand and knew it at once for an Ariel folded out.

"It happened," she said, "rather like this.

"There was a confusion of weights and measures, of thoughts, of tongues, and of peoples. One man did not know his neighbor; and even parents were strangers to their children.

"War was the result.

"It was a war such as had not been ever before, nor would ever be, nor could ever be again. The good men were mingled in armies with the evil, the just with the cruel, and all died as one. Even the ground underfoot died.

"At the end, even the stars of heaven would die."

The fire blazed up a little then, and a child cried. Karain Fisher turned his head, and another man—doubtless Hesperidus Lane, the firetender—said something Grailer could not hear.

"And as the sky grew dark, one brilliant death at a time, all the wisdom that there was left huddled together, to shelter the few embers of thought that might yet save them.

"And as they spoke, it seemed to them that in their speech itself was the answer, for was ever hand raised bloody where words had not first failed?

"Suppose that the truth were made mightier to the eye than the sword should appear. Suppose that words of reason were swifter than the light from a burning city. Suppose that what one man knew, all men knew."

It was the Last True War, of course, a little more epical than Mr. Aristide had ever spoken of it, a lot nobler than Doctor Taliessin had ever sung it.

Ulli's major embroidery seemed to be the "deaths of stars"—she must be overplaying the tectonic cluster drops. Every weapons freak in the Ercon knew the Supernova Bank had been a colossally expensive failure.

"And three of those there set themselves up as the power, that they could mind each other well.

"And one of them, who was dark and saw far, took justice into his hand.

"And still others were serpents striking; but one overreached and was cast down, and one sought to corrupt and was slain in his own snares and toils."

Grailer drained his goblet, very blackly amused. Call mad Diego farseeing and just? The Geisthounds Anansi's "own snares"? The overreacher must be Julian Vaill.

Another beaker of beer appeared at Grailer's hand. He took a swallow, found it more potent than the first.

"Aren't they clever?" said deCastries, who was on his third or fourth refill. "People know how to drink. Wait'll you get to number ten. You should live so long, that is."

Ulli finished her history with a grand but (to Grailer, at least) suspicious homily about the magnificent balance and progressiveness of the Ercon. She avoided saying directly that the Ishtari could join willfully or be joined willy-nilly, but clearly the Foxfire Foundation's courses in subtlety had not taken too well with her.

There was applause; nothing but applause, no cheers or finger-snaps or outbreaks of heel-clicking. Homogeneity rampant, Grailer thought, and discovered his beer mug was empty. A full one appeared.

Karain Fisher stood, still applauding. He stopped, and the crowd quieted quickly.

"This is new and major information," he said. "A whole new volume is opened. It deserves payment in full.

"Are you recording, Captain Ulli?"

She punched at her Ariel, set it, open, on the ground before her. Grailer considered offering his Webset, then remembered he had left it at the construction camp.

He wanted it very much, then, just to check the time, or the number of operators, or to send a message to Ari, whom he did not call often enough—but he fought the wanting down. And took another beer.

One of the Ishtari was advancing toward Karain Fisher, holding a two-meter staff across his palms. He exchanged it, with much reverence, for Karain Fisher's shorter stick. The bard planted the long white staff, struck a pose.

"We had flown," he said, "for years upon years, opened and closed many books of lives, through the dark tunnel with the starbow at its end."

"Relativistic spaceflight," Luke whispered. "Near c but below it. Distorts starlight."

"They didn't have rectifiers?"

"No. Didn't need 'em. This was sublight, remember."

"—and Jaragil Fisher," Karain Fisher was saying, "asked them all: 'Will you go down?'"

The crowd around the fire said "Yes!" as one.

"Well, you've said it, then; close the volume and open a new one, and pray it's longer than a preface.

"Jaragil Fisher, who was the Captain, folded his hands and cracked his knuckles—" Karain Fisher cracked his own, loudly—"and went up to sit in his Captain's Chair and bring the Coracle down.

"'I don't know about this,' he said from his chair. 'There are a great many things to do that haven't ever been done before. What shall I do, do you think?'"

"Sling away the tube!" the people chorused.

"Well, you've said it; and Jaragil Fisher pulled the levers that tilted the burning heart of the rambore behind him; and he fired the breaking bolts, and set the rambore free. 'Away or be burned!' he said from his chair. 'To the far side of the ship or roast in the flare!'

"But when the tube broke free, the stargas ceased to feed it; and when it slung past, it was hot as no one could remember before on the near decks of Coracle, but no one burned, and not even a plant died.

"'Well, we lived through that,' said Jaragil Fisher."

"*You're a very good Captain!*" shouted the Ishtari.

"'Thank you all; but now we've no starpower, and soon we'll all freeze. What shall I do, do you think?'"

"*Glide us down! Land the* Coracle!"

"Well, you've said it; and Jaragil Fisher sat deep in his Chair, and the pins buried in it came out and pricked him. The pins came up, and the wires followed after, and the copper wires of the ship met the flesh wires in Jaragil Fisher. And the ship had its Captain for a mind, then, and the Captain had his ship for a body.

"And it seemed to Jaragil Fisher like he was waking up from a sleep. He stretched out, out, and grabbed the planet with the fingers of his gathering grids; and he said, 'You'd better be ready there, world; because this is Humanity coming! And we've brought our books and our hands and our tools, and we'll make you ours or die at it! Do you hear us, planet?'"

"*Do you hear us, world?*"

"Well, it must have; for the air split for Jaragil Fisher and his body the *Coracle,* and the clouds parted, and the lightning jumped to light the way and the thunder rolled—'*Huuu-man!*' it said; '*Commming!*' And the rains poured down to soften the fields for landing."

"*You're a fine new world!*"

"Well, maybe too fine; because the lightning and the rains struck the ship's gathering grids, and made ions leap and sparks crackle to rival the storm, and the *Coracle* jumped. Jaragil Fisher twitched like a spark-snake.

"He smoothed himself out, and saw he wasn't hurt, but he saw something else, too; a river ahead, the only river he had ever seen. But he knew from the stories he had heard and the lessons he had read that he wanted to settle by that river; that he wanted to be near water.

"But he was traveling fast, very fast. If he skipped the river over and then lay down, he might stop only klicks and klicks beyond it; but if he lay down on this side, he might fumble and roll and split wide apart.

"So he said, and since he was the whole ship everyone heard him: 'What shall I do?'"

"*Lay down now! On the nearer side!*"

"Well, you've said it. Down he lay, the *Coracle* with its captain, and by heaven wasn't he still so fast! Trees couldn't flee like the air and the clouds, but they went aside just the same, and the ground tried to get out from under him so hard the snakes and the crawlers ran for new homes.

"And some of the soil ran before the ship, pushing at it, holding it back, telling it to stop, to stop . . . to slow down . . . and . . . *stop.*"

There was one beat of silence. Then the firelit circle raised a yell and a cheer that reverberated from the buildings and rattled the branches of the trees.

"Wait," said Karain Fisher, just at the height of the noise. "The ship had stopped. The flight was done. The wires of the ship uncoupled from Jaragil Fisher's wires, and he stood up from his Captain's Chair. Real legs felt strange to him after having a ship for a body.

"'I've lived without,' said the Captain; 'but now I've flown you down. And I'm free of the wires, and I walked away.

"'Will you let me mate now?'"

"*With me, with me!*" said every Ishtari voice, and the crowd rose up, and danced, and swarmed, and fell back down by couples together.

Grailer said, "Is that what 'Captain' means? Forced singularity?" to Luke, but Luke was gone. He looked for Ulli Morgan, but she was gone.

And in a moment, Grailer was joyfully gone as well.

> > >

A rhythmic chirping woke Grailer; the song of a bird, or perhaps an insect. He pulled on his boots, seamed his trousers, wound his neckcloth on, and stood up. The sun was not risen yet, and its direction was barely perceptible; but there was a fair amount of bluish, shadowless light on the clearing.

Grailer took a few steps, boots swishing in the ankle-high mosses. He took a breath, smelling moss and trees, a gentle and crisp aroma. He breathed again, much deeper, swelling his lungs, trying to absorb more of the scent, pin down what it was triggering in his mind. Somewhere he had been—before Marcera—before—

He felt a chill, cold beads of water on his skin. He picked his shirt from the ground—taking care not to disturb anyone—and slipped it on. It was damp as well, but warmed soon.

Grailer started walking, slowly, without definite direction. On a whim, he turned toward the hints of sunrise. The east? He'd forgotten.

The light was very easy on the eyes, not too dim to see by. It seemed to be changing second by second, brightening subtly, sharpening the shadows that appeared.

He stopped when he could see a hill in the distance, a blue-black shape surrounded by blue-gray sky. The hill glittered from its top and he knew it was the landing site, the earth piled by the ground-grinding *Coracle*.

He wanted to go to it, in the dawn, to see the place where men had first landed here. From which they had spread—

Spread? Well, no.

The hill flashed light, a star. Grailer took a step.

"Good morrow, and well met."

Grailer turned, nearly losing his balance in the damp moss. Karain Fisher stood a few paces behind him, leaning on his cane.

"I didn't mean to startle. Do you not like to be followed?"

"I don't mind." Grailer saw a distinct dark trail in the moss where he had dragged his feet and disturbed the dew. "I enjoyed the story last night."

"Everyone enjoys that story. But then, most of them know what comes after." They shared a laugh, and the bard went on:

"It is a key volume, and there are not many to match it. If you won't take it as an insult, I hope your information is of less value in the future; my resources are finite."

"I'm not much of a storyteller. I know about rocks and machines.

Tectonicists know where the land comes from—but it's not very romantic. No more than cloth from a fabricator, really."

"Cloth being spun? But there are many stories about that. Arachne and her loom, mocking the gods; Clotho the Norn spinning out all our lives; Penelope weaving and unweaving, all to fool her suitors. . . . Metaphor, trope, strophe—oh, I can think of all those uses."

"I'm no storyteller. Just an engineer, really." Grailer wondered briefly who Arachne was, but let it pass. "Since you're here, though . . ." He pointed at the shining hill. "Might we go up there? It looked fascinating from the air."

"Up—" Karain Fisher shook his head, tapped his cane about. "You must mean *Coracle*."

"That's right."

"No. You have nothing to trade for that."

Grailer was a little puzzled and a little angry, but he let neither feeling out. "I'm not so sure," he said.

"I do not intend you insult, Captain Dominick. But there is more bound up in what you ask than you can know. There are old men here who have never seen the interior of *Coracle*."

"If it's information you want," Grailer said—or, he wondered suddenly, was it the beer in his gut speaking?—"we've got more than you could ever imagine. All on tap at once. Instantly, from anywhere."

"Captain Ulli told me something of that. Understand—and if I offend—"

"You're not."

"We are not interested in information for its own sake. Perhaps the word misleads; we do not want your 'news.'

"You could tell me that the sun rises on other worlds than this, or that men come in many shapes and colors, or that they are making war; but these things I know. By the old theory they are not even information. They communicate nothing new.

"But your stories, your tales, your poems and songs, *those* we will hear, for they take those bare known things and clothe them in surprise and wonder. And love."

Grailer saw that Karain Fisher's head was turning side to side, only just noticeably; and in the improving light he could see that the round eyes did not look at him, but rather past him.

Grailer had seldom seen eyes like that directly, unhidden, unashamed. No wonder Karain Fisher spoke his stories. What use books to a blind man?

What use the Web?

"Do you understand me, Captain Dominick?"

"I'm trying to."

"I will still hear gladly any story you know. The legends of the Earth were very great, I was told; but many were lost in generations apart from the Earth."

"I'm no storyteller."

"Does that matter? I am. Please consider. We have lost so much of the world we left."

More than you think, Grailer thought, and almost said. He cursed himself. Ulli's story had not specifically mentioned the destruction of old Earth. If Karain Fisher did not know of it, to tell him would be a cruelty; if he did, it would be a petty cruelty.

"I must go back to the camp. Are the others still here?"

"Captain Ulli always talks for a long time in the morning, and Captain Luke is a redoubtable sleeper."

Both statements were true, though Luke proved to be a better driver half-asleep than he had been awake.

> > >

Hours to working days, days to weeks, the Bridge crawled toward the opposite shore. Though they looked frail, the beams and rails upon which the city blocks would hang were more stoutly built, with more redundant members, than Grailer could remember seeing on anything of the like.

"It's not that I don't believe in tensegrity," deCastries said. "I believe in anything that stays up when you pull out the falsework. But tension-integrity's a theory-of-minimals kind of building. There's not an element in a Fuller tower that doesn't have to be there. And if one of those elements fails—well, a chain's no stronger than its weakest link, I learned that hard enough.

"But there's another article of faith with people like me: If you're losing sleep over a weak link, *put on another chain.*"

Luke pointed to the arcology frame, traced out its imaginary completed lines. "That Bridge is going up to last until this river's a lake, and then a sea.

"Can you imagine that?" he said, and the roar of the go-tracks and the yammer of the sonowelders and grind and clank of metal-comp on itself seemed to fade, the dust and hard orange sun no longer distracting. "A city bank to bank, shore to shore, no one living on the land. Leave the land for mining and planting, and for wilderness. Can you see that?"

Grailer tried to see. He had seen waterbow arkies before, across rivers and canyons, color-checked arcs of minute motions and lights. He had seen rainbows, and once and always-remembered the double rainbow with darkness between. He extrapolated between the two steel towers, and then tried to swell the image to stretch across the horizon, around half the world.

For a moment he thought he saw it, as though from space. And then the dust and light and sound intruded again.

"It can't last ten million years," Grailer said, and was sorry at once. He felt cruel again, and rather small for it.

"No, I know. If I built it out of granite rock, it would wear down before then. I suppose that's why I'm ordering go-tracks around out here, instead of dancing with all the smart people. Gematria Corporation. Earth Magic. God. What were we thinking?

"I think I'm going to fly my pretty bird, Dom. Do you want to come along?"

"N-no. I've got some measurements to take."

"Tell me if you find anything exciting, will you? A new volcano, or maybe the ocean trench opening up overnight."

"I'll look hard."

Luke laughed, but it was a dry sound. "Always did hear strange tales about the Gaea Society."

"Is the truth any stranger?"

"An improvement," Luke said quickly, "but no, no stranger."

> > >

Grailer looked for Ulli Morgan at the Anthony Relief aid and training station, a set of blowfoamed buildings near the Ishtari town.
He could hear children's voices from some of the domes, teachers
trying to be heard over them; smelled things baking, saw the begin-
nings of what would be a pod gantry.

A drone overhead, a shadow that flickered by, was Luke flying
the shuttle at a crazy speed and altitude. If he should crash it, what
could lift them into orbit? The work Hellmanns couldn't rise ten
meters.

They had the Web, of course. Another shuttle could be here in
days, weeks at the extreme.

The Web—he had not touched it in a week. He was not here, he
told himself, to build Bridges or measure fault heave and throw or
listen to folktales, but to find the reason . . .

"The planets Wayne gets keep failing," Gian had said.

DeCastries thundered by again.

"Somebody is mucking up."

"You have not found a solution." Good old Nick.

"Hello, Dom," Ulli said, and woke him up. "Come to see me?"

"I wanted to ask you some things."

"Go ahead."

"What's it like to work for Anthony Wayne Bayard?"

"Is that Luke flying up there?"

"Yes."

"I guess it's safe, then. All right. I'd say it's all right, but it's confining."

"Can you explain that?"

"Probably not very well, but I'll try. Let's go inside and sit down.
There's some coffee, and I think I can filch some fresh bread from
the kitchen."

They settled into folding chairs, with steaming mugs and thick warm slices of bread with fruit and butter. Grailer put his Webset on a table near them. Ulli unfastened her Ariel and bookprinter and put them down as well.

"Nobody's recording this, right? You're just curious?"

"I thought it would be better to ask when Luke wasn't around," Grailer said, taking care to say nothing untrue.

"I don't think he hates the General. I really don't. I think he's scared of something he remembers."

"Or of hearing something about Bayard he'd rather not remember?"

"Or that. But hate him—no. Look at me. When I was learning 'tockthology at Foxfire, I heard the General cursed black all the time—heard him called a mass murderer and worse. 'The master of the Lorraine Cross,' whatever that was."

"An incident where Bayard supposedly shot his own men, during a disaster of a battle on a planet called Lorraine. The details are hard to come by," he said, as he well knew.

"Oh? I wouldn't have thought—I mean, I *like* the General, in spite of everything they taught me. He cares about his people . . . us. Before we came here, he warned everybody that there'd been trouble with some of the teams, said it openly, didn't leave it to stardust and hearsay. He wouldn't send anybody who wasn't a volunteer— and he gave a stationside job at the same pay to anybody who didn't want to volunteer. He's not a Borgia count—he's really a Bayard."

"And what exactly does that mean?"

"Huh? Oh. Middle Annodomini period, old Earth. The Borgias were militarists who parlayed it into an empire—A-five-forty-six. The Chevalier Bayard was a great knight, the very model of chivalry—A-five-twenty-six-point-seven."

"You've lost me again. The numbers?"

"STI code. The Stith Thompson Index of folk themes. A-five-twenty-six-point-seven is the culture hero, type mighty warrior. You remember the stories, the other night? Mine was a combination of P-three hundreds, nonfamily social relations, and P-seven-hundreds, that's assorted social motifs. Karain Fisher's was an A-sixteen-thirty-two-point-two, the tribe climbing down from heaven. At least that's my preliminary classification. It'll doubtless be disputed."

"Is this a Web system? Assembling stories out of building blocks?"

"Oh, no! The STI is middle Annodomini. Just pre-Space Era, I think. And it's not for assembling, really; it's for classifying. That's why it's lasted so very long. It was designed to stretch to fit everything."

"Is this Chevalier Bayard a folk figure, then? Could I look him up using that code?"

"Oh, the Chevalier was a real man, but he's a lore figure, too, like Lincoln or König Artorius or Alexsandr Aloysius Pryne. You ought to be able to find him using the STI, though. Or try Kuppering's *Intact Chevalerie*, if you can stand to read Kuppering."

"I may. You said working for the General was confining. How is that?"

"Well . . . will you not misunderstand me if I tell you? Because it's not really the General's fault."

"You're sounding like Luke."

"No, I'm not."

"You—I guess you're not. I'm sorry; I don't know why I said that." And he didn't really; it had been a cut, without any cause, like his comment to Luke that morning, like his thoughts at Karain Fisher at the dawn. Maybe I should spin, he thought. Or maybe I should stay away a little longer.

"Well . . . do you understand, this isn't the General's fault?"

"I believe you."

"All right. APRA is a humans-only agency, did you know that? Colony recontact and disaster relief only."

"Yes, I know."

"Well . . . I'm an autochthonologist. Not just an anthropologist. And there's . . . You're a tectonicist, right? What's the biggest, best thing you could possibly find?"

"A planet like this one, I suppose. Still young, pangaeic, volcanic. Wegener II-phase."

"No. I mean big, like in *important*. Like in something you could take back to your Gaea Society and have them get up and applaud you."

"It's tough to do that to the Gaeans."

"Still."

Grailer thought hard. This sort of thing was easier with the Goliards, easier still with a Webset working for him. Garnett was too occasional a disguise to stand too much of this. "Something like a high-order plate junction, I guess. A point where a lot of continental plates come together. Two is usual, three a little rare; I think five is the record. An order-six would be unique."

Ulli nodded. "All right. Well, with 'tockthologists it's finding one of two things: an Antikitheron or an Ozymandias Device. And here there's no chance for either."

She refilled her coffee cup, spread another slice of bread.

"Why isn't there any chance?" Grailer asked, thinking of Luke's metalcomp that must corrode with time.

"You don't know what they are."

"They're not rocks or bridges, I know that."

"Well, they could be. An Antikitheron is a technical artifact found in a nontechnical society. Something not just ahead of its time, but *out* of its time. The original, the Antikithera Device, was a calculator, found in the remains of a culture that shouldn't have had any such thing."

"How could you have plexy hardware without—"

"No, not plextronic. Mechanical. Gears and levers. This was very early Annodomini, before even monoelectronics. There were mechanical calculators a little before electricity—but long, long after this. Over fifteen hundred years after."

One Lifespanned life. "How long in period lifetimes?"

She pushed keys on her Ariel. Her fingers were short-nailed, practiced on the panel, but uninspired at work. "Thirty, about."

The entire Ercon, the Web, were less than a tenth of that.

"But you can't find them on human worlds, don't you see? You can't make the jump on the colonies. Your societal experiment is as much as you can handle, never mind technical research. And do you know how many of the old Fringe Folk set out with scientific laboratories of any worth at all? Four. And *those* were all genetic."

"I don't suppose you need to flee society to build a holospace or a surround-sound player."

"Damn right you don't." She looked a little shocked at what she had said. Grailer wondered why, and at exactly what.

"No offense taken," he said as a precaution.

"I didn't mean any." She took a big bite of bread.

"What's the other big find?"

"Thomf—the Ozymandias Device. That's the real prize. Have you ever read the poem, about the broken statue with the boast carved on it: 'Look on my works, ye mighty, and despair'?"

"Once." Doctor Taliessin had sung it; Grailer and . . . Sharon . . . had been learning each other, though, and had not had time to listen well.

Time, he thought, time, time—*wasn't sixty years—?*

"Tell me about it," he said, and filled his own mouth with coffee and bread, confounding the fruit-butter's delicate flavor.

"That's an advanced artifact too, one you'd catalog as an Antikitheron when you found it. Only it's not, quite. It's not a jump forward. It's a holdover from the past. A relic of an advanced civilization that's crumbled into the one you're studying."

"The colonies wouldn't, of course—"

"Of course not." She looked into her coffee. "There's a small chance, of course, a theory . . .

"A 'Kithi *could* develop in a colony culture. And an Ozi might be left over from an extinct culture, one that had gone right back into the soil, or out . . . out into the stars. . . ."

Ulli was slumped in her chair. Grailer had the feeling she was not seeing him, though her eyes were open and aimed his way.

A voice came from across the courtyard, through the thin wall: *"Children, be quiet, or I'll—"*

"Wouldn't they have shown you such a thing?"

"I don't know. Damn it." She gnawed her thumbnail. "They *trade* information, Karain Fisher keeps saying, but there's— Did you try to go up to the starship?"

"I asked and was told no."

She nodded vigorously. "Something's up there all my stories won't buy, he says. Old blind bard, telling me what I mustn't touch . . . C-five-forty-two. The treasure of the other world, tabu to touch.

"I'm going to tell them a tabu story tomorrow night and see what I get in return."

CHAPTER 11

FIRE AND FLEET AND CANDLE-LIGHT

t happened," Ulli Morgan said to the firemet Ishtari, "rather like this.

"Out Man reached, once his war-ways ended; out to the stars. Humanity bold, humanity watchful—for having destroyed worlds they reverenced them now—and humanity lonely.

"For humans were not meant to live alone, finding loneliness enough when Death should come; and if the hold of the hollow-eyed gaunt had been loosened, broken it had not been."

Except for a dreamless few, Grailer thought, and sipped; without Luke present to match him drink for drink, he was savoring his beer slowly tonight.

"But who was to be their company, as Time piled high in the spaces between the stars? Three companions had those who flew the ships.

"One, their Ships' Companions.

"Two, the Web in which all things strand.

"Three, their books."

A murmur ran through the crowd, whispers and "Ah!"s and two-sentence conversations. Grailer supposed she had a reason for not mentioning the true Pilot's Companion: the brainstream hypnosis and the Mysmemedi in the blood that let one face less-rectified space than the sane folk of the ship.

"Now, for the Companions no mortal needed training—" laughter—"though the Companions themselves were high in their art.

"But of the Web and the book, there was needful skill. All those who flew the ships, the loneliest of the lonely, they were skilled in the written word. But many there were who were not."

Louder murmurings rose.

"And the Literate, the shipsfolk, said together, 'Shall we endanger ourselves with those who cannot read clear warnings? Shall we crowd the wavebands with spoken words and pictures, where letterline would do as well? Shall we share space with those whose only escapes are dancing colors and intertwined limbs?'"

"*No!*" the people shouted to her.

Ulli took a moment to recover. When she did, Grailer could see her face was set, her teeth showing in the firelight.

"So said they: 'No! No! We will give unto you to learn, freely and without limit; let there be none to say he had no chance. But if you will not learn, then come not to us, for we know you not; then die in your ignorance in the place of your birth.'

"And they set up those who would stand at the gates and watch; and if any did not read the words, neither did he fly to the stars."

She went on, detailing First and Second and Third Literacies in the odd stilted speech. Not Fourth, of course, never Fourth Literacy. Grailer wondered what Stith Thompson Index number he would fall under.

The firechime rang.

"This," said Karain Fisher, turning his head so his templechain twinkled, "is a great datum indeed, and one I had not expected to hear.

"This thing speaks to me harshly; it reproves me. For I say it, shamed: I had not expected such a wisdom, even from these people who reached over space, over the General Theory we held so dear, to aid us.

"In this light I will tell a tale that I had not thought to tell. I will tell of *Coracle,* as she lies."

More talk, and people bending close. Grailer saw Ulli strain forward, her audio gear ringed before her. The position looked unnatural and painful.

Karain Fisher took his long staff. "We know, don't we, that there are folk who do not care for life. We know, because it's taught us very young, that there are those who walk on young trees instead of the mosses that grow to be walked on; who will kill from fear, or pleasure of killing, and not merely for needs, and will even kill fellow men without first casting them out—"

Grailer laughed to himself, bitterly; so they had outlawry. A Web-spinner would not be safe here; not even here.

"—but it is time you heard the foulest thing in our past. The thing we truly fled.

"The life of the body is cruelly short. The volume never has pages enough before it closes. And it is not so strange, then, that the fear of death, which touches us all, should sometimes change to a hate of life, for its brevity. This we know. This we can heal, and then forgive.

"But some hate—some fear—the life of the mind. Thoughts. Data. Information."

One person spoke up from the listeners. "How could any hate the thing which makes us live past death?"

"Some fear the life after death. 'Ghosts haunting,' they say, for the memories they wish could be put aside."

"What are ghosts?"

Grailer's stomach turned over. His mouth tasted sour with beer. There were no such things as ghosts, he had heard for eighteen years. And then one had lain with him for ten years more.

Sharon Rose, she died alone, he thought for the first time in three years of physical age.

He turned back to Karain Fisher; there was nothing else to listen to, and his muscles hurt. He had assumed the same arched position as Ulli Morgan. A fresh drink found its way into his hand, and he gulped it.

"The burnings of books," said the bard, "and the men who wrote them. Running into . . . into . . ." He paused. The listeners caught breaths. ". . . into the doors of a closed mind."

Karain Fisher stared at the ground—no, not stared, but lowered his face.

"Because of that closed door, children of the Captain . . . we ran away. We fled, in fear. And we have never quite unlearned that fear. Most of you here have only seen the outside of the ship *Coracle*, or gone just a little into her to borrow parts of her skin. There is a reason for that.

"Deep inside her we left a chest, and a covenant; that the knowledge men would try to kill and to kill for, would murder to suppress, would stay safe. Only a few would open the chest and bring forth the knowledge.

"Now you know where I go, and Hesperidus Lane, and Gethen Gower, and the others. And you know what we go for."

There was silence save for the shifting of limbs and seats.

"Is it not time, then, that you changed?" It was Ulli, raised to her knees. "There's no more need for secrecy. There are no more burnings. There is no more forbidden knowledge!"

If you only knew, Grailer thought.

Karain Fisher did not look up (but why would he?). "Not yet time," he said, painfully it seemed. "The covenant is stronger than our lives. We cannot break it."

"When will it end, then? When your lives end?" She was fully to her feet now, arms outstretched, trying not to trip on her instruments.

"It might."

"Well . . . I respect your oath, then."

Well, indeed. What's the rest of his life to you? Two years. Maybe one.

"Will you hear another story tomorrow?"

"Yes. Gladly we will."

The meeting broke up quickly, quietly. Grailer drove Ulli back in the Hellmann sled.

"Didn't I have it column and line?" she said. "C-five-forty-two, the other-world treasure. The box it's death to touch." She tapped at her Ariel. "All right. Here it is. The Ark of the Covenant. Held supported on poles by ritually draped attendants. Only approached by a special priest in a separated chamber on state occasions. Someone tries to touch it, and *zap!* he's dead. Ark of the Covenant; God and St. Anne, even the *name's* right."

"Sounds like a case of radioactives more than forbidden knowledge. What kind of data storage would these people have had?"

"I'll look it up." Keys clicked. She fumbled, swore silently, and started over. "Paper, tape, disk+card, magdom, crystal."

"Crystal might carry corona shock, or some of the charged-plane stuff. But Karain Fisher didn't say the chest was lethal to touch."

"Didn't he? He said it was 'more powerful than our lives.'"

It made a certain sense. A special kind of sense. "You think they've got your Antikitheron? How?"

"I—I'm not sure I think that. I just—look, Dom, will you let me off here? I want to walk the rest of the way. I've got a light on my belt. Come tomorrow night, will you?"

"Sure."

Grailer understood the need for solitude and was feeling it as well. He let Ulli off, made sure her hand light was working, and glided on down the trail.

When he got back to camp, Grailer drove down to the riverbank below the Bridge, watching the streak of light it cast on the black water. Across the river, over the opposite bank and the hills beyond it, was a trace of blue, the last light of the long-set sun.

Grailer smelled the water, a fresh scent that made him want to fill his lungs with it. The forests around the camp were minty by night. And the camp smelled of sawn wood and metal and electrified air, displacing the sulfur trace of the faraway volcanoes.

He thought about waiting for dawn, and was suddenly very tired. It was as if his body were deliberately trying to deny him the morning. He considered making a pot of coffee. But there would be work to do tomorrow.

He expected uneasy sleep, nightmares. But he did not dream at all. In the morning he was not refreshed at all. And the day passed only in search of the night.

> > >

"It happened rather like this." Ulli had her feet spread and set firmly; she had gone through four graduated beers before starting.

"Johnny Sky was the best portduster that ever there was. When the big ships came down into the thick air, it was Johnny their captains asked for; Johnny to patch the plates, Johnny to polish the Pryne couplings, Johnny to trim the seals.

"Because Johnny was a whole crew all by himself. He could carry the weld-cable in one hand, the deutube in the other, and the fixit-cart on his shoulders. He could wrap a hand with raw metalcomp and patch a whole hull with one swipe. He could drag a coupling across his cheek and polish it on his beard. He could trim the seals with his little fingernail and blow on the hatch to test the job."

Grailer was amused, and a little puzzled. A "culture hero" story, he supposed she would call this. But why? Had she given up on the *Coracle*?

He found he had to refill his own drink; everyone was listening to the story.

"—and he drank his coffee straight from the drum, a hundred liters at a time.

"But do you think the skyport bosses were happy? They were not. Bosses are like that all over." There was a ripple of laughter—but harsh laughter, very little joy in it.

"The skyport boss took Johnny aside one day. 'Johnny,' he said, 'a man like you shouldn't crawl the ports all his life. Why don't you be a liner captain, and own a ship instead of slaving to them?'"

"*No!*" shouted the audience. It made Ulli pause, but she recovered.

"'No,' said Johnny Sky. 'If I mastered a ship I couldn't touch them where it counts. I couldn't carry the cables or patch the plates. And how could I let another man do that to my ship? No, sir, I'm a 'duster born and a 'duster I'll die.'

"'Well, then,' said the skyport boss, 'will you be a hullbanger, and float up in grand free space where there's no weight to drag you and the stars are always out?'"

"*No!*"

"'No, sir,' said Johnny Sky. 'I'm a thick air breather. What would I do when I threw down a tool, and newtoned off to the dark? What would I do when I got feeling cramped, and I ripped my suit to let the breeze in?' And Johnny flexed his big muscles, and r-r-ripped his suit just to make the boss's eyes pop."

She seized her headcloth and tore it in two, top to bottom. Eyes did pop. A raucous cheer went up, and cries of disappointment that the example had not been more literal.

"'Well, then,' said the boss, 'you'd better pick something, for you're going off this job.'"

"*Off?*" roared the Ishtari.

Ulli shrunk down, just like Johnny Sky's boss. "'Off,' said the boss. 'For I've got a machine coming in that'll do the work of a crew.'

"'Will it patch the plates?' asked Johnny Sky.

"'Smooth as still water,' said the boss.

"'Can it scrape the contacts?'

"'Bright as double suns.'

"'Does it trim the seals and check 'em?'

"'Flat and tight as laser light. And it never stops to drink a drum of coffee or eat a barrel of biscuits. You're done, Johnny Sky.'

"'Sir, that may be; but you bring your machine out here, and you bring two of the ships down in the thick air, and I'll show you if I'm done or not.'"

Grailer heard a song going up from some of the Ishtari, elders and children both, with a rhythmic chorus and a "Lord, Lord!" on the downbeat.

"So out they went on the increte, Johnny and the big machine. They called it the Dustermatic Ten Thousand, and it was from he-e-ere to the the-e-ere long, and *that* high. It had arms that spun and fingers that snapped and hands to hold the cables. Johnny Sky saw it, and he got a little worried. And then he got a little mean.

"'Are you ready?' asked the boss.

"'*A-a-all* ready,' said Johnny Sky.

"'Yes-sir-yes-sir,' said the machine.

"And they brought the two ships down from heaven, with a

whoop and a howl. They skidded to on the increte, and Johnny and the Dustermatic went to work. The metal-comp flew as they patched the plates. The couplings shone till they hurt your eyes. The seals would have held back a warstorm.

"And wouldn't you know who was winning?"

"*Johnny Sky!*"

"That's the truth; and not only was he working faster than the Dustermatic Ten Thousand, he was drinking coffee by the drum and eating biscuits by the barrel, and *still* working faster.

"'This won't do,' said the skyport boss. 'This won't do at all.' So he went—sneak, sneak—up to the machine, and whispered to it—" Ulli cupped her hand to her mouth and made sibilant noises—"And what do you think the Dustermatic said?"

"*Yes-sir-yes-sir!*" said an army of robots.

"And when Johnny Sky came back from his coffee, the machine stuck out the arm it held the cables with, and it wrapped the cable from Johnny's ship around Johnny's ankle and spliced it. And Johnny was busy pumping vacuum and never did notice.

"Pretty soon Johnny was done, and the Dustermatic only halfway. 'I guess I win,' said Johnny as they gantried his ship. 'I guess you do,' said the boss.

"But then the cable got tight around Johnny's ankle, and up went the ship, and up went Johnny Sky, riding high into the big black sky."

Ulli paused. Grailer waited. She bowed, walked to where Grailer was sitting, sat down beside him.

"Aren't you going to finish?"

"I am finished," Ulli said.

"*What?* The story's not over. Johnny Sky grabs the cable and hauls the ship back—"

"I never heard that part. Besides, it spoils the whole point that you can't fight the advance of technology with—"

Grailer stared at her, was about to speak when Karain Fisher struck the firechime.

I should have gotten up, Grailer thought, finished the story. I should have—

"Anansi the Spider," Karain Fisher said, "was working in his field."

Grailer held still.

"A Kwaku Anansi story," Ulli Morgan said. "A-five-twenty-two-point-three-point-one. The Trickster. The witling."

"Quiet," Grailer said.

"He's also called 'Ti Malice, and Aunt Nancy—"

"*Quiet!*"

"Now Black-beetle, who lived on the line over from Anansi, had a fruit-tree on his land, and a big, ripe fruit hung down on the prop-er-tee line." Karain Fisher's voice had become strangely rhythmic; not "beautiful," but—but musical, like Celene Tourdemance had had music in her voice.

"And Anansi went out, for to trim up his garden, and he saw that fruit hanging, down on the line. So he swung his big knife—up, and he cut it; split it in two, so it fell on both sides.

"'Hey!' said Black-beetle, 'what do you do? That was my fruit, for it hung on my tree.' But 'No,' said Anansi, 'I took what was mine, for I only took half of what was hanging between.'

"'Death will make me forget this, Anansi you Spider; death to forget, and I'll live a long time.'"

Grailer was fascinated, horrified. He could see Diego Cadiz, that long-lived black-beetle, lecturing Anansi the Webspinner, whom Grailer saw as a vague figure—in red, for some reason.

"Now Anansi the Spider, he went to the King, and said 'Make me a preacher, and I'll bring in all the people.' And the King said 'Fine! But you must have a coat; a coat of fine stuff, for to wear to be a preacher.'"

"Damn it, old man," Ulli said.

"Damn *you*! Shut up!"

"And Anansi hurried home, for he did have a coat, and he washed it and he pressed it and he hung it up to dry. He hung it on the fruit-tree, that stood in the garden, and he went back in the house, for to write his first sermon.

"Black-beetle came out, once Anansi was inside, and he swung his big knife, and he cut the coat in two. A piece fell on Anansi's side, a piece on Black-beetle's, and he stood there and he waited for Anansi to return.

"When Anansi came out, he said 'In death will I forget you!' But Black-beetle laughed and said 'My memory is longer.' And the soldiers came in, the soldiers of the King—"

Grailer was shaking.

"To take Anansi away, for the breach of his promise. For there are promises and promises, and oaths that you swear, but a promise to the King is your life in balance fair."

Grailer looked for Ulli, but she was gone. When he looked back, Karain Fisher was gone as well. The people seemed to be singing a hymn, and going out.

He drove back to camp and went to sleep, alone.

> > >

The near end of the Bridge extended a hundred and fifty meters over the water. It was a double cross now, a second pylon in place, the temporary pillars past it and crawling westward. A raft was tethered out at the pylon's shearwater, a recovery station for the men with wings who clustered about the new work like insects in the autumn heat.

Luke was waving at go-track drivers and giving instructions via Ariel to lifter pilots and wingmen. He was yelling a lot, not always to be heard over machine noise.

Grailer was consulting, but not especially as an engineer. He was telling Luke jokes, and stories of construction jobs he had seen (real ones, in fact), talking about Maracot Falls and its perpendicular infracity. The Anthony Relief kitchen sent a sled of sandwiches and chilled drinks, and he fetched an armload for the two of them. He even talked tectonics, having crammed his head from a book the Web offprinted for him.

"Now the plates are coming up from a trench, like clothes from the slot, but spreading both ways." He put his hands together and rolled them apart. "The trench is near the far bank. When you get to it, you'll want to put in a stretching span; one with built-in false-work to hold it till a new section will fit in."

"Textbook stuff," Luke said, but he was looking at the distant bank, and his sarcasm sounded forced.

"Well, after all, who wrote the textbooks?" Grailer said with equally mock diffidence. And Luke laughed . . . and Grailer thought it was real.

They were working at the H_2/O_2 plumbing of an idled go-track, Luke twisting pipes, Grailer creasing his fingers, when their Ariels pinged. Both at once. Not the slow call sound, but the *tone, tone, tone* of an alert.

Luke dropped his wrench, drew the pocket terminal, and enabled it with one hand, his eyes trained on the Bridge. Faint sounds were drifting down from the open, river end.

"DeCastries. Go."

Grailer had his own Ariel out in a moment more, thinking how like a pistol draw Luke's movement had been. He heard:

"—screaming his head off, and—"

"Identify yourself, dammit!"

"Far forward—Forward Six."

"For God's sake don't try any—" To Grailer: "Dom, get us transport. And wings, helmets, gloves. Go."

"—heroics," Grailer heard, and closed the Ariel and ran for the gear.

In minutes they were aboard a service cart, locked to a Bridge rail and rolling, slipping into their shoulderpack Hellmann wings. Grailer had by instinct looked for full-flight wings, but there were none to hand; only the small ones for high-safety. It did not matter that much. Even full Hellmann flight wasn't half as fast as the rail-cart. And the cart might not be half fast enough.

Grailer noticed the chest buckle on his wings pictured a man with mechanical birdwings spread: sigil for Leonardo Devices. One of Gian's companies. Of course, he made Hellmanns. That would be a good joke to tell Luke. Later.

"Dammit, of course there's a remote power cutoff. There's got to be! *Find it!*"

"Trouble?" Grailer felt like an idiot at once.

"No trouble," Luke said sharply. "I don't think the whole Bridge will fall. Just Number Two pylon. Minor setback."

There was a sound clearly audible ahead—clearly a scream.

"I didn't mean—"

"Go-track operator at an X-beam junction. Got his hands mangled. He's death-what-dreaming. Says he's going to roll right over the edge. And he knows I'd let him, because he's got a half dozen workers pinned down. If he goes, he rolls right over them. And everybody else is too scared to find the remote cutout."

Grailer's Webset was in his room. But he had his Ariel and could work from that. Revealing himself, of course. Was it necessary?

"Have anything in mind, Luke?"

"One particular thing." He put a hand to his shirt, above his waistband, brought out a black rectangular object.

It was a Valkyr Cestus, a gun not much bigger than the two ten-millimeter rockets inside it. There were no barrels to speak of, nor accuracy. Ari had said the big slugs could rip an arm off at the shoulder. Ardrey the Man-Hunter would not carry one.

DeCastries' eyes were hard and his face was blank. "Only if I have to," he said, and tucked the gun in his belt.

There was more noise now. The Bridge was built not to reverberate and magnify noises, but it was still open, and the wind blew through. It was no wonder, Grailer thought, Luke could fly the shuttle like he did. There was no less wind or noise or altitude up here.

Luke stopped the cart. "There."

Grailer needed no directing. Fifty meters ahead of them was a go-track, the man in the control cage holding his arms to his body. The lifting fingers on the track's front end were spread wide, circling around a group of people, fencing them against a panel. The panel was thin, a temporary windbreak of wood; the track would punch right through it. And the people between . . .

"That you, deCastries?"

"Right. Come on down, Randy. We'll fix you up."

"Sure . . . sure you will. I can't feel nothin' from my elbows down, deCastries. My nerves're dead. Nerves don't heal, everybody knows that."

"I'd wait till the doctor had a look at it. We've got a doctor, Randy—General Bayard's doctor, not some foxhole medex."

"You bet on it, Lucas Wolf. With a handful of sleep, that it? And I wake up without—"

The driver lurched forward, squeezing his hands into his armpits. The go-track grumbled and rolled a few centimeters. The workers trapped in front milled about. They wore high-safety wings, Grailer saw. There must be some way they could make use of that.

"Luke," he said very softly, "what kind of circuit is the power cutout?"

Luke did not turn his head. "Relay in the track, wired to its talk-box. Signal comes from a crash panel around here somewhere."

"Weblink or RF?"

"Synapse. Can't use radio worth a damn around all this metal."

The driver raised his head. "What are you talking about, Lucas Wolf?"

Luke muttered, "Wish I damn knew," then said aloud: "What is it you want then?"

"I want you to watch! I want you to *see* this! I *know* who owns Gematria!"

Luke, softly: "He's out of his mind. You'd better get clear." Aloud: "I've got less than a third of it, Randy. And what's wrong with—"

Grailer tore himself away and focused on his Ariel. He would not be without the big set ever again, he swore. Now he just had to hope there were not too many barriers between him and the power relay. And that the driver kept talking.

And that he didn't draw the Hounds—

He went to work. Numbers only, it was taking him twice, three times as long to reach his virtuals, give them working commands. He found the base-camp communications board, seized it. Let them worry about the blackout later; he was committed now. And revealed anyway. He reached out from the board to all the hardware in the camp. Synapse-linked, he felt the touch of machinery around other stars and pulled away at once.

A go-track's combox is lower-right on the control quadrant, his fingers felt out. It runs a wire down, and back, and left-right-left to a plastic-capsuled relay aft and starboard of the driver's spine. A surge current could melt the relay, pop it; but that might fuse it closed. It also might shoot splinters into the soft lower back of the driver.

We are here, Grailer saw in his mind, *past the Two Pylon junction, over the water. The track is here, a few meters farther. The cutout transmitter is . . .* He traced up and down the pylon, back and forth along the bridge.

. . . ten meters above us.

"Luke."

"Go ahead."

"In ten seconds that track's going to die. Tell everybody in front to run for it. Wings on, just in case."

Luke scratched at his hip. Then he nodded. Grailer put out a finger and sent the signal. He could feel the relay snap.

The track fell still, and the wind was suddenly loud.

"Everybody out! Wings on, jump if you have to!"

The driver howled, hurt, in pain. He rolled over the side of the track, colliding with the last worker out, knocking her down. Screaming, he picked up a stick in the two red mittens on the ends of his arms, held it to smash.

A white flame jumped from deCastries' fist. Grailer stared at Luke. He'd drawn and palmed the gun during that hip-scratching move. Grailer turned to the driver.

He was wobbling on his feet, his ruined hands full of wooden fragments, insult to injury. The board had been blown out of his grip.

Without another sound, he ran to the side. Toward an opening in the Bridge.

"Goddamn it, *stop*, Randy," Luke said, and punched the air with the fist that held the Cestus.

The man jumped, where they could see him fall.

When a body tumbled down in Maracot Falls, a close-wrapped corpse buried in the cataract, it flicked in and out of view, now hidden, now spray-obscured, now for just a moment in full view. But there was no concealing blue water here. And Grailer's eyes were drawn to the falling man, as he flailed, as air hammered at him, harder than he must have expected.

If Grailer had only had a Webscreen to draw him away, he might not have been compelled to watch that terrible . . . slow . . . fall . . . to the water.

Luke turned to go, before the splash, which anyway was not very great.

"Luke . . . love." It was Mazey, picking herself up from the spot where she had been pushed down and nearly had died. "I'm sorry, Luke."

"Right. Now tell me why."

"He was angry, I guess; and the pain drove him over."

"It was something more than that."

"Why's it me you're sharp with? You know nobody likes an owner as super."

"I'm not working for myself. If I've been screwing up—"

"No, you haven't mucked up—" Grailer winced, hoped no one noticed—"but haven't you been working for yourself? Who have you been working for, Luke love?"

She started on by, stopped. "And that was a true enough shot. Was it his head you were aiming for, Lucas Wolf?"

They watched her go.

"Tell anybody that asks they're off duty for the day," deCastries said to Grailer. "I'm going flying."

"Should you do that?"

DeCastries spun around, his shoulders raised. Then he relaxed.

"No, I suppose not. Be a long time getting a replacement. For the shuttle, not for me.

"Then tell 'em this, too: I'm not available till sometime tomorrow."

"Even if Gematria calls?"

"Especially so."

> > >

Grailer wandered for the rest of the afternoon. There was some brawling—oh, there always had been, but this was wilder. They were using clubs and stones as well as fists, and snapknives flashed. Grailer broke up a couple of fights, could not even slow down some others, took a share of blows. For the first time since he had arrived, he thought about the Hawkwood 81C pistol in his room.

He went to the Relief center to put himself far away from the gun.

Ulli wasn't there. One of the cooks said she was away at the Ishtari town, and offered him a sandwich and a beer.

The beer was warm, the glass wiped instead of washed. The texture of the bread was pebbly, lumps of dry flour all through it. A bone in the filling scraped his gum and he cursed.

"Fix it y'r own damn self, then," the cook said. "You try cooking for five hundred, three times a day. You just try it."

Grailer threw the sandwich down and left. He passed the sled by—*Be a long time getting a replacement. For the shuttle, not for me*—and walked back, losing the trail several times in the early darkness.

The camp lights were turned up high. The sounds of fights still came from dark corners, but the crew seemed even to be sleeping with every light on.

CHAPTER 12

AND EARTH RECEIVE THY SOUL

He found Luke awake, puffing anodynes in his rooms, surrounded by drawings of the Bridge. Line-faxes, engineering drawings with numbers marking everything off neatly, color renderings of Karain City on completion and after a few years' occupancy, and a spread-out strip-mural of the arky in the far future, vanishing over the edge of the world.

Grailer pointed at the half-empty bottle of offworld whisky. "What's the matter? Starshine not good enough for you?"

Luke, who laughed at everything, didn't this time. "Stuff tastes like it's been pissed in," he said, and tossed his anodyne aside. It landed on the strip-mural, which smoldered and caught. Luke snatched it up, muttering, kicked the door open, and threw the burning paper onto a patch of gravel. He watched it for a moment and closed the door before the mural had burned out.

"Something you want to tell me, Luke?"

"Not a damn thing. You want a drink?"

"I—yeah, I want a drink."

"Take what you want. You'll never catch me."

There wasn't any ice. The whisky tasted hot and metallic, filling the back of his throat with a warm vapor. He could feel it going all the way down inside him.

"Doctor T's right. I'm a wine drinker."

"Wine gets you sick drunk. Who needs it? Dom, will you tell me how you cut out that track?"

A warm fog was gathering inside Grailer's head, and he blinked to clear it. Tell him? He hadn't even told Gian, or . . . or . . . "I'll tell you if you'll tell me why that nickname offends you so much."

"Nickname?"

"'Lucas Wolf.'"

"Hell, that must be a powerful secret. 'Major information,' the old blind man would say. All right, I'll tell you. But you first."

Without including any particular personal details or naming any names—including Grailer Diomede—he explained Fourth Literacy to deCastries, told him how much freedom the Webspinners had in reaching through the strands of the Web.

"That's pretty near anything, I guess."

"It's a lot."

"Nothing's safe from you, then, is it? No secrets. No . . . no privacy. Band of thieves."

"We don't steal," he said, "we're more honest than—" His hands hurt. He found his fists were balled tightly. There was blood on his palms.

"Nev'mind. It's my turn." Lucas threw the bottle onto the other empties, uncapped another, and pulled from it straight.

"My whole name's Lucas Wolfe deCastries. That's Wolfe with an *e.* And everybody called me deCastries until I got in the army. Till I started fighting for Wayne Bayard. That's what they call *him,* y'know. Not Tony. Wayne."

"DEVAFORCE?"

"Don't you goddamn talk to me about DEVAFORCE. I was in the real war. The Last-Real-War. I was on Lorraine with Bayard. But I made it out, in spite of everything. I made it out alone, just me and a rifle and a knife. And I—"

He shook his head. Grailer's vision was poor; he squinted. Was deCastries—

"When I came back—I'd been out a long time, alone . . . I wasn't trained as a guerilla, not me. I didn't know how to long-range, I had to just hit and hit hard at anything that got in my way . . . and this stupid sentry, this goddamn brainless witling, kept asking me for the password, over and over, and I—"

"Did he die?"

"I think so. But . . . I . . . woke up and said, 'Where's the sentry?' and they said, 'What sentry?' and I thought I was crazy. Until Wayne Bayard came in and told me about what had happened."

"The Lorraine Cross," Grailer said.

DeCastries was on his feet, the bottle reversed in his hand. Liquor spilled on the floor. "Don't you ever say that to me!"

"I'm sorry, I—"

"Sorry, yeah, all so goddamn sorry! Wayne Bayard wasn't *sorry*. He went *out* and put his ass on the *line* and *did for*—"

Luke was absolutely still, his eyes wide and white on the dripping bottle in his hand.

Grailer started up, then froze as well. His hand was tight on something in his pocket. It was his snapknife, and his thumb was on the catch.

"Are we all out of our minds?" Luke said.

"I think . . ."

"Don't think, *tell me*! I'm Lucas the Wolf, Dom. I'm the man who crawled out of Lorraine with not a damn thing behind him; that's why they call me that. God only knows—if they knew about the sentry—"

"You shot the board out of Randy's hands, Luke. You could have killed him, but you didn't."

"You can't aim that goddamn palm-gun, Dom. I meant to take his head off his shoulders. Mazey was right."

Luke put the bottle down, gently. He sat and put his face in his hands. He was beginning to shake. "I thought it was over and done with. There's something about this place, Dom; do you feel it?"

"I feel it." Where are you sleeping tonight, Sharon? I don't know which way Skolshold is from here. All my sadness (I thought I had forgotten), all my joy . . . came from loving . . .

Luke's agony. And mine (but mine was buried deeper). All floating up. And . . .

Where was Ulli Morgan tonight?

Grailer opened his Ariel, made a prayer. Damn you, BellStel, it's only a dozen km!

Ulli answered. Her face was oddly lit; her hair was mussed. Grailer wondered if—but no, she had on tunic and sash.

"Yes, Dom?"

"Ulli, I . . . where are you?" Darkness behind her, only a few stars.

"Why do you ask? Look, Dom, I'm really busy." Grailer adjusted the visual gain, and metal ribs came into view, square panels of stars.

—where we borrow from *Coracle.*

"Don't do it, Ulli. Don't. Leave now."

She broke Web.

"Luke, can you drive?" He could have called her back and locked the channel open, but what would be the point?

"I've taken all the detoxicants I could take in a week. What's wrong?"

"Ulli's at the starship. Robbing it, I'm sure."

"What's there to steal?"

"Information," Grailer said, already headed through the door. "The only thing the Ishtari value."

> > >

Grailer drove the hoversled as fast as he dared, not half as fast as he wished. The night was dark, and the trail wound close about the trees. The detox pill was still scrubbing the alcohol from his system—and as he sobered, he got angrier. His forehead was hot and his breath came hard.

On the seat beside him was his Webset, closed but not latched, its strap trailing off his shoulder. On his hip was Gian's gift, in its beautiful handworked holster.

He drove by the light from one headlamp, dazzle-guarded, and he wished for a moon. Starlight was so cold, so faraway, so faint. *Starlight/Painted on the sky/Sunset came without a warning . . .*

He came out of the forest, saw the path straighten and branch, saw the piles of stone he had seen from the air. And the glimmering hill upon which rested *Coracle*.

He dimmed the headlamp, moved on softly singing Hellmann fields among the cairns. As he passed close to one, he saw a plate affixed to one end. A name and numbers. They were graves, out here in the shadow of the ship.

Some people built monuments to the dead, Grailer knew. Some heaped stones. But that was also the way a radiation-poisoned body would be buried.

The Ark of the Covenant. Death to touch. Tabu. C-five-hundred-something.

The lamp picked up a white shape. It was the sled he had left at the Relief center. Its piping glinted golden. Safety reflectors sparkled and the red words stood out: GEMATRIA CORPORATION. The sled hovered, drifting a little in the gentle evening breeze.

Behind it was a ramp of compacted gravel, shining silver in the light. Grailer dimmed the lamp out at once. He fumbled for a handlamp.

The ship rose before him like a castle wall, the hill a battlement to one side, the ramp rising before him to a square opening rimmed inside with pale blue light.

Stepping gently on the crunching gravel, he went up the ramp.

The cold blue light ringed the doorframe, more of it visible up and down the halls inside. Radiation, he thought. But the glow-spots were too regular in shape, too sharp-edged. He got close and touched one. It was cold to the touch, glass. Emergency lights, that's all. Come on, come on, you've got to get her out.

Where was she? Grailer turned the handlamp down, hung it on his belt. His eyes adjusted; the glowstrips produced a satisfactory light, though one that drained color from everything.

He opened and enabled his Webset, made a deep-channel prayer to BellStel, to Ulli's Ariel. Just as the circuit closed, he suppressed the pinger. Or tried to; one tone got through anyway.

What am I doing? Got to slow down.

No answer came. Grailer traced wave displacements, feeling

along the Webstructure. Feeling, not dancing, not roving free. His fingers seemed thick. He was miskeying. But he found the distance and direction and broke Web with relief.

His boots rang in the corridors of the ship; his attempts to walk silently were clumsy, worthless. He was sober, he knew that, and a little sick from the detox pill—why was his head so fogged? Trace poisons in the air, the water? The Ishtari had lived out their lives here, grown old here, died here.

Sharon Rose, she died insane—

He stepped out over void, tottered on the edge of a chasm, recovered his balance. His gasp echoed over and over.

The corridor entered near the curved belly of an enormous cylindrical room. All round its arc were doorways, and the ruins of ladders and platforms and metal stairs, overgrown with moss. Squares were missing from overhead and opposite, space dark and starspecked on the ghostglowing walls. In the center of one flat wall—floor or ceiling, when the ship had flown—was a dome of opaque shiny stuff, thick glass perhaps.

A firedome, in the center of what had been the floor, in the middle of the curved walls. The Ishtari had cut their village out of this chamber and put a fire at its center. Just as the space-born and space-buried generations had had the hydrogen fire below them. Without the synapse to speak in t-zero, this had been their whole world. Without rectifiers to straighten the stars, it had been their whole universe. Without the Pryne envelope, there would have been hundreds—thousands, by the look of this place—who had never known, never been able to touch and feel and see that there was anything else.

Grailer looked across the cool and shadow-crossed vault, and at its bottom he saw a light move. "*Ulli!*" The name echoed and echoed.

The light went out. Then it came on again, cutting across the scattered beams and rails, fingering Grailer. "Dominick?"

"Ulli, get out of here!"

"Dom, come down here and help me!"

And in his rage he did, only too quickly, only stopping when he saw what she meant by help.

A dais had been built on the new-axis "floor," covered with glow-strips pried from corridor ceilings and fitted neatly together. The blue pool lit Ulli Morgan from below, made her look ghoulish. She was straining with a dark box, a meter square and twenty cm thick. A small Hellmann dolly was beneath it, whining under the weight, incapable of adjusting to the movement.

"Leave it, Ulli. Let's get out of here."

"I'm not going without this."

"Was there a guard, Ulli? Did you kill the guard?" They were capable of anything, now, tonight.

"No guards. God protects the Ark, remember? Come on, God, help me taketh away."

"*Leave it!*"

"I'll take it whether you help me or not."

Grailer raised his hand and grasped his own wrist to hold himself back. He was panting. He turned back to Ulli and saw the arch of her neck and the zap pencil in her hand.

"I'm not going without it," she said evenly.

Grailer nodded, feeling helpless and angry.

Together they moved the chest out to the ramp. Shadows preceded them out. Every squeak of the lifter seemed the complaint of a ghost.

They skidded it down the ramp (its weight was not increasing, Grailer told himself, it was grav-grid illusion) and heaved it aboard Ulli's borrowed sled.

"Now," he said, "what are you going to do?"

"After I've recorded it"—she was gasping too—"I'll put it back. Just the way it was. They only go into the Holy of Holies . . . I don't know . . . but they'll never . . ."

"Eden Curtis?" said a voice, a familiar, bardic voice. "Numenor Skora? Are you there?" And out of the darkness the *tap-tap* of Karain Fisher's blindman's stick.

"Come on!" Ulli whispered, and jumped into the sled. She shoved hard on the stick and was away in a rush of fields and draft, knocking Grailer off balance. He clenched his hands. They were scraped. They burned.

"Walden Chang! Gethen Gower! The alien blood has done as we expected!" The old man's voice rose like a storm gathering, a stellar flare. "Come and burn them!"

They're mad too, Grailer thought. We're all mad. He staggered across the dark field, not daring to light his lamp, Webset *bang-bang-banging* against one thigh, pistol riding the other, his hands aching and trembling.

I've got to get away. Spin. I've been away too long. I can't keep control without the Web; I'll spin and it'll bring me down from heaven, down the spiral.

He collided with the sled, climbed on it. He shifted forward too hard, pushing stones on the ground, making noise.

"I know it is you, Dominick Earthdoctor, no-Captain. I know you by your walk and your breathing!" Headlamps washed over Karain Fisher, who stood shouting with his stick raised up. Mr. Aristide had held his stick like that when Grailer had committed some great offense in training; but Ari had never been angry. And Karain Fisher was raging, at the theft of his people's soul.

One more thing Grailer saw, in the bard's eyes; that which their blindness had blinded Grailer to. Karain Fisher's were Romany eyes, deep and imprisoning, the eyes of the old Romany, the ones who had gotten off Earth when she was blue and wet.

Grailer shoved the control forward, nearly running Karain Fisher down, telling himself it wasn't intentional, he hadn't meant to kill him and close those eyes—that were blind anyway—and besides people died open-eyed—

As he drove headlong into the woods and the darkness he heard more voices behind him and saw shadows cast by unnatural, bright actinic light.

He could outrace them easily, though, outrun the cries and the burning light. He had the sled. He had the Web.

Deep into the forest, he steered the sled from the trail, jumped out and knelt before the headlights. He thumbed the catches on the Webset, opened and enabled it. His mind was clearer than it had been for days. He would jump the synapses, call help in t-zero. Call—Nick? No, call Gian Paolo, get the rich man out of his chair. Perhaps his bed. Turn on his bedroom lights, switch off his sleeping grid, and drop him, *plop!* That'd get his attention!

"This is *Florence III*," said a blandly grinning angel. "May I—"

Grailer broke it off, hammering on the keys, wobbling the sticks. They felt stiff, hard to set exactly. He'd been away much too long.

"Nicholas Anders," the set said, though the screen showed numbers on noise. "Messer Sforza is presently unavailable."

"Nick, this is—" What name, what name? "Jim Knight. We've got trouble on Ishtar. All the trouble you wanted and then some."

"James, explain yourself."

"Good—old—Nick. At least somebody knows it's me."

"James, what are you doing on this channel?"

"I'm—" There shouldn't have been any question of that, any indication of anything wrong. But then, he should have gotten Gian, not Nick.

Red lights were flashing on the keyset. He'd made some kind of mistake. Something was horribly wrong.

Then the screen darkened, and there was a long and agonizing howl. The howl of the Hounds.

Grailer broke Web with Anders at once. Another mistake, he thought then; his spinning drew the beasts. More spinning would only draw them faster.

The Geisthounds called again, a distant sound like cries for help across a wide river. As Sharon Rose had called out once.

They were drawing closer and he could not stop them, leaping across the links of the Web at thoughtspeed, hunting for the place where its sanctity had been violated. Thirsting for the Webspinner's life.

If I don't stop them, they'll kill me. They'll kill us all.

They'll kill Sharon—

The keys clickclacked under Grailer's sweating fingers. He was playing antiphony now, one hand countertheme to the other. The Hounds snarled and spat, and static was crackling in Grailer's fine hair.

The Web could not be mechanically linked into an intelligence. But that still left virtual systems: electrical imitations of an intelligence, programming constructs not tied to one particular component. A virtual was a wandering program, resident where it chose, traveling where its structure told it to go.

Or in the case of the Geisthounds, where CIRCE had trained them to go.

(They moved by apport, through the forbidden spaces where time held still, where only signals could pass. Someday men would force matter between the synapses and travel in t-zero, and Humanity and Universe would finally reach congruency.)

A maze of lines built on the Webset screen. Grailer shaped the Web into a plextronic labryinth, saw himself at the center, the Hounds at the edges. As the glowing net reached the limits of the screen, a pale green shape leaped into view.

It was on the edge of the screen. Grailer kept his eyes away from the green thing with a strength partly will, partly fear. From the speaker the high wild sounds of pursuit were joined by ripples of soulless, loveless laughter.

Was there a hand on Grailer's side? Was there someone there that he had to protect? He played an impassioned tune of control commands to an *a cappella* chorus of damnation hurled at the Combined Intersystem Executive. *Why* had they put the beasts into the system? Oh, crime, yes, law, the harder the lawbreaker was to catch, the more vigor went into his punishment—but the trap laid for the Webspinners went beyond justice. They had built blood vengeance into the system, against the spinners, against all their house—

Damn Diego Cadiz, the eternal man, eternally mad.

Lines grew like trailing vines around the Hounds on the screen. They screeched and leapt, burning greenly in the liquid crystal forests of the Web. They could sense the prey out there, and waited to feed on his nerves and brain.

But Grailer struck first, hard. His lines of power intersected, all at once, and spread the Geisthounds' hypothetical bodies through a probability volume. He rattled the trap, altering the Web's internal references to make the Hounds dizzy and cloud his trail. A hundred prayers to BellStel would misroute as a result, but no way around it, not now. Then, guts cold, breath held, he fired them on a pulse of multiplexed energy, on the wings of BellStel which sleepeth not, out to a distant signal storer.

The heel of his hand came down. Power surged, and the faraway machine blew itself to bits. The Hounds died.

He closed his eyes. When the noise of his blood and breath subsided, he could hear the set droning: "—nett, are you there? Respond, respond. I say again, Dom Garnett, are you there? Respond—"

He slammed it shut. Too long away from the Web. It had been taken from him. He got into the sled and drove for the camp.

He found it by the light of flames.

> > >

The Ishtari had atomic-flare torches, no doubt the tools they used to carve out the village from *Coracle*. The jet-flame burned anything— shipmetals, buildings, piles of materials, people. The ground moss was burning all around.

Some of the Gematria crew were running, dodging, long black shapes cradled to their chests. Had there been rip-guns and rifles in the toolroom? It seemed that there had been, in a locked cupboard. Locks could break. Locks could melt. A sonowelder could tear a lock apart.

Ripguns chattered and kicked. Robed Ishtari danced in pain and fell dead. Lines of unbearable light reached out. Engineers fell. There was no place without fire behind. Every standing thing was silhouetted, a perfect target. There were no stars, no horizon. The flames burned away night vision. Away from them there was no light to see by.

The moss, some soft and loathsome, some crisped hard, pulled at Grailer's ankles. He kicked at it. Twice he kicked human hands, but there were no cries of pain. He was looking for Luke, but he could not call his name. He probably could not have been heard anyway.

He saw the sled, with the dark shape of the box in the back, and people around it. One was raising a long pale rod and bringing it down on a burning bush. Firelight winked from Karain Fisher's headchain. Grailer walked on toward them. It had to end. If anyone could stop it, the bard could.

Two Ishtari pointed their torches at him. He saw a heap on the ground, with an elbow up at a sharp angle. He kept walking.

"Is it the Earthdoctor? Yes. I hear his boxes clatter, his boots rustle the moss. Don't kill him."

The torches moved down.

"We have our own. We have done enough. He deserted his; let him live with that."

"*E-Enough?*" Bile came up after the words, and Grailer had to spit it out.

"Enough," Karain Fisher said, and spat at Grailer's feet.

"I tried to make her wait. To ask much later."

"It did not matter. We would never have given it to you. Never. We are Captain's blood, all of us. You have none, and so we called you."

"Was it information you wanted? How much?" Grailer fumbled with his Webset, held it out. "We have more data than you could ever cram in your heads!"

"All worthless," Karain Fisher said, and moved toward the sled. An Ishtari took his arm. "*She* said you were advanced. You all said it. *Liars!*

"You do not *age*, you do not *learn!* Ten years passed, twenty of yours, for each year we flew; yet you speak the same languages as we left behind us, you revere the same false gods. You claim to violate physics, flying faster than light, yet your engineer could not tell Hesperidus Lane how it is done."

"Nobody can—" and no words would come. Grailer fought the spell of the Romany eyes, intensified by firelight.

"You have nothing to trade. We will go. Whoever survives this night may leave our lands in peace."

As they got into the sled, Hesperidus Lane at the controls, Karain Fisher raised his staff in both hands. *"The fires return upon the burners!"*

Grailer fell to his knees beside the smoldering bush. Ulli Morgan lay beside it. And in it was another body.

Grailer grabbed at deCastries' head and shoulders, raised him up. Luke's body was battered soft, the flesh loose on his bones.

Don't die on me, don't die, Grailer tried to say but was too sick. *We'll get you in amber*—but there were no amber vats here.

Luke stirred. "D'mmm . . ." His jaw hung crooked, his cheeks were red and black and smeared with something gray and soft. ". . . Bayard . . . betrayed us . . . th' Lorraine Cross."

—Don't you ever say that—but with the whole world inside out, why not?

The body did not lighten as Luke faded. It weighed a thousand tonnes. The eyes were so bruised Grailer could not tell if they were open or closed.

He let Luke down and stood. The sled was moving slowly away, dodging fire and bodies. It's over, he thought, but it wasn't over, not like this. His nose was full of smoke, his mouth of vomit. His Webset lay on the ground somewhere.

The gun was in his hand of itself, and out and level; the Hawkwood 81C was the finest handgun made. It did the labor. Its trigger begged to be squeezed and responded satisfyingly.

The tracer was a geodesic of red fire between Grailer's rigid body and the retreating sled. It pierced the hydrogen cylinder on the rear deck and went on into Karain Fisher's body in the microsecond before the explosion.

The fireball lit up the river and the Bridge, a yellow double cross above the whole camp.

Grailer just stood, and stood.

There was a stirring at his feet. Ulli Morgan dragged herself up, an arm hanging at a bad angle, a leg twisted.

"Dom," she said from a bloody mouth, "I—"

It was a good thing, then, that he had killed, for worse crimes tempted him; but he was spent. He just stared at her for a moment, hating, *loathing* her heart and soul for being alive, and walked down to the water.

It's someone else's blood spilled in the moonlight,
Another body drifting out to sea

Blood washed into the river, soiling even it. Beneath the Bridge were bodies. Some floated. One hung suspended on high-safety wings, trailing only its toes in the water.

But someone died last night,
Someone died last night

He hefted the gun and threw it as far as he could, and listened for the splash.

Someone died last night
And it was me.

> > >

Nicholas Anders and Grailer Diomede stood on a plain of frozen gas, clouds of vapor rising around them. To one side was a garden of bent trees with flat bands of foliage, giant bonsai. In another direction were buildings exactly like hundred-meter chessmen in the Queen's Gambit Opening. Grailer had seen the buildings move. Off another way was a rickety frame of wood and metal, two hundred meters high; a train of railcars ran on it without Hellmann compensation. The idea seemed to be to feel as much g-force as possible.

Grailer did not look that way. The frame—"coaster," Anders called it—was too much like the Bridge.

"And what was in the box?" Nick asked. He wore his weather-breaker coat, more creased than a year ago, trousers tucked into high boots.

"Books. No miracles of technology, no lost civilizations—well, no artifacts of them. Just books: *fiction about* ideal civilizations. Utopias. One called *Utopia*. And one where the dreamland was an island called Karain. Oh, and a multivolume set, she said; *Everything About Britains*, something like that."

"The *Encyclopaedia Britannica?*"

"Yes."

"What edition?"

"I didn't see them, damn it—but wait, she said that too. Eleven. But I didn't ever see them. And they aren't there anymore—just a melted-down box and a lot of ashes."

Grailer wore all black—beret, wrapshirt, kilt and leotard, black leather sandals. The gas chilled his feet. "You say they danced on this?"

"They danced barefoot. One kept moving. If one did not, one froze to the spot. Strange dances. Vaill was a strange man, James."

"I nearly forgot. She said there was a copy of *Erewhon* in the box as well. Shall we go back inside?"

"Out here is safer," Anders said. The light of three moons, all of them artificial, lit up a film of frost on his radiant hair. "You have not found a solution. That is understood. You have incurred certain costs and obligations. These are nothing to Gian. They are forgotten.

"He asks after you, James. What shall I tell him?"

Grailer took a step on the ice, another. His feet felt warmer, then cooled again when he stopped. He imagined the dancers, moving, leaping, a second's pause a threat to the flesh.

"Does nothing matter to *you*, Nicholas?"

"No. *Hier stehe ich; ich bin Nick Anders.*"

"Eh?"

"'Here I stand. I cannot change.' A pun Gian taught me, long ago."

"Oh . . . Tell him that he will have his information. And to expect the needful action to already have been taken."

Anders nodded and began walking across the moon-silvered ice, each footstep leaving a column of fog. Grailer watched him walk away, through the mist—through the smoke—

"Wait. Don't tell him that."

Nick stopped.

"Tell Gian . . . I'm sorry about his gift."

Anders nodded once more and continued across the ice.

Grailer looked down at the sheet of perfect ice. He slipped out of the sandal thongs, stood upon the leather soles, hesitating. This was, he had no doubt, where Pier Jacopo Sforza had died.

Without stepping on the ice, he slipped them on again and followed Anders to the waiting starship.

THIRD MEASURE:

THE WILL

CHAPTER 13

ANGELS FLIGHT

The starship, a thousand times faster than light, rode the night from star to star. Her name was *Glynarian, Silver Field*, though her hull was a scarred sand color and the Pryne envelope around her was shifting and iridescent; it was a name-conceit. The names of things do not always mean what they say.

Just so, though all aboard her were called "travelers," for most by far the travel was merely the means to the end. Some of her consist were en route to the most urgent of rendezvous, some were ship-working to own their own ships, some fled any and all things and people behind them.

One was hunting.

"*Do* you understand, Ari?" said Grailer Diomede to the man who had taught him everything.

Mr. Aristide's face and voice were distorted on Grailer's portable Webset, from the nearness of the Prynes, from the envelope. But his tone and intent read real pure nova.

"I understand that the choice is to fly on or die. The climate is bad here for Webspinners, Grailer. The climate is *hot*."

"I thought it was spring on Marcera."

"Yes, Grailer, late spring. Late as in close to end. As in dying, as in dead, child mine. I've put three in Maracot's pale blue water."

"Three is rare."

"Yes. Three is rare indeed. Two to the Hounds and one to the black knights . . . that last was a student as promising as you, Grailer. When I saw him dead, I saw you . . . and me . . . and all of us."

"Three in a season."

"Three in spring's pale blue. Must I tell you of those in winter's white? Summer comes, and Maracot's water will run sapphire blue; and I do not want you beneath it. There was killing here, child mine, and I do not wish you dead."

"You've survived."

"I have . . . but I have been forced to long measures, and I am very good."

"So am I."

"I am better."

"True. Ari, what if I fall to earth regardless?"

"We'll share wine and talk, as always. You were the finest student in the hardest school; I would not forget that."

"Then I shall see you when *Glynarian* passes by."

"Grailer. Forty of us to this world's billion, and three are dead. None sleep in amber."

"There is no resurrection for the dead I left behind me, Ari. There were no amber vats on Ishtar." Grailer lifted his hands from the Webset's keyboard, reached them out to the crystal screen. "While a man I held died, he told me that Anthony Wayne Bayard had killed him."

"You have told me a great many things. But you did not tell me how."

"I'll find out how. You are the very best at what we do, Ari, and a good teacher as well, and I have not forgotten your lessons of obligation. I will find the people I am hunting."

"Suicide is no one's obligation."

"Say that again, Ari. Make me believe it."

Mr. Aristide cast his light eyes down, and shadow crossed his face. He sighed quietly. Without another word, Grailer broke Web, adding the commands that would block even Ari from calling back. He detached the sixteen-key Ariel from the sixty-four-key portable, folded the larger set, and latched it.

The fabricator in the stateroom wall chimed and delivered. Grailer stripped and shoved his worn clothing down the deweaving slot. He dressed, smelling the faint pine-oil scent of fiber-binder, the new fabric cool and slightly abrasive against his skin.

He added a few accessories from his permanent kit, some touches from the makeup box. The Ariel slipped easily into the top of a boot. He gave the plate by the stateroom door a series of touches, and the curtain of filaments became transparent—that margin of safety, for occupant and caller both—then loosened. Grailer slipped past into the tubular corridor, tapped the external lockplate, and the vertical filaments sealed gastight and opaqued again.

He walked past more filament doors, emergency dive-throughs, arcane shipservice equipment set into the smooth curving walls— walked alone. He was most of an hour Standard late for the gathering on the promenade deck; for the Dance of the Goliards. He smiled. In the personality he had chosen to wear tonight, he would be late and the others would applaud.

His steps fell crisply on the shallow carpet, and the *thum-thum-thum* of the Pryne tubes answered back. *Glynarian* was lightly built for a liner, not large at two hundred meters long and fifty beam, but she was thus all the better for the Prynes, hermetically sealed in their tubes.

No one not intimately connected with the factory in the Magellanic Clouds knew quite what was inside those canisters. All the omnicorps' magic could not tell exactly. Supposedly they were one sort of thing when they ticked forward and another thing when they tocked without reaction—but that was a long way from an engineering drawing. It was an established fact that those who opened them to find out what made them tick were unpleasantly, expensively surprised. And then there was the unified chaos theory of Koniichev mathematics, and the need to look through rectifiers, through distorting glasses, rather than directly at the truth. In many respects a Pryne tube was remarkably like a human being.

"Why, Count Diamant! No one told me *you* were aboard."

Grailer fixed a smile coldly lustful enough to suit the reputation of *der Graf von Diamant* and brushed past the Ship's Lady. She touched him; he ignored it, with some difficulty, then ignited a long white anodyne and stepped onto the broad promenade deck, breathing jasmine smoke.

The deck was a circle thirty meters across. From waist level down it was all white, soft edges and deep furs, seats and tables hovering on humming Hellmann grids. Upward to the ceiling, barely too high for Grailer to touch, the surfaces were black; cool planes of rectified space, false windows on the real universe.

Against the stark interior, all black and white, were people all polychrome. All of them were wild and unique, and as such all the same, in formal dress, court dress, and undress—traders and thieves, who glittered when they walked; soldiers, each with his tale to tell, each one a sole survivor of the '46 Plot; dancers and murderers, artisans and whores of all sexes, in filmy clothing and brilliant skin. Eyes and daggers flashed, hands were busy, tongues and hearts went casually about wickedness and the idle teasing of fate.

There were no gray-robed Wandersmänner, no coral-surpliced Alvanians, no Keelyites staring intently at their pocket perpetual motions. Grailer had not the dazzle of the drabbest one there, and because of that he stirred all the talk.

"Graf von Diamant, there—"

"Diamond G! Of course!"

"What's he trading in now, I wonder—"

Grailer was dressed in tan riding breeches, spitpolished boots, and nothing from the waist up but a black Holbein-hilted dagger strapped to his left arm. His hair was chemically curly, his skin darkened by Ishtari sun and Transagua water during a personality now stuffed down a clothes slot.

The Ship's Lady caught his glance again. She idled with the clasps of her green gown and serpentine collar, and Grailer made his eyeflick a deep long gaze, his gunmetal-colored eyes partly hooded. She laughed silently, the toss of her head putting a hungry shiver into Grailer, and was gone to await him. He puffed at the anodyne and hoped she would not wait too long. He squared his smooth shoulders and took up a prominent position by the forward

screens, knocking ashes to the spotless carpeting and watching it
eat them.

The role of Diamond G excited Grailer less than it once had,
and not much at all now; but it was still wise to Dance with the
Goliards on occasion, to keep up with the measures of the pavane.
And they loved von Diamant for a proper rogue in black and tan, a
real pure nova deathman. Conversation fluttered vampiric around
him, never quite alighting:

"—silks and women, I hear—"

"—no dreams save those he sells you—"

"—gems brighter than your eyes, my dear—"

A CIRCE operator stepped onto the deck then, his steel-shod
boots scuffling loud in the deep rugs. By twos and threes people
paused, looked, then went back to their affairs, as if a spectacularly
lewd joke were being discreetly passed.

Grailer rested his eyes on the black knight. Black the boots, black
the loose trousers and tight jacket of heavy bulletweave, black the
impact gloves that killed with a slap. His/her—ah, hists—helmet
was a dark, shiny globe not unlike the panels of space overhead.
Even the shockwand in its belt loop was black, meaning that its
carrier was given the power to visit death.

Grailer fed his anodyne to the carpet and felt amusement, distance, even lust drain away, hate bubbling up to displace them.

His dagger would go through the Combined Executive's "bullet-
proof" jacket on a solid thrust. Grailer only needed one thrust. And
then the black knight would be dead, dead as Sharon Rose, who
died alone. . . .

But he could not, not here, not now. No hand would restrain
him. None would stop him, before or after the fact. And he would
spin the Web from his room and von Diamant would simply disap-
pear from the ship as if he had never existed.

But he would not. *Timor licentiae conturbat me*, Ari had said
once about the terrible simplicity of the whole procedure.

Grailer turned to the bright false stars in the walls. Once he had
wanted to see past the machinery that distorted the universe back

to reality, see Space as it really was in an envelope of Pryne pseudo-velocity. He was young and had a Webset. He was also a very lucky young man. He was one of those who survived.

Sometimes the truth is too much, Mr. Aristide said (later he would teach Grailer Latin), but though he had sworn on his name never to speak of the incident, his look, the angle of his hands were enough to remind the boy, to cause him agony, over a ship dead and drifting, its Prynes blown like burst hearts and all on board uncaring because the mad mind and the dead don't care.

The boy had had a mother and father. Once upon a time.

"I didn't know," said young Dian—ah, Grailer Diomede, "it all came so easily," and Colonel Augustine, whose name was also Aristide, said indeed so. This is how the training of a Webspinner begins.

But now the hate was souring Grailer's blood, making him crazy, like Sharon Rose, who died insane . . . he wanted suddenly to say, Look, you—I am Diamond G, whom you don't dare even question despite my crimes; but behind the mask I am Grailer Diomede, Webspinner, whom you might shoot down on sight!

Grailer lit another anodyne to control his hands. It wasn't enough. He needed the machine beneath his fingers. He needed to spin the Web.

"My dear Count."

It was the Supersteward, not the Captain. The Captain was indisposed flying the ship, watching an approximation of Real Space under brainstream hypnarcosis. An intravenous trickle of Mysmemedi kinked his timesense; an hour would have passed for him before you reached the second syllable of Hello. What Lifespan gave, the immoral Mem took away.

"Can I provide for you?"

The Supersteward was a little man, not quite a dwarf but spaceship-cargo-sized. His head was as round and white and bare as a hen's egg, and his hands were short and fussy. He was the unhealthy pale of spaceborne people, who hide even from mild ultraviolet after a few massive sunburns. He wore a puffed black tunic with razor-creased white trousers and blended nicely with the wall.

Now he provided just what Grailer needed; a chance to drop into character again. Grailer wrapped a bare, muscular arm and gloved hand around the Supersteward's shoulders, adjusted his expression to clinical disdain, and whispered as if for the stage.

"I require a Web terminal."

"Of course, a range shield for your portable. Shall I have it retrieved?"

"You—shall—*not*. Not if you value the integrity of your hulls. When I *say* I require a terminal . . ." The sentence trailed into an insinuation.

His advance rebuffed, his attempt at omniscience shattered, the Supersteward did not lose poise. Those in his position often suicided over loss of poise. But this one, who loved life and rich foods and the hands of his Ship's Lady, caught himself, fell silent, and led Grailer to a roomful of paraplex electronics. And, thus distracted by the nearness of death, he never wondered what a man traveling under Second Literacy, capable only of operation on the Web, could do with a full programming console.

Not much at all. But Grailer was not Second Literacy. He could of course program from the sixty-four keys of his portable. He could even program from the sixteen keys of an Ariel or public booth; a slow and desperate measure. Meant to save lives, though so recently it had helped take one. And Mr. Aristide had in the depths of Grailer's training taught him to send binary code using two wires scraped bare.

So what could he do with two hundred and fifty-six keys, rows of knobs and slides, a double band of matrix sticks, and a dozen crystal screens spread in a hemisphere before his seat? Only miracles. He played hot Web jazz on his portable; the master console was a four-hundred-piece orchestra with which to play sweet symphonies to Bell Stellar.

Grailer slipped off his gloves and rested his hand lightly on the enable lever. The Prynes heartbeat through his fingertips, his spine, and he thought about what Ari had said. But he did not think for long. He kept thinking of Luke deCastries, burnt and broken and

betrayed. And he had been Bayard's loyal soldier. He thought of
Sharon Rose, who died for love . . . he could not help that. And he
enabled the console. The silver screens flickered to life.

```
ENABLED.
BELL STELLAR COMMUNICATIONS CORPORATION
WEB LOGON 01/32/79 21.33.18
GNOSIS COEXED CODE
??
```

Grailer ran fingers over keys and sticks and the words vanished.
The screens all went silver. He was past the gates of the Web, giving
no name nor password.

opstat, he typed, *nihil opstat*. Strings of numbers went in, slides
were moved just so, and channels closed to common men opened.

```
SERVICE? banquor.
HOW MANY ERCS? unrestricted.
WARNING—WARNING—THIS PROCEDURE IS IN VIO Lauthor
     override subj code auth: banquors ghost.
```

Grailer's music had charms to soothe the savage circuits, hundred-
eyed security routines falling gently to sleep as he danced past.

It was not computer programming. The Web was no computer,
but a construct as large in theoretical size as human civilization,
more complex than many living things. If it were all to be integrated
at once . . . well, that was not possible. Too much of it was perpetu-
ally occupied with normal work. And it was said that the nominal
twenty percent continuously free would not be sufficient for intelligence. That was said. Certain little-known devices attempted to
preserve its truth.

But what Grailer did was not really Web programming either.
Was the Web everywhere? Yes. Was it complex? The word was
scarcely adequate. The Web did not think, it could not. Safeguards
against that had been built in—at least a lot of people hoped. But

programming the thing still required a special mindset, a particular kind of intelligence; a little bit psychiatry, a little bit poetry, a little solving of shifting-block puzzles, a little fourth-order insufficient-data reasoning power. Third Literates were not so much made as born.

Grailer was Fourth Literacy. It was a self-applied term, not official like the other three. He could no more carry it in his Gnosis card than he could breathe vacuum. It was a poor term as well; "Webspinner" was no less precise and more evocative.

Programming was a science, Webspinning an art.

Third Literacy was a talent, Fourth a genius mutation. (Mutation? A loaded word. Ask not what exposure to Koniichev-space might do to fragile sperm and delicate ova.)

Glitchkilling was a richly paid profession. For what Grailer did, CIRCE was authorized to terminate with extreme prejudice.

This is why:

Grailer touched out a complex instruction—a chord. Magnetic bubbles rose to the screens and burst, spelling out the holdings in deuterium, gold, and crystal of a legendary Mysmemedi concentrator on Blejdamsvei. Numbers said that a rich load was arriving at one of the Memking's dark rocks, to be unloaded by men with purchased souls and lacking last names.

It was pure nova Mem, grown under high, high gravity in an atmosphere soupy with arsenides, and none of your synthetic environments. Not a stick, not a leaf of foreign life sullied the iridescent stalks and filaments of the wonderful dream fungus. Grailer knew that load well. He had spun it up himself, from numbers in the *Mysmemedi Grower's Handbook* and from a small text on Mem concentration that was printed on flash-ash film and carried the death penalty for possession.

A run down the flight lists of the Asgard Complex turned up a Freya Pharmaceuticals chillship in just the right place. Its pilots got a midnight callout, which they obeyed cursing. The portdusters had had choice words too; it was as well they did not know they loaded stolen goods.

And now the Memking awaited the ship's arrival, and the main threads of the theme joined harmony:

An officious voice invoking the Combined Intersystem Regulation and Control Executive, its visage blackly masked, told the chill-ship pilots they were secretly transporting corpses infected with Theta Fever delta-strain—execute stellar disposal, return home, tell no one.

The image of a mousy little man told the unloaders on the cold rock that they were there as a blind to fool the black knights—the drop would not be made. Stand down. Forget it.

A square-jawed face with a scar stitched across an empty eye-socket appeared to the Memking, and through a screen of obscenities announced that the deal was a flameout, the Mem was all weed.

"Did you deal with those involved?" The Memking was trying to remember when and where he had hired this man.

"Cold solid, lord mine. In fact, we're not done with a couple of 'em." Square-jaw grinned.

"You did right. Keep the magic." The man with the missing eye saluted and broke Web. The dreamtrader smiled after the good new soul he'd just bought. The man had looked right all along.

Grailer was always amused by the readiness of people to listen to his angels. Send audio-only and they would suspect every word, but have a generated image mouth along and the barriers all fell down.

The fugue for dreamtraders drew to a finish:

The pilots remembered tales of whole planets wiped clean by the mere *gamma*-strain of Theta Fever and did their job with dispatch. They fell back to earth to find a month's paid leave waiting.

The men on the rock, roared at by mice and disillusioned once too often, began plotting their break with the trade.

The Memking, who for professional reasons could not confront his leading supplier, was forced to sever ties. And when the supplier discovered the loss of a shipment of Limbex-290, a rare and elusive substance that paralyzed the will while leaving the muscles directable, he of course countersanctioned.

And a generous number of ercs were coded and fired from one legitimate bank memory to another. On the way, however, the signal detoured briefly between synapses and passed through a low-range repeater that altered the Gnosis code of the recipient.

It was an elegant, subtle, complex diversion, more satisfying and much, much broader in effect than the ercstacker tampering of Grailer's childhood. "It has two virtues over money spun from Web noise and error," Mr. Aristide had said after a demonstration of the technique. "One, it's backed up by something, somewhere; no one can put his hand beneath and discover it floating unsupported. Two, there is a moral satisfaction for the honest outlaw in cheating the dishonest citizen."

"How will I know who I may take from?"

"*You will be honest,*" Ari intoned, his dark brows knit, his knuckles white on his white wand and red cloak. "Any man you can be honest with, and still touch his possessions, him you may take from freely. You will find this to include two types: better men than you think exist, who will not be hurt, and men on the other extreme, who deserve the injury. Both will have reasons not to cry transgressor."

There was a green flicker on a peripheral screen. Grailer's fingers arched. His neck stiffened. But there was no howl, no prickle. The flash was gone; it had only been a transient. A fluctuation in the Webflow.

Grailer sat still, air forced from the ventilators drying the sudden sweat on his back and chest. It seemed to him that Diego Cadiz must be laughing.

But not for long, he thought quite calmly, for I have killed over the Hounds, and I shall not be diverted from my goal now.

Words contract. They mutate. *Parallel multiplex electronic devices* become *paraplex electronics* become *plextronics* and occasionally even *plexy.* Just so, *prae judico* becomes *prejudice* becomes the catchphrase *terminate with extreme . . .* among the black knights of CIRCE, who did not, who could not show signs of even so base and elementary an emotion. CIRCE in fact killed with extreme nothing.

Grailer's hatred had simmered down to a thick, heavily sweet syrup of revenge. No, that was too severe a word; what he planned was not reprisal but riposte. Grailer would have revenge for the thousand injuries of CIRCE, but a master's revenge. No slaughters. One drop of heart's blood.

First Bayard and his accomplices, and then you, Diego. And you never cease bleeding, do you? Only tape the wound over.

He reached a hand into Seren Glasu Transport's booking center and shuffled the cards a bit. Green Star was fashionable but fly-by-starlight nonetheless. The parent omnicorps of Thor Lines or Venice Space or Starwinds were a good bit more difficult to finesse.

Pick a card, keep it; it records that one Dominick Garnett, consulting engineer (and Gaean), Third Literacy, boarded SGT's *Glynarian* at Agramonte, destination Perdition Twenty.

The magician cuts the cards. Look at yours again; the jack is now a king. Magnetic domains have changed their tiny minds to say that the Count von Diamant, trader and speculator, Second Literacy, is aboard, destination The Dolichrone. A special notification flies automatically to CIRCE Sector Headquarters concerning the motions of the notorious Diamond G.

Grailer closed the file, wiping away the fingerprints of his work. Then he broke Web and began deliberately entering miskeys, lighting enough ERROR signals on the console to lock it up. He pulled the Ariel from his boot and paged the Supersteward and asked for—demanded, rather—the portable Webset and travel case from his cabin.

To his everlasting personal credit, the bloodless little man did not even hint at a smile when he saw the goof-locked board and *der Graf* drumming his fingers upon it. Only when he was safely back in his own cabin, with the door and annunciator jammed, did he burst out laughing. Grailer watched him, from the new room he'd ordered up. Then he went to find the Lady in waiting.

Neither did the Steward laugh at the Marcera fall, when a First Lit named Perceval Demonde departed. Demonde was an obvious St. Audrey, carrying just enough education to pass him offworld, who had never once been visible all his flight from who-cared-where and entered the portpod wearing garish red and green doublet and hose and—Morning Star Shining!—a *rucksack*.

Ah, well, mused the Supersteward. Next planetfall was The Dolichrone. One would not find a Perceval Demonde *there*.

CHAPTER 14

THAT WHICH WAS

The first man on the planet had been of narrow vision. He had seen the blue falls fading and named her Marcera, Withering World. He was purely wrong. It was a beautiful and ever-new planet, even to those who loved space best. There was more water to land than had even been on wet old Earth, broad blue oceans and thick white clouds that gave it a searchlight albedo. Her land was all dense green woods, and tan savanna, and mossy riven rocks, with nothing like a desert or steppe, with no sterility anywhere. There were plants, tall and colorful, on the icepacks.

And if your taste in worlds ran to violent scenic wonder, there were the cliffs. Two- and three-km planes of perpendicular rock stood where plate had slipped past plate, bands of strata like madras silk risen stark into the sky. Some of the cliffs were especially high, and some had waterfalls, and some changed with the seasons. The very best, on which was laid the city of Maracot Falls, did all of these.

Maracot's water ran pale blue with spring. Late spring now, and day by day more salts of copper leached into the falls. Soon it would be summer, and the blue of the water would be electric; as transparently beautiful as toxics are, as bitterly sweet as life. Fall would come, and a falls of silver, bouncing and ringing like a shower of coins through a miser's fingers. Some would leave the city then, and not see winter's white; but those who stayed spoke of moonstones and lace and a column of light three thousand meters high.

Grailer fell to earth, to Marcera, to his home of gone years, riding the ballistic spiral from heaven to rushing rapids. He saw the city as an animal of colored glass crouched upon the falls for most of their length, the beast's talons deep in mossy rock, back arched. Maracot Falls, the vertical city, with elevators and linears instead of heliportransit, ventilators a thousand meters long, arched crystal bridges and echo tubes and viewdecks built in the awe and the love of the falling water.

He saw the city as a new thing, relearning it, and it made his eyes sting.

The pod touched with a rolling bump and shelled open. As the portdusters wheeled it away, four smiling people in seasonal color met Grailer. He gave his hand to the woman and asked for the vending wall.

He dropped magic in the slot and punched up heart's desire; a salted double-helix of meat and crisp dough, sweet fruit that fell from a tree behind the vendor's glass. The current fashion in drinks was a punch that sparked and puffed vapor. Grailer passed it up for swirlcolor wine in a stiff-film disposable goblet. He ate well, from hunger. He had been eating tiny meals for the most part; his stomach had seemed insulted by food.

He ran out of coins quickly. Percy Demonde's Gnosis card went into a slot, red-striped, an eyepopper. Grailer stared into the goggles mounted on the bank terminal. The Web read the card, shot pulses to parts of itself on a dozen planets, came up with a backwater file that was quite convinced that a man of the given identity had several thousand ercs on deposit. In fact, the memory said, the card has not been recently updated: Mynheer Demonde has through self-application and study learned to program and code upon the Web. The terminal cut his elevated literacy rating in at once. Then it flashed green incoherent light into Grailer's retinas and showered jingling magic into his hands. He shivered, without wanting to. He could get new eyes, no problem, but it would be a long, dark, lonely wait. It would slow his motions down. It would interfere with his vengeance.

He held a one-erc coin up to the light, looked through its center. White light bounced from the microgrooves inside the ring, casting the clear color image of a raptor-bird poised for attack. Grailer tossed the coin to the guide girl. One erc was a dismissal. Five would have been an accolade, ten an invitation, fifty a command, point five an insult. Despite the Economic Reference Counter, based in energy and power rather than metals of romantic association, hard money had its uses.

He dropped another coin, made a prayer to BellStel from a public booth, and Ari shuffled together on the screen. No, his test pattern did—a calculated affront. But his voice was there, and, fully aware that he spoke with an angel, Percy Demonde announced his arrival and imminent appearance, following a walk and a talk and an elevator ride. Then he broke Web and went to the falls. He missed the falls.

Grailer stood on a railed plateau that crossed falls-head, water rushing beneath his feet and leaping into space, sheets and veils thrusting and shattering into rainbow with sounds of thunder and steam. The skyport was set back from the brink, and on either side a wing of the highest-priced apartments on the planet arced out and over. Marceran architecture was typical of scenic worlds; spare and angular, in metal and maximal glass. Grailer saw colors, and leaded pictures, and numberless panels of photochrome turned dark in the afternoon sun. Here and there solar cells glittered gilt, open windows showed dull, elevators crawled twinkling. Grailer saw through the wall of a distant elevator and used his imagination.

He hitched up his rucksack and went to find Amanda.

> > >

"You shouldn't have had any trouble," she said. "Amanda Jordan Whiteriver, Elevator One-sixty-three on Maracot Falls. Ask anyone."

"I didn't have to. I remembered."

"What did you remember, Dio? Times have changed. I've changed."

How had she? Her legs were still long, long, smooth, and turned so fine, her breasts aimed perfectly, her hands light-boned with long pink nails. Grailer reached out and put his fingertips on her coppery throat, just near the collarbone, and when she twisted away as if burned, he knew there was something there he had not touched before.

Then she turned back, and there was a tension in the movement that he had not before felt, a hollowness in her cheeks that he had not lain with, a light in her eyes that he had not reconciled to his own.

"Amanda, it was not so long."

She fingered the heavy magnetic key that hung from her chain belt, the symbol of her station. She hesitated as if waiting for something to be said. Then she unclasped the belt, opened a small door in the elevator's command panel, and inserted the key. She paused again. "CIRCE can override this. I never knew that."

Grailer nodded. "I can fix it." He reached for his Webset; she grabbed his hand.

"No, if you know you're safe you won't understand." She touched his doublet seam, opened it. The elevator continued slowly down.

His name had been Philip, she said, Philip and Phelps and Pell *et alia*. Mr. Aristide had shown him the values of plural personality, and he had taken to it as a black swan to flight.

Grailer kept control. "Oliver Pell? Was that one of his names?"

"Oliver Pell—Philip Otto. Yes. Did you know him, Dio?"

"I met him once. That was all."

He had been nova, this Philip. In the first few years of Grailer's career he had established four identities, could produce documents for them in a few hours, had opened a line of credit in five figures. In the same time, Philip Otto had six selves, all check-tight and free-traveling, who drew on a megerc balance. Four of him ran a charitable organization called The Fifth Horseman that was (on magnetic file) a close competitor to Anthony Relief. He was loose, untight with his plans in Amanda's car (some things haven't changed, Grailer thought), said he couldn't believe in rivalry among the merciful. Even if his nine digits of Economic Reference Counters were more magnetism and less deuterium than General Anthony Wayne

Bayard's, magnetism was as spendable, felt the same from this side of the Webscreen. . . .

"Oh, no, Amanda, he didn't. Ari would have warned him."

"Mr. Ari did."

But he went to Bayard anyway, card in hand, sales proposal wired neatly on his Webset. Buy me out, Oliver Pell had said, my angels grow weary. Fuse our businesses, serve the starving and the homeless with doubled efficiency and reduced overhead. My magic is at your service, my terms most reasonable.

And perhaps we'll even get you a seat at the Sidi el-Kutra.

Grailer felt his knuckles sting with the crack of a wand. Ari had let him have a pair upside his head too, for emphasis. "Learn the lesson again, child mine, learn it well or the next blow will be another's and sharper: *You must be honest.* You must be honest with all men, Spinners or not. Lie to the Web; you can spin it and blinder it, and the damage you do can be mended. But men are hurt beyond repair, and they always avenge their wrongs."

Had Philip's hands and head been whipped numb, Grailer wondered, or did he mistrust, or did he love lies too well?

No matter why. They had been close, Amanda and Philip, on the soft pile of the elevator floor, and had not noticed its stop. Fingers had pressed on her throat suddenly, a hand in an impact glove; and a voice from behind a black face bubble said "Combined Executive. We're CIRCE. You'll be all right." Four hands held her down, not roughly; four spread Philip against the wall. Two hands assembled a quiet gun and fired it into his body. Four times— their trademark. Once through the brain, instant death, then into the throat. Through the heart. Down, penetrating the diaphragm. Let the victim have the hardest of amber contracts; let them freeze him. Let him wait for a cure for those wounds.

Amanda ran long fingers down the new glass, pausing where a slug had left a dent and fracture in the old, leaving imaginary prints in ghost blood. She looked at the crumpled carpet and shook. "For the love of the Spirit, why? Why does Mr. Ari stay locked in his rooms, and drink wine, and weep tears into the falls? What is it your kind have done to men that they have the right to kill you?"

"We have something they don't have. No, that's too bitter, too simple. We have a power they don't really understand and wouldn't trust themselves with if they did."

"You're the only people I know that I *can* trust."

"Oh, we love our friends, but there are so many others." Grailer looked at the city rising past him and felt very small. "The Second Poet Dylan said, 'To live outside the law you must be honest.' Philip tried to swindle a man. He gave CIRCE what they want from us." He laughed without humor. "But I'm hunting that same man for mass murder. Was Philip really the honest man, then? Whose morality is the lie?"

"Dio, I need an answer to a question."

"Amanda, I only wish I had one."

Half an hour passed.

There had been a time for Grailer when all women were Sharon Rose. He loved well and hotly, and knew it was only a prelude to madness and death. But he could not stop loving, because he had loved her, and he could not save them, because he had not saved her. The Geisthounds had killed someone, and it was him.

Ten years—ten long years in love with death. And as he had drawn close to a year of bodily age, Amanda had taken him into her arms and her starsprinkled coarse black hair, and made him see a world of light and falling water, and see her as red-skinned Amanda and not pale Sharon Rose. He was close to her, and she did not die; and he was suddenly free to be close to anyone again.

Now Grailer lay beside her and knew that someone had died, and it was her. For her, now, all men were Philip Otto; and he could not do for her what she had done for him.

Half an hour passed, emptily.

Amanda pulled her key, and the elevator opened. Grailer slung on his pack and went out, hearing her call after: "For the love of the Spirit, come back!"

But he knew that she meant later, when there was something to be said, and kept walking.

Oliver Pell, the clever devil, who bid so sharp at the DESA auctions but never seemed to win one.

Was that a reason to kill him? The players at the Sidi had given him the right to join the game, and his close play had forced the others into a little more honesty. It would have been a true crime only if his plexy organization had taken on a real contract.

Was his swindling of Bayard reason to kill him? It broke even the Spinners' own laws—but the Spinners did not kill. There were only two possible causes of his death: CIRCE, for a Webspinner, or Bayard, for a thief. For the first there was no answer. The second could have been set right without—another—death. . . .

Grailer felt responsible in a great and terrible way. He had let the fears he'd forgotten he held sidetrack him. He might have saved Pell, if he only had not seen him as an enemy.

It would be small service indeed to avenge him, now that he knew his enemy. Now that he had the Web in his hands once more.

He went to see the man who could help him.

>   >   >

Mr. Aristide lived down near falls-impact, where the carpets were less deeply piled, the colors more muted, the art in the narrow high corridors more classically representational. The sound of falling water was less violent, more sibilant, with an accompaniment of cymbals crashing below. An older sort lived here, a more established and introspective group. Only the rooms on the brink rented for more than these.

Grailer keyed Ari's door. It did not open. Instead a calm female angel Grailer knew as Ariadne said, "Please identify."

"Perceval Demonde, for Mr. Aristide."

"Physical identification is requested."

Grailer thought a moment and fumbled Percy Demonde's credit flash into the slot.

"I will page Mr. Augustine."

At last the door opened. Grailer stepped through and saw Ari, and his smile froze on his face.

Ari's cool blue eyes were sunken and threaded with blood. His cheekbones thrust like wings. He no longer had a mustache, and his dark hair was brushed straight back; evidently he now found a splash and a stroke more appropriate than careful depilation and styling. His gown and trousers were too clean, too crisp; red and white cloth-silks that he could not have been living in, that must have been put on for show. Or worse yet, that he had been sitting in passively, still. He held a tall sweating glass garnished with a fading flower, and took a gulp from it before speaking.

"Come in, Grailer. Since you must come, come in."

The apartment was low-ceilinged and broad—rare and exorbitant in the vertical city—decorated in white wood and red leather, with accents of gold. There were leather-bound books in carved racks, mirrors flat and curved, half a wall of blinking plextronics, and racks of tape. Holographic musicians pounded out a beat in their cube, and surround sound played. The song was "Polydore Virgil Magus"; Grailer tried not to hear it. He was playing lead guitar in the holospace. Somewhere in the background multicymbals chimed. Rang on Sharon's fingers.

I may not be here when you waken from your dream

From your dream

Ari's taut face softened a bit, and he killed the music with a wave of his signet ring.

"I am sorry if it brings the evil things back. I thought it might cheer me to hear your hymn of praise. But there is little joy in pride gone stale . . . and mine has all grown stale.

"But you are here now, and if I fear for you, I am glad to see you. Wine?"

"You know me better than that."

A pass of the ring, and a bottle and two cut-crystal goblets revolved from the wall. Ari sniffed the open bottle and poured. "An . . . interesting vintage. There are biscuits, if you wish."

Grailer sprayed a mouthful against his palate. His eyes widened. "Excellent. I've never tasted one just like this."

"And you might not have, nor even known its like. It's a freak, a miracle hybrid, from the Stanvery vineyards on Pandarai. They meant to keep it locked away till Time turned to vinegar, marketing a case every century or so at an . . . appropriate price."

"I presume there was an error somewhere?"

"Alas, a transposition of coordinate numbers caused vine stocks to be shipped hither and yon, beyond all recovery. And with each stock went a case of this superb grape-juice . . . since, after all, *in vino veritas*."

"What of the Stanverys?"

"They have most of a vineyard and most of a cellar. Just not the only vineyard and cellar. Here's to Pinot Pandarai, premier grand cru."

"Real pure nova." They clicked glasses and drank. For a few minutes the only sound in the room was the rumble of the falls. Ari had single-pane windows, closed now but hinged to open inward, and sonic dampers turned up halfway. Nothing delicate or water-soluble was near the window.

"You intend," Ari said quietly, "on hunting General Anthony Wayne Bayard, and avenging upon him. Let us hold burning court, then."

Grailer put down his glass. "Simple enough. I was working on Ishtar with an engineer named Lucas deCastries. We were uphanging an arcology—that's all. Anthony Relief was supplying food and teachers.

"There was tension, I could see that clearly enough.—Tension, nothing! We were at each others' throats by the end of a few weeks. Then someone did a very stupid thing—I can't say her name again. But who would have expected all the killing? So—much—killing."

"Your friend died."

"A lot of my friends died. But Luke—I could have been there to help him. He could fight . . . but there wasn't any fight left in him anymore. With someone there with him, he'd have survived. But I was trapped, caging the Hounds. I got rid of them just in time to see him die. And to—and to *kill—I should have trapped them quicker!*" Grailer's fist on the table made his wineglass jump.

"And you think the teachers and feeders were responsible."

"Luke said something to me, while his brains spilled in my lap. His last words were 'Bayard betrayed us. The Lorraine Cross.' And up until then he would have cut his own throat before saying any such thing."

"True or not?"

"True or not.

"When I first got involved in this, Ari, I was told that Anthony Relief was taking Development bids on desperate terms. But the real secret is the violence. This—*thing*—has happened before."

"Perhaps they're cutting too close, hiring untrained people. The omnicorps make it steadily harder for small business."

"No. It was Gian Sforza himself who gave me my data. And it wasn't the omnicorps who were pressing the case; it was Philip Otto. And Luke wasn't untrained, nor undertrained."

"I bow to superior counsel. Your investigations afield seem to have produced more than mine at home."

"You've been investigating Bayard?"

"He is not far from here, Grailer. And when I heard of the track you were on, I did what I could to preserve your life. I have been hired."

Ari had never in his life used that word.

"Why didn't you tell me?"

Ari faced the window. "Because I knew it would bring you here, Grailer. I have stood with this window open, watching and listening as my students and friends were buried in the rapids. Men and women with their nerves eaten by Geisthounds, with their bodies shattered by . . . justice. . . . Grailer, I see you, and I know your work, and I think, perhaps . . . I need not worry, there will be no problem . . . but there is. There is, and will be.

"And there is another facet to the matter. I do not trust my employers' motives."

"You wouldn't work for CIRCE." Why had he said that?

"Child! Your travels have unhinged you! I made the first joke about what that cruel lady changes her men into. In fact . . . well. A moment. The Foxfire Foundation hired me."

"Foxfire? *She* was Foxfire. They thought Bayard was a murdering . . . she said . . . but she also said they were wrong."

"I suggest you ask them yourself what they think of him. Not mentioning our connection, of course. They might provide you with some cover."

"Will I need cover?"

"You have seen Amanda." It was no question.

"Philip made an error. I saw him setting up Bayard financially. He wouldn't have wired Bayard; why should he?"

"Philip had something else on his mind." Ari swept a pile of loose change from a stiff folder on the table. He handed it to Grailer, who saw the CIRCE sigil at the top—the balances supported by a sword.

"You spun CIRCE directly—" Grailer took a swallow of wine from the bottle.

"Gentle with the rosé, Grailer. The teacher knows things that the student must learn on his own."

Grailer snapped open the folder, uncertain of what to expect, unprepared for what he found.

CIRCE DIRECTIVE	
OBJECTIVE	Termination W.E.P.
SUBJECT	Pell, Oliver/NOT RELIABLE
	SEE DESCRIPTION
REFS	Bayard, A W, General CIGF (Ret)
CLASSIFICATION	Strike Directive/ /
	PARTICULARS FOLLOW
	Final Strike
	No Witness Prejudice
	No Disposal
AUTHORITY	UniComCode Sec 20

"Then CIRCE didn't just find him out."

"No, child mine. He was far too good a Spinner for that."

"Ari—Ari, I thought—"

"Yes?"

Grailer went to Ari's wall Web. "During the flight from Ishtar I looked this up in Kuppering."

"Oh, God, child, not *Intact Arthur*. What a dreadful . . ."

"No. *Intact Chevalerie*. It doesn't make much sense . . . but it makes enough."

Bayard

And those who bore the guns?

Aide

                                        They all are slain.

Good knight, what does provoke thy fearful wrath
Toward cannoneers, when those with sword or bow
Receive unending mercy from thy hands?

Bayard

Canst speak to me of chivalry, when knights,
The flowers of true chivalry, are dead,
Ungodly slain, by missiles hurled on flames,
The demons of this—*anti-chivalry*?

Aide

They are but weapons.

Bayard

                                 Weapons forged in Hell.

Aide

Good knight, let not revenge possess thy mind.
There was that Danish prince.

Bayard

                               I knew him well.

"I'm beginning to wonder what General Anthony Wayne Bayard is really capable of. And also if there's any limit to the amount of hate that I can feel."

CHAPTER 15

IN THE BEGINNING, IS NOW

Grailer wasted an hour trying to sleep. He settled for another hour of relaxation exercises and breath control, which soothed raw nerves and enervated muscles, but only recharged, did not refresh.

Morning was near. The sun rose all at once for Maracot Falls. Orange light sprayed across the glass face of the city, striking veins of gold, turning the spring-blue water into the green of dead Earth's seas.

Grailer dressed in clothes fresh from the fabricator and went to breakfast in an echo tube, enveloped in comforting pink noise and slow air cool from the night.

He entered a linear, dropped magic in the slot and punched up heart's desire. The linear car hummed and shot upward, the Hellmann in its floor keeping Grailer's weight constant and his inertia null. The car moved a thousand meters up and ninety across in twenty seconds, counting five seconds to switch tracks. Grailer did not, however, take the linear for speed. He rode it because, just then, he could not have enjoyed an elevator ride.

He was dressed as a Wandersmann, in sandals and hooded robe of thick gray felt. A thermal pistol and telescoped battlestaff were thrust into the white cords around his waist.

The Foxfire Foundation's corridor was decorated in forest. Grailer stepped from the car and felt living grass against his feet, cool and wetly sensual. Woody stems and dangling vines lined the close high walls, green-leafed branches diffusing the overhead light. The air was moist, misty. Surround sound played bird songs and wind and the rustlings of unseen animals. The office door was carved wood, burl with a sweeping figure. There was no keypanel, nor slot, nor screen; just a heavy brass mallet hinged on the door that fell against a worn brass plate. He lifted it and let it fall, and a woman opened the door.

The receptionist had long red hair that was so clearly natural it made Grailer's heart jump, wore iron jewelry with a handmade look and a bare-shouldered wraparound of red cloth just rough enough to be natural product. She led him to a waiting room, dressed in more of the same: long grass on the floor, wingbacked chairs woven from plant fiber, light angled to simulate wild-world sun. There was a holospace in the corner, but even it was framed in wood and had no visible controls. A loop program called "Change—For the Better?" offered five minutes of war, famine, pestilence, and death, all brought on by the march of civilization to the boundaries of the universe. Grailer watched it three times.

A deep, rolling voice came from the curtain of vines the secretary had vanished through. "Mr. Gray? Come in, come in."

"I come," Grailer said, and brushed the plants aside. "Mr. Coughlin Delaplane, I am Damian Gray. I am sworn."

The hall had been grass, reception wood. Delaplane's office was stone. It was paneled with a light, smooth marble, rising to a high arched ceiling cut in relief with dragons and eagles. On the walls were fixtures of black wrought iron and hangings of tapestry and parchment.

Delaplane sat behind a desk of heavy dark wood set with bronze rivets and a top of flawless rose quartz. He wore a gown of bulky brocade, deep blood red and vaguely priestly, like an Alvanian might wear but more opulent. Gian Paolo Sforza wore such cloth as a matter of course, but Gian was wealth incarnate.

It was very quiet in the office. Grailer saw Maracot's water roll over the brink through a hingeless double-pane window with dampers up all the way.

Delaplane was stout, but not fat. He pressed the tips of thick fingers together, fixed Grailer with twinkling brown eyes, and grinned. "So, Wandersmann, what may we do?"

"I am told that you know of an imBalance."

"We do, oh, we always do, as you must know if you know what we do here."

"You attempt to preserve the Balance."

"As you seek to correct it. Oh, yes, Mr. Gray, the Foxfire Foundation has worked well with the Wandersmen, well and closely."

"You then have facts for me?"

Delaplane pressed a button hidden beneath his desktop. The secretary appeared with a cassette, which Delaplane snapped into a concealed wall slot. One of the tapestries on the wall sparkled and dissolved into a holographic image.

It was a war scene, hellfire lighting and blinding explosions. The picture was silent. The pickup tightened on a man in CI Ground Forces officer's uniform, red and green singlesuit with a white raincape. A communications coronet was on his head, three general's bands on his shoulder. All around him men were running in all directions. He seemed to be screaming something at a group of them, and fired a Masada Works ripgun from the hip. One of the bursts caught three men, tore them into spurts of blood and pieces of flesh, shocking splinters of metal and bone through their bodies. The pickup zoomed, showed the corpses in a dirty heap. They wore the same uniform as the general.

"General Anthony Wayne Bayard, Defender of the Progressive Faith," Delaplane said. "Presented here in ten minutes of concentrated murder."

Death from the muzzles of guns. Beneath the treads of wartracks. Death from near orbit, descending on the intense blue geodesics of radpumped lasers, on the glider wings of strike shuttles, on the flow-charted winds of biochem aerosols.

All that was lacking, Grailer thought, was some record of a tectonic drop; but had Bayard actually ordered one of those? He couldn't remember.

"Lorraine. Six thousand dead. Two hundred of them Bayard's own men, forced to withdraw into his command position. The incident became known as the, ah . . ."

Bayard betrayed us. The Lorraine Cross.

"Driocchi. Twenty-one thousand. No wartracks on the other side, no orbital support.

"Hammerschmied, Griesheim, Lict's Keep. Griesheim, I should say, had no weapons larger than a small arrow-thrower. And no explosives, no, no gunpowder at all."

"War is not our concern. War Balances itself."

"I am surprised that you consider the actions of DEVAFORCE to be war."

"You have not yet named or shown a DEVAFORCE action."

"Oh, my, yes. Data is so hard to come by concerning that period. But there is later data. Ilse! Second cartridge. Ah. Here."

This time the pictures were fuzzy stills, flicking larger and from shallower angles. They seemed to have been taken during a fall to earth.

A horizon appeared, green jungle. A smudge on the trees, a clearing, a village, huts.

Bodies.

A woman, limbs askew, cut, torn. Ripped—

Grailer was sick, felt cold sweat drip down his back onto the Webset buckled over his kidneys. But Damian Gray could not be sickened by anything he spent so much time with. So Grailer hid inside Damian and stayed cool, calm.

"Is this a DEVAFORCE action?"

"No. Mr. Gray, there is a chemical you may know of called Ceptex-Four. It is, bluntly, a sterility drug."

"Is it harmful?"

"Harmful? It is not toxic. I take it, in fact. Many take it; you would not, I suppose you do not, ah, such. Not toxic, no. Effective, safe, yes. Unlike some such drugs, there is no, ah, damping of the drives. But *harmful*?

"What is a child, here, now, Wandersmann? You see everything, as you go; you surely know. Children are a surprise, a brief joy but an inconvenience, something to be handed away and raised by others and preferably not seen except to—well. The family no longer exists, Mr. Gray. It has been so casually destroyed that who gives a thought to whether birth is allowed or inhibited?

"But on nobler worlds children have a meaning. They are the continuance of the species. They are the proof of human strength. They are immortality, of a purer kind than Lifespan treatments.

"The people of this village were hungry, until Anthony Wayne Bayard fed them. Then they were sterile. They thought it was witchcraft, thought it was uncleanness. How could they have guessed the truth?

"And then there was an explosion. A madness."

Grailer raised his hood. "It is not just. I will seek him out. Shall any be spared?"

"A man named Ardrey. He is a hunter. He has his own tasks."

"I did not think you dealt with hunters."

"Not of innocent animals."

>   >   >

Grailer returned to his room to change clothes and selves again. Damian Gray had been a good choice to meet Delaplane, he thought. The Wandersmann saw every sort of falsehood the human mind could project, and shuffled it off as just some more of the omnipresent imBalance.

He had expected Delaplane to be as phony as any other True Believer. But the man was much *too* transparent. He was putting on a deliberate show for a man he thought was a soul-sworn killer.

There had been no fertility riot on Ishtar.

Perhaps Delaplane played the glaze-eyed fanatic to impress the hooded fanatic. Perhaps that was how he put distance between himself and the murderers around him.

>   >   >

Grailer stepped into the linear car, dropped a coin, and punched for Anthony Relief. He looked through smoky photochrome at the plain below Maracot's scarp, forests and fields with only a little regularity imposed upon them.

He didn't care at all what worried Coughlin Delaplane, he found. He would do what he had set out to do with the man's help or in spite of it. He was no more than another source of data, another weapon.

The car stopped short. The door opened. Grailer had his hand poised to knock down, his legs tensed to run.

Green dense cloak and soft shoes were what he saw, black bushy hair and opaque glasses. Dylan Treece.

"Good day, Doctor. Or is it Lord Doctor today?"

Dr. Taliessin stepped aboard, gave the command panel a rap with his knuckles, and the car started again. "Not every cape confers nobility, lad." He put both hands behind his back, beneath his cape, brought out the disk of crystal and gold.

> *"My Geordie will be hanged in a golden chain,*
> *'Tis not the chain of many—*

"Why are you hellbent, lad?"

"What do you know of it?"

"I know you came back from a disaster, and you talk like you're going to make another. You've worn staff and sidearm, and I've a feeling they're not purely for show."

"Did Gian Paolo Sforza tell you?"

"We haven't spoken of late. His aide, the crackly man, and I do not get along."

"How about Ari?"

"Is he home?"

"He's home. So you just found the data on an open file?"

Dr. Taliessin shrugged. "Only lies care if they're believed; truth, never. I'm not here to condemn, lad. Only to warn. Take your vengeance. But start no wars."

"This is a war."

"Grailer, lad, the Last True War was before your birth. If you'd ever looked at it, you'd have learned: Anybody will war on anybody, once there's a capital-letter Cause.

"The minstrel boy went forth to war,
  A kingly crown to gain—

"But he ends up dead, like they all do."
"I'm a Webspinner like you, and—"
"The Eschaton is immanent, and I'll slit your eyes if you say different. What's Webspinning, lad? A word. Take your vengeance, lad. Kill your one, but do no more. Take care of the Joyful Plague.

"Two brothers on their way,
  Two brothers on their way,
  One wore blue
  And one wore gray—
  All on a beautiful morning."

Grailer had his feet planted, his hands clutching his engineer's sash. "It's not what you think."
"Lad, it never has *anything* to do with thought.

"Two girls waiting on a railroad track,
  Waiting for their Johnnies to come back,
  One wore blue
  And one wore black—"

Grailer closed his eyes tightly. When he opened them again, Taliessin had vanished. He had left behind a card, on the floor; Grailer stared at it.
Its motion had been stopped with the tide rolled out, the body on the sand high and dry where the ten white swords pinned it.

> > >

Grailer waited barely five minutes after his arrival at the relief agency. He brushed imaginary dust from the shoulder of his light metallic singlesuit and shook hands with Bayard.
The General's fingers were rough, his movements slow. But his

gray eyes were bright behind gold wire glasses, and he smiled easily, brushing silver hair from his forehead. He was dressed in a single-suit of military cut and color, with white trim added and without insignia. He wore no medals or badges at all, and his boots were heavily scuffed.

The floor and ceiling of his office were grids of white squares. The ceiling panels cast shadowless light. One wall was cork, one magnetic, one plextronic, and the fourth books and screens. Desk and chairs were free curves of black plastic.

In one corner, near an open, fully damped window on the falls, stood an oddly tall woman in a metal-silk dress that covered from her chin to the floor. She held a silver walking stick hilted with ebony. A smooth white pack was clipped to her shoulders.

"Victoria, this is the engineer who wants to join us. Jim Knight, this is Doctor Victoria Osmanli, our cultures expert."

Cultures. A part of the guilt must be hers. What?

"Pleased," she said, in a beautiful smooth soprano.

"Very pleased," Grailer said. He could not help examining her face. One eye was blue, the other brown. The skin of the brown-eyed side, the left, was tight and slick. She was smiling, but the left side of her mouth bent down.

Grailer caught himself staring. "You've got wings," he said, as an excuse.

Dr. Osmanli laughed, high and ringing. "It never fails, Wayne, you see? Men, they fly free, without thinking, to build their towers. But show them an old lady who scrapes the ground, and wings are something strange again." She put a hand to her waist. The Hellmann pack changed tone and lifted her a few centimeters.

"My legs will walk, but not carry. The wings will carry, but not walk. It's a partnership."

"I regret—"

"Oh, you regret nothing. At least you spoke up about the damned thing, didn't wait for me to drift sidewise or dance on the ceiling. Wayne! Hire this fellow."

Bayard was lighting an anodyne from a golden crux ansata on a black base. He put the lighter down next to a pair of sculptured gold hands bearing a bowl of flame. The fire formed a stylized A.

"Right, Knight. You're hired," he said, grinning. "Just one thing before you go to work. What is it exactly that you do?"

"I should tell you, General, Doctor, I'm not looking for a permanent job. I like to free-lance."

"Fair enough."

"I'm a computer engineer. A glitchkiller."

Bayard broke his anodyne in his fingers. He spoke evenly.

"I know where I've seen you. You were at the DESA once, with that ball of barb-wire Anders. You don't work for Florentine?"

"I'm a free-lance, like I said. Everybody's got glitches. You'd be surprised at the magic I do. . . ."

"Why us?" Dr. Osmanli said coldly.

Grailer clenched his teeth, blew out a breath. This was tougher than he had thought it would be. "Alphabetical order," he said, and waited to be struck dead.

"Knight," Bayard said, laughing with an almost hysterical relief, "name your price."

Grailer grinned, rather stupidly, but did not laugh. He was pleased by the openness of these people, but not disarmed. Never disarmed. *Bayard betrayed us. The Lorraine Cross.* He knew that he inevitably must find what he sought: some secret weapon to destroy the General with.

> > >

The Agency proper was built on the plateau above Maracot Falls, a few kilometers back from the edge. An asymmetric rosette of formcast buildings, low, with walls angled up and out, the complex spread like a huge white version of the lichens of Marcera's ground.

A breeze blew, carrying low-pitched mechanical noises, smells of cut wood and grain. Atop the structures, wind turbines whistled. Transfer cranes, stark and bowed, lay in the distance, and beyond them a precise row of launch gantries. Robot go-trains wheeled from building to building, slipping past each other at closer quarters than any human operator would have dared. A cart rolled to a halt, stopped as if puzzled, then came round on silent tires and waited for the three people to board it.

Bayard pointed out a tower with a brick-shaped, glass-fronted top. "Monitor," he said. "Doesn't miss a damn thing. Especially not his boss."

They showed him how the wheels of succor revolved. There were classes in rescue, medicine, construction, the teaching of those, and more. "This one's my favorite. They call it Makeshifting." Inside, instructors and pupils were turning fishbones into fishhooks, making twigs and plant fronds into windmills.

There was a Traffic Control room, where two hundred people at a hundred plexy consoles read screens and printouts, talked with suppliers and delivery teams, kept spacecraft moving. It looked like—

"—a War Room, sure. I was in CIF too long not to pick up something. And they can and will bust you from anything to nothing for lousy organization."

"It looks like it takes a lot of people."

"It takes an army." Bayard paused. "That is—there are five people to a planet, what we call a Home Team. Two of the five are on duty all the time, on lapping shifts."

"Lot of data passes through here, then."

"I guess that's your department, isn't it?" Bayard went to a corner of the overlook platform, to a machine that looked much like a Web terminal. He tapped at its keyboard, and a screen lit up with rolling columns of characters. He played the keys very well, Grailer saw. Rough fingers, but agile.

"This is the Atropos device. The most advanced triage computer there is. It's what keeps us one step ahead."

Gian and the Florentine Group would be happy to hear that, Grailer thought. "Triage?" he asked, innocently enough.

"Death control," Bayard told him. "Oh, no—you say it, Victoria. You've got the pretty voice."

"Atropos," she said, and, oh, her voice was pretty, "sorts out worlds in crisis. Before any of the Aid Teams go in, First Teams send us all the data they can—not just standard questions on diet and local gods and toilet facilities, but anything and everything. Do they eat their peas with honey? Is the god of love male or female, for or against? Can you stir your berry malted with your left hand? Atropos takes cultural factors into account, not just genetic and biological ones. It tells us who we can help—"

"And who we can't, supposedly."

"—and, more importantly, how to help. When and where to give food, drugs, training—even arms, sometimes. Our Aid Teams have a reference. Something to anchor them."

"We don't send guns often," Bayard put in again. "But some cultures need a lot of protein—and most protein on the hoof fights back."

Grailer nodded slowly. He saw his weapon. He could feel its keys under his hands already. Atropos would know why Luke deCastries had died with his head clubbed in. He would have gambled his life that the data in the triage machine had brought Philip Otto four CIRCE bullets.

Of course, he was gambling his life already. But he had found the marked deck.

"I'd like to play with that thing for a while."

"That's what I—"

A red light flashed on one of the Traffic Room consoles. A chime rang, three soft notes.

Grailer saw Bayard stiffen, as if struck by a great pain. Dr. Osmanli tapped her cane on the floor, marking time with the triple gong.

Someone on the cluttered floor below them looked up, raised a hand, and waved it, not a salute but a signal.

"Come on, Knight, Victoria. Let's look around the plant."

"Wayne, there'll be—"

"Yeah, and it'll still be there later. Let's go."

The longest building of the rosette reached out from the complex center to the flightpad and gantries. A flight of portpods was tripping down the ballistic spiral like stiff-winged, gravid birds.

They touched the skid pad, one, two, three, splitting the air with sound as they braked.

A windsooted glider rolled past, bouncing and ungraceful on its thin shock struts. It slipped between the spider legs of a transfer crane, stopped with a curtsy and a nod. The crane let down its arms, felt about the shuttle's shellback, came up with a pair of dull cylinders cradled in its steel grip. The glider sighed as its suspension relaxed, then taxied away. As it moved out of view, soiled and relieved of duty, an alarm wailed from the gantry row, and three sparkling sootless ships rode the rails up and away on clear light-distorting columns of ultracompressed air.

The crane handed the cylinders to a go-train, which carried them inside the building. From the train they rolled into a vertical rack, dropping one by one to a magnetic conveyor like cartridges working through a weapon action.

"Grains," Bayard said. "High protein, amine rich, low fat. Just damn near perfect. This way."

They followed a high railed platform suspended above the processing line. Bayard's boots rang on the steel grille, Grailer's soft shoes echoing softly after. Dr. Osmanli's wings hummed faintly and her cane tapped the catwalk.

The grain was dried in ten-meter stainless drums tended by a handful of persons in orange singlesuits and dust masks. It was ground and pounded (hammers on the ears and soles), airblown and blended (clouds and fountains of white-gold powder.) The finished product was funneled into brown paper bags lined with plastic film and stamped with the hands-bowl-and-flame.

Grailer knew those bags well. He felt as though he were standing by an open grave. Nine yards of bag had been Luke's shroud—

"Staple concentrated powder," said the General. "You can eat it dry, you can mix it with water and eat the dough, you can bake the dough, or fry it, or stuff it in a bird and roast it. Name the diet and we can fit Staple into it."

Grailer remembered the white bread they had eaten on Ishtar.

It had meant nothing particular to him then. He was too used to white bread.

Below the catwalk, cylinders were racked, running valves and hoses that wound across the floor. Their ends were marked with bands of color and numbers.

"What are those?"

"Chemical additives. Colorizers, odorants, flavorings. Pure Staple is as neutral as we can make it—has all the flavor of silicone sealer, actually. We customize the product just like its application."

"And the Atropos device tells you what to add."

"Lord. Knight, I can see you're going to get paid plenty. Let's get back to the office."

On the way out they passed a stack of Staple bags piled for shipment. Grailer muttered a meaningless phrase and walked around the heap, palming his snapknife. When he rejoined Bayard and Osmanli, he had a pocketful of white Staple powder.

> > >

"Our private glitch concerns Ceptex-Four." Bayard leaned forward, elbows on his desk, eyes glowing like the anodyne in his hand. The even white light from the rectilinear ceiling did not soften his face.

"There's sterility drug in the food?"

Bayard looked puzzled. "Of course there is. There has to be. That's the glitch; it's not working. Watch."

Bayard tapped at a keypad set into his desk. Dr. Osmanli turned to face the plexy wall. Grailer followed her look. A graph labeled *POPULATION × TIME* flashed on the highest wall screen. A heavy black line crawled from Time-zero, flat and parallel to the Time axis. Population was stable. Then a red circle appeared around the line, and the word *ARRIVAL*. The line curved up, ran faster. It became a parabola, zooming toward the top of the graph. Just before impact it stopped, and another red circle appeared, and another word: *BREAKDOWN*.

"First graph," Bayard said, "improved nutrition in a primitive culture, without contraception. The population rises in proportion to the increased nutritional capacity, out of proportion to cultural capacity. In a short time the culture breaks down, usually violently. Our triage engineers call it a Malthus Burnout."

"Colorful phrase," Dr. Osmanli said. Her left hand was on her knee, massaging it. "From where I was, it looked like a war."

"Victoria was injured during a native—"

"Injured, hell!" She told Grailer exactly how her legs had been ruined, her face changed. He saw Bayard's lips twitch once at the word *ripgun.* The Doctor went on, sparing nothing, describing the explosion of slugs in her flesh, the stitching pain of bone fragments, the rough crawl to an amber vat, and finally the burn and tear and hot needle pricking of her legs and face and eye in thaw, because the cryostat batteries had been shattered with gun butts.

She pulled up the long sheath skirt. Grailer saw, and blinked, and nodded. "I'm sorry."

"It's been longer than you've lived."

Another graph appeared beneath the first. The line again ran flat to the ARRIVAL circle. This one increased in a gentle slope, then leveled off. Slant, plateau, slant, plateau, and the annotation *MAINTENANCE.*

"Second graph. Ceptex-Four population maintenance. This is what's supposed to happen—what *has* happened until lately."

"Where does the growth come from, if they're all sterilized?"

"They're not. The natives that come to special education classes are taken off the contraceptive. At the end of a four-week training period, they're fully fertile and stay so for about four more weeks. The performance of the technically trained natives inspires the others to go to school. But the growth is gentle, under control."

"Nor," Dr. Osmanli said stiffly, "do we keep them drugged forever. We teach control as well as impose it."

"Graph number three."

The bottom graph followed the first two to ARRIVAL. Then it arced up, slowly at first, twenty degrees, then thirty, forty, and a skyrocketing near-vertical leap that hit a red circle and stopped. The word appeared: *INCIDENT.*

"This is the new pattern."

"Ending in violence?" Grailer felt hollow inside. He was being handed deCastries' murder as a puzzle to solve. Was the blooded warrior trying to trap him? Get him to tip his hand as Philip had tipped his?

"Listen." Bayard's fingers danced on the keyboard. "This is what that red light meant, back at Traffic." The fingers were light, limber, playing almost—almost—like Grailer's own.

A voice sounded in the office. It was a man, and he was straining the words. His tone was broken. There were sounds of burning as well.

"This is an emergency record. Team Medic Tchaka . . . Acting Team Leader Tchaka . . . taping.

"Team Leader Walsh is now dead, as are Sung, Tellenor, Rhodes, and Fine. Hanna is critically wounded. Duvreis was severely burned about the face, and is blind." A gun chattered somewhere, there were breaking noises and a woman swore.

"We are under attack with torches, clubs, and knives. Though several of the natives have . . . acquired firearms, they have made no serious attempt to use them . . . except as clubs. Communications Specialist Tereshkova has protected the shuttle . . . with gunfire and will continue to do so while capable . . . due to my oath, I may not . . .

"We cannot lift, we cannot lift." He said it as though he were arguing with someone.

"It must be made clear that the Team Leader at no time . . . violated protocols even though . . . tensions had reached a high peak . . . before . . ." There was a long burst of ripgun fire, a crash of glass, howls and screams.

"They are through—" Tchaka's voice grew fainter. "Why are you doing this? What have we—*Rosnya! My God, my God, what went wrong?*"

There was a moan of sick, helpless, hopeless agony, long and low, ended by the squeal of a broken transmitter.

It was Ishtar, all over. He was pinned down by his work, and just—too—late to save Luke.

But the names were changed. And they were engineers on that miserable planet, not teachers. They had fought back. In a way, they had "won."

Grailer hurt inside his body and head, and wished he had Damian Gray to hide within, or Diamond G. Jim Knight was a harmless man, with nothing but a common man's will and strength to shield him.

He looked at Bayard, wanting to reflect the hurt back on the General. And thought he had, for a moment. Bayard was trembling, his lips pressed bloodless.

Then Grailer realized it for what it was. Shaken even worse than before, he sank into one of the curved black chairs.

Bayard stood up, walked to the screens, slammed his fist into one. He went to the open window and threw his anodyne into space. "They don't learn. They keep making babies, and they don't learn. And then they kill our people, our teachers. They burn them and ax them and drown them. Lord, it's like the battle on Griesheim, where they hit the bargaining party with ballistas and Greek fire.

"And it's taking less and less time to happen. That one planet—what was it, Victoria? Island? Insel? The one where my Lucas died . . ." *My Lucas*, he said, his eyes pressed tight, leakproof.

"Knight, have you ever heard stories about computer thieves? I don't mean blind-eyed men who tried to gimmick their moneycards. I mean nova operators who can waltz in and make the machines do tricks like a pet dog."

Lies must follow on lies. It does matter so much to a liar that he is believed. "General, I'm Third Lit and I'd lose my eyes if I tried to steal a kiss. But, yes, I've heard stories."

General Bayard ran his fingers through his hair. "I've led men for—oh, my whole damned life. I thought I was through with leading them to their deaths.

"Let me tell you what I want done here. If you know me at all, you know I brook no betrayals, on any level; there's a phrase about it. A backstabbed man says he's been 'given the Lorraine Cross.'"

An edge of lightning and steel had come into Bayard's voice. "Do you know what that really means? It means that a man who tried to sell ten lives for his own had to pay reckoning in hard coin. I shot two hundred men down on Lorraine because they had run back to hide behind me instead of going where they had been ordered. Where they could have saved two thousand of their supposedly fellow soldiers.

"Knight, I want you to dig through this organization, with a shitscoop or a helltorch if you have to, and find me who did murder."

"And if . . . what if . . . it isn't a thing that can be traced?"

Bayard's voice had a cool electric crackle. "Then I've failed, and I'm to blame, and I'll pay. Knight, do you know what you have to do?"

"Yes," Grailer lied a third time.

CHAPTER 16

AND EVER SHALL BE

This time he walked from point to point, because he did not know where he was going. And so that he would not meet anyone to tell him the way, he entered the infracity.

Maracot's infracity began where the talons of the beast clutched the rock, infiltrating by tunnel and trench deep into the scarp. Pipes and cables ran up to falls-head, down to where the hydrostats drew power from crashing water, alongside veins of sparkling gneiss, smooth-planed schist. Here and there a shaft felt out to daylight. For a while Grailer sat on a worn stone block and watched the day from behind the blue curtain of the falls.

A worker came by, doffed his helmet, and politely asked for a little space on the stone. Given it, he pulled a violet cloth from a pocket and carefully spread it out. Then a battered leather case that Grailer had taken for an Ariel was unhooked from his belt; a tiny key drawn up on a neck chain, and inserted in the latch on the case. Out came a long narrow deck of cards . . . of tarots.

They glittered, but were not shiny: worn pasteboards with metal-leafed illuminations rather than plastic and image-ink. The pictures did not move. Nor had they really any depth; the faces were flat cutouts against collage backgrounds. Even so, there was a singular quality of life in the flat eyes and lips.

Grailer recalled where he had seen that look. In Gian Sforza's collection of ancient art were paintings called ikons, portable images of the old gods. Those were innocent of perspective and shade, and the heads seemed always to incorporate a solar disk—the precise symbolism escaped him. But in the ikons there was always a peculiar attraction. As if the painters had made up for lack of skill and limitations of form with a magnificent excess of love; had mixed blood with the cadmium in their reds, sweat with sienna, tears in titanium white.

So while these cards were not much at all like Celene's animate dreams, or the lightdeck of Astre d'Ouranos, or the polychrome visions that dark Doktor Dakhra called his Book of Thoth, they drew Grailer and held him.

"Would you read for me?"

Powerful fingers, that Grailer was quite sure would not lose their grip on a hundred-kilo slab of increte, quaked and let a card fall: a baroque Tower, its crownlike capstone riven by gilded lightning. The man crossed and uncrossed his fingers. Perhaps for a raiser of works that was a bad omen indeed. "There're better readers than me. Anywhere up, down the city."

"Are you turning me down?"

The man frowned, put on his helmet, took it off, and scratched his head.

"Wouldn't you like to read for me?" Grailer prompted, knowing the true answer (there being only one) but hoping he did not sound too hungry. If the fellow felt too much rode on the turn of the cards, he'd pack them and go.

The trouble was, Grailer wasn't certain just how much *was* staked on the shuffle.

"Okay, I guess. Do you have a Significator?"

"Knight of Swords," Grailer said at once.

Down they fell. Covering, crossing. Below, behind. Above, ahead. Fear, friends. Dreams . . . destiny.

The Two of Swords cut, blindfold. Seven wands flew past, perilously near the ground. Beneath five pentacles cut in stone two people stood huddled in the snow. Death danced, as it seemed always to for Grailer; not a black-armored CIRCE rider, but bones swinging a scythe, leaving a field full of—cut-up corpses.

Grailer gasped and the reader looked up. "I'm sorry."

"Why?" said Grailer in a whisper. "It's not you who stacked them, is it. She said the very first time that she didn't trust my machine; perhaps I shouldn't trust hers."

The reader put spread fingers lightly on the cards, protecting them. "Who do you mean?"

Why not say? She had told him to say it. "Celene Tourdemance."

The man stacked and cased the cards, with great care but rapidly. "Why didn't you say? The Lady of the Tower—please tell her you didn't warn me; tell her I meant nothing—you must."

Grailer looked at the purple cloth, tried to recall the pattern that had lain upon it, but he could not find the proper mental keystrokes. And in a moment the cloth was tucked away as well.

"You *have* to tell her."

There had been no hope in the pattern; that he remembered. There had been swords, as borne by the angels of vengeance, but no banners of victory or landing-markers within the Celestial Kingdom.

"I'll tell her. But you've nothing to fear. She's kinder than you imagine." Surely; she had warned Grailer. But who listens to such verdicts? They're all only a pack of cards—

Grailer found himself alone, watching the falling water that was supposed to be so healing. Would he have to return to Juvenal upon Brass, find her among the Romany and the CIRCEs? Or go further back, see Space as not God but Pryne had intended, and—join his ancestors—

He stood and took several lurching steps toward the falls. Not many, he knew, leaped from inside. This was his chance to do something monstrous clever, keep his final measure within the Dance . . .

He turned his back on the water and walked on.

He found a better-traveled area, built perpendicular upon a Hellmann grid; feeling braver, he grabbed a stanchion, kicked off from his platform, swung unsupported over five hundred meters of space while his center of gravity slid up and down his body—and landed with a pleasantly tingling shock on a floor that moments ago was a wall.

He felt suddenly giddy. Wall was floor; he could see the tire marks on it. Truth was lies; Coughlin Delaplane was as false as down on a Hellmann. Lies were straight truth; Grailer had seen the pain in the General's face when he had spoken Luke's name, and Grailer thought how all his rage and grief seemed petty next to that one look of agony. Anthony Wayne Bayard, whatever he had done, had not killed Luke. He was suffering for someone else's crime.

But whose—?

Grailer, the space of his mind curved by massive doubt, walked the infracity of Maracot Falls. And then it merged with and dissolved into the infracity of Skolshold, long ago and far away. Where he fled the memory of a woman who lay with nerves burned out, mad by grace, mercifully dying.

Sharon Rose, she died insane/And no one knew who was to blame/Except the man she spoke of in her dreams/A knight of ghosts and shadows/Who had a dozen names.

Skolshold's angel-boned daughter would come to his room and spin; and he would teach her as Ari had taught him, and learn from her in ways he had not. "Does she show promise?" Mr. Aristide had asked, in the too-few times they had talked. Grailer looked past him and said, "She fulfills it. . . ."

Sharon Rose, she died alone/And who was there who could have known/The only man who knew what had been done/Was a Lochinvar who'd loved her/And into darkness gone.

"Gry, they sound like banshees. Or Johnny Sky, riding up."

"What—*the Hounds?*" He snatched the set from her. He hadn't expected the Geisthounds. He was just dumb enough for that. He distanced them, but slowly, a little cleverer than a hare but not so much as a fox, yet, and he could feel their hot static breath on the small hairs of his neck. She lay a white hand on his side, and skin prickled to skin.

"Grailer, have I learned enough to—"

"Not enough, never enough! Sharon, they're breaking, *get clear!*"

She dug in her nails, and the pain in his side outbalanced the pain in his hands; he picked up speed, and was going to trap them and win. When Sharon, who did not know to keep her eyes away, saw a Geisthound face to face.

Ask it again: Is the Web intelligent? Answer again: no. But would the fly call the pitcher plant intelligent? The Hounds were meant to kill Webspinners. In that sign, they had been given, or developed, a face that no one understood, not then, not now. But this they knew too well: they appeared as an awful, fearful thing, and all people see fear differently. So Grailer never knew just what Sharon saw that gave her the strength to hurl him aside, and his conscious mind never shaped the green bolt that leaped from the screen.

She threw out her arms as the Hound tore into her breast and throat, her slim body bent in rictus, her hair straight and sparking with the corona; she hung at an impossible angle as muscle tore against muscle and neurons exploded. The air smelled of burning hair and ozone. Sharon fell then, twitching, as dead as it mattered.

He broke Web, because there was nothing to do. He packed and left by dark corridors, because there was nothing to say. From deep in the infracity he made a prayer to BellStel and spoke to Emergency Medical with the test pattern up, because he did not want her to lie dead and alone in the room . . . and he did not know whether she had let the Hound out of its trap, or he had. He would learn more about the Web, become old and wise on the Web, and never have a certain answer to that question. Dr. Taliessin had found him, and from there was a great darkness.

Sharon Rose, she died for love/What was it she was thinking of?
Grailer had never finished the song.

And now he thought he heard the whoop and whine of a rescue van, bearing by on Hellmanns and fans, stutter and blaze of lights warning the world that the enemy was still Time, that if lives were to be saved from the amber vats 'twere best done quickly.

Dusty air woke him, and he leaped aside; the van was real. It passed him without dodging a millimeter, banked hard on air and warring g-fields, and was swallowed by light. Grailer's eyes stopped down, and he saw vans lined ready and humming, cool pastel tile, bands of colored light directing hospital personnel swiftly, swiftly to their places.

Grailer walked through an air curtain and entered the flow. Jim Knight's silver-pale singlesuit was close enough to medic's clings to pass. He knew the rigmarole well: look sharp and disdainful at the medexes, smile and ignore your fellow medics, don't speak to doctors unless spoken to, and ditto plus a slight bow to the cape-wearers.

It also helped to know where one was going. Hospitals were great knots of colored yarn, and Security was quick to stop anyone who looked unraveled.

Grailer walked a yellow line and counted door numbers. At Six he stopped, rapped on the frosted glass.

The door opened a bit, and a face appeared: black pencil brows, liquid eyes, a shark nose. Gold braid on collar and red shoulder cape, and a widening smile.

"Gray! Not in years."

"Too long, Simon."

"Old dear, you look like death centrifuged. Come in and get drunk."

Grailer held a laboratory flask of clear, potent liquor, drawn from a distillation rig in one corner of the glassware jungle of the hospital lab. It burned his throat and brought tears to his eyes, and was surprisingly comforting in its warmth.

Simon Jonas poured himself a beaker of straight-up water. He tossed his red internist's cape over one shoulder and sat down lightly. He crossed a leg horizontally, brushing away specks that fell from a slipper to a crisp white trouser leg.

"Simon, I've got a need."

"Ah, dear, I wear the red, not the purple."

"Not psych—well—no. I want this analyzed." Grailer pushed glassware aside and set a bag of white powder on the counter.

Jonas took a long swallow from his beaker. He rose, went to Grailer's side, and picked the bag from the table. "Something sinful, I'll wager. What is it, Gray? Resublimated Mem? Of-death-what-dreams? Or something prosaic from the opiate spectrum?"

"Staple Concentrate."

Jonas put his drink down, went to the wall Web, and made a prayer. The screen churned for full minutes. "And this is a hospital call. Gray, could you teach me that talent of yours?"

"There's—no." The more spinners one was woven with—

"That's what Ari says, too." Finally a bright young face appeared on the screen, coronet pickups on her forehead.

"Arseau, I have a special series of tests to run. Lab Six is inviolate until further notice."

"But, Lord Doctor Jonas, you were to do the Ostrovik series."

"Are the samples drawn?"

"Yes, Lord Doctor."

"Then have the patient scraped and chilled for surgery."

"But, Lord Doctor, the Lord Doctor Teng P'ing has asked—"

"You can *tell* that knife-grinder in green to quit wasting my time and the patient's magic and *open her*; he'll find the same adhesions this week that I told him about last week, only there'll be a little extra plumbing to replace now. And if Madame Ostrovik asks about the tests that she insisted Lord Doctor Teng order, tell her that not one of them has any value beyond describing them to one's friends—and that if she persists I will gladly return every specimen to its original location, giving her enough stories to last for *years*!

"Have you got all that, Arseau?"

The medex nodded, a little dazed. "Good. You may wear the cape yet, old dear." He tossed his own cape across himself, like an ancient Roman senator, and gave the medex the test pattern before breaking Web.

"Simon, you didn't have to."

"I'd been wanting to. After all, a medical Fellow has his privileges." He fingered his cape and laughed. "But all that doesn't matter. You wouldn't have brought me food powder unless you were cold solid. Give me a history."

Grailer told him all that was relevant. Remembering an earlier time, he included Sharon.

"I'm not sure I understand this computer affair—but again, no matter. Draw yourself another cup of starshine; it won't take a quarter to test for Ceptex."

Twelve minutes later: "Here's your Ceptex-Four."

"Are you sure?"

Jonas raised an eyebrow. "According to a reliable proprietary test, yes. But privately, no. Let me try something else.

"Did you know, Gray, that once doctors had to ask other doctors to do their tests for them? I wonder how anything ever got done."

The single additional test took another hour. "But here's what you wanted," Jonas said.

"It isn't Ceptex, is it?"

"No, not quite. There's an isomer of the real thing present. It'll pass all the bottled tests for potency—but not the *in vivo*, of course. Very exotic, expensive sort of thing; someone went to a lot of trouble for a practical joke. I've heard of dreamtraders using the isomer trick to pass inerts off as miracles and vice versa; but this usage . . . well. At least it explains their population problem."

"Yes, that. But the questions it asks—I can't see. I can't see why, or who."

Jonas stepped close, faced Grailer, laid a hand on his. On the doctor's ring a Libra-the-scales sparkled in ruby. "Can I help?"

Grailer squeezed the offered hand and looked up. "It didn't work, Simon."

"She was between you and love."

"She is again."

"Gray, perhaps you're too close. You're too near the business; you need a changed perspective."

Grailer stood quickly. "Simon, I love you and always will."

"Was it something I said?"

"Yes, about perspectives. Is there a Web console in the building? A programming console, a two-fifty-six?"

"We're a very modern hospital."

"Can I get to it?"

"I'll raise bane and deviltry if you can't. Drop my name; that should inspire fear enough. Now will you tell me why?"

"Give me half an hour, and I'll tell you things you might rather not have known."

> > >

The Atropos device was not formally part of the Web, but for the sake of communication and convenience it would be linked somewhere, along some well-guarded channel.

Grailer was in no mood for artistry. He killed the guard and entered the Atropos with intent to ransack and loot.

He played with it first, to take his and its measure. He set up planets, watching them develop under careful guidance, the invisible hand. He meant to try it two or three times, but went on for a fourth, a fifth, another. It was a curious feeling, like spinning the Web but a louder, wilder music. Grailer had played games with Webwork lives before, planetsful of them, to save real lives or take magic from the wicked or just as a chess excursion. But this had a startling ring of reality, as the machine asked him for strange and unexpected details of the societies he imagined for it and sent back its predictions; peace, plenty, health, death. Always death. In the most placid of situations, after the most generous of aid programs, there was always a residue, a number for Death.

He probed deeper, feeling cautiously through the keys, looking through the screens. And in time he found what he was looking for. It was nothing so casual as, say, a set of double-entry books. The spinning of the Atropos might be likened to the erasure and replacement of figures in a ledger, if the obliteration were done by a trompe-l'oeil artist and the new work by a master forger. But even that was inexact. The Atropos device had been not so much changed as slanted . . . as corrupted. Its premises, the equations by which it delivered guns or butter, seeds or pills, were altered in a subtle and deadly direction.

Grailer might never have found it had he not expected to, and expected more than a simple alteration. It was not a thing that anyone but a Webspinner could have done. Or discovered.

There was another layer yet to the mystery. The changes set up in the machine merely primed a situation. Triggering that situation required one more element; and now Grailer knew what that element was.

When he went back to the lab, he was as much awed as horrified.

"Simon, if I described a hypothetical drug, could you look for it in that sample?"

"Depends. I can analyze for any number of things, but I've got to have some fair idea of just what."

"This would be a psychoactive. It'd . . . well, just gradually drive you crazy."

"I'll call a purple doctor for you if you wish."

"You can't help me?"

"Be more specific."

"We were all sad and angry. Violent. I couldn't play the keys. Luke couldn't shoot straight. Ulli"—there, he'd said it—"did things her training should never have allowed."

Jonas drew a hard drink, downed it at once. "I can analyze that without soiling a tube. What you're looking for, old darling dear, is a positive cyclothymol, encapsulated for oral administration. Do you know how we treat cyclic psychosis? We, not the psychists? We inhibit the action of certain chemicals in the nervous system. We've been doing it for centuries.

"But there's a chemical that reverses the process. There shouldn't be, but there is."

Grailer clenched his teeth and nodded. Fear led to realized fear. Bread with fruit-butter and fowlsmeat sandwiches.

"I spent a twelvehour extracting it from a man's CS fluid. Oh, he was the pride of the purple doctors. They thought we were on our way back to the days of witchcraft, of non-chemical, nonstructural psychoses. For it's a subtle thing. I find dreamtraders hard to live with, God knows there're enough legal dreams—but the man who made this I'd happily see flayed alive."

"Who was the patient? Where is he now?"

"He was a drifting canrunner, between consignments, no identity and wouldn't provide any—vicious character, no mistake. Nor would the Web help. Curious, yes? Well, it doesn't matter now. If he'd had a soft amber contract, it was voided. Whoever blasted him went for brain tissue."

"He was killed here? In the hospital?"

Jonas fingered his cape. "By a man in red and white. They laughed at us for weeks, dammit—didn't occur to anyone at the time that doctors seldom carry zap wands with them—"

"Enough, Simon, please." Realized fear led to determination, a taut cable from brain through heart deep into gut. Grailer's eyes were wide, white. "You mentioned sinful things, Simon? I have to return sin for sin, now."

"Sit down, Gray; tell me."

"Not now. I have to go."

"Surely, surely. Tell me why."

"Because I have an oath to fill. I have to end this."

CHAPTER 17

THE END OF THE WORLD

The man who made the prayer wore a transparent silk shirt slit to the waist, gems and metal, bracelets, and an ankle band of cord and leather. He had long hair the color of yellow sunlight and a gold band around his head.

"I hight Dido," said the man on the Web, "Dido Kupler, and I live by my wits." He raised a fingernail that was overlong and dull black; such things were often poisoned.

The spark, the Goliardic dazzle, and the indelicate words were enough to blind and deafen Coughlin Delaplane to the man he spoke to, to make him see only the picture.

Image was all there was. A few grace notes played on the public Web's sixteen-pad had called up an angel, so that Grailer Diomede stood dressed in wrinkled and dusty silver on one side of the screen and quite differently on the other.

Delaplane tented his fingers. "What do you have for me that I might want?"

"Three, and you *do* want them. One known, probably; one known, possibly; one not known, guaranteed."

"One probable?"

"But one you want."

"Ah. Ah. So. For your three, three sniffs of wonder."

"And the black knights, then? No."

"Ah. Then a soft touch for three of your nights."

"There is no accountancy of taste. No."

"Then three thousand straight magic."

"Two thirds in advance?"

"One third."

"Half."

"Contracted." Delaplane's hands went to the buttons beneath his desk; Grailer watched the magic transfer. "And now my three."

"One, probably known: The man Ardrey put one of your careless men in amber."

Delaplane gave an ugly grin. "Known, and not entirely accurate. You forfeit a thousand."

"Two, possibly known: Ardrey is warm with the black knights."

"Hah! Suspected, but meaningless; there is a commonality of interest. You forfeit five hundred. I hope this last brings some results, witling."

And so do I. "Three, not known. The man Knight has discovered what Bayard wishes to know. All of it."

Delaplane turned purple. He called for his secretary, then made half a prayer before he realized Web was still unbroken. Grailer managed to slip him a few seconds of test pattern before the call ended.

He transferred the magic back into Delaplane's account. He had never intended to take it; it was just part of the charade. And he could not take it honestly.

Grailer waited about ten minutes, watching the door of his room from the public terminal.

He saw Mr. Aristide examine his sleeve, slip one of his gold-tipped white wands into it. Then he pressed the door-panel of Grailer's room.

"Yes?" the angel said.

"It is I, child mine. Matters are urgent. I must enter."

"Why don't you turn around instead."

But since Ari had a self-aim weapon, Grailer fired into his back. The impact drove him into the door, face first; his nails scraped down as he sank trembling to his knees. He passed out as Grailer keyed the door and dragged him through.

Grailer's face was a blank mask as he dumped Ari's limp body in a chair. He did not answer the other man's groans as he stripped the zap wand from Ari's forearm, handcuffed his wrists before him, wrapped cord around his ankles and the legs of the chair. He had a hard time tying the knots.

Mr. Aristide rolled his head back. He had a look of terrible resignation—almost of boredom.

"I never . . . taught you . . . cruelty."

"No. You taught me honesty, though. And a sense of justice."

Ari twitched. "I'm sorry," Grailer said. "I know you need to move, after the shock. But I promise this won't take long. And if I'm wrong . . . I'll make up for it. But I don't think I'm wrong."

"Tell me what I've done."

Slowly, his eyes not leaving Ari, Grailer opened his Webset and put it on the table before Ari. Then he pulled a chair over, sat, turned the set, and began working the keys. "I have to tell you exactly why I'm doing this."

"No, you don't. You're in control, Grailer; you need justify your actions to no one."

"Don't, Ari."

He held out the cuffs. "What choice have I?"

"*Stop it!*" Bitter bile rose in Grailer's throat; he gulped back his feelings. Now he had no character at all to hide within but his own. "I'm spinning the Atropos device, Ari. I spun it a few hours ago and found I wasn't the first."

No response.

"Whoever twisted the machine was purest supernova. Better than me, in fact. That meant you."

"And for that—"

"No! Not for that. Atropos was high-order Webwork; I'm sure you had a good reason, at first. You must have had a reason."

"Then for your engineer . . . Lucas." Ari's back arched as his stunned nerves racked him.

"Not for Luke, though your work killed him. All he did was build bridges, Ari; it wasn't his fault he landed on one of your special planets. *Hadn't he been through enough?*

"The work was brilliant, I will grant you that. Anyone examining the files might have found the slant to the data block, but such a delicate slant as to be meaningless without the special increase of tension. The drug, the damned hate-drug. And if Luke and Ulli hadn't blown earlier than they were supposed to, I might never have found either one.

"You were good enough to fool Dr. Osmanli, but did you know Luke saw through you? It was my error to misunderstand his last words. I heard 'Bayard betrayed us.' Luke wouldn't ever have said that, not even dying, not even insane. What he said was 'Tell Bayard someone betrayed us. The Lorraine Cross.' And he meant the last in Bayard's sense, not the common one. He meant someone had abandoned the troops for himself."

Grailer looked at his hands on the keys, then at Ari's hands on the table near the Webset. "But that's not the reason, either. You were Webspinning, Ari, and we do hurt people. But . . . *timor licentiae*, Mr. Aristide, *conturbat me*, do you remember? Are you not a member of the brotherhood?"

"Then . . . for Philip? Surely not for Philip!"

"No, not for Philip. Maybe for . . . but ultimately, no."

"Then for what?"

"You will know, very soon."

From the Webset came a sound like something dying.

"Oh, *God*," Ari said, and strained. His face was white as his silks, and sweat slicked his forehead. "It's for your dead Rose of Sharon," he said, his voice metallic, the death rattle already in his throat.

"Yes. You know who I would kill for. Who and only who.

"Did you mean to warn me, when you showed me the thirty silver coins and the CIRCE document? I didn't see; did you expect me to take such a hint? I had Bayard to hate. Even when I talked to him—"

"He knows nothing. Less than nothing."

"Nor did I. I would never in all the wide Web have believed you would have given someone over. But when I saw you had, for no better reason than that another Webspinner—*another one of us*—had in his own work stumbled on your Atropos secret . . . then brick fell on brick. The lights all went out at once."

"If you know the truth, child mine, tell it."

"We had so much trust, Ari, that common sense got lost. CIRCE was too easy to hate for me to have seen one thing: they could not have created the Geisthounds. *Only a Webspinner could have done it.*

"I think I did suspect, long ago; if I was so nova and couldn't touch them, how good would their master have to be? But of course I couldn't have believed, because if I'd believed I would have had to act. And I could not have come to terms with the action. How many people would be alive if I had?

"Ari, you're going to die. Then I'll die, for having killed you. The Hounds will bite, and no one will ever know—so tell me, for the sake of the dead *tell me!*"

Mr. Aristide looked at the ceiling. His face was old, streaked, hollowed out from within.

"It was an accident.

"I was experimenting, looking for an improvement on the active virtual—for a machine intelligence, if you will. I taught it Web-work, and . . . perhaps I taught it too strictly. I kept increasing the range, the power, and . . . I lost them, that's all. They reproduce, they move . . . you know the rest."

There were snarls from the Webset. Grailer felt the hair rise on the backs of his hands. He spoke quietly. "You could have said something. Perhaps all the Spinners together could have done something."

He stood up, turned the Webset to face Mr. Aristide, then slid it across the table. Ari reached for it, to the limit of his rope—and the keys remained barely a centimeter beyond his fingertips.

"Those are hospital restraints Simon gave me. They're very gentle. They can't hurt you. Just like the drug. But they hold. I thought about dosing you with your own medicine, but it works too slowly . . . and it would numb your perception. You've got to feel it. *Feel it.*

"It isn't any way to die, is it, with your salvation just beyond your reach?" *Push it!* he thought, trying to keep the wheels of retribution turning. He had expected, if not a thrill of triumph, at least the fullness of satisfaction. He had waited for this for sixty years—and now felt only a mountainous duty, next to which death would be lighter than a feather.

The sour-spice scent of tension thickened the air. Ari stretched, and again, uselessly. "Grailer, this is no reason to die."

"Then tell me what is."

"Nothing. There are no good reasons for dying."

"Only for killing?" He argued with Ari, but more with himself. A deadly trap is always laid for the torturer; for he must either love the pain he inflicts or hate it. A clever victim can play on either passion, to seduce the inquisitor or revolt him, and turn the pain back on the giver.

Mr. Aristide was inhumanly clever, and he knew where every passion lay.

The sickening whine climbed the scale. They heard the terrible, insane laughter.

"The channel's wide. It won't be long."

"Grailer?"

"Yes, Ari?" I won't listen, though, no matter what you say—

"Enter what I tell you. R, C, I. Thirty-two, fourteen. Stack shift, again, again and back."

"Ari, it's too late to trap them."

"It's no trap. The countermands are Stapledon and Grimpen—"

"Ari, if you sit still your muscles won't tear so badly."

"Streak-shift twice! Stairstep roll, and a Gardner curve!"

The air crackled. A buzz came from the console, and laughter and howling were loud in the air.

"For the love of God, Grailer!"

Grailer took the set, entered the codes, and at once the Hound noises died. There was a fading whine, then nothing.

"Now tell me why, Ari."

"To control the competition."

Grailer's heart stopped.

"Child mine, we are one in ten million now. A small proportion, to be sure, but who can count man's billions? Still a small number, yes, *now*. I love spinning, Grailer; it is my art and my soul's joy—but I love with my eyes open. And there is a critical mass of Webspinners, child. Reach it and no social structure can survive. Web, worlds, works, everything—all goes chaotically Cosmeg Bang."

"And for that you worked with CIRCE? You killed?"

"Someone must feed the Fenris Wolf. CIRCE is a vicious thing, Grailer, hairy and slavering . . . but it has its place in the universe. As have I. As have you."

Grailer turned back to his Webset. "Is it so recorded?"

Voices came from the speaker. "It is."

"Aye."

"Recorded."

Mr. Aristide closed his eyes. "You held court just now, didn't you?"

"Burning court. Trial by ordeal. If I had been wrong about you . . . I know one way to protect a companion from the Hounds."

"Do I know the jury?"

"Yes."

"Well, then." His voice was steady. "Let the last comment of the prisoner be that Doctor Taliessin envied me Grailer Diomede as a pupil, Haafetz the Eyeless was a student I ejected for incompetence, and Magdalena Athanasia loved me once when I did not love her. All are, however, Webspinners of the highest order. As they know."

There was a burst of simultaneous conversation. "Finding!" Grailer shouted.

Magdalena Athanasia spoke, and if there was ice in her operatic contralto, there was also sorrow. "We cannot but find guilty . . . but . . . neither can we fix sentence."

"Then I shall," Grailer said. "He shall be stripped naked and his parts flung to the Hounds."

Grailer waited several seconds, listening for a word from Dr. Taliessin, a note from his harp. There was only silence as he went to the keys.

Every scrap of magic in Mr. Aristide's accounts was scattered beyond recovery. The pass codes of his palaces, his cars, his ships—all were scrambled. The Geisthounds ravaged his identities, his angels, all memories of him in mechanical minds—and by so doing killed some human memories as well.

When they were done, had chewed the last scrap to bloody bones, Grailer set the Hounds on guard, gave them his scent, and the command to kill should he ever step across the boundaries of the Web again.

When Web was broken, Grailer unlocked the shackles holding Mr. Aristide—no, call him that only by courtesy, for in the links of the Web he had no name. He was no longer even First Literacy; he would die on Marcera.

"I think it a just fate," was-Ari said, "and deserved for one found out such a hypocrite. Bravo!

"A unique punishment as well. You should not have mastered their control so quickly. You have invented something new."

"The student can have secrets from the teacher," Grailer said tiredly, "if the teacher is distracted. I planned this end for a long time; but I never told you. I was afraid of disappointing you in me."

"I told you my name, Dian—"

"*Don't say that!*" Grailer screamed in pain.

"You told me yours. We were never safe from one another—but I had thought. I had thought."

"I said I would punish her killer. I never cared who."

"Ah." Was-Ari straightened his gown and cloak. "I taught you even better than I hoped."

"You taught me not to kill. But I have anyway." Grailer closed the set, staring long at his hands.

"No teaching can prevent all killing," the man said, turning Grailer's head. "Words are not iron bands. But I taught you to hesitate. To consider; to weigh; to stay your hand until the weight of duty crushed it down.

"You did to me what you did because of your woman, who even you thought was forgotten. And of that I was guilty.

"But of spinning the Atropos device I was not. Philip Osmanli— oh, yes—did that. For the sake of mother love. For that I gave him to CIRCE, for Oedipus was better dead than blind. I even killed a canrunner outright—too late, I see. And for those things, too, you are justified.

"Now it is time to end the game; to promote the knight. Have you ever heard the tale of Anansi the Spider?"

"He's dead . . . Black-beetle trapped him."

"I see you are learning history. Very good. More than past time. But you learned wrongly. Anansi is not dead—or, more correctly, he is only just dead. Up until moments ago, I was Anansi the Spider. And now you are."

Grailer held his set to his chest. "Anansi was killed by the Hounds."

"Celene Tourdemance still calls you 'tumblebug,' did you know? I wonder if I shall ever see her again.

"But, yes, Grailer, Anansi was killed by the Hounds. Two times, now. And someday your pupil will snare you and kill you. Because there can never be more than one of us to deal with CIRCE, nor anyone to know. CIRCE alone is a leashed wolf. CIRCE with an army of Spinners would devour the moon.

"You did not show the burning judges, did you? They do not know you are the Master of the Hounds? I thought not. Poor Taliessin. He thinks he is the devil too, who numbers all the dead. And that is why I was your teacher."

Grailer felt suddenly weak, horribly sick, as though rising from a ghastly nightmare to discover it was no dream at all.

"Good-bye, Anansi, White King. Do not let Diego frighten you; he is a kind man in truth. But he is so, so lonely, having only me as a friend . . . now, only you. Only kings cannot be captured."

The door opened, and the nameless man stepped out. From the

corridor came strumming, the music of a harp. One of Dylan
Treece's songs:

> I have a sin of fear, that when I've spun
> My last thread, I shall perish on the shore;
> But swear by thyself that at my death thy Son
> Shall shine as he shines now and heretofore;
> And having done that, thou hast done;
> I fear no more—

The door closed.

CHAPTER 18

AMEN, AMEN

General Anthony Wayne Bayard was at his desk, penciling notes on hardcopy. A dish by his elbow was full of anodynes, each one less smoked than the previous one.

"Knight? I didn't know—"

Grailer pulled back the hood of his Wandersmann's robe. "General, I've found what you . . . wanted. Listen." He told the story without omitting one cold betrayal, murder or attempt, no trust misplaced—not even his own grief and guilt.

Bayard listened, nodded a few times, looked out the window and at the papers on his desk. He spoke coolly.

"Are you telling me this because you have a gun?"

Grailer's hand went unwilled to the thermal pistol in his belt. "No, because I think I can trust you."

"After all that."

"You didn't know, though, did you?" Grailer's eyes were wild, his voice quavered. Even Damian's false front was inadequate now. "You wouldn't kill for your own ends."

"If the ends aren't my own, I'm with the wrong army."

Grailer shook his head. "No, not you. Not you too." He drew his pistol, looking at it as though he had never seen it before.

Bayard stood. His hands appeared from beneath the desk holding a hard-chromed rocket pistol. "I've killed a lot of people who made bad decisions. But I would never take away the freedom to make those decisions. As someone has done, in my name."

"I knew you weren't guilty, General, not after . . ."

"The question of my guilt is not yet settled, Knight." He snapped open a drab green Ariel and made a short prayer. He held the speaker to his ear, muffling the sound from Grailer. Then he shut the set, slid it and the pistol into pockets.

"Come along."

"Where?"

"The plateau. We're expected."

> > >

The mill was silent and dark in the night. The machines stood still around the two men, gleaming like idols in moonlight. Bayard walked with his gun drawn, taking deliberate steps that made no sound. Grailer followed, his pistol out but unready.

A muffled slam came from ahead of them, and a light went out. Shadows bent. Something clicked like a footstep overhead.

Grailer threw out his arm and fired, a wobbly line of red light that lit the room up like the foundries of Hell. Metal crackled and spat high above. There was no one there.

There was laughter, bouncing off drums and walls, impossible to tell the source of but impossible to mistake the soprano voice. Then there was a whistle, ending in a crack. Whish-*crack*.

Bayard whirled, shoving Grailer behind him. They faced an office, fronted with translucent panels and illuminated from within. Silhouetted against the door was a human figure.

Bayard fired, a rocket screaming off the pistol rack, pure geometry of fire impacting in a bright star of shattering plastic.

Cracks tessellated the shadow on the door, centered on what should have been its heart. It shifted but did not fall.

"He's dead or I'm blind." Bayard lowered his gun, went to the door, and pulled it open.

A thick body in heavy clothes fell stiffly to the floor. Coughlin Delaplane stared unseeing at the distant ceiling, black burns on his face and upraised hands, a deep charred scar on his throat. The hole in his chest did not bleed. In death his fingertips were still tented together before his red brocade collar, exactly as in worship.

Behind him, among scattered papers, disordered charts, overturned chairs, Victoria Osmanli hovered on her wings, her hands folded in imitation of Delaplane.

"Welcome, Wayne, the great knight. And the lesser Knight as well." Her eyes, the blue and the brown, roved over Grailer. "A new costume, I see. My son was fond of costumes and name games as well. He also played tricks with machines, you know. I think they killed him in the end for it.

"Poor bloody infantry," she said in her lovely voice. "They fight like fiends, but they never do see how war is waged. Coughlin saw things falling apart for him, tried to bind himself to my side. Stupid man, did he think he could cheat me of my revenge and live, when my own son could not?" Her feet touched the floor. She picked up her cane and wound fingers on its hilt. "It was a nice affair we had, Wayne, you and I and Coughlin."

Bayard swallowed hard. Grailer remembered something Delaplane had said. *There is a commonality of interest.*

Dr. Osmanli moved forward, leaning on her stick. "Such love, such fulfilled desire, Wayne. You salved your battle-scarred conscience and never really knew or cared what the Agency did. Coughlin's concern for primitives stemmed from their value to him in charitable donations. Innocents kept him in brocade and redheads. Hypocrites all." She prodded the corpse.

"And you, Victoria?"

"I dissipated both your energies, playing you against each other. I got the intense satisfaction of destroying two corrupt organizations. And you with them. My Philip was preparing the final stroke, the one to wreck your fortunes utterly . . . but."

"I never hurt you, Victoria."

"Didn't you?" She seized her silk skirt, rent the seam open. When they saw her legs, their gun barrels dipped, and they could not look away. "I grew up working with the natives you burned down because they were in your way or pledged to something they half understood. No, they weren't always peaceful and ignorant; they weren't sheep. They cut me, and stabbed me, but I healed. I healed, and went back, and beat their spears into pruning-hooks. There may be no noble savages, but they can be *taught* nobility. That is, until they bite the apple—

"Thou fool, thou bloody fool, who thought that war was the natural state of things, that guns were just another tool. I learned a great lesson while I waited for new flesh. You can't till soil with a ripgun, Wayne!" She lashed out with her cane. The gun flew from Bayard's hand. He clutched his wrist. "It's not a deep burn. It will heal. Slowly, I hope." She whirled on Grailer, her wings humming. "And you?"

Grailer looked at the thermal pistol in his hand. He tried to pull the trigger, he did try, but it was much too late in the day. He threw it aside, drew and telescoped his battle-staff.

"You duel fairly. Good. Good. You use a noble weapon. Better." She swung, her charged cane striking sparks against Grailer's staff. He braced, swept at her legs, thinking at once, *Useless!* She laughed and glided out the door.

Grailer knelt to help Bayard. "Fool," the General said as they rose. "I'd have waited beyond the door and stabbed you when you turned."

She called from the catwalk overhead, her voice echoing high and beautiful in the dim steel cavern. "Come up and joust, Knight! Tilt on my log, Robin Hood! There are two kingdoms up for grabs; winner takes them all!"

Grailer took a step. Bayard grasped his shoulder with his wounded hand. He held Grailer's pistol in the other.

"A soldier can't be stupid. You don't fight on the enemy's terms, especially not crazy ones. How d'you think she got up there? She can fly. Can you?"

"You can't just shoot her down like that."

"Hell you say," Bayard said wearily, flipped the gun, and fired wrong-handed.

The bolt caught Dr. Osmanli in the thigh, fusing her wing controls. She dropped her cane, crashed through the railing, slammed into the wall, leaving a mark; slid all broken the long distance to the floor.

"Damned thing is, everything she said was true. Everything. My guilt is now established, Knight. You're witness." Bayard pulled the Ariel from his pocket and made a prayer to BellStel. It went unanswered. The General cursed and started again. Grailer unbuckled his Webset from the small of his back, slid it from his robe, and offered it. Bayard accepted the set.

"Get me Launch Control."

"General, they're in countdown—"

"*Then abort it!*"

"One moment, sir . . . I'm sorry, General, but they've just shot the last—"

Bayard broke Web with a violent swipe. "Knight. These tricks you do with machines. Can you control a ship remotely?"

My very first program. "I can do that."

"There's more. But get started now.

"Launch Control, this is Bayard. I want a glider ready, with the following equipment." Carrying the Webset, he started for the far end of the building, where the launch rails waited. "Come on, Knight! Do you know the value of two minutes?"

> > >

Grailer's Webscreen showed a curved bank of instruments, a man's hands on them, and through a sloping windshield a long skeletal launch track. The sky was blue-black with hurrying dawn.

"General, we are set for launch in sixty seconds," said the tech nearest Grailer, without looking up from his own instruments. The poised white glider was easily visible through the huge window of the monitor tower. But no one looked.

"Booster tank pressure is yellow-line. Rotate gas valves."

"Minus forty seconds."

"Flightpath registers green all stations."

"Minus twenty."

"Sound the warnings." Sirens came faintly through the walls.

"Minus ten. Shuttle crew please secure." The tech bit the words off as he said them. On Grailer's screen Bayard's hands drew out of sight.

"Five. Four."

"Diverter valves, full rotation."

"Three. Two."

"Launch locks ready for release."

"One. *Launch.*"

There was a crack as the locks released the ship, and wind trembled the monitor tower. The blue of the shuttle's windscreen darkened rapidly. Stars came out.

"All secure," one of the techs said, and they took off their coronets and left Grailer alone. Only a few cast brief glances back, and none more than that.

In space, on the Webscreen, General Bayard's hands moved back to the shuttle controls. "Now, Mr. Knight, find me that ship."

Bayard was a real nova pilot, breaking spin and homing on locus with easy, offhand grace. Grailer thought of his hands on Webkeys and of the burn on his wrist. Five minutes passed of wheeling past the stars, ten, and then the vessel, *Agnus Dei,* hung huge in the screens.

She was a barge, a cage of metal and filaments kilometers long, solid masses and delicate threads hung together. She was not beautiful in a classic, faired and streamlined sense, but rather as a dynamic creation, balanced without symmetry.

"First, Knight, tell me: You'll do what needs be to clean up the rest of this damned mess. Tell me, I trust you."

"I will, General . . . what needs to be done."

"Won't take all that much. The men we're fighting, they love power more than life and are ignorant of honor. Just remember—in any war there are always more of the enemy than you think, and there are always allies you never knew you had.

"Now, get the conning capsule."

The image of Bayard's controls dissolved. Grailer loaded commands into the brain of *Agnus Dei,* took over her hands and relaxed them. Out in space, clamps opened, and the only part of the barge that contained men drifted clear. It tumbled, then caught itself on ion-stream. Its crew was bound for a safe planetfall.

"Give me more light."

Grailer opened the secondary hatches. He cut back to shuttle pickup and saw them swing, light spilling out from a square a hundred meters on a side, illuminating Space. Within the barge's flank were levels upon levels of poisoned food and weapons that were not also tools. Some unfastened gear drifted out, as if reading the portents and fleeing the end.

The open port drew closer; Grailer cut back to cabin pickup, saw thrust needles bound up on Bayard's panel. Grailer reached for his keys.

"Knight!" Bayard's hands drew out of view again. He had locked thrust wide open. "Remember what I said? About shooting the man who was kneeling to help?" The hands reappeared, holding a power hammer.

Grailer lunged as the screen went dark. He was a Webspinner; he had a hundred eyes. He found a satellite view of a small star approaching a large one, aimed for the flood of light from its side. A small, fast package, full of the explosives Bayard had claimed he was only going to plant on the barge. Grailer moved to stop him.

But Bayard had smashed more than a vision pickup. He was no longer a part of the Web. He was beyond Grailer's reach.

Agnus Dei was not. He switched tracks, began nudging the barge out of the line of fire.

Dawn came early and suddenly to Maracot Falls, a second sun flaring high overhead. Some took it as an omen, some as a terrible accident, some as a mathematical inevitability. All of them had small fractions of the truth.

Grailer folded his arms on the Webset, put his head down, and wept.

After a few moments he felt a hand resting on his neck. The touch was encased in an impact glove and rested not heavily but on the most delicate of nerves. It was a come-along grip; the user could suggest with it, or punish, or with those black gloves even kill.

The voice behind the hands was calm, unhurried. "Is the present crisis ended?"

"It is." Grailer rose slightly, felt the fingers firmly placed but not quite hurting him. "What are your instructions in that event?"

"Your predecessor left rules for the succession." Grailer sucked in breath, was rewarded with a knife in his spine. "You have abided by these rules. The present situation is therefore closed."

Rules of succession. "*I have my place in the universe, as have you.*" Teacher to student. To—"There will be changes made, Executive."

"Your privilege."

"There will no longer be—" he stopped. There are no good reasons for dying, he thought; but good men sometimes find bad reasons adequate.

"No longer be?"

"Not now," Grailer said. "The present matter is closed."

"Very well. By the rules, then, I am required to tell you: Death exists. CIRCE waits."

The hand let go and Grailer nodded. The CIRCE operator turned away, then back. "Will you answer a question, for myself?"

"I might."

"Whatever CIRCE has done, we always drew our right from law. From whence does yours come?"

Grailer said instantly, "From a fleeting voice in the soul. From honesty, and honor. From the best perception of the truth."

Dawnlight shone in the black knight's mask. "That is no answer to the question."

"Perhaps not for you."

The person in black bowed and left.

Grailer massaged his throat and folded his Webset. He would return to the city. He would find Amanda, and at last know what to tell her.

And he knew he would go back to Diego Cadiz, this time without a gun. He could feel the Spider's mantle settling on his shoulders like that black impact grip. *Having only me as a friend . . . now, only you . . .*

He could comfort Amanda. He could argue with Doctor Taliessin. But he would need a friend.

For to the question the black knight had asked, he did not know if he would ever find another reply.

Well, they're saved from the blessings of civilization.

from *Stagecoach*

ABOUT THE AUTHOR

David Dyer-Bennet

JOHN M. FORD was, in his lifetime, a favorite author of many writers better known than he was, including Neil Gaiman and Robert Jordan. He won World Fantasy Awards for both his novel *The Dragon Waiting* and his poem "Winter Solstice, Camelot Station," and he won the Philip K. Dick Award for his novel, *Growing Up Weightless*. His Star Trek novel *The Final Reflection* essentially created the nuanced Klingon culture seen later in the feature films, and his other novel in that universe, *How Much for Just the Planet?*, was a Star Trek tale told as a Gilbert and Sullivan musical, complete with songs. He was a genius. He died in 2006.